The Way You Love Me

A Dangerous Kiss
With Just One Kiss
A Seductive Kiss
It Had to Be You
One Night With You
Nobody But You

A Family Affair Series
After the Dawn
When Morning Comes
I Know Who Holds Tomorrow

Against the Odds Series
Trouble Don't Last Always
Somebody's Knocking at My Door

Invincible Women Series
If You Were My Man
And Mistress Makes Three
Not Even If You Begged
In Another Man's Bed
Any Rich Man Will Do
Like the First Time

Standalones
Someone to Love Me
The Turning Point

Anthologies

Twice the Temptation
Let's Get It On
Going to the Chapel
Welcome to Leo's
Della's House of Style

The Way You Love Me

FRANCIS RAY

St. Martin's Griffin
New York

Published in the United States by St. Martin's Griffin, an imprint of St. Martin's Publishing Group

THE WAY YOU LOVE ME. Copyright © 2008 by Francis Ray. All rights reserved. Printed in the United States of America. For information, address St. Martin's Publishing Group, 120 Broadway, New York, NY 10271.

www.stmartins.com

ISBN 978-0-312-94684-5 (mass market paperback)
ISBN 978-1-4299-4632-2 (ebook)
ISBN 978-1-250-62403-1 (trade paperback)

Our books may be purchased in bulk for promotional, educational, or business use. Please contact your local bookseller or the Macmillan Corporate and Premium Sales Department at 1-800-221-7945, extension 5442, or by email at MacmillanSpecialMarkets@macmillan.com.

First St. Martin's Griffin Edition: January 2020

10 9 8 7 6 5 4 3 2 1

Dear Reader,

I want to thank you for your tremendous support of the Graysons of New Mexico Series. However, once Ruth married off Sierra to Blade Navarone in the fifth and last book, *Only You,* you wanted to know about the friends and family members you'd met in *Until There Was You, You and No Other, Dreaming of You, Irresistible You,* and *Only You.* Because of your overwhelming requests, my publisher has allowed me to write the stories you clamored for.

First up in a new series called "Grayson Friends" is Shane Elliott, a man who piqued readers' attention from the moment he appeared in *Dreaming of You.* Bold, gorgeous and deadly—Shane doesn't have time for a woman— until he meets one he can't forget, Paige Albright. Hired to protect Paige from an unscrupulous boyfriend, Shane is caught in a dilemma that his sharp intelligence and training as an Army Ranger can't help him solve. He wants Paige for himself, but if she learns the real reason he's insinuated himself in her life, she'll hate him forever.

The next book in the Grayson Friends Series is *Nobody But You,* Cameron McBride's story. We first heard of the McBride curse—unlucky in love/lucky in business—in *Dreaming of You.* In the same book we learned of Cameron's heartbreak of still loving a woman who had left him at the altar. But why? Was she a heartless tease or was there a compelling reason for betraying Cameron? We'll find the answer as we enter the fascinating world of NASCAR where Cameron is one of the top ten drivers. Will the McBride curse rule, or like Faith, will Cameron finally be lucky in love and win the woman he'll love forever?

I can't close without expressing my thanks to you, the faithful readers, and my publisher at St. Martin's Press for reissuing *Until There Was You,* slated for December 2008. We've waited a long time for this to happen and I couldn't be more pleased. To celebrate this wonderful event, and as a special gift to my readers, I've included a bonus story, *Christmas and You,* where you can share and delight in Luke and Catherine's first Christmas.

Happy reading,
Francis

Email: francisray@aol.com
www.Francisray.com

THE GRAYSONS OF NEW MEXICO—THE FALCONS OF TEXAS

Cousins by marriage—friends by choice
Bold men and women who risk it all for love

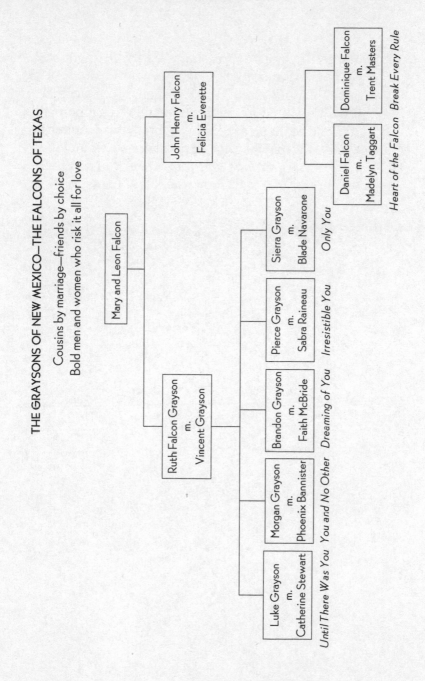

Mary and Leon Falcon

John Henry Falcon
m.
Felicia Everette

Ruth Falcon Grayson
m.
Vincent Grayson

Daniel Falcon
m.
Madelyn Taggart

Dominique Falcon
m.
Trent Masters

Heart of the Falcon Break Every Rule

Luke Grayson
m.
Catherine Stewart

Morgan Grayson
m.
Phoenix Bannister

Brandon Grayson
m.
Faith McBride

Pierce Grayson
m.
Sabra Raineau

Sierra Grayson
m.
Blade Navarone

Until There Was You You and No Other Dreaming of You Irresistible You Only You

The Way You Love Me

Prologue

She moved him.

For longer than Shane Elliott could remember nothing and no one had touched his heart, made him remember he had a soul, except the two men who had walked through hell with him . . . until that night, until Paige Albright.

In the stillness of another restless night, he lay awake in bed and watched the shadows of the trees sway on the wall of the cottage behind the main house of Blade Navarone's estate on Riviera Maya. Hundreds of miles away from where they'd first met, in Dallas, he could still feel her incredible softness, smell her haunting scent.

Most of all, he could see the fear in her eyes after he'd thrown her to the ground, covering her small body with his.

The terror that had leaped into her eyes, the uncontrollable trembling of her body would forever haunt him. That he had been protecting one of his closest friends and employer, Blade Navarone, hadn't mattered. Then and now, Shane felt as if he had destroyed something precious.

At the time, he'd consoled himself that his actions were necessary; yet a part of him had been grateful that he'd had on night-vision goggles and that they were in the deep shadows of the trees so she couldn't clearly see his face. His search of her body for weapons was quick, methodical, detached . . . until his hand, passed over her small but perfectly formed breasts that fit his hand as if made just for him. Her sharp intake of breath had caused her breast to quiver, then push against his palm.

Shane's hands fisted on the bed. He was disgusted with himself for that night's sudden tightening of his body, the hard, hungry arousal he couldn't hide.

She'd trembled worse, her teeth chattering, then she'd started to fight once again. His arm under her chin had effectively stopped her struggles. Words wouldn't have helped calm her, not with his thick arousal pushing against the junction of her thighs. For both of them, he had to complete the task of searching for weapons as quickly as possible.

Thankfully she'd stilled and he'd hurriedly finished, then pulled her to her feet by her slim arm, keeping his back to the meager light coming from the house fifty feet away. He flashed a beam of a light into her frightened, heart-shaped face, then pushed her hand away when it automatically lifted to shield her eyes.

"Don't move and you won't be hurt."

Her eyes widened. Her soft lips trembled. Shane locked the curse behind his teeth. "Hurry." He'd rasped the one word, wanting Corbin to finish feeding her driver's license number into the handheld computer Shane had devised for fieldwork.

"Everything checks. She's clean."

"Who . . . who are you?" Her voice was cultured, with a hint of the Deep South. He'd guessed that an expensive private school had negated the accent until now . . . until he had made her realize how defenseless she was.

Shane wasn't used to answering questions. He had no intention of starting now. "What are you doing here? And I want the truth the first time." His voice was cold; he'd learned to be. Killers had no respect for race or gender or county.

"I—" she began, then faltered.

He could see the lie start to form in her darting eyes, her tongue moistening her lips. He immediately dismissed her as a threat. She couldn't lie her way out of a paper bag.

"The truth or I'll have to search you again."

She gasped. Horror widened her eyes. She quickly stepped back. Knowing that the thought of his hands on her was abhorrent to her shouldn't have mattered. He couldn't have cared less what people thought of him . . . until her.

"Talk," he snapped, hoping to jar her into telling him what he needed to know.

She jumped and began talking. Strange, but as she finished in a strained, embarrassed whisper, he felt even worse. He'd recognized her name, Paige Albright, and knew she'd told the truth. Just as he knew the person she sought would do everything in her power to ensure Paige never found the answers she sought.

The accusing look in Paige's eyes stabbed him worse than any blade could have. He'd taken something from her, made her more vulnerable than merely tackling her should have.

He'd taken a swipe at her pride.

He'd give anything to undo what had happened, but that was impossible. Stuff happened.

Shane reached for the handheld. He quickly scanned the data, entered more, then exchanged it for her black designer handbag, which was at least twenty by twenty-four inches. Picking up the flashlight she'd dropped, Shane shut it off and stuck it inside the hand-bag.

When she'd stopped within rifle range of the patio where Blade and Sierra Grayson and the couple they were visiting, Dominique Falcon-Masters and her husband, Trent Masters, chatted, Shane had made the decision to take the unexpected visitor down. He had no way of knowing she'd been looking for the binoculars he'd seen the instant before his body covered hers.

"You'll be escorted back to your car. My advice would be to take an earlier flight rather than the one in the morning."

Surprise flickered in her eyes, then a spark of defiance. "It's a free country."

"Would you want her to find out why you're here?"

Anger mixed with fear flashed in her eyes. "You bastard."

Good. She was regaining her footing. "Remember that and be on the next flight to Atlanta."

She snatched her purse from him and hooked the wide leather strap over her slim shoulders. After one look filled with distaste, she turned and walked away, never looking back.

Corbin followed to make sure she got back in the rental she'd left on the FM Road a mile away. A patrolling sentry had notified Shane the moment she stepped onto Dominique and Trent's property.

Eyes closed now in bed, Shane threw his arm across his forehead. She wasn't a threat to Blade or Sierra, but in the weeks since, she had become a threat to Shane's peace of mind. The one woman who moved him, and he disgusted her.

And he couldn't get her out of his mind no matter how hard he tried.

Chapter 1

Tired of chasing sleep and battling memories, Shane silently rose from his bed shortly after six the next morning and headed for the shower. It was a good thing he didn't need much sleep, he mused, as he stepped naked into the glass enclosure and turned the jets on full blast.

The pelting streams of water did little to take his mind from the reason for his inability to sleep. It was almost three months since he'd encountered Paige Albright, and his memory of her was as vivid as if it had happened last night.

Why her? Why was he unable to forget her?

Over the years he'd encountered many women, taken more than his fair share to bed. They'd enjoyed each other, but when he'd walked away he hadn't looked back. His body had only covered Paige, yet the imprint was more indelible than any other woman's.

His large hand paused in soaping his chest. He hadn't been intimate with her; perhaps that was the reason she haunted him. He was shaking his dark head before the thought completely formed. Women passed through his life in large numbers. He didn't fixate on them. Even when he'd discovered the woman he'd thought he loved, thought loved him until he caught her cheating, he'd walked out of her bedroom despite her frantic pleas for him to stay and erased her from his mind. No woman ever made him think twice about her.

Until Paige.

Ducking his head under the spray, he rinsed off the suds. He'd figure it out. Nothing and no one ever got the best of him. Shutting off the water, he grabbed a towel and absently ran it over his body. It wasn't like him to live in the past. He *did* know the reason for that.

From his earliest childhood, when he'd learned that stealing and conning people wasn't the way he wanted to live, he had been in a constant battle to rise above the sordid, wasteful lives of his parents and older brother. The army had been his way out, his salvation.

Tossing the towel into the open hamper, he went to the dresser and pulled on a pair of silk briefs. The light blue shirt he slipped on next was also silk. The tailored slacks were made of the finest cotton.

He didn't care about clothes or shopping, but his job as head of security for Navarone Resorts and Spas, located around the world, meant that on occasion he mixed with some of the wealthiest and most influential people in the country. He had to dress the part.

Snorting, Shane put on his alligator belt and thought of Rio, a rule breaker if ever there was one, and Shane's second in command. Rio conformed, but only to a certain degree. As groomsmen less than a week ago on this very property, they had both worn tuxedos for Blade and Sierra's wedding on the beach at Blade's compound. Only his love and respect for Blade had gotten Rio into the tux. "The supreme sacrifice," he'd called it.

Finished dressing, Shane hooked on his cell phone and the radio that connected him to the various guards on duty at Blade's estate. All of them knew it was only a matter of time before a relative let it slip or an inquisitive reporter learned billionaire real estate mogul Blade Navarone had married Sierra Grayson, his exclusive broker for Navarone Place in Dallas. When the news leaked, things would get crazy, but until that time Blade and Sierra wanted their privacy, and that was where he and Rio came in.

In the front room of the guest cottage on Blade's estate, Shane glanced at the sofa. Rio's long, muscular body was stretched out with a sheet up to his flat stomach, his eyes closed, one hand over his wide chest, the other on the floor. Shane knew the pose was deceptive.

Rio's left hand was very likely near a concealed weapon under the sofa. He never let down his guard. Shane didn't have a doubt in the world that Rio had heard every restless move Shane had made during the night and early morning. Rio had the ears of a bat and the eyes of a cat. Combine this with the tracking skills of a bloodhound, and he was a force to be reckoned with.

"I'm going to the main office." Shane had moved the command center for the security of all the Navarone properties to Riviera Maya when he learned Blade and Sierra were getting married here. As long as he had a computer, he could connect with his security team wherever they were. As an Army Ranger he had learned to be flexible and mobile.

"Trouble sleeping." Rio said without opening his eyes. It was a statement, not a question.

Shane glanced out the door. "A bit. See you later."

Rio opened his eyes and uncoiled. His long bare feet hit the wooden floor. "For a time Blade was the same way, and we both know how that ended."

Marriage to Sierra. "He was conflicted about Sierra."

Rio kept his unreadable gaze on Shane. "That's my point."

Shane blew out a breath. They didn't lie to each

other even when the truth was uncomfortable. Shane didn't question how Rio knew a woman was involved. Although he hadn't been in the field when Shane met Paige, he'd read the report, and with his uncanny perception Rio had come up with the reason for Shane's restlessness. "That's not about to happen to me."

Rio, his gaze intense, asked, "Is the impossibility the reason for the sleeplessness?"

Shane stared. "You always see too much."

Rio came to his height of six-four, a scant quarter of an inch taller than Shane. The sheet fell heedless to the floor. "Keeps me from making the same mistakes as others."

This time Shane had no ready comeback. All three of them, Shane, Rio, and Blade, had various reasons for steering clear of serious relationships with women. Sierra had helped Blade overcome his fears. Shane had little hope for himself, and none for Rio. The man simply did not forget or forgive. "You know where to find me."

Not waiting for a response, Shane continued out the door and down the winding path that led to the front of the house. He paused by the driver's door of one of the two black jeeps parked in front. He studied the darkened house for a moment. Inside Blade and Sierra were in bed, sleeping or not. His mouth curved into a smile. After all, it was their honeymoon. It hadn't been easy for them, but here they were, and nothing this side of heaven could tear them apart.

For some, happy endings were possible. For others there wasn't a chance in hell. Getting into the jeep, Shane pulled off. For the first time he was seeing his lonely life ahead of him and not liking what he saw.

A little after ten that morning Shane was leaving checkpoint five, the outer perimeter of Blade's property on the beach, when his radio went off with two beeps. Yellow Alert. He'd been too restless to stay at the command center for more than an hour. He'd left and personally checked in with all of his men on patrol.

He snatched the radio from his belt. "Talk."

"Checkpoint one. Three visitors without clearance. Dominique and Trent Masters. Joann Albright. They say Mr. Navarone expects them. Over."

At the mention of Paige's mother's name, Shane's heart thumped. It annoyed the hell out of him. While he was assessing his reaction, his cell went off. One note. Blade. "Hold. Over," Shane said into the radio, then answered the phone. "Shane."

"Shane, three guests are due to arrive this morning. Dominique and her husband, Trent, and Joann Albright," Blade said.

"They're at checkpoint one, awaiting clearance."

"Sorry, I forgot to tell you last night."

"My fault," Sierra said, then giggled.

Blade's laughter joined hers. He'd been doing that a lot lately, Shane thought. It was about time. Sierra had healed the tortured places in Blade's soul. For that, she had Shane's undying gratitude and allegiance.

"Please let them through, then bring them to the house," Blade finally said.

"Done." Shane disconnected the cell and spoke into the radio. "Let them pass." As soon as the orders were given, Shane was moving. He had just enough time to meet them in front of the house. Blade had asked him to bring them, which meant he wanted Shane there as well.

Dominique and Trent had been at the wedding and so had Mrs. Albright, flying in on the private jet of Daniel Falcon. She'd been one of the first to leave after the ceremony. Now she was back. The reason must be a good one to interrupt Blade and Sierra's honeymoon, and why did Shane have the feeling that he wasn't going to like hearing it?

"I was told you could help me."

Shane prided himself on keeping his thoughts hidden; he did so now. He didn't look at his employee and friend, Blade, or Rio, or Trent Masters, the man lightly holding the hand of the woman who had just spoken, Joann Albright.

As soon as the introductions had been completed, Sierra and Dominique had left the room, but not before Sierra playfully told Shane she was armed. Then she winked and gave Blade a kiss. She'd done it more for Blade than Shane. Although getting better, Blade remained a bit skittish when she wasn't in his sight. After almost losing her to two kidnappers, he had good reason. Especially for a woman he loved more than his life.

Mrs. Albright took a seat beside Trent on the sofa in the great room, then fixed her gaze on Shane. "I was told you could help me," she repeated.

"In what way?" Shane asked. Through his work in army intelligence he'd learned never to volunteer information or make assumptions. Although Mrs. Albright might have seen him at Blade and Sierra's wedding, Shane had seen her on two other occasions. All three times she had been obviously happy. Now lines radiated from her pursed lips, across her forehead. Her troubled eyes were light brown, unlike the startling gray of her daughter's.

Mrs. Albright's hands clenched. Trent's long arm immediately curved around her shoulders. She sent him a smile filled with love and affection. Sitting next to the six-foot man, she looked small, delicate like her daughter. "Keep my daughter, Paige, from making a horrible mistake."

Shane couldn't prevent the barest flicker of his lashes, the clench in his gut. It wasn't any consolation that only Blade and Rio would have detected the slip, but they had been looking at Mrs. Albright. At least he knew Blade was. You never knew about Rio. "Please continue."

"She's seeing a man, Russell Crenshaw. They dated a couple of times when Paige was a freshman in college, then went their separate ways. However, he's been calling on her regularly since her father's death from a . . . stroke five months ago," she said.

Shane wasn't surprised to hear the hesitation, see the loathing in Mrs. Albright's face. In his capacity to protect Blade and now Sierra, Shane made it his business to know about everyone they were in close contact with. He'd read the official police report of how her husband had died, not the story she'd circulated to keep their children from finding out what an adulterous and distasteful man their father was. "You don't approve?"

Mrs. Albright's eyes chilled. "No. Russell is after her money."

Anger whipped through Shane, but his expression remained impassive. "Have you spoken to your daughter?"

Mrs. Albright visibly swallowed. "Since the death of her father we . . . we aren't as close as we once were. His death devastated her. Russell's father and Paige's were business associates. Her father always wanted her and Russell to marry."

Shane could figure out the rest. "Seeing Russell is her way of honoring her father's memory."

"Yes," Mrs. Albright said, the one word full of

disgust. "Russell was there initially to offer comfort, and now he's ingratiated himself with Paige."

"Perhaps he really cares for her," Shane said, wondering why the words left a bitter taste in his mouth.

Fury flashed in Mrs. Albright's eyes. For the briefest moment he recalled the fury in her daughter's eyes, the reason. Only years of training kept him from twisting uncomfortably in his seat. "What he cares about is the five-million-dollar trust that will be turned over to Paige when she's twenty-seven. That's less than four months away."

Rage, hot and lethal, shot through Shane at the thought of any man using Paige. But he'd learned long ago that the world wasn't always pretty or fair. Stuff happened. His job was to make sure it didn't happen to those in his charge.

"I can do a thorough background check on the man she's seeing," Shane suggested. Besides his silence, he owed Paige after his ill treatment of her. But he wasn't getting in the middle of this. Perhaps Mrs. Albright was wrong. Sometimes parents overreacted.

Mrs. Albright was shaking her head before he finished. "No, I want you to come to Atlanta. Russell is the epitome of an upstanding citizen on the outside. You might not find anything in your search." She sent Trent a pleading look, then gave her attention back to Shane. "I heard how you helped find information when Sierra was kidnapped. Ruth and Daniel said you and Rio made the difference. I want you. Blade agreed. Please."

She'd pulled out the big guns. She'd used her connection to Trent Masters and his to his brother-in-law, Daniel Falcon, and to Blade Navarone to find a man with the expertise to investigate a man she believed wanted to use her daughter. Blade would let Shane make his own decision, but Daniel had helped as well when Sierra, his cousin, and Blade's lover at the time, was kidnapped. There was nothing Daniel and Blade wouldn't do for each other.

"You can be my houseguest," she said, pushing her point.

She'd just derailed Shane's suggestion to send Rio. He was as intelligent as they came, had the dangerous, compelling looks that turned women's heads, but his eyes were colder than a blizzard.

"Sierra suggested I could introduce you as the protégé or son of one of my old college roommates," Mrs. Albright continued.

Shane wasn't surprised Sierra was in on this. She had a way of ferreting out information, then giving her opinion whether it was asked for or not. She'd made Blade whole again, and Shane would do almost anything for her.

But not this.

"We'd appreciate it and of course pay you whatever your fee is, but we know money is not the issue," Trent said. "Sierra's brother, Luke, could do some preliminary investigation from Santa Fe, but we know without asking that he won't take a job that will keep him away from his wife."

Trent was on target. All the Graysons were the same love-struck way, and so were their extended family members and in-laws. Shane had never seen couples so committed and in love.

The first time he'd seen the Graysons, the Falcons, the Taggarts, and the Masterses all together was when Sierra had been kidnapped. Shane had thought the crisis had brought them closer together. However, they'd been just as devoted at Blade and Sierra's wedding. Shane had subsequently learned that their love was the real deal. It wasn't for show. Where one went, the other wasn't far behind.

"The situation is delicate," Trent continued. "We need someone we can trust to investigate. That's why we didn't consider a private firm."

A dull flush stained Mrs. Albright's cheeks, but she kept her gaze level. Secrecy was needed more than they knew. Paige was on to her, but she hadn't connected the dots yet. When her daughter did, there would be hell to pay. Telling Mrs. Albright that her daughter was suspicious of her would solve nothing and only worry her more. She had suffered enough.

Staring across the room at the attractive but obviously worried woman in her early sixties who reminded him so much of the daughter she wanted to protect, Shane made the only decision he felt logical. "I'll find out all I can about Crenshaw, but I take my responsibilities here seriously. I'm sorry, but I can't leave at the moment."

"I admire your loyalty. Perhaps if you saw her picture." Opening the designer croc handbag on the seat beside her, Mrs. Albright stood.

Shane came to his feet, as did all the men in the room. "See. This was taken the day she interviewed and got her first job. She works with a nonprofit agency and has taken a special interest in foster children."

Shane briefly wondered if Mrs. Albright had influenced her daughter's decision. Trent had been raised in foster care.

Stopping in front of Shane, Mrs. Albright's delicate hands clenched for a second. Her voice firmed. "Paige gives so much. I won't let her be used."

Shane stared at the wallet-sized photograph of the beautiful, laughing woman with a heart-shaped face, her eyes bright with happiness and a hint of mischievousness. He was unable to keep the picture of her frightened and trembling in his arms from overshadowing the image. Seeing her might put that memory to rest, but he wasn't sure how he'd handle seeing another man with his hands on her.

"If Shane won't help, we'll keep looking until we find someone who will." Trent's arm went around Mrs. Albright. "Don't worry, Mama."

And that was the secret that Shane knew instinctively would tear Paige's world apart. She'd snuck onto Trent's estate to find out the connection between Trent and her mother. Paige hadn't found what she sought, but that didn't mean she'd stop trying.

As far as he could determine, she thought she and her brother, Zachary, were their mother's only children. What would happen when she learned differently? She'd lost a father she loved and was worried about her mother. There was a distinct possibility that a man wanted her money more than he wanted her. If ever there was a person who didn't need any more problems heaped on her, it was Paige.

Still, he'd learned never to take on an assignment without knowing what he was getting into first. "I'll think it over and give you my final answer in a few days."

"Thank you," she said.

"I haven't said I'd help," Shane cautioned her.

"You didn't say no. I have to hope," Mrs. Albright said. "I won't let Paige ruin her life the way—" Her voice trailed off. Swallowing, she turned away to pick up her handbag. "Thank you for listening."

Shane watched Mrs. Albright and Trent leave, knowing full well what she hadn't finished saying and how painfully true it was. *The way I ruined mine.*

"Mother, why do you keep disappearing?" Paige Albright whispered the question that she had been trying to find the answer to for the past three months. Sitting on the stairs in her mother's house with a clear view of the front door, she shivered and wrapped her slim arms around her jittery stomach. She knew the *where,* but the answer had come at a steep price.

Paige's bungling attempt to find out why had ended in disaster and humiliation. Clamping her eyes tightly shut didn't prevent the image of the powerfully built man towering over her, pinning her body to the ground. He hadn't hurt her, but he'd frightened her, made her feel foolish and helpless . . . which was inexplicably worse.

Those feelings were too much like those of the young Paige before she'd finally started to come into her own the summer she turned seventeen. From that point on, she no longer had to wonder what cruel genie had mistakenly dropped her into a beautiful family of high achievers with outgoing parents and a gorgeous and musically gifted older brother.

She'd blossomed and become what she'd always longed for, the delight of her father's eye. Tears misted in her eyes. She missed him so much. And since his death, her mother was somehow different.

It wasn't just the out-of-town trips she'd started going on; it was something else. At times she seemed unbearably sad, staring into space. Paige might have thought her mother was mourning the loss of her father, but a few weeks after the funeral she'd accidentally heard her mother talking with her lawyer in the library.

After thirty-five years of marriage, Paige was shocked to learn her mother had been preparing to file for divorce. With her father's business in trouble, her mother couldn't have picked a worse time to add to his problems.

Six weeks after her father's death, her mother had put up their house for sale. It sold in three weeks. Even before the sale was final, her mother had moved into her parents' house, which she'd kept after their deaths. With Paige's apartment complex being sold to a developer, she had grabbed the opportunity to move in with her mother and try to figure out why she had changed and become secretive since Paige's father had died.

Thus far Paige wasn't doing very well, but she refused to give up. Until she had concrete information she wasn't going to worry her brother Zachary. Her Grammy-winning brother was in the middle of producing an album for one of the biggest pop stars in the country. Yet he wouldn't hesitate to help or come home if she called him.

When they were growing up, Zachary had tried so hard to help her overcome her shyness and be assertive the way he was. And although she'd failed miserably, he loved her anyway. He never minded if she wanted to tag along with him. Not once had he complained about babysitting her when their parents went out. She looked up to her brother. She was handling this on her own.

Headlights speared through the fourteen-foot windows on either side of the recessed double front doors. Her mother's Lexus was in the garage. Paige unfolded her arms and straightened her spine. A few minutes later the locks disengaged, the arched steel-and-glass door swung open. Her mother was finally home.

"Where have you been?"

Startled, Joann Albright dropped the small overnight case in the foyer and swung around, her hand pressed to her chest. "Paige! I-I didn't expect you."

Exactly the reason Paige had chosen to surprise her mother and perhaps get some answers. Aware that her mother hadn't answered the question, Paige slowly rose from the foot of the stairs and walked to her. "Where have you been?"

"Been?" her mother repeated, her eyes darting away. Bending, she picked up the case. "You know where."

Paige barely stopped herself from hissing, *Don't lie.* "Where did you—" Again she caught herself. The word on the tip of her tongue was *sneak.* Her mother was one of the most honest, loving women she knew. Or at least Paige had thought she was until her father's death. She was sure it had something to do with Trent Masters; Paige just couldn't figure out exactly what.

She'd thought of putting the question to her mother too many times to count, but was almost afraid of the answer. Her father certainly hadn't wanted to speak of the afternoon Paige dropped by their home to watch the photo shoot for a home interior magazine.

Paige had found her mother hysterical, her father in a rage, and a man she later learned was Trent Masters asking her mother a question that seemed to have no reason. If Trent and the people with him were con artists as her father insisted, why would her mother visit him? She'd hired a private investigator to find out that much, then dismissed him. She hadn't wanted him to learn any information that might prove embarrassing or detrimental to her mother. She just wanted answers and things to be as they were before.

"I thought you were taking a business trip to Chicago?" her mother said, moistening her lips.

"So you thought you'd be free to do whatever it is you do when you disappear," Paige said, watching her mother's eyes dart guiltily away.

"I love you, Paige," her mother said, her gaze finally meeting hers, her voice soft and quivering.

Paige's hand clenched. She could easily hear the countless echoes of those exact words while growing up in a world where she often seemed out of place. No matter that she wasn't a class officer or a cheerleader or any of the things she so desperately tried to be, her mother always gave her a smile and a hug, and those words to hang on to.

"If you love me, then why won't you tell me what is going on?" Paige went to her, forcing herself to say the unthinkable. "Is it a man?"

Shock raced across her mother's unlined face. The relief that Paige felt was instantaneous, but so many unanswered questions remained.

"I honored my marriage vows," her mother said, her voice hushed.

"Mother, I'm sorry, but I don't understand why you disappear from time to time."

Her mother laughed, but it was laced with nervousness. "I don't disappear. You can call me on my cell. The spa doesn't allow phone calls in or out on their switchboard." She lifted her hand, paused, then placed it on Paige's shoulder as if she wasn't sure it would be accepted. "You can always reach me."

The uncertainty tore at Paige. Once she and her mother had been the closest of friends and confidantes; now they were uneasy around each other.

"I'm home now and I'm not going anyplace. I'm here," her mother continued.

For now. "I'll take your things up." Paige reached for the overnight case her mother held, breaking contact. In the past Paige would have hugged her back.

Her mother caught her arm, staring at the jeweled bracelet on her right wrist. "Is this new?"

Paige glanced at the platinum bangle bracelet circled with diamonds. She'd forgotten she had it on. She frowned. "Russell gave it to me today as an early birthday present."

"Your birthday is four months away."

Paige's mouth curved. "You know Russell. He said he wanted to be the first to wish me happy birthday." Her smile faded. "He said he had been looking at it for a while and had shown it to Father."

Her mother set her case down, her intent gaze on Paige. "Are you going to accept it?"

The disapproval in her mother's voice was obvious. "Russell loved my father." Paige hadn't meant the words to come out so accusatory. Her mother flinched. "I'm sorry. I—"

"It's all right." Her mother picked up the luggage, trying to smile and failing. "You're probably tired."

For some odd reason, tears clogged Paige's throat. Her mother always accepted her, never criticized her. "Russell asked me to wear it to remind me that he is always there for me."

"That's an expensive gift for a friend," her mother said, searching Paige's eyes.

"He's hinted that he wants more," Paige confessed. "He was hoping there might be an announcement at my birthday party. Father wanted us together."

This time her mother touched her arm without hesitation. "What do you want?"

"For my father to be alive, for things to be the way they once were." Shrugging from her mother's hold, Paige took the luggage and turned toward the stairs.

"Paige."

Quickly climbing, Paige heard her mother call her but refused to look back. Unless her mother explained what was going on, the closeness they once shared was gone. The secret she refused to divulge stood between them, and Paige wasn't sure it was possible for them to regain their once loving and open relationship.

And it had something to do with Trent Masters. She

just hoped and prayed whatever it was hadn't contributed to her father's stroke.

Shane's cell rang a little after midnight. Instead of trying to sleep, he was pulling an all-nighter at the command center. He answered without taking his eyes from one of ten computer screens in front of him. "Shane."

"You have to come and save Paige," Mrs. Albright's hysterical voice pleaded.

Shane's gut clenched. He spun away from the computer and stood. "What happened?"

"Russell gave her an expensive bracelet, then hinted that there might be something more to announce at her birthday party," Mrs. Albright said. "He lied and said her father had seen the bracelet and approved."

"How do you know he lied?"

"Because Russell is too selfish to give a woman a ten-thousand-dollar bracelet. It was another way to sway her feelings for him. Unfortunately she believed him. He's going to ask her to marry him. That can't happen. He's a manipulator, a selfish, greedy man. You'll see once you investigate him."

Shane had received an extensive report on Russell less than two hours after he'd met with Mrs. Albright. He hadn't liked what he'd learned. Believing that Mrs. Albright might be right in her belief that Russell's private life was vastly different from his public persona, Shane had enlisted the aid of a highly recommended investigation firm in Atlanta. According to the report they sent, Russell was two weeks into an affair. Shane's temper had spiked on reading the information, and he'd yet to fully cool off.

No woman deserved that kind of ill treatment. He was going to Atlanta. What he couldn't figure out was

if he was accepting the job because of Paige, or her
mother, or because he couldn't help himself. Probably
a bit of all three. Shane hadn't had a moment's peace
since Paige's mother visited the compound.

He owed Paige, and he always paid his debts. "Give
me a couple of days to set things up and I'll be there."

"Thank you." The relief in her voice was obvious. "I
knew you wouldn't let me down."

"I haven't done anything yet," he reminded her.

"But you will. You'll save Paige. You'll do what I
couldn't do."

"Mrs. Albright—"

"Good night, Shane. I can sleep now."

Shane disconnected the phone. At least one of them
could.

Chapter 2

Shane turned into the almost hidden driveway of Joann Albright's estate shortly after eleven on a clear Saturday morning two days after he'd last spoken with her. The mile-long drive curved through mature trees and flower gardens bursting with color. As the car straightened on the last curve, the house came into view. It was a beaut. Three stories, pristine white, with Doric columns and wide balconies running the length of each floor.

The house had belonged to Mrs. Albright's parents, second-generation millionaires whose own parents had made their fortune in banking and insurance. Both had died over two years ago. She could have sold the prime piece of real estate for millions, but instead had kept the house and the employees needed to maintain its grandeur. She was a woman with a strong sense of family, and she'd lived a hellish life because of it.

Water spewed from a stone fountain rimmed with late-blooming azaleas as Shane pulled in front of the house behind a silver Audi. Shutting off the motor, he climbed out of the rental sedan and grabbed his luggage from the trunk. He would have preferred his specially equipped Porsche, but he was supposed to be an unemployed video game designer trying to figure out what he wanted to do and where he wanted to do it.

Sierra had been overjoyed he'd kept her cover story that he was the protégé, not the son, of an old college roommate of Mrs. Albright. With any cover story, it was always best to stick as close to the truth as possible. His mother had barely finished high school.

From Rio there had been a look that warned Shane he was playing with fire. Wouldn't be the first time, and thus far he hadn't been burned. He went up the three stone steps and rang the doorbell. Lush, flowering vines flowed from huge stone urns on either side of the porch.

One of the heavily carved double doors opened. A slender olive-skinned woman, wearing a gray maid's uniform answered the door. "Yes?" She appeared to be in her midfifties.

"Good morning, I'm Shane Elliott. Mrs. Albright is expecting me."

A warm smile washed over her face. "Good morning, Mr. Elliott." She stepped back. "You can leave your luggage here. Sirus will take it up to your room. I'll show you to Mrs. Albright. She's on the terrace reading."

"Thank you." Stepping inside the wide foyer, Shane set his suitcase on the white marble floor. He'd barely straightened when he caught a movement out of the corner of his eyes. His head slowly turned. Somehow he knew who he would see.

Knowing didn't prepare him for the punch to his gut on seeing Paige Albright, one graceful hand on the polished oak balustrade, the other carrying a brown leather attaché case.

The light from the high windows bordering the front doors bathed her in the morning sun. Her lustrous auburn hair, pulled back from her captivating face, hung past her shoulders. She had on a black silk shell with thin straps and a straight skirt that stopped at the bend of her knees. Strands of pearls of varying lengths graced her slender throat. Paige glowed.

Suddenly she stopped, her head slowly coming up and around. Shane wondered if anything about him would trigger her memory—or had he been the only one to relive that night over and over? Curiosity flickered in her gray eyes. Eyes he'd spent countless hours thinking about.

"Hello, you must be Paige Albright. I'm Shane Elliott." He might as well get it over with. Since he had been wearing the night-vision goggles, she wouldn't recognize him. Besides, fear and time distorted the memory, as proven by the number of wrongly accused people in prison thanks to an eyewitness. The intonation of his voice was another matter, but it had been deep and raspy back then due to his arousal, and anger at his lack of self-control.

Finally her exquisite face curved into a warm smile. "Mr. Elliott." Continuing down the stairs, she reached the bottom riser and extended her hand. "Welcome to Atlanta and Fountain Oaks."

His fingers closed around her small, delicate hand. He expected the softness, the leap of awareness, the assault of her fragrance he'd been unable to forget. He expected them, but the reality gave him another punch to the gut. He released her hand. What he really wanted was to continue holding it, hold her.

He lifted his sunshades. "Shane, please, and I hope I can call you Paige."

"Of course," she said, a frown knitting her brow for a second before it was gone. "I hate to run out on you, but I have a charity luncheon I organized to attend."

"I understand." He reached for the black jacket in the crook of her arm. "May I?"

For the briefest moment he thought she might refuse,

then she nodded again and allowed him to assist with the jacket, switching the attaché case from one hand to the other. His finger lightly brushed across the nape of her neck as he pulled her hair free. He felt her shiver seconds before she stepped away.

"Thank you," she said, her gaze not meeting his as she turned to the maid. "Please tell Mother I'll see her at the luncheon."

"She wanted to see you before you left," the maid explained.

Paige's pleasant expression slipped for a brief moment. "Please tell her that I was in a hurry and will call her. Good-bye, Shane." She headed for the door.

"Paige."

Paige jerked to a stop at the sound of her mother's voice. Slowly she turned, her hand clenched the handle of the case. "Good morning, Mother. I'm in a hurry."

"Then I won't keep you," Mrs. Albright said, her smile bright and forced as the maid left the room. "You've met Shane."

"Yes." Paige flicked her gaze toward him.

"I thought the luncheon would be an excellent opportunity for Shane to meet some of your friends," her mother continued bravely. "He could use my ticket since the luncheon is sold out."

Surprise, then relief shone in Paige's eyes. Shane knew her mother saw it as well when her smile wavered, then firmed. "It will give me a chance to work in the flower garden."

Paige nodded and turned to him, her gaze sweeping over his jeans and polo shirt. "It's business attire."

"I'll try to grin and bear it," Shane said, thinking that mother and daughter were doing much the same thing.

"The address is on the invitation," Paige told him.

She started for the door, then swung back. "There's always a seat available if you change your mind."

This time her mother's smile was real. "I'll be fine. You go on. I know you always like to get there before everyone to ensure everything is in place."

"All right." Paige looked at Shane. "We're at table five. I usually don't stay seated very much, but I'll tell Jackie Weaver, the foundation president, to expect you."

"Thanks."

"See you later. Good-bye." Once again she started for the front door.

"Let me get that." Shane quickly stepped around her and reached for the brass doorknob at the same time she did. Their fingers brushed. She jerked hers back, then quickly went through the door he'd opened.

He watched her throw the attaché case in the passenger seat of the Audi, then speed away. He'd touched her on purpose the first time and just then, to see if the heat, the leap of awareness, had been a fluke or wishful thinking on his part.

It wasn't. Knowing she was as aware of him as he was of her would present a problem . . . if he let it.

He closed the door, resisting the urge to stare after her, just as he resisted the urge to dwell on the awareness between them. He was here to do a job. Allowing his emotions to get in the way would only complicate matters. Complications screwed up a mission.

"Thank you for coming," Mrs. Albright said when he came back to her.

There was such optimism in her face, her voice, that he hated to disappoint her, but he wouldn't give her false hope. Shane picked up his luggage. "I'm not sure how much more I can do in person."

"Once you meet Russell you'll see for yourself that

he's not the man for her," Mrs. Albright said. "You'd have to be an excellent judge of character to work for Blade."

"Is that the only reason?"

She sighed. "No. Paige is suspicious of the times I've left to visit Trent and his wife since Paige's father died. It's created a wedge between us. Having you here will make things less tense between us."

"I'm sorry." He didn't know that much about a mother's love until he'd met Sierra's mother and her extended family. He certainly hadn't been the recipient of it.

Mrs. Albright smiled sadly. "So am I. Paige has always been shy, except when she is helping others. She's nothing like her take-charge, outgoing older brother, Zach. She loves deeply and is hurt easily. I promised her that I wouldn't leave again."

"I'm not sure that will solve the problem."

"Neither am I, but it will help I think." Mrs. Albright glanced at the suitcase. "You need to get dressed and to the luncheon. Russell will be there."

"I can't wait."

*I*t had finally happened. After Paige had given up, had accepted that, along with her other faults, she also carried a genetic malfunction, she'd just been proven wrong. The impossible had finally happened.

Her hands trembling, her stomach not any steadier, Paige eased to a stop and shoved the car into park as soon as she was out of sight of the house. Her wobbly fingers touched the nape of her neck, the exact spot Shane's callused fingers had brushed across. She shivered.

The awareness, the leap of her pulse that had yet to return to normal, had been as unnerving as it was exhilarating. After all these years, she'd finally experienced the heat of desire that she had read about, dreamed of, and, yes, yearned for.

She could see why Shane wore sunshades; he was lethal without them. One look and the woman would be mesmerized, lost in the depths of his beautiful black eyes. Just as she had been.

But it was for the wrong man.

Her eyes shut. She leaned back against the headrest. Russell, not a virtual stranger, should be the one she was attracted to. He was the one her father had picked out for her. Tears misted in her eyes. She missed her father so much, wished there had been some way to erase from his face the worry that had become increasingly more evident in the few months before his death.

He hadn't wanted her help, had brushed off her attempts. That had hurt, but she had understood that her father was from the old school. He felt it was his responsibility to care for his family. He'd worked hard to do just that. The night of his fatal stroke he had worked late in his office, then checked into the hotel room he kept for clients.

She leaned her head forward until it rested on the steering wheel. He'd been alone when he'd become ill, but had the presence of mind to call an ambulance. No matter the differences they were going through, her mother had rushed to his side. She'd been with him when he died.

Zach had been in LA, and Paige had been there visiting. Their father died while they were on a chartered plane heading back to Atlanta. Their only comfort was that he hadn't been alone.

Opening her eyes, she brushed away the tears, shoved the car into drive, and pulled off. She hadn't been able to help her father, but there were others she could help.

First, though, she had to see Russell. She pulled onto the highway and headed for the freeway.

Just the thought of the coming conversation with him made her hands clamp on the steering wheel. She hated confrontations, hated letting people down, but there was no other way around this. She'd been conditioned to please people, to get them to like her, for as long as she could remember.

She hadn't fit in growing up. Her father was a business whiz, her mother the consummate hostess, her brother the most popular boy in school, and then ordinary Paige had been born. Her main goal, her only goal, had been to somehow have people accept and like her. Now that they did, she hated to see disappointment in their faces.

Russell was not a man to accept defeat, but neither was he the man who made her heart beat faster, her body heat.

She'd always thought that, perhaps in time, the special connection she wanted between the two of them would happen. Now she knew it wouldn't. It wasn't fair to keep him hanging. The problem was, Russell had a way of talking over and around her.

His persuasiveness was the reason his consoling her after her father's death had gradually turned into dates. She'd tried for the past three days to talk to him, but he was always too busy. Today she planned on pinning him down.

She threw a quick glance at the attaché case on the seat beside her as she pulled up to the downtown Atlanta hotel and stopped in front of the valet stand. Today there would be no excuse. She was giving the bracelet back. It wasn't fair to him to keep it and hope her feelings would deepen when she knew there was no chance of that happening.

Slipping the car's claim ticket into the pocket of her jacket, she entered the hotel lobby, searching for Russell. Last night he'd told her he had an early-morning golf game with two clients who were staying at the hotel. She'd called the country club and was told Russell wasn't on the course. If she was lucky, or perhaps unlucky, she'd catch him. Being punctual and fastidious, he would drop off his clients, then go straight home to shower and change for the luncheon.

Directly in front of Paige, one of the six elevator doors opened on the other side of the opulent lobby. People piled out. She paused when she saw Russell. He was one of the last two people to emerge. The other passenger was a voluptuous fair-skinned woman in a tight pink dress, black stiletto heels, and a pink-and-black Chanel bag. Something about the woman seemed familiar to Paige.

"Excuse us," said a male voice from behind her.

Paige murmured an apology to the large group trying to pass to get to the elevator and quickly moved aside. By the time they had moved past her, Russell was heading in her direction.

As he crossed to her, one hand negligently in the pocket of his golf pants, she had to admire his erect posture, the trim leanness of his body that he worked so diligently to maintain, the boyish handsomeness that had a couple of women turning to watch as he passed.

She couldn't help the traitorous thought that the number watching Shane would be significantly higher. Groaning, she massaged her temple with unsteady fingers. Thoughts like that would only lead to problems, and she already had enough.

"Paige?" Russell greeted, surprised delight in his face, his voice, just before he gently took her shoulders and kissed her on the cheek. Not one current or one tiny jolt coursed through her. The sixty-two-year-old gardener who had been in her family's service since she was a teenager might as well have kissed her. "You must have missed me as much as I've missed you."

His statement made her feel worse. "Russell, we need to talk."

He must have caught the seriousness in her voice, seen it in her face, because his smile slowly died. "What is it? Can I help?"

Why couldn't she be attracted to a man who was so kind and caring? she thought. "Let's talk over here." She pulled him to a quiet corner, thankful most of the people were rushing out for sightseeing or other business. Placing the attaché case on a small table, she opened it and picked up the bracelet. "I can't keep this."

His brown eyes, always so gentle, narrowed on her face. He barely looked at the bracelet. "Why?"

There were probably many ways to explain things to him, but she knew only one. "Because, despite how much I want my feelings for you to deepen beyond those of a friend, they haven't and I don't think they will."

Distress tautened his face. His hands lifted, closing on her upper forearms. "Don't say that. I lo—"

"Russell, please." She bit her lip. She didn't want him vowing love when all she could give was friendship. She didn't want another failure.

His hands flexed on her arms. If she didn't know better, she'd think he looked almost desperate. "I care about you. Your father wanted us together. It was one of the last things we talked about the day we lost him. He was so pleased that I was going to ask you out, that we weren't going to disappoint him or my family."

The weight of his words slammed her into the chest,

almost bringing her to her knees, where she'd spent too much of her life already. Repenting for being a failure.

How many times had her father told her over the last years after they'd gotten closer that he didn't want her to disappoint him the way her brother and others had. And although she loved her brother, Zach, to her shame, she had stopped trying to defend him. When she did, her father had ways of showing his disapproval that made her feel insignificant and inept, the same way she used to feel before he'd finally loved her the way she had always wanted.

Zach said it didn't matter, to save her breath. He and his father hadn't seen eye-to-eye since he'd graduated from high school and didn't go to Stanford as his father had demanded. The tension between them had grown worse after Zach began producing music. Her brother letting her off the hook hadn't stopped the guilt or her feeling like a coward.

"Just give it time," Russell continued. "You're still grieving. Your feelings are mixed up."

Not mixed up enough that she wasn't attracted to her mother's houseguest, and that embarrassed her. Her head lowered.

"Sweetheart," Russell murmured, drawing her into his arms. "Everything will be all right. I'll keep the bracelet if it will make you feel less pressured. I'd do anything for you."

Her mind was in turmoil. One hand fisted on his chest, the other clenched the platinum bracelet. Everything wouldn't be all right, but he wasn't listening, and she was too big of a coward to make him listen. She reverted to type, going along to get along. Her head lifted, she stepped back and handed him the bracelet. "Thank you."

Taking the bracelet, he slipped it into his pocket.

"When you change your mind it will be waiting for you." He kissed her on the cheek before she could tell him that wasn't going to happen. He closed her attaché and handed it to her. "You better get moving or the luncheon guests will arrive before you."

She glanced at her watch and knew she didn't have time to argue. This time he was right. "See you later." Paige hurried toward the revolving front door, never looking back.

If she had, she might have seen the woman in the pink dress crook her finger toward Russell. After one panicked look at Paige going out the door, he hurried toward the woman with a wide grin on his face.

Chapter 3

Most people didn't realize all the behind-the-scenes hard work and synchronization needed for large events to go off flawlessly. Paige wasn't one of them.

From short wait staff, to misdelivery of items needed for the meal, to errors in the programs, things could and did go wrong. When it happened, people looked at her as manager of special events and fund-raising to quickly solve the problem. It was her job to see that everything ran smoothly. She prided herself on excelling.

In the kitchen just off the Majesty Ballroom where five hundred guests expected dessert after their meal, she made a slight adjustment after only half of her order was delivered. If the serving of cheesecake was small, there might be a few comments, but with so many women dieting or off dairy products, there were always desserts left.

She smiled at a passing couple, pleased to see that the elegant tables set with crystal, sterling, and beautiful pink and white lily flower arrangements were filling up nicely. No matter how many times she chaired an event she was always afraid that people wouldn't show up. A case in point was her guest speaker. His plane had taken off late from Detroit. Luckily he wasn't due to speak until after lunch, so there was still time.

She glanced around the crowded room and her breath snagged. *Shane.* Although he was a big man with broad shoulders and long, muscular legs, he moved easily through the throng. He didn't seem to notice the blatant stares of the women. Instead he appeared to be searching for something. Or someone.

Their gazes met. Clung. She went hot, then cold, from the sizzling impact. The noise of the room receded, yet she would have sworn her senses were more alive, more attuned. A moment later she knew they were. To Shane.

"Paige."

Caught ogling, Paige flushed and swung around, and barely missed bumping into a passing waiter with a pitcher of tea. She always had a horror of making a misstep in public and embarrassing her family.

"I'm sorry," she told the waiter, but he'd already moved away.

"No harm done," Jackie said. "My fault for startling you." She leaned over and whispered, "I don't blame you, though. Eye candy at its finest."

Paige couldn't keep another flush from her face. Denial was impossible. Jackie smiled in that warm, nonjudgmental way of hers. They'd hit it off from the moment Paige had been hired at the agency. Jackie was good at what she did, helping others be the best they could. In her early fifties, she had stylishly cut red hair, freckles, and a creamy complexion. She was committed to her job as president of the nonprofit organization.

"Since I'm a newly engaged woman I shouldn't have been looking, but he's kind of hard to miss or ignore," Jackie continued, with a grin on her pretty face.

"He's my mother's houseguest." Paige said the only thing she could, but Jackie had never been more on target. Shane in a suit was devastatingly male. "He'll be sitting at our table."

"And you were trying to catch his attention to ensure he found it," Jackie said in understanding. "Well, why don't we make sure he does, and on the way you can tell me how much longer it will be before our guest speaker arrives?"

"I wish I knew." Paige and her boss got along so well because they were honest and respected each other. "His plane should have landed twenty minutes ago. All I'm getting from the airport is that there has been a flight delay."

Jackie lifted her thinly arched brow. "I guess we could always let you stand in."

Paige stopped and stared at Jackie before she realized the other woman was teasing. In small crowds Paige had no problem, but even Toastmasters hadn't been able to get her over her fear of public speaking. "For that, I might tell Aaron you're a grouch before your three cups of coffee in the morning."

"He already knows that and loves me anyway," Jackie replied, a dreamy smile on her face.

"That he does," Paige replied just before they reached Shane, wondering again what it must feel like to be loved and be in love.

"Hi, Paige. Miss." He dipped his dark head, a smile tugging the sensual corner of his mouth. "Quite a gathering you have here. Your mother said you were good at this."

"Thank you." One thing she never doubted despite the uneasiness between them was her mother's support of her. "Jackie Weaver, president of Carl D. Rowe Foundation and my boss, meet Shane Elliott, my mother's houseguest."

"Pleased to meet you, Ms. Weaver." Shane extended his hand.

"My pleasure, and please call me Jackie." She glanced around the room, bustling with guests and wait staff, and whispered, "I have a birthday coming up, and calling me *Ms. Weaver* will only remind me of it more."

"If you'll call me Shane." He leaned over and whispered, "I don't know the birthday number, but you're too attractive to have to worry about it."

Jackie laughed aloud. "If my fiancé wasn't heading this way, I might hug you."

"There'll be no hugging except for me." Aaron Baskin joined them, slipping his arm easily around Jackie's rounded waist. He was tall, thin, and several inches taller, and the opposite in body build. Their love was evident in the little touches, the warm looks they exchanged when they were around each other.

Paige introduced him to Shane, still marveling that he had so easily charmed Jackie. Perhaps Paige should be worried about her mother.

"Are you all right?" Shane asked.

"Yes," she answered, frowning at him. She would have sworn his full attention was on Aaron.

"You looked like a woman with something on her mind," he said, his gaze so piercing that she was afraid she might have spoken her thought aloud.

"Probably hunger," Jackie said. "At these events she never eats before or during the event, and seldom, if ever, sits down."

"Then why don't we take our seats and see if this can be one of those times she eats?" Shane's long fingers curved easily around Paige's forearm. "Shall we?"

The heat from his hand burning through her light jacket was overpowering, and so was the command in his voice. A frown flittered across her brow.

"You're frowning again."

"Hunger," Jackie repeated, and headed toward table five. "Let's take our seats."

Paige glanced away from the sharp look in Shane's eyes. For a moment, just a moment, there was something in his voice that tugged at her memory of a time she didn't want to think about. Of a time another voice had been commanding, and made her feel like a foolish child.

"We're right behind you." Shane followed with her arm still in his grasp and, although it wasn't threatening, she had a feeling his hands could be.

"Is this all right?" Shane asked, his hand on the chair beside Jackie.

No. What she really needed was a moment to sort out why she was reacting so strongly to him. "I need to—"

"Sit," Jackie ordered, sliding into the chair Aaron held for her. "I'm pulling rank on you. Perhaps a full stomach will help us think better."

Paige doubted it, but she took her seat, then introduced Shane and Aaron to the other three people sitting there, a bank president, his wife, and their teenage daughter, who had looked bored earlier but perked up considerably on seeing Shane at their table.

"Anything I can do to help?" Shane asked, spreading his napkin on his lap.

"Not if you aren't Houdini," Paige answered, trying to be witty. Not her strong suit.

"And if I were?" Shane asked, with all the assurance of a man used to doing the impossible.

Jackie cut into her special order of baked fish. "Tell him, Paige. We're among friends. The foundation couldn't survive without the generosity of Mr. Usher's bank."

The distinguished man in a charcoal-gray three-piece

pin-striped suit nodded his thanks. "And we're glad to do it."

Strangely, Paige had been about to confide in Shane before Jackie told her to. There was something in the way Shane looked at her that made her want to open up to him, which was unusual. She was a private person. Quickly, she explained their problem with the missing guest speaker.

"Have you tried him lately?" Shane asked.

"Not in the last five minutes," she answered, her finger fiddling with her flatware.

"Hello, everyone," Russell greeted. The smile on his face died a quick death on seeing Shane sitting next to Paige. A hard frown on his face, he stared at Shane. Shane sent him a cocky grin and stared back.

Paige moistened her lips. For a moment she felt like a bone two dogs were about to fight over. A first. "Russell Crenshaw. Shane Elliott. Russell is a close friend of the family. Shane is Mother's houseguest."

Russell's face cleared and he took the only seat left, between Aaron and the banker's daughter. Paige liked the reserved table to seat eight instead of ten to give the honored guests more elbow room. She had never been less pleased about the seating arrangements.

Neither Russell, Aaron, nor the banker's daughter seemed particularly pleased they were sitting together. Russell gazed at the plate of chicken on a bed of wild brown rice in front of him, and dismissed it with a look. "Plan on staying here long, Elliott?"

"Depends." Shane cut into his chicken and forked in a bite.

Annoyance flattened Russell's lips into a thin line. "You're here on business then?"

"You might say."

Paige didn't know if Shane was giving such ambivalent answers to annoy Russell or because Russell was being rude and deserved them, but one of their main benefactors was at the table. "Shane's mentor and Mother were roommates at Vassar. He's a video game designer."

"Wow!" The teenager perked up again, propping her arms on the table. "Cool. What's the name of some?"

"Unfortunately the company went into bankruptcy before they could be developed," Shane explained.

"Bummer. I bet they were hot," she said, leaning back in her chair.

"I'd like to think so," Shane said, placing his fork on his plate. "One was a mind game where you were required to solve certain equations before you were allowed into the next level."

"Then you're jobless." Russell flung the accusation.

A dangerous glint in his eyes, Shane slowly turned to stare at Russell. The condescending smile slid from his face. Paige blinked at the quick change in Shane. He might be charming, but he wasn't a man to be slighted.

"You shouldn't have any trouble finding employment here," Aaron said into the charged silence. "Atlanta is growing with lots of opportunity."

Russell, trying to regain his composure, picked up the printed program in front of his plate. "Aaron knows. Did your company do these?"

"It would have been a conflict since we're engaged," Jackie said, her voice cool.

Russell didn't seem to notice. "Surely there should be extenuating circumstances since his company is so small. Two-man operation, isn't it?" He turned to the bank president, dismissing Aaron as if neither he nor the answer mattered. "Since the foundation is about helping people, surely the sponsors would understand."

"I certainly have no problem with Mr. Baskin working for the foundation," Mr. Usher said, a benign smile on his face.

"There." Russell turned, all smiles, as if he had healed the ills of the world. "You'll be getting more business, Aaron, and we all could use more business. I was in Beijing last month and have to go again. Heading operations for ten states with over five thousand employees keeps me stretched thin." He smiled across the table at Paige. "But whenever I go and no matter how busy, I never forget who I left behind."

Shane grunted. Paige didn't dare look at him. She was aware that Russell thought Jackie was marrying beneath her, but he had never been this condescending.

"But it's worth it," Russell continued. "Management isn't for the faint of heart." He looked pointedly at Shane. "Some people will always be the underlings, to do the bidding of others."

"And make the company successful," Shane said. He didn't back down from the gauntlet Russell had flung. Paige hadn't expected him to. "Giving orders is the easy part. Making them work is the difficult task." He turned to the banker. "I'm sure Mr. Usher would agree that all of his employees play an important part in the success of the day-to-day operations of his bank."

The man nodded his gray head. "That's very astute of you, Mr. Elliott, and exactly right. A bank has to be client-friendly. No employee is less than any other. A hostile clerk can be just as detrimental to business as a hostile loan officer. There are too many other banks out there for a customer to accept less than the best with every contact."

Russell's mouth tightened for a few seconds. "But under your leadership the bank has thrived, and it gives back so much to the community. It's in the genes. Family will tell."

"On that we agree," Shane said, the words coming out as anything but a compliment.

"Well, I'm not following in my daddy's footsteps," the teenager said, a mischievous smile on her face as she sipped her iced tea.

"Fashion design, perhaps?" Russell said.

She sent him an annoyed look. "Aeronautics."

Shane chuckled. Russell twisted uneasily in his seat. "I've got a feeling you'll do it. Women are as smart as men."

"Sometimes smarter," the banker's wife said, eliciting more chuckles from everyone around the table. Except Russell.

"That's obvious from the women at this table," Shane said, turning to Paige. "You don't talk, you just do."

"Exactly," Jackie said, with an emphatic nod.

Paige just stared. No one was better at the word game than Russell. Yet Shane had gotten the best of him. He'd won over the president of the largest bank in the city and his family as well. She didn't know what to think of him. Thankfully, her cell phone vibrated, giving her a way out.

"Excuse me. I need to take this call." Russell jumped up to pull her chair back, but Shane, who was closer, beat him to it. Shane smiled at Russell. A muscle flickered in Russell's clenched jaw. Paige's cell phone vibrated again. She didn't have time to pacify Russell or referee.

Thanking Shane, she hurried behind the partially drawn maroon velvet curtain near the podium. "Hello."

"Roscoe Thompson."

Relief swept through her. "Mr. Thompson. It's so good to hear your—"

"We're sitting on the runway," he interrupted. "The storm early this morning has everything backed up. We're the fifteenth plane back."

Paige quickly calculated the time it would take to deplane, then get to the hotel, and groaned. "You're set to speak in twenty minutes. You'll never make it in time."

"I'm sorry. I guess I should have come in last night as you originally suggested," he said.

Saying *I told you so* to one of the top motivational speakers in the country wouldn't help. "Things happen."

"Problems?"

She didn't jump, but it was a near thing. For a big man Shane certainly was quiet on his feet. "The guest speaker. His plane is fifteen back to the gate and the airport is thirty minutes from here in good traffic." She shook her head at the futility of things.

"If he has a BlackBerry with Internet or if he can borrow one, he can send his speech to another computer."

Paige was happy for all of two seconds. "But someone will have to read it."

"We'll cross that bridge when we have to," Shane said. "Just ask him."

She did, then turned to Shane. "He does and his speech is on it."

"Let's go find a computer." He took her arm. "You might want to check to see if the hotel has a helipad."

"Helipad?"

"My employer found them invaluable," he said, never pausing on the way to the door of the ballroom.

She followed. She didn't have a choice unless she wanted to be dragged. She couldn't help thinking that he certainly touched her a great deal, and that she liked it way too much.

Chapter 4

Shane enjoyed helping Paige. She was as sweet and loving as her mother had said.

Bent over the laptop computer, Shane grunted. He wasn't attracted to women who were sweet and loving. He glanced up at Paige, hovering over him, her lower lip caught between her teeth, and he thought how much he'd like to do that for her.

"Is something wrong?" she asked.

"No," he answered and went back to watching the file download. He hoped another part of his anatomy stayed down. What it was about Paige that got him excited and ready, he didn't know. He did know that it wouldn't lead to anything. He never mixed business with pleasure.

And although Russell had spouted a lot of crap, he had been right about *family will tell.* Paige wouldn't condemn him for his family background, but he knew there was no way he'd ever want her to know where he had come from.

"Are we about set?"

Shane looked up at the sound of the sultry voice of the news anchor for a local TV station, Veronica Wilson. Beautiful, long-legged, full lips with a smile that said *Your place or mine?* No strings, just hot sex.

He couldn't be less interested. "Since you're used to reading teleprompters, I've set up another laptop for you on the podium."

She rested her hand on his shoulder as she looked at the computer in his hands. "Nice work. We could use someone with your skills at the station."

Shane ignored the caressing fingers. "Thanks. We're ready when you are."

"We're thankful you're taking on this extra duty, Veronica," Paige said to the news anchor.

"My pleasure," she said, letting her hand slowly slide off Shane's shoulder. "I hope we have a chance to talk again."

"I'm sure we will," Shane answered. "Jackie, are you or Paige going to explain the change? The chopper is in the air and should be here in fifteen, but the guests are getting restless."

"I am." Taking Veronica's arm, Jackie headed for the steps leading to the stage.

"I still say I could have given the speech." Russell joined them, pique in his voice. "I'm more familiar with motivating people."

"And annoying them," Shane muttered. From Paige's and Russell's gasps, he guessed he hadn't been quiet enough. He grinned.

Jackie, on the stage with Veronica, stepped to the mike. "Due to unforeseen circumstances our guest speaker, Dr. Roscoe Thompson, will be a few minutes late. However, we have a treat in store. Veronica Wilson will begin with an introduction of Dr. Thompson's work, some of his anecdotes. He should be here in about twenty minutes to sign copies of his best-selling book, *Change*. Ms. Wilson."

"Thank you, Jackie, for this awesome opportunity to

share the podium with a man I admire and a book I've read." Veronica lifted a copy of the hardcover. "How many of us want to change something in our lives? Yet how many of us are afraid to do exactly that?"

Hands went up in the audience. Shane sensed Paige going still beside him.

"A direct quote from Dr. Thompson's speech says, 'It all begins with you.'" Veronica glanced offstage where Shane sat. "Go after what you want or be left behind. I know I plan to."

Applause erupted from the ballroom. *Not this time.* Shane planned on staying out of the woman's way. There was only one woman he was interested in and he couldn't have her. He didn't believe in substitutions or wasting his time.

"Thanks to you and Shane, the luncheon was a success," Jackie said as she stared fondly at Veronica, standing by the single and bookish-appearing Dr. Thompson.

"Glad to be able to help." Shane wished the doctor luck. He couldn't seem to keep his eyes off Veronica or his glasses up on the bridge of his nose. She hadn't looked Shane's way since the doctor announced he'd just signed a multimillion-dollar publishing deal.

"Veronica certainly seems to be enjoying the benefits," Paige said, frowning at the other woman.

"Dr. Thompson is a big boy," Jackie said, then hugged Paige. "Fantastic job, as always. See you Monday." She extended her hand to Shane. "Come visit us sometime."

Shane shook her hand and that of her fiancé. "Nice meeting you."

"Same here," Aaron said. "Perhaps we can grab a bite together or catch a game."

"I'd like that." Shane watched them join the crowd

leaving the room, Dr. Thompson and Veronica among them.

"Paige, something has come up and I won't be able to go to the apartment with you this afternoon," Russell said.

Paige's brows knitted. "But we're supposed to help Noah and Gayle paint their new place."

"I know." Russell smiled apologetically, showing perfectly capped teeth that Shane had a strong urge to rearrange. Instead, he watched Russell pull a couple of gift cards from a home improvement store out of the breast pocket of his suit jacket. "Perhaps this will make up for my not being there."

Paige took the cards without much enthusiasm. Russell's hundred-watt smile lost some of its voltage. "This is very thoughtful of you, Russell, but you know it's important to be there for them. You promised. We both did."

For a split second, irritation flashed in his eyes. "I know and I feel terrible about this, but I just received the phone call. You know I wouldn't miss going if I didn't have to. The amounts are very generous." His hands closed around her forearms, and Shane wanted to knock them away. "The company's president wants me to personally handle the problem, otherwise I wouldn't go." He kissed her on the cheek. "I'll call you later tonight."

Shane watched Russell merge with the crowd and make his escape. Shane had no doubt where he was actually heading, and it wasn't business. He was smooth and out for himself, just as Mrs. Albright had said. "You're painting?"

She glanced up at him, a bit distracted, and nodded. "Noah and Gayle are getting their first apartment ready, and we promised to help."

"Newlyweds?" Shane asked, although he knew the answer.

"Brother and sister," Paige answered, her natural smile returning. "They're complete opposites in personality. Gayle is shy and a bit naive. Noah is street-smart and assertive. They're coming out of foster care. For the first time they'll be on their own."

"An exciting time until the bills start rolling in, and you find you can only stretch money so far."

Paige paused in placing the centerpiece of pink and white lilies in a cardboard box. "You were in foster care?"

"In a manner of speaking." He grabbed the box and went to the next table, leaving her to follow. "What else do we have to do before you can leave?"

No one except her mother had ever asked that before. Even Jackie would depart with the other guests. "After this, I have to see the manager of the wait staff and make sure the laptop and other extra AV equipment is returned."

"Then all we have left is this and the manager." He moved to another table, this time picking up the centerpiece himself and placing it in the box. "I took care of the computers."

She frowned. "When?"

"When you were getting Dr. Thompson ready for his signing." It had given Shane a good excuse to escape Veronica until she found another victim.

A centerpiece in each hand, she came back to the table. "I can manage this. You go on. You must be tired from your trip."

"I'd rather stay and help you," he said easily. "It's not as if I have a lot to do."

Paige set one of the arrangements down, then reached

out to touch his arm. "There are lots of job opportunities here, you'll find something."

He was the one frowning. "What's a woman like you doing with a man like Russell?"

Her pretty eyes widened. She snatched her hand back.

"Ms. Albright, was everything to your satisfaction?" asked a man in a black tux.

"Superb, as always." Opening her attaché case, she handed him an envelope. "Please thank your staff."

"We thank you." After shaking her hand, he was gone again.

"That was nice of you," Shane said, trying to get back on an even footing after sticking his foot in his mouth, something he couldn't recall doing before.

"For a woman like me," she quipped, but there was hurt, not pique, in her shaky voice.

He realized she thought he had taken a swipe at her. "A woman who is kind, generous, caring, efficient. You don't forget anyone."

She blinked, then tucked her head, but not before he saw the softening of her features. "Serving a group this size is difficult, but I've always had top-notch service." She glanced at her watch and looked around one last time. The room was empty except for the hotel staff. "We can leave now."

"You sure you don't want to pick up the others?" he asked.

She seemed surprised that he'd asked. "The florist should be here shortly. I'm getting these for the dining tables at a retirement home. We have so many events; it's a shame not to let the flowers be appreciated for as long as possible."

He might have known. "When are you going to the apartment?"

"After I go home and change." She started toward the ballroom door.

"Mind if I tag along? It will give me a chance to see more of Atlanta," he said. "Plus I'm a pretty good painter."

She smiled at him as they started down the escalator. "I can't image you not being good at whatever you did." Her eyes widened and she tucked her head again. He had a feeling that if she hadn't been carrying her attaché case she might have clapped her hand over her mouth.

"Thanks. After seeing you in action, I can say the same thing about you," he told her, watching as she slowly lifted her head, a shy smile on her face.

P aige couldn't imagine what was wrong with her. First she was having all these irrational sexual feelings; now she was blurting out things without thinking. She threw a glance into her rearview mirror at Shane following in his rental. What had possessed her to say such a thing?

Perhaps it was the coming Masquerade Ball. The biggest fund-raiser of the year, and the most ambitious event she had ever attempted, taking over the entire fifteen-thousand-square-foot Carrington Estate with an expected crowd of two thousand guests. Tickets were three thousand dollars each. Failure was not an option, and she was in total charge. The stress must be getting to her. That had to be the reason for her uncharacteristic behavior.

Feeling more in control, she pulled up by the front door and got out. Shane exited his car as well, a sexy smile on his too-handsome face, as if he didn't have a care in the world. Women would fall all over themselves for him. And who could blame them? He was charming, sensitive, intelligent. But there was steel and a hint of danger beneath the easygoing facade. All in all a fascinating combination. When you added the devastating good looks, he was lethal. She was certainly finding it hard to resist him.

"You're frowning again."

Caught staring at him—again—she hoped she didn't blush. "I was just thinking that you might not have any old clothes with you."

His fingers closed gently around her arm. "A T-shirt and jeans will do, and I have those."

"All right." She started up the stairs—anything to get moving so he would release her arm. Her skin was too sensitive to his touch, and she enjoyed it too much.

Her mother met them at the door. "I've already had a couple of calls from friends who said the luncheon went fabulously. I knew it would."

"Thank you." Paige was used to the critiques of her parents' friends. If any of her mother's friends had anything negative to say, she never heard. Her father had been a different story, but he'd pushed himself to excel as well.

"It certainly was, and it didn't stop there," Shane said. "She's dropped off the flowers from the luncheon to a senior facility, and now she's going to help paint an apartment. I'm not sure where she gets her stamina."

Paige's mother smiled fondly at her as they walked toward the stairs. "She's always been full of energy. She single-handedly helped raise awareness and funds for scholarships for young adults coming out of foster care while she was still in high school."

"Mother, please. Shane doesn't care to hear about that," Paige said, not wanting her to get started. She'd go on and on about her children, given the least enticement.

"Sure I do," Shane said, and Paige barely kept from rolling her eyes.

"You should be proud," her mother said, smiling at her. "You gave up your allowance, held garage sales to raise the first thousand dollars, and challenged your father and grandparents to match you."

"Father met the challenge just as I knew he would," Paige said.

Her mother's smile wavered. "Yes, he did."

"We better get going, Paige, if we have to pick up the paint," Shane told her.

"Yes," she agreed and started up the stairs with him, wondering if he had noticed the happiness leave her mother's face at the mention of her husband, then thought, of course he had. He didn't miss much. What Paige continued not to understand was why the mention of her father's name seemed to dampen her mother's spirits so much.

And if it had anything to do with her trips to Texas and a man named Trent Masters.

Paige wasn't a pushover. There were times that afternoon when Shane feared she was, then he'd remember her standing up to him the night she had gone to the Masters family estate. At times she was bold, then others a bit of a shrinking violet.

He now understood. Paige might let you get one over on her, but not on those she cared about. She'd gone to Dallas to ensure that her mother was all right, become annoyed with Russell when he'd backed out of painting the apartment—and now the salesclerk in the home improvement store was trying to blow her off.

Five-three, with her brother's oversized white shirt over a white tank top and a pair of slim-fitting jeans, she looked adorable with her hair swept back from her face in a ponytail under an Atlanta Braves baseball cap. The clerk outweighed her by ninety pounds and had tattoos running from his wrists to beneath the sleeves of his T-shirt.

Folding his arms, crossing his legs, Shane leaned back against the shopping cart and waited for the man trying to get her to leave to get it through his thick head that for others, Paige was as bullheaded as they came.

"Lady, that is your order," he said for the third time in as many minutes.

"No, it isn't. It's the wrong color, and the amount is incorrect as well. There should be a five-gallon can of pale blue, five gallons of yellow, and ten of white." Paige patiently handed him the receipt. The annoyed young man behind the counter was in his midtwenties and wore a paint-splattered apron and black T-shirt. He barely looked at it before handing it back. "That's the name on the can."

"Then someone has made a mistake."

He shrugged. "Sorry. You'll have to talk to the manager." He looked behind her pointedly and beckoned to the next person in line.

Paige didn't budge. "Then please call him."

"I will if you'll step—"

"I'm not moving until you call a manager," she said, folding her arms.

"Lady, there are—"

"Call the manager," Shane said, not moving from the cart, his voice deadly quiet.

The young man jerked his head up and around. His eyes widened. He took a step back.

"Shane, I can handle this," Paige said, without turning around. She was having enough trouble dealing with the heat of his hard body burning into hers. Perhaps she should have left him at her mother's house. Or perhaps she should ask him to step back. Both sensible ideas, but she did neither. Her reaction annoyed her, yet somehow it made her feel more alive than she'd ever thought possible.

"Sure you can," Shane said easily. "I'm just the muscle to carry the paint. All twenty gallons of it."

The man behind the counter threw a frantic look at the one-gallon can of paint on the counter in front of Paige and grabbed the phone. "Manager to the paint department. Stat."

As soon as he hung up, Paige told him sweetly, "You might want to tell those behind me that you're sorry for the delay, but you'll be with them as soon as you've corrected my order."

He eyed her, and then Shane, before saying to the people behind her, "Be with you in a minute."

Up strode a tall man with bags under his brown eyes, wearing a frown and a red plaid shirt. His stomach pushed out the orange apron with the store's logo. "What seems to be the problem?" he asked the young man behind the counter. The clerk in turn pointed to Paige, but she had already stepped up to the man.

"Thank you for coming so promptly." Paige stuck out her hand. "Paige Albright, and you are—?"

The man blinked, then hurriedly offered his callused hand. "Dennis Yearly, the paint department manager."

The man continued to stare down at her while holding her hand. Paige simply smiled. For some odd reason people often did that when they first met her. She'd come to the conclusion it was her gray eyes staring out of a light brown face. "Mr. Yearly, as you can see by this receipt, my paint order is incorrect." She handed him the receipt. "It's imperative that it be corrected.

The painting has to be completed today for move-in to-morrow."

He studied the receipt, then turned to the young man. "Where's the paint?"

He dutifully pointed a paint-stained finger to the one gallon of paint. "Her name is on it."

"Miss, if your name is on the paint, there is—"

"Mr. Yearly," she said, cutting him off. "From the receipt you can see that this is not what was ordered or paid for. It is certainly not the type of service I expected. Can you correct the problem or do we need to talk to the store manager and, if he can't solve it within the next five minutes, the district manager?"

Annoyance swept across his face. "I'm doing—"

Paige cut him off. "Let's cut to the chase and call the store manager." She took out her cell phone.

"What are you doing?" the department manager asked, frowning down at her.

"Taking a picture of the paint you're trying to shove off on me. Then I'm taking a picture of you, the man behind the counter, and the clock." She held up the camera phone with his picture frozen for him to see. "In the meantime please call the store manager. I don't want to miss getting him and his photo in on this dispute, which a seven-year-old could clear up."

The department manager reached toward the camera phone. Shane stepped to her side and shook his head. The man's hand clenched, his mouth narrowing into a thin line.

"Did I miss you calling the store manager?" Paige asked sweetly and took the photo of the clock on the wall behind her. "Time is wasting."

"And you have customers waiting," Shane reminded him.

The manager blew out a frustrated breath, then shot another look at Shane.

Paige didn't want to look over her shoulder at Shane, but every time either of the men looked in his direction, they became nervous. Surely they'd seen well-built men before.

"Do we need to call him for you?" Shane asked, his voice flat.

The department manager gulped. Paige couldn't help but look this time. Shane smiled at her. Her stomach shimmied. She quickly turned back around.

"No need to do that," the department manager said jovially. "You have your receipt. We pride ourselves on happy customers." He turned to the young man and handed him the receipt. "Take care of this."

The young man sent them a killer look, but he took the receipt.

Paige turned the cell phone to the manager so he could see his frozen image, pressed DELETE, and then put the cell phone back in her purse. "Thank you, Mr. Yearly. While he's getting our correct order, I need to pick up a few more things. Would you have time to help me with this list?" She pulled a sheet of paper from her purse. "The paint is latex and oil-based. I believe we need different brush types for each kind of paint."

Mr. Yearly reached under his apron and tried to pull his pants back over his stomach. "You're right, miss, and, like I said, we pride ourselves on customer service." He firmly turned to the man behind the counter. "I expect her order to be ready when we get back." Then to the people in line. "Sorry for the wait, folks. When it's your turn, we'll give you the same personal service."

"I can attest to that," Paige said, smiling at the long

line of disgruntled customers behind her. Her smile didn't waver when only one or two smiled back.

The manager threw back his shoulders. "This way to the paintbrushes."

Shaking his head, Shane followed. She could be tough if need be. Now, if she could just cop that attitude with Russell.

Chapter 5

The apartment complex was located in a quiet, well-kept residential neighborhood in the midst of an older section of the city. Paige drove through the open black iron gates that shut at midnight and opened at 5:00 AM, past the one-story office building, and pulled up at the second unit. "This is it."

Shane looked at the elderly couples walking down the sidewalk. There had been another group of older people congregated in front of the rental office. He saw the well-kept yard, the ring of marigolds and caladiums around every tree, the clean sidewalks and streets of the complex. "I can see why you'd pick the place, but I can't imagine them going along with it."

"They weren't too pleased until I had a friend pull a police report on the other apartment they wanted. The burglary rate was incredible, whereas this apartment complex has only had one burglary in the past six months," Paige told him.

"I guess thieves figure senior residents here weren't worth the effort," Shane said. "They don't understand that older people can pinch pennies better than anyone."

"Did your grandparents?" she asked, wanting to know more about him.

"Not that I ever knew." Shane reached for his door handle.

Reluctantly, Paige did the same, then she smiled. "They must have been watching for us."

Shane saw a handsome young man in paint-splattered jeans and a white T-shirt showcasing impressive shoulders racing toward him. The teenager stopped and beckoned a pretty young, full-figured woman in an oversized shirt and pants walking at a slow pace behind him to hurry. Smiling, she did as he bade. They both reached the car at the same time.

"Hi, Paige, you had Gayle worried," the young man said, still grinning as he stopped by the driver's side of the car.

The teenage girl slanted a look at Shane and momentarily tucked her head. "I was not. I knew if you said you'd be here, you would."

The boy threw his arms playfully around his sister's shoulders. "Just teasing." He gave Shane the once-over. "I hope you're here to help."

"I am." Shane liked the brash young man. He didn't take him at face value, and the sizing-up probably meant he had tangled with the police. So had Shane at one time.

Getting out of the car, Paige popped the trunk. "Shane Elliott is a houseguest. This is Gayle and Noah Mathis."

The young man shook his hand; his sister nodded and went to the trunk where Paige waited. "Noah and I can handle the paint if you ladies will get the rest of the things Paige bought."

Paige threw Shane a dismissive look. "Mr. Yearly said I could bring back anything we didn't use as long as we had the receipt."

"Which will be most of the things." Shane picked up two of the five-gallon cans.

"Is Russell coming later?" Noah asked, picking up the other cans.

"No, he had unexpected business, but he sent both of you a gift card to the home improvement store in case you needed something else," Paige said, her arms tightening around the bulging paper bag she held.

"You can always depend on Russell," Noah deadpanned.

Paige glanced up at him sharply.

"How does it feel to be in your own place?" Shane asked from beside Gayle.

Gayle looked startled that he had spoken to her. "Exciting." She clutched another paper bag and a long-handled roller. "A little scary."

"I can imagine," Shane said as they started up the stairs to the second floor. "I went straight into the army out of high school. I didn't know what to expect."

"Paige made sure we did," she said softly. "We had to search for the apartment, compare prices, look for furniture, grocery shop."

Leading the way, Noah opened the door to the apartment. "She even had us cutting out coupons for anything from cleaners to groceries to restaurants." He shuddered. Gayle laughed, and he threw a look of affection back over his shoulder.

Whatever the problems that had led them to this point in life, they had each other, they had Paige. That was a better start than most had. It certainly topped his experience. He had a biological family whom he detested as much as they detested him.

Inside the apartment the walls were freshly plastered. There was painter's tape around the baseboards and where the thin wooden cabinets in the kitchen connected to the walls. The carpet was dark and threadbare in places. It was a palace compared with where Shane had come from.

"Not much to look at," Noah said with a shrug.

"Now," Paige said firmly. "You and Gayle will change that. The important thing is that it's on the bus line for your jobs and college in the fall, and near a grocery store."

"Where you can use those coupons," Shane said, earning a shy smile from Gayle. "You guys have done a good job getting things ready."

"Paige's doing again," Gayle said. "We went online and talked to a decorator before we started. I'll miss the computer at the home."

"We might be able to squeeze it into the budget," Noah said. "We'll be able to get one with the new credit card that companies are so anxious to send to people." He looked at Paige. "That we will pay off before the first bill."

"Then why not wait until you have the money?" she questioned. "There's a reason for the credit card mailing out those applications. If something happens and you can't make the payment, the twenty-eight percent interest is going to hit you hard. It'll dump money into their account and take it out of yours."

Noah shook his head. "Somehow I knew you'd say that."

Shane was curious. "Then why mention it?"

"Because she has our best interests at heart, because she tells me straight, not what I want to hear." Noah blew out a breath and looked at his sister. "I guess we wait."

"We wait," she repeated.

"Where do we start?" Shane asked, easily seeing why Paige wanted to help them. Unlike his parents and brother, Noah and Gayle wanted to help themselves, not sit on their collective butts and wait for a handout, or scam people.

"Gayle's room. She deserves to be the first," Noah said, his face serious for the first time.

"I—"

"Don't argue with your big brother." Noah picked up the five-gallon can of pale yellow paint.

"Gayle, speaking from experience, I'd say save your breath." Paige placed her cap on the passway between the kitchen and the living area, then pulled two large blue bandannas from her pocket. Giving one to Gayle, she tied the other over her head. "Zach never let me win an argument. Now let's get this show on the road."

Working together they painted the two bedrooms and then the living area. Shane and Noah were finishing up the kitchen while Paige and Gayle did the single bathroom.

"Thank you for helping us," Noah said, carefully going around the edge of the cabinets.

"You're helping yourself." Shane ran the roller brush up and down the wall, giving it its second coat of glistening white paint where the refrigerator would eventually go.

Noah stopped painting and turned. "You're nothing like him. Maybe I won't have to worry about Paige anymore."

Shane didn't need two guesses as to who the young man was talking about. He kept working. "Paige can take care of herself. Besides, she wouldn't like us discussing her."

"I guess not. When I first met her, I thought she was one of those do-gooders who volunteered to make themselves feel and look good."

"What changed your mind?" Shane asked, aware that they were doing just what he said they shouldn't do, discussing Paige.

"No matter how much I messed up, getting into

trouble at school, at the foster home, losing a good job—if I bothered to get one—because of my mouth, she never stopped trying to get through to me. She kept telling me that I had the brains to make something of myself." Noah shook his dark head.

"I was headed to hell or jail—maybe they're one and the same—as fast as I could go until she made me realize that if I didn't straighten up, there would be no one to take care of my sister. She never missed a day of school, was never in the principal's office, and she finished third in our class. My sister is going places."

"You both are," Shane reminded him.

"Now. Six months ago it was a different story," Noah admitted with a shake of his head. "It scares me sometimes to think of how close I came to being a statistic."

"But you made the decision to listen. Some people never learn." Like his family. Shane dipped his roller into the paint tray.

"That's what Paige says. We're twins. Our parents died when we were five. After my mother's brother used up the insurance money, he didn't have much use for us." Noah shrugged. "Uncle said he couldn't take care of us. Our family and the state might have left us to fend for ourselves, but Paige hasn't. She's one cool lady."

"Why, thank you," Paige said from the doorway, then she bowed her head and laughed. "But don't think because you gave me a compliment that you can slack off." She folded her arms and looked at Gayle. "Since we're finished first, perhaps we should go eat by ourselves."

"I'm painting." Noah quickly but carefully finished the second coat around the cabinet.

Shane said without turning, "I guess you didn't consider we had a larger area."

"We considered. That's why we didn't just leave," Paige told him, a smile tugging the corners of the mouth that he had thought too much about. He'd never seen her this carefree. He hated to put a damper on things. But there was no way around it.

"While we're finishing up, Paige, why don't you gather the drop cloths, extra brushes, sandpaper, and all the other things we didn't use? We can return them after we eat."

Her smile slipped. She wrinkled her nose. "I was hoping you might have forgotten that."

"Not a chance." He almost smiled. He could get used to that smile, to teasing her. Instead he placed his roller over the paint tray and opened the door to the cabinet. "With some varnish and some molding these would look a lot better."

"I was thinking the same thing. Perhaps some chair railing in the kitchen as well," Gayle said, then bit her lip.

"Why didn't you say something before?" Noah asked.

"It wasn't in the budget," Gayle said as if that explained everything.

"It is now," Paige told them. "When I take the unused merchandise back you'll have a refund on your gift card to use for future purchases, and the gift cards Russell sent can be used to buy the molding. So, Gayle, if you have any other ideas, let's have them while we have two men who are probably as good with a hammer as they are with a paintbrush."

"Well, there were one or two other things," Gayle said, then smiled.

Since all of them had paint on their clothes, they chose a small barbecue restaurant. Noah insisted he pay. Aware of a man's pride, Shane let him. They selected seats in the back of the restaurant. Halfway finished with their meal, Paige nixed Gayle's idea of forgetting the crown molding and inserts.

"You want to make your place as welcoming as possible." Paige delicately licked sauce from the corner of her mouth.

"And besides, if we stick with smaller molding, it won't be as expensive. Wider pieces would overpower the area," Shane said, trying not to stare at Paige's quick little tongue and imagine it on his body. "And as Paige said, Noah and I can handle the grunt work."

"If you're sure. I—"

"We're sure," Noah said, interrupting his sister from his place beside her in the booth. "Your thing is interior design. You're good at what you do."

"Oh, Noah," she bemoaned, shaking her head at him. "Helping Mrs. Hill and a few of her neighbors is no testament to my ability."

"It is since more of your foster mother's friends want your services." Paige picked up her cola. "But next time they pay you."

"But—"

Again Gayle was cut off, this time by Paige. "But nothing. They pay for your bus ride plus an hourly salary."

"As a grunt worker, I'd agree. People will use you unless you stop them." Shane polished off his sliced beef sandwich.

"I bet no one ever got one over on you," Noah said.

"They tried," Shane said. "Now if everyone is finished, we can get to the home improvement store if we're going to go back and do the molding." Before his words were out of his mouth, Noah, Gayle, and Paige were scrambling from the table.

* * *

Shane hadn't been around young adults very much, but he couldn't imagine two happier ones than Gayle and Noah selecting exactly the perfect molding, then proudly carrying the pieces of lumber to the cashier.

"Thank you," Paige said, standing beside Shane as Noah and Gayle watched the clerk ring up their purchases.

"For the muscle?" he asked.

"For treating them as if they matter, for validating Gayle's ideas," Paige said in an aside as they stood a few feet behind them.

"She'll get over her shyness and gain the confidence she needs," he said. "She reminds me of someone else I kn—"

"I'm telling you there's not enough on the cards to cover the purchase," the cashier said, turning the readout around for Noah and Gayle to see.

Worried, Paige rushed up to the register. "There must be a mistake. How much is the total?"

"Ninety-nine dollars and seventy-eight cents." Noah, his lips tight, dug into his jean pocket for his wallet. "I have the rest."

Gayle's hand on his stopped him. "No. That money is earmarked for groceries and a deposit on a phone. We'll just put everything back."

"No, wait. Russell said . . . ," Paige began, then looked at the fifty-dollar total of the gift cards and reached for the purse slung over her shoulder.

"I got this." Shane handed the clerk a fifty-dollar bill. "Consider it my contribution. Besides, I want to see how Gayle's and my ideas work."

Paige flushed. "I'm sorry. There must be some mistake. Russell assured me it was a generous amount."

Shane handed the receipt and bag of inserts to Gayle. "Come on, Gayle, we'll have the man in lumber cut these for us."

"Gayle, Noah, I'm sorry," Paige repeated.

"You have nothing to be sorry for," Gayle told her, catching her arm and following Shane. "Without you, I don't want to think of where we'd be."

Noah caught her other arm. "She's right. Things happen. Besides, we learned one of those valuable life lessons you're always talking about."

"What?" Paige asked as they stopped behind the CAUTION sign at the cutting area.

"First impressions are generally on target."

Shane saw Paige flinch. Even the kid had Russell's number. Shane just hoped Paige woke up as well.

After returning to the apartment, they varnished the cabinet moldings and painted those for the kitchen walls. As everything dried in another room, they sanded, then washed, the cabinets. Shane attached the crown molding, inserts, and chair railing. Paige, Noah, and Gayle varnished the cabinets, then watched as Shane, with Noah's help, affixed the front molding.

"It's beautiful. Shane, you and Gayle were right," Paige said, staring at the sparkling kitchen with cabinetry that now stood out, and the distinctive yellow crown molding and chair railing.

"Instead of a computer, I think we'll get a few area rugs." Gayle frowned down at the faded linoleum on the kitchen floor, the threadbare carpet in the living area. "The floors really stand out now, and not in a good way."

"The furniture will take care of that," Noah, ever the optimist, assured her. "Just think, tomorrow night we'll be sleeping in our own place."

Excitement shone in their faces. "What time did you say the mover was coming?" Gayle asked.

"One o'clock," Paige said, her face not as bright as it had once been. "Let's lock up, and we'll take you home."

Gayle and Noah looked around the place one last time, then headed out the door. Paige started after them, but stopped when Shane caught her arm. "His fault, not yours."

"How . . ." She shook her head. "You wasted your talents in computers. What else are you good at?"

His black eyes, hot and penetrating, stared down at her. "Any number of things."

She'd meant it as a joke. The sizzling passion in his eyes was anything but. Her awakening body stirred, yearned. She wondered what it would feel like to have his strong hands all over her body loving her, stroking her. The little smile on her face died. "Shane—"

"Are you two coming?" Noah yelled.

Breaking away, Paige quickly escaped. Shane let her go. This was worse than he had anticipated. He wanted a woman he couldn't have, and there was nothing he could do about it.

Paige was determined that there would be no more nonsense between her and Shane. He saw too much and she felt too much when she looked at him, saw him looking back at her. As soon as they entered the house, she thanked him again, said good night, then hurried to her room. But that wasn't the only reason.

Picking up the phone by the bedside, she dialed Russell's cell. It was past twelve, but he kept it on all the time for his clients to reach him. She knew Noah didn't trust or like Russell. Perhaps with good reason.

Russell had insisted he drive them during Noah and Gayle's search for an apartment. At the first stop they'd come back out of the apartment with the manager to hear Russell on his cell telling someone that he was busy with another of Paige's charity cases.

He'd tried to explain that he meant her work in general and not them. She had wanted to believe him, but thought it best for Russell to take her home to get her car. Knowing how Noah and Gayle felt about him, she'd never involve Russell again. He'd volunteered to help paint and offered the gift cards.

"Hello," he said after the sixth ring, sounding out of breath.

"Russell, are you all right?" she questioned. Russell took great pride in taking care of his body. He ran three miles every morning.

"Paige," he said, surprise evident in his voice.

She'd never called anyone except Zach this late. "I'm sorry to disturb you, but this is important. The gift cards you called generous were only twenty-five dollars each."

There was the briefest of pauses, then, "What! There has to be some mistake."

Paige had been holding her breath, then felt disloyal for ever doubting Russell. He wouldn't be that cruel. Yet for a little while she'd thought that perhaps Shane and Noah were right. "Do you have the receipts?"

"No, I didn't think it necessary."

"How much was each for?" she asked, almost blurting out the question, pacing as she waited for an answer. "You said it would be generous."

"Two hundred dollars each" came the quick reply.

Relieved, she plopped on the side of the bed. "Thank you, Russell. They could really use that money."

"Sorry you had to supplement them. Of course I'll reimburse you."

"Not me, Shane." For some odd reason she became restless and stood.

"He was there?"

You weren't, she almost told him. Instead she said, "The entire afternoon. He really made a difference."

"Be careful, Paige," Russell warned, his voice sharpening. "You're so naive and trusting. He's unemployed and sponging off your mother. He looks shifty."

Mouthwatering always, shifty—never. And she was tired of people thinking her naive. Yes, she trusted people, expected the best out of them. And because she did, she was willing to give Russell the benefit of the doubt.

"He stepped in at the luncheon to help, at the apartment, and then tonight. He's been there when I needed him." As soon as the words were out of her mouth she wished she could call them back. She should have said *when we needed him.* From Russell's silence, he had caught the slip.

"My skills with the computer probably rival his, and anyone can paint," he said dismissively.

Pointing out that he hadn't offered a solution at the luncheon and that anyone *couldn't* paint would only lead to an argument, and she was tired. "Russell, I have the receipt and the gift cards. Monday we can go to the store and straighten this out. You always pay with your credit card so it should be easy to track."

There was dead silence on the line.

"They could use that money, and I don't want a computer glitch shortchanging them," she said.

"I'll be busy, but I'll try to work it in," he said slowly.

"Thank you, Russell. Good night." She hung up, the niggling doubt creeping back. She pushed it away. Russell wasn't fond of her working with foster children, but he wouldn't lie about the amount on the gift card.

Would he?

Chapter 6

Paige was awake when her alarm went off Sunday morning at seven. She'd slept poorly and had finally given up, gotten out her laptop, and set to work. She'd planned to work on the list of donors for the next fund-raiser, but hadn't been able to keep her mind off Shane.

Sighing, she closed her eyes and leaned back against the headboard. He moved her, scared her. Her body reacted too hungrily to his. Once her body awakened she didn't seem able to control her response to Shane. Not only that, his opinion of her mattered. Too much. She didn't even try to tell herself it was a reflection of the old Paige who wanted, needed to please everyone so they'd like her.

She wasn't that needy anymore. Yet every time she had required help, Shane had been there. No situation seemed to throw him. It was comforting to be around someone that self-assured.

And like Noah, Shane thought she'd let Russell get one over on her. She'd seen that pitying look too many times in the past not to recognize it. Blowing out a breath, she saved the document and shut down the computer. She wasn't looking forward to seeing that look again. She'd purposefully set the alarm early so she'd be gone by the time he and her mother got up.

Placing the laptop on her desk in the corner by the French doors, she picked up the undergarments she'd laid out the night before and went to take a bath. Then, dressed in a white suit with a small crownless black hat and black patent-leather heels, she picked up her purse and hurried down the stairs.

"Morning, Paige."

On hearing Shane call her name she stopped dead in her tracks and whirled, her breath hitching when she saw him coming from the direction of the kitchen. How could one man be so breathtakingly handsome? He wore a cream-colored sports jacket that showed his wide shoulders and incredible physique to perfection.

"Shane," she finally managed, when she got her tongue unstuck from the roof of her mouth, and continued to the foot of the stairs.

"Your mother has breakfast ready," he said, coming toward her with that slow, sexy walk of his.

She just had to ask. "How did you know I was up?"

Stopping in front of her, he gave her another heart-stopping smile. "The pipe in your bathroom knocks when the water in the shower or tub runs."

Her face grew warm at the thought of Shane knowing she was naked. From the way the smile slowly slid away, the way his dark eyes narrowed on her mouth, he had thought about it, too. Oh, mercy.

"Breakfast is getting cold," called her mother.

"Coming," Shane answered. Taking Paige's arm, he led her to the kitchen and held out a chair.

"Good morning, Mother," Paige greeted, hoping her voice sounded normal instead of hot and bothered.

"Good morning, Paige," her mother called. She was standing in front of the stove scrambling eggs in a large skillet. "I know you have a big day, and I wanted you to have a good breakfast."

Paige looked at Shane as he patiently held a chair for her. "Guilty," he said. "I hope you don't mind."

"No, of course not." Paige gratefully took her seat at the table set for three. Her legs weren't too steady. If just a look, a touch unsettled her, what would happen if he molded his sensual mouth to hers? Caressed her tongue with his? Heat flooded her face. She tucked her head. "Thank you."

"My pleasure," he said, his voice deep. His sensual gaze swept over her like a velvet caress. For a wild moment her breath stalled, her gaze clung to his tempting mouth, then he turned away. "I'll get the platter of eggs."

"Thank you," Mrs. Albright said, following Shane to the table and taking the chair he held out for her.

"Thank you for cooking." Shane took his seat. "Another wonderful reason for waking up in the morning."

Desperately seeking control over her wild reaction to Shane, Paige looked up, knowing she'd find him watching her. Her stomach muscles quivered. She might be fighting a losing battle.

"I'll say grace so we can eat," her mother said.

Paige quickly bowed her head to pray, silently asking to remain the sensible woman she prided herself on being. Finished, she lifted her head, saw Shane's mobile mouth curve into a seductive smile across the table at her, and accepted that Shane was the kind of man who could make a sensible woman enjoy sin.

"What's the agenda for today? Do you plan for us to be there before the furniture arrives?" Shane asked, passing her the platter of meat.

The platter wobbled in her hand. "Us?" Without being asked, he was volunteering to help. Again. She didn't even think of trying to talk him into not going, and was a bit ashamed that she had planned to leave him out today because of her inability to control her body around him. Her problem. Not his. "Yes. But knowing how impatient Noah is, he'll be there by twelve."

"I can't blame him," Shane said, exchanging the meat platter for one of eggs. "I'm no decorator, but the place looked great." He handed the pancakes to Mrs. Albright. "You should see it."

"I'd like to, if Paige doesn't mind," Mrs. Albright said, a bit tentative.

"Of course not," Paige quickly said, finding that she meant it. Shane had accomplished something else: He'd eased the tension between her and her mother. "You took Gayle to estate sales and persuaded your friends to donate or sell furnishings at an affordable price. Thanks to you, their place is going to be fabulous, but even more, a real home with furnishings they can be proud of."

"Seems you two make a good team." Shane cut into his pan sausage.

"I enjoyed it," Mrs. Albright said. "Gayle has a good eye for color and detail. She'll succeed."

"So will Noah." Paige drizzled maple syrup over her pancakes. "He's a natural."

"For what?" Shane asked.

"Psychology. He likes to figure people out," she said, thinking of his opinion of Russell. "He's good at it."

"He's had to be to survive, but for others it takes longer," Shane said.

Paige busied herself with her food, wondering if he was right, and if he was talking about her.

Holding Mrs. Albright's and Paige's arms, Shane escorted them down the steep steps of one of the largest churches in Atlanta. It had been a long time since he'd been inside a church. If there was one place that supposedly accepted you as you were, it was here. The problem with that was the *people* in the church didn't always have the same forgiving attitude.

"Joann. Paige."

Shane felt both women tense beside him. Rushing toward them was a smartly dressed woman in a tight-fitting lilac suit with a hat, bag, and gloves to match. He recognized her immediately. Russell's mother wore the same disapproving expression as her son on seeing Shane for the first time. Stopping in front of them, her critical gaze swept from his bare head to the off-the-rack wing tips.

"Hello, Tess," Joann and Paige greeted, then Joann continued. "Tess, I'd like you to meet Shane Elliott. Shane, this is Tess Crenshaw, Russell's mother."

"Mrs. Crenshaw," Shane greeted.

Mrs. Crenshaw barely tilted her head, causing the lilac feather in her wide-brimmed hat to waver slightly. "I heard you had a houseguest," she said, speaking to Joann.

"Yes," Paige answered. "Shane's mentor and Mother were roommates at Vassar."

"Really," she said, then ignored Shane and spoke to Paige. "Russell is at his place working. When we spoke this morning, all he could talk about was you." She touched Paige's jacketed arm. "We all love you. I was hoping that you two might unite our families the way your father wanted."

"I . . . Russell knows how I feel." Paige flushed and threw a sideways glance at Shane.

Tess frowned as if she didn't know how to take that answer. "His father and I are going to the club for brunch. We'd love for you and your mother to join us. Your guest, too, of course."

"Thank you, Mrs. Crenshaw, but we have other plans," Paige said.

"Oh?" Mrs. Crenshaw responded, lines pleating her forehead.

"Two of Paige's friends are moving today, and she's helping them," Joann explained.

"Anyone I know?" Tess asked.

"No, but you met them," Paige said. "Noah and Gayle Mathis."

"The two indigents I met at your parents' house?" Mrs. Crenshaw asked with an affronted lift of her perfectly arched brow.

"Hardly," Paige said tightly.

"They're smart, resourceful young adults and Paige helped them get to where they are." Shane was tired of the condescending woman.

"And how would you know all this?" Tess asked, a barely concealed sneer in her voice.

"Because unlike some people I could name, I took the time to get to know them. I didn't prejudge them because they had less money," Shane said. "You know, like the pastor just said in his sermon about judging others."

Russell's mother's mouth tightened. Her angry eyes stabbed him.

"Tess, if you'll excuse us," Joann said into the charged silence. "We're on a tight schedule. Good-bye."

"Of course, good-bye," Mrs. Crenshaw said, finally dragging her hostile gaze from Shane. "Paige, be sure to call Russell. He'll be so glad to hear from you."

"If I have time," Paige said.

The shocked expression on Russell's mother's face was priceless. Shane tipped his head and led the women to his Ford rental. She'd taken a swipe at Paige's charges.

A definite no-no. Paige was gradually coming into her own, and he couldn't wait.

Paige was right about Noah and Gayle being there before the appointed time. The two teenagers were getting off the bus when Shane pulled into the apartment complex a little after noon. "I'm so glad they didn't beat us here," Paige said.

"Why?" her mother asked from the backseat.

"You'll see," Paige said. "Shane, hurry and park so all of us can go up to the apartment together."

After parking by the black wrought-iron stairs leading to the second floor, Shane opened the passenger door for Mrs. Albright. Paige was already out and waiting for the new apartment dwellers at the bottom of the stairs.

"I see you couldn't wait," Paige said with a laugh after everyone had spoken.

Gayle smiled a bit sheepishly. "We came directly from church. Mrs. Hill and her husband are bringing over our things later this afternoon."

"I can't wait to see what you've done, Gayle, and how the furnishings you selected will look," Mrs. Albright said.

"Me, too, but the place already looks great. You won't believe the difference," Gayle said, animation in her voice. "Shane was a big help."

"I was glad to do it," Shane said.

"Why don't we all go up to our place and wait?" Noah said, his face serious for all of two seconds before he laughed. "*Our* place. I've waited a long time for that to become a reality. I can't imagine any better-sounding words."

"You will in time," Mrs. Albright said, looking meaningfully at Paige.

"Friends, respect, loyalty," Shane said.

"Don't forget love," Gayle blurted.

"Not a chance," Shane said.

Standing beside Shane, Paige felt the softly spoken words all the way down to her soul. What would it feel like to be loved by a man who championed you, who believed in you unfailingly, who stood by your side no matter what? The Black Knight that she had dreamed of since childhood come to life. She was afraid she'd never know.

"I didn't," the young man said. "Friend. Sister. Love. Respect. Loyalty. And that's why our place is so awesome." He extended his arms to Gayle. "Let's go open our door and greet our first visitors."

"Let's." Gayle stepped up beside him.

Shaking away her momentary melancholy, Paige hurried behind them. This was about Gayle and Noah, not her foolish dreams from childhood of a Black Knight to slay her dragons.

Noah unlocked the door, pushing it open for those behind him to enter first. His sister stepped aside as well. Paige rushed inside, putting her finger to her lips as her mother and Shane followed her into the apartment.

Noah and Gayle were barely inside before they stopped abruptly and looked down. Plush gray carpet stretched beneath their feet. She squealed. He yelled. They both lunged for Paige.

"When? How?" the twins asked almost in unison.

Paige laughed with them. "Since I was with you when you leased the apartment, I was able to convince the apartment manager to let the men in early this morning to lay the carpet," she told them. "My boss is redecorating her house with hardwood floors and wanted to get rid of her almost new carpet. I asked for it and she said yes. She also has enough gray tiles to do the kitchen floor when you're ready."

"Thank you for this, for not giving up on me," Noah said, swallowing, then swallowing again.

"Someone didn't give up on me," Paige said, her gaze going to her mother, who was biting her lower lip.

"I hear a large engine," Shane said. "Maybe the mover is here early, too."

"Oh, my! The furniture and appliances," Gayle said and took off, this time leaving her brother to follow.

Shane took immense pleasure in watching Paige, working with her. He delighted in the warm smiles she and her mother exchanged before either of them had time to guard their emotions. Both were giving women, but life, as it had a tendency to do, had dealt them a cruel blow.

Just as it had to Gayle and Noah, but to look at them as they helped unload furniture, debate over where to hang a picture, place a chair or table, Shane knew life also gave you a second, sometimes better chance.

Walking from the garage Sunday night after putting his rental away, he paused and stared up at Paige's brightly lit windows. She'd worked as hard as anyone. She was a good person, but good meant squat in this day and age. Good people were even more likely to get stepped on and used.

His expression hardened. That wasn't going to happen to Paige. He wasn't sure how he'd manage it, he only know that he would.

Locking the kitchen door Mrs. Albright had left open for him, Shane headed for the stairs. His cell phone went off with a familiar ring the moment he entered his room. He jerked it from the inside of his jacket, knowing he wasn't going to like what he heard. Rio didn't do small talk.

"The honeymoon is over."

Shane didn't waste his time cursing. It was inevitable that Blade and Sierra would be discovered. "How bad?"

"A photographer was able to take pictures of them kissing on the beach before he was interrupted and his camera inspected," Rio said. "He probably cursed a blue streak when he learned the images on the film were blurred."

"Blade and Sierra?"

"In the air thirty minutes after it happened."

"How is Blade taking this?" Blade had dreaded their discovery with good reason. Rich men and their families were often targets, and that was where Shane and Rio came in.

"Better than I thought. Sierra is good for him," Rio answered.

The right woman could change a man's life, give it purpose, depth, change his way of thinking. Before Shane could stop himself, a picture of Paige entered his mind.

"The jet is taking them directly to Santa Fe for the press conference at Sierra's sister-in-law's hotel to make the morning papers. All the key players who made the wedding happen will be there or available by phone to give Sierra's hometown media another scoop."

And annoy the hell out of the general media. Again.

When the press had descended on two-time Tony-winning Broadway actress Sabra Raineau, Pierce Grayson's lover at the time and eventually his wife, it had been Faith, Brandon Grayson's wife and executive manager of the Casa de Serenidad Hotel in Santa Fe, who had helped Sabra coordinate a press conference. Shane heard it had gone off flawlessly. Faith had been chosen again and prepped for that very reason.

"The entire extended family is on their way to Santa Fe."

And that meant Trent, Dominique Falcon's husband, would be there as well. There was no reason for Trent to be caught up in the media frenzy, but his wife, as the official wedding photographer and Sierra's cousin, would be there—and where she went, Trent went. Shane just hoped Trent stayed out of the glaring eyes of the cameras.

If Trent's picture and the date of his wedding appeared in print, Paige might recall that her mother was missing during that time. If that happened, Paige would be reminded that her mother was keeping secrets. The tension between mother and daughter would return.

"Dominique and her mother, Felicia, have the story and photos ready?" Shane asked. It had been Sierra's idea for her first cousin and aunt to write the story of the wedding and reception. Good thing Dominique and Felicia were working together, because her parents had left the reception early and gone back to the yacht.

"Yes. Blade and Sierra will select the photos they want to share with the media, the exclusive ones they plan to auction off to benefit the Darfur Foundation, and the ones they plan to keep private."

They'd tried to plan for every contingency, but things happened. "I'll be there in three hours."

"You don't trust me to handle things?"

"That doesn't deserve an answer." Shane pulled from the closet a bag that he always kept ready. "I'll be at the airport in thirty minutes."

"Harris and the smaller jet are waiting for you," Rio said.

"Are you in the cockpit?" Shane asked, unzipping and double-checking the bag that held his shave kit, electronics, traveler's checks, and clean clothes for two days.

"Yeah. I thought I'd let them have some time alone since things are about to get wild."

Shane grunted. Rio admired Sierra and loved Blade, but he still didn't get the kissing/hugging thing. "I bet there are a couple of other reasons."

"There is that. There'll be a car waiting for you at the Santa Fe airport. Don't be late for the fun."

"Wouldn't dream of it." Shane disconnected the call, checked his watch. He had one thing to do before he left. Placing the bag outside his door, he went down the hall to the rooms on the farthest wing. Passing Paige's room, he didn't slow his steps. Curving around the hallway, he went the last room and knocked. "Mrs. Albright."

"Shane," she called. Moments later the door opened. She had a book in her hand. "Is everything all right?"

His gaze swept down the hallway before answering. He thought he heard a door opening. "A photographer was discovered on Blade's property. I need to go and help control the media."

"Oh, no! They were so hap—" Panic leaped in her eyes. Her hand clutched his arm. "You'll be back, won't you?"

That she had thought of Blade and Sierra first told him he had been right about her. She was a good woman caught in an impossible situation. "I'll be back. A plane is waiting for me at the airport."

He hesitated for a moment. She didn't know Paige had followed her to Texas, but she had to be prepared. "He'll be there. I'm not sure if he'll be in any of the dozens of photos the media will likely take."

He saw the words sinking in, the panic and fear as well. "She saw him once. She can't—"

Shane lifted his finger to his lips, sure of the sound he had heard earlier. He lowered his voice and said one word, "Paige."

Mrs. Albright jerked, her head turning to see Paige in the hallway, condemnation in her face. "Paige—"

Without a word, Paige disappeared around the corner. Moments later a door slammed.

Mrs. Albright's head fell. "I thought after today . . ." Her words trailed off. "Why do I keep hurting her?"

He wasn't the comforting type, but something about her pulled at him. Seconds later he knew what it was. A mother's love. "You've done nothing but try to protect her. Perhaps too much. Without all the pieces, Paige is jumping to the wrong conclusion. But she should know you better than this."

Mrs. Albright swallowed. "This is hard for her on top of losing her father."

"You lost, too, and a lot more," Shane said meaningfully. "It's time Paige realized she's not the only one hurting."

"She might not listen." Mrs. Albright bit her lower lip.

He'd seen Paige do that so many times when she was conflicted or worried. "You won't know until you've tried."

Nodding, she went down the hall in front of him to Paige's room and knocked. "Paige." There was no answer.

"Be as bold with her as you were *for* her," Shane said. "I'll see you when I can." Picking up his bag, he nodded toward Paige's door, then continued down the hallway.

Swallowing the lump in her throat, Joann entered the bedroom to see her daughter standing by the closed

French doors with her arms wrapped around herself. The distance between them hurt.

The idea that her daughter thought she was having an affair hurt even more. Perhaps Shane had been right; perhaps she was too protective of Paige.

"Shane came to tell me he's leaving tonight to help a friend. I thought you knew me better than what you're thinking. You've insulted us and shamed yourself. You owe both of us an apology."

Paige stopped pretending to look at the window and finally turned, saw the tears glistening in her mother's eyes, her hands clamped around the hardback novel she had been reading. Shame hit her, and not for just the reasons her mother stated. For a moment she had been jealous.

"Mother, I'm sorry."

"You might want to hurry and tell Shane that before he leaves," her mother said. "I'm not sure when he'll be back, and I'd hate for him to leave thinking you thought badly of him."

Paige didn't waste time. She hugged her mother briefly on the way out the door, then hit the stairs running. Her mother also didn't want Shane to think her daughter a judgmental snob. Shane's rental car was in the garage in the back. He had to pass the house to get to the main road.

Seeing headlights coming from the direction of the garage, she cut across the yard, her slipper socks sinking into the thick grass. As she ran, she knew it wasn't just important for her mother's sake, but for hers as well.

Paige stepped out into the one-lane driveway to and from the four-car garage. Lights blinded her. Brakes squealed. She threw up her hands, then heard a door slam and a muttered curse.

"Don't you ever do anything so idiotic again! You could have been killed!"

For a moment she had the strangest feeling, as if this had happened before. She couldn't see Shane, could only hear his voice. Then he was there, blocking out the beams of the headlights.

"Paige, are you all right?"

"I—" She shook her head. "For a moment I thought . . ." Her voice trailed off.

"What?" There was sharpness in his voice that hadn't been there before.

"Nothing." Her breath trembled out over her lips. "I owe you an apology."

"Your mother deserves one as well," he said, his voice less gruff.

"Already given. I just wanted to tell you before you left." She shoved her unsteady hand through her hair. "You're coming back?"

His eyes stared into hers for a long time, as if searching for something. "Yes."

Happiness shot through her. She'd worry about her reaction later. She stepped back. "Safe travel."

His hand lifted toward her face. For a heart-pounding moment she thought he planned to touch her, take her in his arms, kiss her. To her disappointment, he did neither. His hand fell. "Go back to the house and take care of yourself while I'm gone."

"I will." With one last longing look, she turned and did as he said. Through the windows beside the front doors she watched his taillights disappear. He'd be back. And then what? She wished she knew.

Now she had one more thing to do. Climbing the stairs, she went to her mother's room and knocked.

"Come in, Paige."

Paige drew in a deep breath and pushed open the

door. Her mother stood by the bedpost at the foot of the bed as if she needed the support at her back. Her own heart winced at the sight. Once they had been as close as a mother and daughter could be. Paige couldn't help but recall all the times her mother had come to her room to comfort her when she'd been miserable and lonely.

"Did you catch Shane?" her mother asked.

"Yes. His first thought was of you," Paige told her, wishing she knew how to close the distance between them.

"He's a good man. He's coming back."

"Yes." Paige's hands flexed. *Just spit it out.* "I'm sorry for jumping to conclusions."

"You should be." Her mother crossed to her. "You know I love you. I would never do anything to jeopardize that love."

"If only that were true," Paige said before she thought.

Her mother flinched, shook her head, then turned away. "Good night, Paige."

She couldn't get her feet to move. "Why won't you let things be the way they used to be?"

"Paige," her mother said, her voice weary. "You have no idea what you're asking."

"Then explain it to me. Please, make me understand." She stepped around her mother to face her.

Tears crested in her mother's eyes. "I love you, Paige. Why can't you just trust me?"

Because this has something to do with Father and Trent Masters, she almost said, but thankfully bit back the words in time. She had a feeling that if she went too far, the rift might be irreparable. "Because you've changed. You're secretive. You're not the woman I grew up loving."

"Does that mean you don't love me anymore?" her mother asked, the words seemingly as difficult to say as they were for Paige to hear.

"You're the first person I loved, the first person who loved me unconditionally," Paige said, the words thick in her clogged throat. "If I didn't still love you, I wouldn't be here." Unable to stand seeing the pain on her mother's face, Paige whirled to leave.

"Thank you for telling me that. I know it wasn't easy."

Opening her mother's bedroom's door, Paige closed it, then leaned back against it. Her mother was keeping a secret that was destroying their once close relationship. A man Paige had just met was making her body burn with desire.

Pushing away from the door, she continued down the hall to her room. Her personal life was in a crisis and she had absolutely no idea how to fix it.

Chapter 7

"Shane, we appreciate your coming, but have you considered what will happen if you're caught in a photo with us?" Blade Navarone asked as he stood in one of the smaller ballrooms in the Casa de Serenidad Hotel in downtown Santa Fe.

It annoyed Shane that he hadn't until he was sitting on Blade's private jet. He always thought of every contingency before an assignment. Once taken, nothing ever interfered with his ability to complete a job.

Until now. Until Paige. "So I'll keep out of the way."

"There'll be times you won't be able to." Rio, tall and imposing, arms folded, leaned against the partition behind them, watching the hotel staff hurriedly set up chairs, tables, and microphones for the press conference.

Being right didn't alter Shane's annoyance. "My job is here."

"And we appreciate it, Shane, but if being here with us will make helping Paige more difficult, you might not have a choice," Sierra said, standing next to Blade, their hands linked just as their hearts were.

Annoyance changed to irritation. "Blade and you are my main responsibility."

Blade placed his large hand on Shane's tense shoulder. "If you hadn't felt there was a need, you wouldn't have gone to Atlanta. You've never taken on an assignment with me, and few while we were in the Rangers, that you didn't finish to your satisfaction. Rio is here, the men you've trained are here. Let them do their job."

Shane's surprised gaze cut to Rio. The look they shared lasted for only a few seconds, but it was enough. *Blade had changed.*

Before his marriage, he would have wanted as much protection as humanly possible between him and the unknown. Married less than two weeks, and he'd stopped being afraid of living, of caring, and it was all due to the woman with her head resting trustingly against his shoulder. Shane had seen the pose dozens of times. It was as if their bodies each drew the other, needed the other.

"Trent is counting on you to help Paige and her mother," Sierra reminded him. "We all are."

Shane didn't doubt her for a moment. The bond of the blended families of the Falcons, the Taggarts, and the Masterses that now included Blade was strong. Although Shane had never been a part of such a close bond, he understood its power and its need to protect and keep the family safe and happy. And Paige didn't even know she was part of such a caring family or how lucky she was.

Unless Mrs. Albright changed her mind, Paige might never know.

"We'll see how it goes," Shane finally answered. He had no intention of backing himself into a corner or limiting himself.

Rio straightened as Faith, her husband Brandon, Luke and his wife Catherine, and Sierra's mother Ruth—followed by a horde of media—came into the room. Conversation stopped for a full ten seconds when the journalists saw Blade and Sierra. A woman raised a camera. Shane and Rio stepped in front of Blade and Sierra, shielding them. There was no need. Luke put his hand over the telephoto lens of the Nikon.

"No photos at this point," Luke said. "Break the rule, and you're out. No exceptions. No excuses."

"We hope that won't be necessary," Catherine said, soothing the wide-eyed reporter now clutching the camera to her chest. "You're all here because the Grayson family has always been able to count on you, and thus wanted you to be the first in the world to hear some exciting news. I'd hate for anyone to break any of the stipulations and miss out."

"Sorry," the woman said, obviously relieved she wasn't going to be asked to leave. "I guess I just got excited on seeing Mr. Navarone."

"Understandable," Faith said. "Now if you'll take your seats, we'll get started."

Shane and Rio moved aside as Ruth and her oldest son, Luke, made their way to the front of the room. Through the back door of the ballroom the rest of the extended family members entered.

Showtime, Shane thought.

Over an hour later, after countless photographs and questions ranging from where Sierra and Blade had met to wedding details, Sierra's mother started winding down the news conference. "Thank you for coming on such short notice, but we wanted to share the news with our own first."

A chorus of "Thank you" and "No problem" came from the media. Cameras flashed.

"Thank you again and good night," Ruth said graciously. Blade and Sierra stood next to her. Luke had moved to the back of the room shortly after the press conference began.

Reluctantly the journalists got to their feet and began gathering their belongings. As planned, Sierra's four brothers along with Daniel Falcon and his two brothers-in-law, Kane and Matt Taggart, began gently nudging people toward the double door that Trent held open. He'd stayed in the back of the room the entire time. Rio, as he had been all evening, remained to the far right of Blade and Sierra.

Out of camera range, Shane stood several feet to the left of the newlyweds. He wasn't too happy with the way things had worked out.

He didn't like compromising one job because of another. Yet he knew he'd like it even less if he ended up in one of the dozens of photographs taken and Paige happened to see it. He wanted to be there to protect her from Russell. The job had somehow become personal.

"Please wait," cried a reporter near the door. Earlier she had identified herself as a reporter for *Santa Fean* magazine. "Mrs. Grayson, it's a well-known and documented fact that you've had a hand in your son's choice of wives. Were you instrumental in your daughter's selection as well?"

The crowd stopped, turned, their ears almost twitching. Cameras were quickly raised. Sierra's brothers, along with Daniel, Kane, and Matt Taggart, stopped, too.

Shane had heard of Sierra's mother's matchmaking scheme during Sierra and Blade's engagement. Sierra had teased her brothers about being the only one to choose her life mate.

Shane wasn't so sure. Ruth Grayson was as outspoken as her children. Yet she never confirmed or denied her involvement, just smiled as she did now. And if Felicia Falcon—Ruth's sister-in-law and partner in

Ruth's plan to marry off her five children—was around, the two women would share a knowing look when they thought no one was looking. What he didn't understand was why he'd caught the two women watching him and Rio.

"I'll answer that for Mama." Sierra laughed, hugging her mother with her free arm. The other arm remained around Blade's waist, just as his was around hers. Turning to him, she lifted her face to his and cupped his cheek. Her engagement ring, a four-carat red diamond center stone surrounded by flawless white diamonds, sparkled as much as the light and love in Sierra's eyes. "My heart chose."

With the hand that bore the platinum wedding band Sierra had placed on his finger, Blade tenderly palmed Sierra's cheek. His dark head descended until their mouths were inches apart. "Just as mine chose you."

Cameras flashed. Several women sighed. Sierra's brothers, cousins, and extended family members connected gazes with their spouses. Shane felt the sizzle, the passion, but also the undying affection. Their love would last a lifetime and beyond. Against the odds all of them had found that one person who grounded them, made life so much richer, happier.

Shane sensed Rio's stare and turned. The warning in his best friend's enigmatic gaze was as clear as if he had shouted the words. *Home and hearth aren't in our future.* There was one little problem: The warning might have come too late.

Paige's life was in turmoil. She honestly couldn't say if it was because of the tension between her and her mother, or the sexual attraction between her and Shane. She tried to see leaving the house Monday morning before her mother woke not as cowardice, but as a nod to the pressing need to see Russell and straighten out the gift card mess.

She didn't want to think she'd made a mistake in judgment of him. The mixup wasn't his fault.

Getting into her car, she backed out of the garage and headed for Russell's apartment instead of to her downtown office. If Russell couldn't come to her, she'd go to him. She hoped he wouldn't see her visit as pushy, but as a way to help expedite matters.

In less than twenty minutes she pulled into the exclusive gated apartment complex, spoke to the guard on duty, and waited for the black iron gates to swing open. She'd been to the upscale complex only once before. It hadn't been a pleasant experience.

After an early-morning tennis match with Russell at the country club they'd decided to go out to eat breakfast. Russell insisted on going to his apartment first to change clothes. He said it didn't make sense for him to take her home, then come back to his place.

She hadn't thought anything about it. But once inside he'd tried to kiss her. She'd been surprised and pushed him away. He'd tripped over an ottoman and almost fallen. The incident had embarrassed them both. He'd apologized, but she'd never visited his apartment again.

And it looked as if she wouldn't this time, either. His new red Cadillac convertible wasn't in his assigned parking space. There was no use looking to see if he had parked elsewhere. He'd often boasted that after he had several cars towed, no one dared park in his space. Disappointed, Paige sighed and reasoned he must have gone in early after working late last night.

Turning the car around, she headed for the freeway and the bumper-to-bumper traffic into downtown

Atlanta. She wasn't giving up. Gayle and Noah deserved that money.

Forty-three harrowing minutes later, she exited the freeway and drove straight to Russell's office building. Getting through security took another ten minutes. While waiting in line for clearance she called his office. His secretary, Ellen, said he hadn't arrived, and that his first appointment wasn't until late that morning. There was something in the woman's tone that bothered Paige, then she saw Russell and forgot about his secretary.

"Good morning, Russell."

Shock registered on his face. "Paige. What are you doing here?"

"You said you'd be busy today so I thought I'd drop by so we can straighten out the misinformation on the gift cards," she explained. "We can call the credit card company from your office."

His mouth thinned. "I have a busy day. Can't this wait?"

"No." She refused to back down. "Gayle and Noah need to know that they can trust people."

"They're questioning me?" he snapped. "I didn't have to give them anything."

Paige glanced around as people stared at them. She didn't want to cause a scene. "I know that and so do they. If that's the way you feel, forget it. Good-bye."

"Wait." Russell grabbed her arm.

She shook her head. "Shane gave them fifty. I'll give them the rest."

Russell looked as if he would explode at the mention of Shane's name. Releasing her, he pulled his billfold from the inside of his light gray tailored jacket and extracted a credit card. "Here."

She hesitated. "If you don't want—"

Taking her hand, he slapped it into her palm. "The next time you need anything, call me. Not him."

She didn't have to be a mind reader to know who *him* was. "Thank you, Russell. I'll take care of this and bring it directly back. I tried to get you earlier at your place, but of course you weren't there."

"What?" he stiffened.

"I called your office just before I saw you. I wondered where you were," she told him. "Your secretary said you didn't have an appointment."

"Car service," Russell said. "Ellen doesn't know everything."

Paige held up his credit card. "Thanks again. I'll be back as soon as I can." She walked away hoping that she hadn't gotten Ellen into trouble. Paige had forgotten. Russell, like her father, didn't like his whereabouts questioned.

One person in particular whose whereabouts she wished she knew was Shane.

Shane had always been able to compartmentalize his thoughts, but late Monday morning he was having difficulty. He'd learned to do so as a child in order to survive the harsh realities of his home life, then he'd done it as an Army Ranger in some of the most dangerous places in the world. He multitasked with ease . . . until he'd tackled a woman on a dark night in Dallas.

"Shane."

Shane glanced up from one of the seven screens of the computer bank on the second floor of Blade and Sierra's estate outside Santa Fe to see Trent Masters. He didn't look happy. Shane didn't need two guesses. "Mrs. Albright."

Trent nodded to a seat next to Shane. "May I?"

Shane inclined his head. "What is it?"

"I'm not sure," Trent began, settling his long body into the rolling leather chair. "I just got off the phone with her. I think something else is bothering her besides Paige and Zachary finding out about me." He rubbed the back of his neck. "Sierra and Blade's wedding is being covered heavily on the news and the entertainment programs. I've tried to stay out of the limelight."

"Hard to do," Shane said with disgust. The "castle"—as Sierra referred to the house—was exactly that, complete with a drawbridge, which came in handy considering the throng of media from around the country camped out front.

"She sounded shaky, really frightened," Trent said, lines radiating across his forehead. "Did anything happen while you were there that might have caused this?"

"No," Shane said. If the situation between Paige and her mother had worsened, it had nothing to do with her seeing them talking outside her bedroom door. Of that Shane was sure.

"When are you going back?" Trent asked.

"Wednesday afternoon."

"All right." Trent stood. "If you get any more information, I'd appreciate it if you'd let me know."

"You got it." Shane turned to the computer screens, studying them for all of five minutes before he picked up his radio. "Number one to number two. Over."

"Number two. Over."

"I need you to monitor the computer. Over," Shane spoke into the radio to Rio.

"I'm moving. ETA five minutes. Problem? Over."

Uncharacteristically, he paused. "Not sure."

There was another pause. "I am. Over and out."

As soon as Rio arrived, Shane left and went to his room down the hall. The castle had thirteen

bedrooms in all, along with a wine cellar, movie theater, and spa, in over fifteen thousand square feet of
living space. Jacques, Blade's decorator for all of his
properties, called the castle a challenge at first, then his
masterpiece.

In his room, Shane pulled out his modified cell
phone and called Mrs. Albright. From his vantage point
on the balcony of the second-floor bedroom, he could
see the front and side grounds, the guards patrolling,
the cars and vans of reporters; helicopters buzzed overhead. Blade was quietly buying the property around
them so the media would be pushed back even farther.

In the meantime they were wasting their time in trying to get an interview or photo. Blade and Sierra were
in an underground cave beneath the castle that Blade
had designed to resemble a tropical paradise. He and
Sierra had gone "to relax" three hours ago and were
still there.

"Hello."

"Hello, Mrs. Albright. It's Shane."

"Shane, are Blade and Sierra all right?" she asked.
"It's all over the news."

"Fine," he said on hearing the tension in her voice.
"I'd like to know about you."

"I guess you've been talking to Trent. He worries
too much." The laughter that followed sounded forced
and hollow.

"What happened between you and Paige after I
left?" Shane asked.

"The same thing that always happens. Paige pushes
for answers that I can't give her. Not if I expect her to
continue being a part of my life. We're growing farther
apart," Mrs. Albright told him.

The hurt and futility in her voice were unmistakable. "You might be giving Paige too little credit."

"I can't take the chance."

"The secrecy will keep coming between you," he told her, watching the drawbridge lower and Trent drive across, then the mad scramble of the media to attempt crossing the downed bridge. His men, as instructed, were there en masse to turn them back. "You're taking a chance this way as well."

"It has to be this way," she said, her voice tense. "There's too much else going on."

His antenna went up. "Like what?" His question was met with silence. "Mrs. Albright, is something going on you haven't told me or Trent about?"

"I've told you everything you need to know to help Paige," she finally said.

Shane had evaded enough people to know when it was being done to him. "Then why do I feel certain you're holding out on me?"

"I can't answer that for you," she said. "When are you coming back?"

His original plan was to stay at least three days. "Late tomorrow possibly."

"Good, we'll see you then. Good-bye."

Shane disconnected the call, then dialed another number. He had to know how she was doing.

"Paige Albright."

She sounded all right, but he knew with Paige that could be deceiving. "Good morning."

"Shane," she said, her voice a bit breathless.

"Yes." It hadn't occurred to him until then that he had expected her to recognize his voice just as he recognized hers. "How is the day going?"

"Hectic, but that's a good thing," she said. "How is the friend you went to help?"

"Better than expected," he answered truthfully.

"Good, then you'll be back soon."

He caught the same wistful sadness in her voice that
he'd heard in her mother's. He shouldn't, but he heard
himself say, "How about lunch tomorrow? I can take
Jackie up on her offer and you can show me around
your office."

"You're sure you'll be back by then?" she questioned.

"I'm sure," he said. "Is it a date?" he asked, then
winced. He did not date.

"It's a date," she confirmed, sounding pleased.

Perhaps the date thing wasn't so bad. But no sense
going overboard. Time to end this before he said
something else he shouldn't. "See you then. Bye."

"Bye, Shane, and thanks for the call."

He didn't like knowing she was sad and there was
nothing he could do about it. "I'll be there tomorrow
without fail."

"I know. Bye."

"Bye." He disconnected, wondering how she knew
he always kept his word. And why knowing that she
did made him feel so darn good.

Shane parked his rental in Joann Albright's garage
thirty-six hours after he'd left. He was a day earlier
than he'd planned. He didn't like to think too much of
the reason. Paige was becoming a complication. He
couldn't let her become a distraction as well. The less
they were alone, the better.

He'd never run from a problem. He wasn't doing so
now, he reasoned. He was simply keeping a major
complication out of the equations. He was here to do a
job, but in the meantime something else wasn't right.

Yesterday Mrs. Albright had sounded distracted on
the phone when they'd briefly spoken. The cause hadn't
been Paige. Trent had felt the same about it. Something
else was bothering her. Shane intended to find out what.

He'd purposely returned when Paige would be at work.

He knocked on the back door, then waited. A cook, maid, or other house staff member was usually in the area. When another knock didn't bring anyone, he tried the door. It was open. He'd have to talk to Mrs. Albright about that later.

He was leaving the kitchen when he heard the raised, mocking voice of a woman he didn't recognize. He quickly moved in that direction. His instincts on alert, he slowly opened the door. Intent on each other, the two women in the room didn't notice they had company.

"Stop stalling and write out my check," the woman ordered, her voice husky. She stood in front of the oversized desk in the library. Mrs. Albright sat behind the desk.

"You weren't supposed to come here," Mrs. Albright told her, her voice unsteady and frightened.

"I go and do what I damn well please, and if you don't want your pitiful daughter or that irresponsible son of yours to know what their daddy was doing the night he died, you'll write out the check," she sneered.

Joann shot to her feet. "Don't you dare say anything about my children!"

"Ha!" The woman folded her arms. "Like you have a backbone? Marshall walked all over you and you took it. Now write the check. I'm accustomed to a certain standard of living and you're going to see that it continues. Or else."

"I've already given you a hundred thousand dollars," Mrs. Albright said.

"Chump change." Greed in her eyes, the woman looked around the elegant room. "You're worth a fortune, and I plan to get my share." She giggled, a high-pitched annoying sound. "You should thank me for keeping Marshall out of your bed."

"You're vile," Mrs. Albright said with loathing.

"Write the check, and I'll be on my way." When Mrs. Albright didn't move, the blackmailer took out her BlackBerry. "Write it or I'm calling Paige. In case you think I don't know her office number, it's 555-877-7777."

Mrs. Albright briefly closed her eyes, then sank heavily into her chair and pulled out a checkbook from the top desk drawer.

"Let's make it an even thirty thousand this time. I need a few things."

"Then I suggest you work for them," Shane said coldly. The blackmailer swung toward him. Her heavily lashed eyes widened, sweeping over him, assessing him.

"Shane, I didn't expect you this early," Mrs. Albright said, coming slowly to her feet.

"Obviously." He advanced into the room and didn't stop until he stood in front of the curvaceous woman wearing a tight red designer dress. Her inch-long nails were the same vivid color. She reeked of expensive perfume. "You won't get another cent from Mrs. Albright. You won't call or come here. Now leave."

Her thin brow arched. "Who are you?"

"Someone you don't want to cross," Shane said, his voice low and taut.

Her gaze swept him again from head to his plain leather shoes. "I don't scare easily, especially by some unemployed nobody."

"I'd ask how you knew so much about me, but I already know." Shane's eyes narrowed. So this was the woman Russell was secretly having an affair with? Like him she was hard, cold, calculating, and a user. She'd used his connection to the Albright household to keep abreast of what went on in the house while she blackmailed Mrs. Albright. "I bet he hasn't figured out why you sought him out."

She started, her heavily lashed eyes widened in surprise.

"Leave," Shane repeated, his tone ominous.

The woman slowly turned to Mrs. Albright. "Is this the way you want to play it?"

"Shane—"

His fingers closed firmly around the woman's forearm. She yelped, her free hand coming up clawing. He easily caught it and marched her to the door, where he released her. "Let me give you fair warning. Mrs. Albright has been through enough. Cause her any more pain or uneasiness, and you'll have me to deal with."

Rubbing her arm, she glared at him. "No one treats me this way. You'll pay for this."

"You do not want to mess with me. But take your best shot, because you'll only get one."

The woman took a few stumbling steps back, then quickly got inside a new silver Jaguar. Shooting him the finger, she sped off.

"She won't go away," Mrs. Albright said, her voice shaky. "She preys on vain, stupid men. I'm a meal ticket. She won't give up easily."

Shane tuned to Mrs. Albright. Knowing that her husband's mistress at the time of his death was having an affair with Russell would only distress her more. "Her name and all you know about her."

"Alisha Brown, thirty-two. She was Marshall's last mistress, the one he was with the night he died." Clearly embarrassed, Mrs. Albright flushed and briefly looked away. "She called 911, but only after she left the hotel. He might have lived if she hadn't run out to avoid being found there with him. I'm sure he wasn't the only one. She is too grasping and greedy for that."

Shane agreed. "You shouldn't have paid her."

"I'd do anything to protect my children," she said fiercely.

"But what you did only made them and yourself more vulnerable," he told her. "If she's as vicious as we both think, she'll want to show me up and hurt you."

Mrs. Albright gasped, pressing both hands to the lower part of her face. "She'll tell Paige. You've got to stop her."

"I will." Shane pulled out his cell and hit SPEED DIAL as he raced back through the house, the shortest distance to the garage. Jericho Black, head of the Atlanta investigation firm Shane had hired, answered on the second ring.

"Jericho."

"Get to Paige Albright's office building now. Alisha Brown, African American woman, five-six, a hundred twenty pounds, reddish-blond hair, in tight red dress is on her way there now. Stall her in the lobby until I arrive. In the meantime have someone dig deep deeper into her past. I want everything you can find."

"Done."

Shane shut off the phone and jumped behind the wheel of the rental. Jericho had proven to be discreet, dependable, and trustworthy. He also didn't ask questions. He had the kind of looks that would attract a viper like Alisha. And this time when Shane stood in front of her, the gloves would come off.

*T*he thief had struck again.

Fire in her eyes, Paige sat behind her desk Tuesday morning. As soon as she'd arrived at work, she discovered the twenty-dollar bill she'd left last night as bait gone. As if dealing with Russell yesterday and the growing tension with her mother weren't enough, she now had to contend with a thief.

Whoever had been rambling in her desk for the past two months had been careful to put things back just as they were, but they had tripped themselves up this time. The handle of the white coffee mug decorated with red hearts Noah and Gayle had given her wasn't aligned with the gold pen, a high school graduation gift from Zach; the desk drawers weren't almost closed.

More tellingly, the crisp banknote she'd left under her desk calendar when she went home last night wasn't there. The other times money had come up missing she'd thought she had just forgotten to put the change in her purse. She might have kept believing that if she hadn't left her gold hoop earrings on her desk, then discovered them missing.

No one in the twenty-member staff admitted to seeing the earrings. Nor had anyone in the cleaning crew seen them. Building security had blown her off. They all thought she had just misplaced the earrings. Now she had proof that someone was stealing from her. She just had to figure out a way to catch them.

Her ringing phone interrupted her thoughts. Her heart rate sped up. It might be Shane, letting her know he was back in town. She'd thought about their luncheon date all morning, had worn a figure-flattering white jacket with a round neckline over a slim skirt to look her best. "Hello."

"Paige Albright?" asked a husky female voice.

"Yes, this is Paige Albright. How can I help you?" she answered, picking up her pen, trying not to be disappointed. She didn't recognize the woman's voice, but she had several feelers out for their major fund-raiser, the Masquerade Ball, in three weeks. They'd already reached their financial goal. Not a seat was left for the banquet, but she was still accepting donations.

"It's important that we talk. Can you meet me in the lobby in five minutes? I assure you it will be financially beneficial."

"Of course." Paige had had stranger requests. "How will I recognize you?"

"I'll recognize you."

Paige stared at the droning phone, then shrugged. Her office was in one of the tallest buildings in Atlanta, and it could be a pain getting past security from the lobby, which meant the thief wasn't a visitor.

Paige checked her watch. Eleven seventeen. She should make it back in plenty of time to meet Shane. She'd already given his name to security. Opening her door, she headed for the bank of elevators.

Seeing that his instincts were right didn't make Shane feel better. He was just thankful Jericho had the suave, wealthy looks that would make Alisha pause and consider him for her next victim.

"You don't listen very well, Alisha."

She spun. Fear leaped into her eyes, but it was quickly replaced by calculation. "Benjamin, this man is stalking me. Call the police."

"I can't do that since he hired me," Jericho said, then smiled into her furious face. "I'll wait over here."

"I was only interested in your money," she hissed.

"And I wasn't interested at all," Jericho said before moving several feet away.

She gasped. "You—"

"Save the indignation for someone who cares," Shane said, taking her arm to move to one side of the busy lobby. "You're going to listen and, when I finish, you're going to leave this lobby and not bother Mrs. Albright or her children again."

"I'm in a public place. All I have to do is scream."

"That would be a mistake, a very costly one." His smile was colder than ice. "You're dealing with something that is over your head and beyond your comprehension. I'm merciless and as vindictive as you are, with the money and power to back it up, to make nuisances disappear." With each word her eyes grew wider, her skin colder until she was trembling, her bravado gone. "Play Russell, but forget you ever heard of Mrs. Albright and her children," he warned. "Otherwise you'll never know how big a mistake you've made until it's too late." He leaned in closer, the smile on his face at odds with the cold promise of retribution in his voice and eyes. "You won't even have time to scream."

Alisha clutched her throat, backed up two steps, then ran from the lobby, her heels rapidly clicking on the marble floor. The armed guards followed her progress all way to the door. They didn't seem to pay attention to the well-dressed, handsome man who left behind her.

Shane turned toward the elevator and stared straight into Paige's worried face. She couldn't have heard them talk, but from the look on her face, she'd seen Alisha take off like a woman running from hell.

Chapter 8

"Hello, Paige," Shane greeted, his sensual mouth curved into a beautiful smile.

For a moment Paige lost track of what she was about to say. "Th-that woman—"

"Was late for an appointment," he said dismissively, cutting her off. "Are you ready to go to lunch?"

Paige studied him for a few moments longer, still trying to reconcile the impression of lethal danger on his face a moment ago with the easygoing man before her now, the man who had teased two teenagers, the man who made her silly heart race, her body believe. "I'm meeting a potential donor."

"Oh," he said casually.

"Yes," she said, glancing around. "She said she'd meet me in the lobby."

He looked around as well. "Where specifically were you to meet her?"

For some reason Paige felt a bit foolish. "We didn't set a location. She said she'd recognize me."

His warm, appreciative gaze swept over her. "You'd be hard to miss."

She blushed. A first. "Perhaps she's running late."

He gently took her arm. Her skin warmed. "Why don't we stand by the door and give her a few more minutes? And while we wait you can tell me what you're working on."

Paige was taken by surprise. No one except her mother and Zach ever asked about her job. Since she'd been seeing Russell, he'd asked to be her escort when he was in town, but never what the events were about. "It's a masquerade ball. We've already met the projected financial goal, but I'm still accepting donations. I thought the woman wanted to contribute. She said it would be financially beneficial."

Something, a coldness, flickered in his midnight-black eyes, then was gone. "Maybe she changed her mind."

"Perhaps. I guess she'll call again. How about lunch?"

"Barbecue?"

She laughed. "Not in this white suit."

"Pity. Maybe next time."

Paige had chosen a small eatery with only four tables. She'd eaten there before and knew the food to be good, and it wouldn't put a dent in Shane's wallet. When she'd stopped in front of the door, he'd given her a look as if he suspected the reason she'd chosen the restaurant. "The food is fabulous and plentiful," she told him.

The server had greeted her by name and quickly served them. Seeing Shane eat with gusto confirmed that she'd made the right choice. He suddenly stopped, grinned, then reached across the table with his napkin and brushed the corner of her mouth.

"Ketchup."

"Was not," she said, smiling. She'd barely dabbed the French fry she'd just eaten in the ketchup.

"My eyes must be playing tricks on me," he mused, rubbing them. "I'll be more careful the next time."

With her skin still tingling, she certainly hoped there would be a next time.

"Is everything still all right with your friend?"

"Yes. Thanks for asking."

There was another question she wanted to ask. "The woman in the lobby seemed upset."

"She did, didn't she?" He took a long swallow of his sweetened iced tea.

"Did you know her?"

"Never saw her before today." He bit into a turkey sandwich three inches thick.

Paige frowned. It was certainly difficult getting information out of Shane. "I only caught a glimpse of her, but she looked familiar."

His gaze sharpened. "Oh?"

"Doesn't matter, I guess," she said and forged ahead on another, more delicate matter. "Yesterday Russell gave me his credit card to buy a $350 gift card for Noah and Gayle."

Shane grunted dismissively and took another long swallow of tea. "Noah and Gayle settling in all right?"

"Yes," she answered, watching the strong column of his throat, wondering if she'd ever get a chance to press her lips there. Sighing inwardly, she pulled herself away from that fantasy.

She hadn't expected handsprings from Shane, but she had expected some kind of indication that Russell wasn't as bad as he'd thought. Noah's reaction had been almost identical when she'd given them the card last night. Clearly Russell wasn't one of their favorite people. "They received their first piece of junk mail, and that made it official."

He chuckled, a deep rich sound that she was beginning to enjoy too much. "They're good kids. You should be proud of what you've done for them."

She shook her head. "They deserve the credit. I've tried to help others and they didn't make it." She shoved her plate aside, not wanting to remember the failures.

"All you can do is show them you care, show them the way," Shane said, causing her to raise her head. "For some, that's enough. For others, no matter what you do, they'd rather take the easy way."

She heard the bite in his voice. "You knew someone who took the easy way?"

Astonishment flickered in his dark eyes as if he hadn't meant to reveal so much. "Yeah."

Sadness mixed with anger lurked in his face. She wanted the teasing Shane to return. "Do you know anything about surveillance cameras?"

His wide shoulders snapped back; his gaze narrowed. "A bit. Why?"

In the blink of an eye he'd changed again, his body alert, poised. There was more to Shane than met the eye, she was sure of it.

She leaned over the small dining table, telling herself it was because she didn't want to be overheard—not because she wanted to be closer to him, inhale the spicy cologne that made her want to sniff, then bite. "Someone is going through my desk every night. The money's not very much, but last week they stole a pair of gold earrings Zachary gave me. I want them back."

He copied her pose, their faces inches apart. "Did you report the theft?"

She moistened her lips, watched his intense gaze follow. For a second her mind went blank. She fought to recall what they were talking about and not speculate on what Shane's mouth would taste like. "That's the problem. No one in my office believes it was a thief. No one else has missed anything except me. Building security didn't even want to make a report or contact housekeeping about the matter until I asked to speak to their supervisor."

"Nothing like going over someone's head," Shane said.

"Mother taught me that early and Father later on, although both went at it differently," she told him.

"After meeting your mother, I bet she opted for the talk-softly-and-carry-a-big-stick approach," Shane teased. "Just as you did with the manager of the home improvement store."

Paige wasn't surprised by Shane's astuteness. He seemed to have a knack for reading people correctly. For some odd reason, she wondered what he would have thought of her father, who brought out the big stick from the get-go. "She did."

"Any reason for you to be singled out?"

She was grateful he was listening and not looking as if she'd lost a couple of screws, the way the others in the staff and building security had. She hadn't even mentioned it to Russell. But that didn't mean she wanted to tell Shane everything.

"Paige?"

She sighed. He wasn't going to give her a choice. "It will sound as if I'm bragging."

"Let me be the judge of that."

She forged ahead. "Besides Jackie and a few others, I'm the one who usually has money around payday. I've gotten into the habit of buying pastries on Fridays, keeping the coffee replenished, and always making sure the snack basket is full in the break room."

"You don't drink coffee."

She was inordinately pleased that he remembered. "Jackie can't function without her third cup. The same goes for a few other workers."

"So let them buy their own."

"It's no problem."

"How many people work in your office?"

She hesitated before answering. "Twenty paid employees, but we can also have from two to five volunteers on any given day."

He studied her for a long moment. She resisted the urge to fidget. "It's all right to want to help others, but don't let them take advantage of you."

Her mouth tightened. "That's what Russell said when he stopped by the office and found me restocking the coffee."

"Forget I said anything then."

Paige laughed. Shane made her laugh, and it felt good. "Russell can be very nice."

"I'll take your word for it." Shane picked up the bill. "Let's go back to your office. A camera might not be your best bet."

"Then what?"

"Me."

It took Shane all of three minutes to check Paige's office. He could have easily installed a surveillance camera, but he had a better idea. "When you leave this afternoon, I'll hide in your office and catch the person or persons stealing from you."

"No," she said, her voice adamant. "The thief might be dangerous."

"I can handle it." Shane patted the cell phone hooked to his waist. "But if it will make you feel better I'll call the police or building security if anything happens."

She nibbled on her lower lip. "I don't know, Shane. Perhaps we should think of another plan. I don't want you hurt."

"I won't be. Trust me," he assured her, wanting for

one crazy moment to take her into his arms and comfort her with a kiss.

"I guess." The worry in her face didn't clear.

"I'll be safe. I'll hide in your closet."

"You'd never fit. Your shoulders are too wi—" She
stopped abruptly, her face reddening.

"I'll manage," he said, not wanting to embarrass her,
but pleased he wasn't the only one looking even though
it wasn't going to lead to anything. She wasn't his type—
experienced, easy to forget, buxom. Paige was inexperienced, unforgettable, and her breasts fit his hand as if
made for him. "What time did you plan on leaving today?" he asked to distract her.

She hesitated. "No later than five. Russell is leaving
for Beijing in the morning and he's taking me to dinner
and the theater."

He glanced at his watch to combat the urge to ask
her not to go. "Five hours. I'll be back at a quarter till."

"What about the visitors' log the guards keep?"

"Meet your new computer guy, who is going to run a
diagnostic on all the office computers—which can't be
done until he has free access to them all."

"That's a brilliant idea. You think fast."

"Occasionally." But what he was thinking about Paige
might land him in trouble . . . if he let it. "See you later."
Closing the door, he walked away without looking back.

"You seemed preoccupied all evening, Paige,"
Russell said when they were leaving the restaurant later that night. "I think I know why. You wish I
didn't have to leave you."

She didn't know what to say, how to respond. His
leaving had nothing to do with what she was feeling.
She was such a coward. "I understand how important
your job is."

"Do you?" He stopped, taking her forearms and staring down into her upturned face. "You're so beautiful. I ache with wanting you."

She looked away. "I'm sorry, but you know how I feel about intimacy before marriage."

"I know, but that doesn't keep me from wanting you," he said, his voice harsh.

"Russell, I don't feel—"

"No," he cut in, his voice panicky. "I shouldn't have pushed. It's just that I'll be gone for two weeks. I don't want us to argue."

"Neither do I." He had been a good friend, had helped her cope with her father's death.

"You seem tired. Why don't I take you home so you can rest?" he suggested.

She should tell him no, be with him on his last night in the States, as he had been with her while she grieved for her father. "If you don't mind."

"Your happiness and well-being are all that I care about." Holding her arm, he started down the street to his car.

"Thank you, Russell," she said, her mind already busy with plans.

Shane had been on dozens of stakeouts with his unit in the army, and despite the sand in his clothes, bugs biting him, rain beating down on him, he had remained focused. He was in Paige's functional but plush office, her door slightly cracked so he could watch the outer office of the assistant she shared with Jackie, and all he could think of was that she was with that arrogant lying bastard Russell. He didn't deserve to touch her after being with Alisha.

Shane cursed. What kind of man chose a slut over a loving woman who always put others first? A conniving, greedy fool, that's who. But what was killing Shane was the unknown. His instincts told him Paige wasn't sexually experienced, but there was a hell of a lot more they could be doing.

His phone vibrated and he jerked it from his waist. "Everything all right?"

"I called to ask you that."

Shane almost looked at the phone. "You checking up on me, Rio?"

"You missed your ETA coming here, and advanced your time to leave by sixteen hours. It's not like you to do either."

Shane had always thought it was a good thing that Rio and Blade knew him better than anyone, since he didn't have a family who cared if he lived or died. Now he wasn't so sure. Blade, in love with Sierra, would understand. Rio was a different matter entirely.

Shane had been late getting to the airport because of Paige and had returned early thanks to the same woman. "It was a good thing I came back early. I interrupted the woman who was with Marshall Albright the night he died, and she was blackmailing Mrs. Albright."

"If she doesn't listen to your warning . . ."

There was no need for Rio to finish. "Taken care of, but for further insurance the zero balance in her checking account should bring home the fact that she's in over her head."

"You're paying her a visit in the morning."

Yep. They knew each other well. "As soon as the bank—what?" The receptionist's door opened slowly. Paige peeked through the small opening.

"Problem?" Rio asked.

"No, it's Paige. I'll call later and explain."

"Somehow I doubt that." The line went dead.

Shane returned the cell phone. Rio was probably right. Shane might explain about the stakeout, but not how Paige affected him. He was still trying to understand it himself. He opened Paige's door wider. "You're not supposed to be here."

Dressed in black from head to toe, she straightened. "My office. My problem."

So, she took her responsibilities seriously. He'd already learned as much. "This is unknown territory. Things could get crazy."

She slipped past him into her office. "We'll cross that bridge when we come to it."

He frowned at her. He didn't like her throwing his words back at him. "Paige, I'm serious."

"So am I." She turned to face him. "You said you'd call the police or building security and that's what we'll do. I'm not leaving."

He tried again. "I thought you were on a date."

Her pretty little chin lifted. "We decided to end the evening early." She raised a paper sack from the restaurant they'd had lunch in. "I thought you might be hungry."

"I could have eaten the snacks in the break room," he said, the need to send her home warring with pleasure that she had thought of him, and that she wanted to be with him instead of Russell.

She tilted her head to one side. "It's down the hall. You would have had to leave my office and chance someone seeing you, and I don't think you'd do that."

"Good reasoning," he said, a smile tugging the corner of his mouth.

She handed him the take-out bag. "Eat, and I'll stand guard."

He watched her go to the door and crack it open.

From the light he could see her slender shape, the enticing curve of her hips. She'd pinned her hair on top of her head, exposing her delicate neck.

"You tell your mother where you were going?"

"I told her I had some work to do at the office," she replied. "She offered to come back with me."

"Sounds like Mrs. Albright."

Paige nodded. "She always thought of Zach and me, worried about us. That's why . . ."

"Why what?" he asked, although he had a pretty good idea what she had been about to say.

"Eat your food."

He decided that eating might take his mind off the woman who shouldn't occupy so many of his thoughts. He opened the bag. Less than five minutes later he'd finished the turkey sandwich.

The entire time he'd been eating, his thoughts had been on Paige and not the sandwich that he'd eaten because she'd brought it, not because he was hungry. On a mission they'd learned to ignore hunger, the elements. But nothing in his training had prepared him to ignore Paige.

Finished, he went to stand close behind her just to torture himself. "Anything?"

"No-o," she answered, her voice unsteady.

Inhaling the sweet scent of her fragrance, feeling the innocent brush of her hips against him, he wasn't too steady, either. He'd like nothing better than to spend the next hour or so searching for, and then kissing all the enticing places she'd put the perfume. Paige was definitely turning into an irresistible problem. "This might take a while."

She looked back over her shoulder. "You've done this before?"

"Army Ranger," he answered, willing his body and mind to behave.

Somehow she managed to face him, her breasts and tempting body torturing him in an entirely different way. "I knew it," she said, smiling up at him. "At the home improvement store, the men kept looking at you as if they expected you to rip their heads off. Then this afternoon, when you were talking to that woman, your face was like . . . *Mess with me at your own risk.*"

He would have bet he did a better job of hiding his other side. Rio would never let him live it down. "I think you saw more than there was. That life was a long time ago."

"It's probably instinctive. It must be wonderful not being afraid of anything," she said, her voice dropping to a whisper before she turned back to stare out the small opening in the door.

Without thinking he placed a comforting hand on her shoulder. "Everyone fears something. In my first six weeks of training in the army, I was afraid I wouldn't make the cut. And when I was selected for Ranger training, I had to fight the fear that I really didn't belong, that there had been some kind of a mistake. When I realized it was really happening, I had to get over the fear I wouldn't let myself or my team down."

Slowly she turned, her eyes searching his. "You aren't just saying that, are you?"

"I'd never lie to you."

Her smile was slow and twisted his insides. "Thank—"

Laughter sounded on the other side of the receptionist's door. Shane tensed; his hand gently squeezed her shoulder as the outer door opened.

A slender black man in his midthirties pushed a

cleaning cart into the room. He was followed by a tall
Anglo woman in her early twenties. Both wore T-shirts
and faded jeans. Keys dangled from their belt loops.

His hand firmly on Paige's shoulder, Shane backed
them farther into Paige's office and into the tiny coat
closet. The fit was tight. Too tight.

His hard body pressed intimately against her softness. He just hoped his lower body behaved this time.
With each breath he inhaled her scent. Her fragrance
teased, beckoned him once again to find and lick all
the delightful places on her body she'd put the seductive scent.

He gritted his teeth and tried to concentrate on the
man and woman in Paige's office and not how she much
tempted him.

Chapter 9

Paige had to remind herself to breathe, to take in a slow steady breath, then blow it out the same way. Her senses were heightened, narrowed to the man behind her.

She felt the hard, warm muscular imprint of Shane's body pressed against her from her shoulders to her hips, felt his arm around her waist as he held the knob of the cracked door, smelled his masculine scent mixed with hers.

She had the strangest urge to press against him. She wanted to feel his body, feel both of his strong arms around her. Her brilliant idea was suddenly fraught with seductive danger.

"You're safe."

Shane whispered the words in her ear, his warm breath causing her skin to ripple with pleasure, goose bumps to form on her arms. Paige would have laughed if she'd had the ability to do so.

She'd never been in greater peril. If Shane propositioned her as Russell had, she wasn't so sure she would turn him down.

"Let's see if she left anything tonight," the cleaning man said as he took a seat behind Paige's desk.

"Be careful." The woman emptied the trash can into a half-filled fifty-gallon bag. "Hope it's better than the

twenty she left last night. I hear she's some kind of do-
goody socialite. With her money, she can afford it."

"And she can't prove anything was stolen." Through
the crack in the door, Paige watched him lift up her
desk calendar. "The key is not being greedy or having
more than one mark on the floor. Being in charge of
fund-raising, I figured she'd have more petty cash on
hand."

"I hate that we have to pawn those earrings." The
woman plugged in the vacuum cleaner.

Paige gasped. Shane's hand tightened.

"They looked good on me when we went out Saturday night," she bemoaned, her crossed arms braced on
the handle of the upright vacuum.

"Pay dirt." He held up a fifty-dollar bill. "This is one
stupid woman."

"Stay here," Shane whispered when Paige tried to
surge forward. He'd heard more than enough. Opening
the door, he eased past Paige. The woman screamed;
the man shot to his feet and jammed the money into the
pocket of his jeans.

"Looks like we interrupted a little something-
something," he said. Grinning, he began to ease from
behind Paige's desk. "No problem. We can come back
later to clean."

"That might be a while since you're both going to be
in jail," Shane said.

The woman whirled toward the door. Shane beat her
to it, slamming it and positioning his body in front as
he took out his cell phone.

"Where are my earrings?" Paige asked the woman,
heading for her.

"Paige, stay where you are," Shane shouted.

"No, I—"

The man lunged for Paige as she passed. One hand

clamped around her waist, the other around her chest. She shrieked, trying to twist free, her frantic gaze going to Shane. He was a blur as he propelled himself across the room. Paige saw him grab the man by the neck. The next second her attacker slid bonelessly to the floor.

"Call security and stay here," Shane ordered as he whirled and ran after the fleeing woman.

Trembling, Paige picked up the phone on her desk and dialed, her worried gaze glued to the door. "This is Paige Albright in the Carl D. Rowe Foundation office on the fortieth floor. Two of the cleaning crew just tried to rob me. Please come. My friend is going after one who got away."

Paige moved farther away from the unconscious man as security asked her more questions. She wasn't in a mood to answer them or stay on the line. "I've got to make sure he's all right." Hanging up, she started out of the office only to pull up short when she saw Shane with the subdued woman.

"I was worried about you," Paige said, her voice as unsteady as her knees.

His mouth was tight. "I should have sent you home."

Paige stuck her trembling hands in her pocket. "I wasn't much help. I'm sorry I got in the way. Security is coming."

"Paige, you could have been hurt." His eyes and voice were unyielding.

"I wasn't." She turned away before he could see the tears in hers. She had been worthless. Why did she think that would change? He was right. She should have stayed at home.

Just then two men in security uniforms, guns drawn, burst into her office. The weapons wavered among the three people standing as if they didn't know where to point them. Paige didn't recognize them.

"What's going on?" the youngest asked.

"Put the guns away," Shane ordered. "She's not going anywhere and neither is the man behind the desk."

"He's the one you should lock up," the woman yelled, trying to twist free. "You fellows know me. He attacked us for no reason."

The security guards traded worried looks, backed up, and trained their guns on Shane. "Turn her loose."

"No!" Paige shouted. The guards' hands weren't too steady on their weapons. "I'm Paige Albright and this is my office. I called you. These two stole from me tonight and before. They admitted it."

"She lying," the woman said, beginning to cry. "We didn't do anything. I swear."

A city police officer entered the room just then. With him was a third building security guard. The brawny man had SUPERVISOR on his nameplate.

"I'm Officer Dawson. What's going on?" the policeman asked.

"Officer Dawson, before this goes any farther, do you think the guns could be put away?" Shane suggested. "The good guys obviously outnumber the bad, and I wouldn't want one to go off accidentally. Especially when Ms. Albright and her mother are personal friends with the mayor *and* the governor."

"Put 'em away," the policeman ordered. The two guards fumbled to do as told.

"Thanks," Shane said, then began to explain. "The moan you hear is coming from the other thief behind Ms. Albright's desk. This woman is his accomplice." Shane handed the woman to the nearest security guard.

Officer Dawson went behind the desk, grabbed the thief's arm, and helped him to his feet. The man held the side of his neck with his free hand.

"Building security records will show that Ms. Albright reported the theft of a pair of gold earrings she left on her desk last week." Shane's hard gaze swept the three security men. "She was blown off and nothing was done. They didn't even contact the cleaning service as she suggested, which was a mistake."

"He's crazy!" the woman yelled. "Tell them, baby! We didn't take nothing!"

The groggy man's head lifted. "He attacked me 'cause we caught them doing the nasty."

Shane ignored the lie. "You'll find a marked fifty-dollar bill in his right pocket."

The man's eyes bugged. "He must have planted it in there while I was out."

"Then your fingerprints shouldn't be on the bill," Shane remarked.

The officer patted the man's jeans pocket. His eyes hardened, his grip on the man's arm tightened. "You want to change your story?"

The man wet his lips. "I-I . . ."

"Think of something!" the woman shouted. "I don't want to go back to jail."

"Shut up," her accomplice yelled.

"I've heard enough," the officer said. He read the man his rights, then the woman, and finally handcuffed them. "I need you and Ms. Albright to come downtown to make statements."

Shane went to stand beside a silent Paige. "I'll bring Ms. Albright, but before we go, you should know that they were bragging about having marks in different departments," Shane told the officer. "The woman was bemoaning having to pawn Ms. Albright's earrings. You'll probably find the earrings in their car or home. Since security was slow to take Ms. Albright's complaint, they might have been the same way with others, which inadvertently helped the thieves."

"Are you in law enforcement?" Officer Dawson asked.

"Computers," Shane said. "Ms. Albright asked for my help since she wasn't getting any from her building security. It's a shame she had to apprehend the thieves herself, risk injury, then have a gun drawn on her."

The police officer looked at the three security people with disdain. "I want a copy of Ms. Albright's complaint as well as that of any other person in this building faxed to the station. I also want you to contact the cleaning crew supervisor of this shift and have him meet us downstairs. Maybe you can do that without messing it up."

Paige was too quiet. She hadn't said three words to Shane since they had left her office building. She simply sat, her hands folded, her face turned away. The dejected pose tore at his heart. Not even being told they'd found her earrings in the woman's purse had any effect on her.

Shane wished for just fifteen, even ten seconds with the creep who had frightened her, called her stupid because she trusted people. He'd show him what it was like to be scared. Since the thief was locked up, that wasn't possible.

"Are you all right?" he asked when he pulled up in front of her house. He'd taken a cab to her office that afternoon because he hadn't known how long it would take, or even if the thief would try anything that night. Earlier when he'd asked for her car keys in the parking lot of her office building, she'd wordlessly handed them over.

"Yes," Paige finally answered. She opened the passenger door just as the front door flew open and her mother raced down the steps to meet them. Mrs. Albright didn't stop until she held Paige firmly in her arms.

After a long moment Mrs. Albright leaned Paige away to stare down at her. "Are you sure you're all right?"

"Yes, Mother. I think I'll go to bed." Paige barely glanced at Shane. "Good night, and thank you."

Mrs. Albright waited until Paige entered the house. "What's the matter with her?"

"I think I know, but I can't tell you."

She stepped in his face. "If something else happened, you *better* tell me."

The fierceness of a mother's love. He'd seen the same warning look in Ruth Grayson's face when she thought he was withholding information about Sierra's kidnapping. Without thinking he lifted his hands to rest on Mrs. Albright's tense shoulders. "It's nothing you should worry about."

She relaxed only marginally. "She's my daughter and I love her. I've never seen her this . . . remote. She's been through enough in life."

Shane could well imagine. "I'm going to talk to her." Taking her arm, they started inside.

"Tell her I'm preparing her favorite breakfast," Mrs. Albright said as they entered the house. "What's yours?"

"I don't have one," Shane admitted. As soon as he'd been old enough to scrounge up his own meals, his mother had let him have the job. He couldn't have been any older than four or five.

As an adult, he enjoyed good food, and since working for Blade, he'd eaten at the most expensive and best restaurants in the world. Blade's personal chef once worked at the only five-star hotel in Texas. Still, Shane couldn't say he craved one food over another.

But there was definitely a woman he desired above all others. "Anything will do."

"We'll have to change that before you leave." She smiled at him, then looked up at the stairs. "I'll leave Paige to you while I go see if everything I need is in the kitchen. If not, Macy can bring it in the morning. Don't forget to tell Paige."

"I won't," he promised.

"Just make sure Paige is smiling at breakfast in the morning." Leaving him in the foyer, Mrs. Albright headed for the kitchen.

Tall order. He had every intention of making it happen. Taking the stairs two at a time, he didn't stop until he stood in front of Paige's door. He rapped. "Paige."

"I'm rather tired."

You're also hiding. "You and I need to talk and I'm not leaving until we do."

"There's nothing to talk about," she said. Her voice sounded thick, as if she were fighting tears. He cursed under his breath and took matters into his own hands. "Then listen." He opened the door.

Paige bounded up from sitting on the side of the bed. Thankfully she hadn't changed. Conversation would have been impossible if she'd already dressed for bed.

"Please, Shane, just leave." Her voice quivered. She glanced away.

"Not until I have my say." He crossed the room until he stood in front of her. "I never apologized for putting you in harm's way tonight. I'm sorry. You had no idea of what to expect. I did, and I let you stay anyway."

She wrapped her slim arms around her tiny waist. "There is nothing for you to apologize for." She swallowed, bit her lower lip. "I'm the one who needs to apologize. I was useless. You could have been killed. I let myself get caught and all I could do was—"

"Look to me to help you." He finally touched her, just her arm. Her skin felt like warmed porcelain and just as fragile and delicate. She was nothing like any woman he'd been with before, and the thought pleased him immensely. "Do you know how much that touched me—even as it angered me that he would hurt you, frightened me that he might have a weapon, that I hadn't kept my promise? You trusted me to help you."

She frowned up at him. "What promise?"

"That you wouldn't be hurt," he said.

"Thanks to you, I wasn't."

"I don't know what I would have done if you had been," he admitted softly. Even now the thought made his chest tight.

Her arms slowly unfolded. Her gaze glued to his, she lifted one hand and placed it on his chest, easing the constriction there and causing his heart to race. "I was frightened for *you*," she said softly.

Only Rio and Blade ever thought of his safety. "We're both all right. Your earrings were recovered *and* you showed your co-workers, the owner of the cleaning company, and building security that you were right about there being a thief. Quite an accomplishment."

The corners of her sweet, sexy mouth lifted. "Jackie kept apologizing when I called her."

He wondered if she knew her fingertips were stroking him. "You'll probably get more of the same from your co-workers tomorrow," he told her. "And well you should. Despite what they were telling you, you weren't afraid to prove them wrong."

"The real credit goes to you," she said softly.

"Why don't we share it?" he said, happy to see that she was less tense. Watching her closely, his other hand lifted to her waist. Her fingertips paused, her body tensed almost imperceptibly for a tension-filled moment, then she relaxed and her fingers went back to caressing him.

"I'd like that."

He liked holding her. "Good. I'll see you at breakfast. Your mother wanted me to tell you that she's preparing your favorite."

"She is?" Surprise widened Paige's eyes.

"She is, and I've been invited to join you." Reluctantly he stepped back. Her stroking was having the wrong effect on another part of his anatomy. "See you in the morning."

"Shane," she called when he had almost reached the door.

He stopped and looked back. "Yes?"

"Do you think you can teach me to be less of a pushover?" she asked, her gaze direct and hopeful.

He hadn't expected the request. Still, whatever it took for Paige to feel more in control of her life—if it was within his power, he'd see that she got it. "We'll start tomorrow after you get home from work."

Her smile lit up her face, made his blood heat, made him wonder what the hell he was letting himself in for. "Good night."

"Night."

P aige woke up with a smile. It was all because of Shane. She didn't know what it was about him that excited her, drew her, but she wasn't going to fight the attraction.

He was her Prince Charming, her Black Knight, all rolled into one. Throwing back the covers, she quickly showered and dressed in a figure-flattering sage-colored sheath. She didn't delude herself that she wasn't dressing for Shane. She wasn't running away any longer.

Paige opened her bedroom door and saw the man who occupied her thoughts more and more. "Shane." She hoped her voice didn't sound as breathless as she felt. He wore a white polo shirt that stretched across his impressive chest and showed off his muscular arms. She bit back a sigh of delight.

"Good morning, Paige." His eyes raked her in one maddeningly slow sweep that caused awareness and, yes, anticipation to sweep through her of the day he'd do more than just look. She held her breath until their eyes met. "I don't know how you do it, but you always look more beautiful every time I see you."

You do, too, flashed through her mind, but the words never made it to her tongue. She wasn't that brave yet. "Thank you."

"Shall we go down to breakfast?" He offered his arm. Her fingers curved through the crook of his arm. She felt the heat and hardness of his conditioned body as he drew her closer. "Did you sleep all right?"

"Yes," he answered as they started down the stairs. "And you?"

"Wonderful," she answered, then dropped her head for fear the breathless quality in her voice might have given away her fascination with him.

In the middle of the stairs, he stopped. Strong, insistent fingers lifted her chin. "Lesson number one. Always keep your head up."

The warmth of his touch made her skin tingle, then heat. Running away from personal conflict was what she did. "I don't know if I can."

"I do," he said softly, stirring her senses. "You're conflicted between your heart and your head. You'd rather hurt than hurt others."

Her head started to fall, but his strong finger wouldn't allow it. Neither would he let her look away from him. "I have no backbone," she admitted.

His eyes narrowed, darkened. "I don't ever want to hear you say that again. It takes courage to reach out and help others. If not for you, Noah would have been lost. You helped him turn his life around when others had given up. It took courage for you to keep fighting for him to help himself. You just have to learn to do the same for yourself."

"I'll tr—"

"Lesson number two," he said, cutting her off. "Even when you're on your backside, never give up. And lose the negative thinking."

She bristled for all of three seconds, then blew out a breath. He was right. "Any other lessons?"

"Lots." He grinned at her. "I'll tell you as we go along. Now let's get breakfast."

They reached the bottom of the stairs and headed for the kitchen. "Whatever your favorite food is, it sure smells good."

"Blueberry pancakes with whipped cream and fresh blueberries," Paige answered. "Mother doesn't cook very often, but when she does, it will make you smack your lips."

His gaze centered on her mouth, sending a ball of fire through her. "Now, that would be an experience."

Paige couldn't hide the blush, but she did manage to keep her chin up. She couldn't begin to imagine what Shane's sensual lips would feel like on her. Would they be hot or warm? Gentle or persuasive? Whatever, she knew she'd never forget the taste of him.

Dragging her gaze away, she followed him into the high-ceilinged kitchen with its black granite island and copper pots overhead. At the stove, her mother turned. "Good morning, Paige. Shane. Breakfast is almost ready."

"Anything I can do to help?" Shane asked, releasing Paige to pull out a chair at the century-old square oak table.

"No, thank you." Expertly Mrs. Albright slid three pancakes off the griddle onto a platter, then turned over the ham sizzling in the cast-iron skillet. Dressed in a cotton eyelet sleeveless shirtdress, she had an apron around her waist and looked as calm and as cool as she did when entertaining guests or speaking to one of her many social clubs.

Paige just stood there, memories sweeping over her of her mother in the kitchen preparing her favorite food when life had slammed her down, as it had so many times. In the South, food was a panacea for wounded souls. Her mother had given her that and so much more. Unconditional love and encouragement no matter how many times Paige had failed.

Her father hadn't been so forgiving. She shivered.

"Paige?" Shane said, his brow furrowed in concern.

"You sure you don't need any help, Mother?" Paige asked.

Smiling, Mrs. Albright shook her head. "Macy helped me get things started before she went upstairs to start cleaning in my room." Mrs. Albright stirred the grits. "Please have a seat."

Paige finally accepted the chair Shane held so patiently. The table was beautifully laid with two place settings of her grandmother's fine china and sterling flatware. Neither her grandmother nor her mother believed in saving the "good" china and flatware for guests. Family came first to them, and it showed . . . or it had until shortly after her father's death. The center-piece was a Waterford vase filled with white roses, Paige's favorite flower.

Her mother placed two fruit plates on the table. "You aren't joining us?" Paige asked.

Mrs. Albright laughed. Paige didn't realize until then that her mother hadn't laughed, really laughed as she did now, free and happy, in a long time. "You know I sample as I go."

"I don't blame you." Shane rubbed his hands together. "I can't wait."

Her mother picked up two large platters and placed them on the table. One held an eight-inch stack of fluffy blueberry pancakes browned to perfection; the other, an assortment of breakfast meats. Next came two bowls of cheese grits and freshly squeezed orange juice. "I'll say grace so you can eat."

Paige bowed her head as her mother blessed the food. She was one of those women who was at ease in any situation and did everything well. That was why her being so secretive caused Paige such concern. What was her reason for visiting Trent Masters? His accusations couldn't possibly have any validity.

"Would you like coffee, Shane?" Paige's mother asked.

"Please. Black," he answered, passing the pancakes to Paige just as the phone on the granite countertop rang.

Paige's mother threw the instrument a look of an-noyance. "Let it ring," she advised.

Paige frowned, then placed two pancakes on her plate. Her mother was usually too well bred and cour-teous to ignore a ringing phone. "I can get it."

Her mother was already shaking her head. She placed a delicate cup of steaming black coffee by

Shane's plate and a glass of juice by Paige's. "No. You eat while your food is hot. It's probably someone else calling about last night."

Paige's frown deepened. "I can't believe Jackie told that many people."

"She didn't." Shane held out the platter of meats to Paige. "The newspaper printed the story."

"What?" Paige ignored the food. "You've got to be kidding."

"I wish I were," he said with annoyance. "You were giving your statement when the supervisor of security arrived, talking loud and posturing. He wanted anyone and everyone to know that the building is safe. A reporter happened to be there covering another story. The supervisor was only too happy to talk to the reporter and do damage control. He promised a thorough investigation would be conducted on why your complaint wasn't dealt with more efficiently."

Shane snorted. "He knew there is bound to be fallout with all the high-profile businesses in the building. I bet his phone hasn't stopped ringing since the story hit."

"I'm sorry you were involved in this," she said, finally taking a slice of honey-cured ham on her plate although her appetite had waned. She hadn't thought past getting her earrings back.

"It's not me I'm concerned about," he told her. "I just don't want the media bothering you."

She might have known. She picked up the crystal pitcher of syrup. "The media can be useful."

He snorted again.

Paige opened her mouth to ask him why he felt that way just as Macy came into the room carrying a portable phone. "Ms. Paige, Mr. Crenshaw is on the phone. He's on board his flight and wants to talk to you."

Chapter 10

Paige couldn't help but look at Shane. His expression was unreadable, but her mother's lips, pursed in annoyance, spoke volumes. "Excuse me." Standing, Paige took the phone and moved a few feet away. "Hello, Russell."

"Paige, you said you were going home last night, and this morning I read you were involved in a burglary in your office," he accused.

"I did come home," she told him.

"A mere technicality," he snapped. "What were you thinking of to try and catch a thief? I thought you had more sense."

She hadn't tried. She and Shane had succeeded, she thought with an unexpected sense of pride.

"The newspaper said that freeloading Elliott was there with you," Russell fumed. "I knew he wasn't any good when I first laid eyes on him."

Arguing would settle nothing. Russell was as single-minded as her father. She didn't know why, but the thought made her uncomfortable.

"Paige?"

"Thank you for calling and for your concern," she said. "I'm sorry to have upset you, but they stole the earrings Zach gave me for my birthday. I wanted them back."

"Good gracious, Paige. You are so childish at times," Russell said with growing annoyance. "They were just earrings."

Paige hadn't expected Russell to understand. It wasn't lost on her that Shane had grasped immediately the importance of recovering her brother's gift and the sentiment it carried. Russell never would, and that made her sad for him.

"I want you to stay away from Elliott. You wouldn't have attempted anything so idiotic if he hadn't influenced you. Now promise me you'll stay away from him before I have to hang up."

"What did you say?" She put her hand over her ear. "You're breaking up."

"Stay away from Elliott!" Russell shouted, then muttered under his breath, "I have to go. I'll call as soon as I land."

"Good-bye, Russell. Have a safe flight." Cutting off the call, she gave the receiver back to Macy. Paige wondered if Russell would suspect she had lied about not hearing him.

Shane stood and pulled out her chair as she returned to the table. "Are you all right?"

"Couldn't be better," she said, meaning every word. She picked up her napkin. Russell had called her senseless, childish, idiotic. The thief thought her stupid. She was none of those things, and it was time, as Shane had pointed out, that she acted like it.

She took a bite of her pancakes. They were warm instead of hot, but she couldn't recall tasting better. "These are wonderful, Mother. Thanks."

Her mother beamed at her, reminiscent of all the times she'd been so proud of Paige just for trying. Paige smiled back.

"I can see how this could be your favorite breakfast,"

Shane said, forking in another bite of blueberry pancakes. "I'll miss this when I move out."

"What?" Paige and her mother said at the same time.

Shane stared across the table at Paige. "I can't continue to take advantage of your hospitality. If you'll help me look, I thought I'd rent a place while I check out the city for a job."

"You'll do no such thing," Mrs. Albright said. "You're staying here."

"I agree with Mother," Paige said, trying to keep her voice level. "I don't mind helping you look for a place, but I have more lessons to learn."

"Lessons?" Mrs. Albright said, looking between the two.

"Self-defense," Paige explained. "You said you would, and you said you'd never lie to me."

He stared at her a long time. "I'll stay for a while."

"Good." Paige picked up her glass of juice. There was still time to see if the searing of attraction went anyplace. And when Russell returned, she'd make him listen. And the very man he'd warned her away from was the one who was going to enable her to stand up for herself.

"She hugged me good-bye," Mrs. Albright whispered, her voice unsteady as she watched Paige drive away.

"She loves you," Shane said. "She talks about you all the time."

"She does?" The older woman brightened even more. "What does she say?"

Well aware that she was greedy for any information that would mean the chasm between her and her daughter was closing, Shane told her of their conversation at lunch the day before. "She knows you love her."

"Thank you." Mrs. Albright blinked back tears. "I knew you'd make a difference. Ruth said you would."

Shane had a difficult time keeping the shock from his face. "What has Sierra's mother to do with this?"

"I told you. She credited Sierra's safe return to the investigative work you and Rio did." Mrs. Albright lightly touched his arm. "She said you would save Paige, and she's right."

"Mrs. Al—"

She held up her hand. "No. I'm too happy to hear anything negative. I'm going to clean up the kitchen, then put her roses in her room."

Shane was left standing on the front porch.

S hane rang Alisha's doorbell shortly after nine. The upscale condominium was subleased in the name of a married man in his late sixties. He was one of three men Alisha shuffled to keep the bills paid and herself in designer clothes, jewelry, and the Jaguar in front.

The door opened. Her hand clenched on the knob, then she relaxed, lifting her hand to press against the door frame. The motion lifted her unbound breasts and parted the sheer white robe. "What can I do for you?" she asked, running her tongue slowly across her red lips.

Disgust rolled through him. Shane didn't want to be around her a moment longer than necessary. "I thought I'd save us both time and aggravation with a small demonstration. I know you're having an affair with Gerald Letts, the owner of Letts Car dealership, with Bob Johnson, the owner of Stylish Designs, and with Russell Crenshaw."

"Is that how you get your kicks?"

Shane ignored her taunt. "None of the men knows about the others. If you want it to stay that way, remember our discussion. Just in case your memory becomes faulty, I wanted you to see this." He held up a five-inch handheld computer. "Your checking account has exactly one dollar in it."

"What!" she yelled, trying to grab the computer. "I don't believe you."

"See for yourself."

She whirled away and snatched up the phone. Less than four minutes later, half of that time spent yelling and cursing at the person on the other end of the line, she slammed the receiver down. "I want my money back," she screeched.

"That depends on you," Shane told her, his voice cold and devoid of emotion.

She swallowed. "I won't go near Mrs. Albright or her children. Just put my money back."

"The money will be returned at exactly nine tomorrow morning. Minus the blackmail money Mrs. Albright gave you."

Alisha opened her mouth, then wisely closed it.

"Disturb the Albright family again and all of your money disappearing permanently will be the least of your problems." Shane went to the door. "Your checking account is flagged. Trying to withdraw the money or transfer it into another account won't do any good. I'll find it, just as I'll find you. Last warning. You won't get another one."

Stepping outside, he closed the door just as something heavy smashed against it. Shane continued down the steps. Let her vent her anger. But if Alisha contacted the Albrights, she'd reap the unpleasant consequences.

She'd been warned.

*   *   *

Paige didn't know what to expect at work, but she was ready for it. After parking in the garage, she got out and joined the other employees heading for the elevator. If anyone called her *stupid* or *idiotic* she wasn't going to be responsible.

Stepping off the elevator on the first floor, she continued through the glass doors to security. She'd no more than swiped her identification card when Harris, the nearest security guard, came around the waist-high counter.

"Good morning, Ms. Albright."

"Good morning, Harris." She knew most of the morning security guards and occasionally brought them doughnuts.

"I heard about the incident last night." He hitched up his belt. It immediately slipped back under his bulging stomach. "We all wanted you to know that we're sorry we didn't take your complaint more seriously."

"Apology accepted." Last night at the police station the security supervisor had apologized over and over. The owner of the security firm had also called.

The guard relaxed. "Glad to hear it." He glanced around the busy lobby and leaned closer. "I told the other guys you weren't the one."

"The one what?" she asked.

He shifted from one foot to the other. "Guess I should have kept my mouth shut."

"Harris," she said, with the stern tone she'd heard her mother use when someone was being difficult.

He nodded his head toward a quiet corner. She followed. "The boss said he had a complaint that the guys on duty didn't check Elliott thoroughly before letting him go up. Everyone on duty when that Elliott fellow came through security, and the guys who overlooked your complaint, were called on the carpet."

Paige had a good idea who had lodged the complaint. Russell. She barely kept her temper in check. How dare Russell! "Without Mr. Elliott, the thieves wouldn't have been captured."

Harris adjusted the utility belt. "From what I hear, that's true, but that guy could have hurt you. If Elliott hadn't been there, then neither would you."

Paige was finding it more difficult with each passing second not to show her anger. "If security had done their job, neither of us would have had to be there," she said tightly.

"That was brought up, too," the security guard said slowly. "A complaint from you, and heads are going to roll."

"I don't want anyone to lose their jobs, but neither do I want security to ignore my complaint or anyone else's again," she told him.

"You got it." He tipped his head and went back behind the check-in counter.

Paige crossed the lobby and rode the elevator to her floor. Taking a deep breath, she stepped off and continued down the hallway and opened the outer door to the main office.

The receptionist saw her, stood, and began to applaud. People came out of office doors to join in. Jackie pushed to the front. "Paige, the woman of the hour."

Paige shook her head and laughed. "That's enough."

The receptionist gave Paige several phone message slips. "You've been getting calls all morning from people congratulating you. Oh, there it goes again."

"I'm sorry I—" Jackie began.

Paige touched Jackie's arm, silencing her. "It's forgotten. I'm getting my earrings back and the thieves are in jail. Let's just focus on the Masquerade Ball."

"Everything going well?" Jackie asked as they started down the hall to Paige's office.

"Yes," Paige answered. "Even if we don't get any more donations, we've reached our goal. This will be the most lucrative fund-raiser event in years."

"Oh, my!"

At Jackie's exclamation, Paige turned to see what had caused the woman's eyes to widen, for them to gleam with unmistakable appreciation. Paige's own heart dipped. How well she understood her boss's reaction.

Shane, his gaze locked on Paige, came toward them with that sexy walk of his that caused her heart rate to accelerate. Noah and Gayle were with him. Shane carried a large bouquet of white roses in his hands.

He didn't stop until he stood in front of her. He was temptation personified. "Look who I met in the lobby."

"We called the house, but your mother said you had just left," Noah said.

"The newspaper said you were all right, but it also said there was an altercation," Gayle added, her expression worried.

"I told her Shane could handle it." Noah grinned up at Shane. "Glad to see you didn't make a liar out of me."

"Wouldn't dream of it," Shane said, then turned to Paige. "These are for you. You want them in your office?"

"Yes. Thank you." The long-stemmed white roses in the elegant crystal vase, at least two dozen, could have been from her mother, but somehow Paige didn't think so. "I'll get the door."

Opening her office door, Paige paused, remembering

letting herself be captured, the security men with guns aimed on Shane. Her fault.

"No negative thoughts, remember," Shane whispered in her ear.

The caress of his breath sent delicious shivers racing over her, sweeping everything away except the sensual awareness of the man standing so close to her. "Please put them on my desk."

Shane moved around her to do as directed. Paige's gaze lowered to the jeans cupping his tight rear. Grade A.

"They look beautiful. I've never received flowers." Gayle sighed, admiring the bouquet, a wistful note in her voice.

"You will," Shane said. "Give it time. I've never given a woman flowers."

Paige's eyes widened in undisguised pleasure at the admission. She tried to tell herself he was just being friendly. But Shane's scorching gaze said something entirely different. "Thank you. This is a first for me, too. I've never received two dozen roses."

"I'm happy to be the first," Shane said, the deep timbre of his voice caressing her.

"You sure know how to set a precedent," Noah said, his astute gaze shifting between the two adults. He nudged his sister. "Ah, we'll catch you two later. Bye."

Gayle frowned at her brother, then said, "Oh, yes. Bye."

"Good-bye," Paige said, seeing them to the door and closing it softly after them. Shimmering awareness coiled though her. She was almost afraid to turn.

"What are your plans for today?" Shane asked.

Facing him, her heart skipped a beat. Arms crossed over his rock-hard chest, he leaned against the front of her desk with his legs crossed, looking good enough to eat with a spoon. Paige's cheeks heated. Shane had the worst effect on her.

"Working on plans for the Masquerade Ball," she finally told him. "It's our biggest fund-raiser of the year and I'm in charge."

"You'll succeed," he told her. "Anything I can do to help?"

Stop making me think and dream of things that can never be. "It's just a lot of phone calls today to ensure everything is in place."

He pushed away from the desk. "I guess I better get out of your way and let you get to it."

She glanced at the flowers, beautiful and beckoning, much like the person who had given them to her. "Thank you again for the flowers. They're lovely."

"Seeing you smile is all the thanks I need," he said, his gaze direct, his voice low and deep, stroking her.

Her silly heart simply melted.

The brisk knock on the door behind her probably saved her from doing something stupid, like touching Shane or, worse, leaning into him and seeing what his sensual mouth felt like on hers. She turned just as the door opened, almost grateful until she saw who it was. Doris Betts, the accountant, entered, her man-eating gaze finding Shane in an instant.

"Paige, I'm so sorry to interrupt, but I have a problem."

"That's all right," Paige said, trying to be gracious when she really wanted to ask the other woman to leave. "Doris Betts, Shane Elliott."

"Ms. Betts," Shane said, briefly shaking the extended hand.

"Mr. Elliott," Doris said, smiling seductively up at Shane, and not moving back when he released her hand. "Please call me Doris. I need a huge favor." She flashed an apologetic and totally false smile between Shane and Paige. "I'm sorry to interrupt, but my computer is down and Jackie said you might be able to help me."

"What seems to be the problem?" Shane asked.

Doris shrugged, causing her D-cup breasts to demand attention. Paige marveled that Shane didn't seem to notice.

"The monitor and tower won't come on. I have a stack of reports to put in and the service we use can't get out until late this afternoon."

"Why don't I have a look at it?" Shane suggested.

"Would you?" Doris cooed, grinning broadly. "Thank you." Her grasping fingers curved around his bare forearm. "I'll bring him back."

Helpless, Paige watched Doris waltz out of her office, clinging to Shane like a drowning victim. It was common knowledge that if Doris wanted a man, she didn't mind stepping on another woman to get him.

A couple of months ago, the luckless woman had been the receptionist, Chy. Jackie had had to intervene when the two women had a shouting match in the break room. Personal matters were to be left outside the office. If not, both women would be dismissed.

The receptionist, a single mother of two adorable little girls, had let the matter drop. The man she thought was "the one" had started dating Doris, but it hadn't lasted two weeks. Paige had heard that the man wanted to get back with Chy, but she wasn't having it. Paige thought Chy's decision had been a good one. Who wanted to waste time on a man you couldn't trust around other women?

The more Paige thought of Doris sinking her claws into Shane, the angrier she became. She reasoned that he was a houseguest, and thus it was up to her to protect him. Jackie wouldn't like an altercation, but Paige was not letting Doris win this time.

Having no idea how to stop the shameless woman, Paige opened the door to her office and started down the hall. Passing the receptionist's desk, she saw Chy's sympathetic, angry face. She had already concluded that Doris would win again.

But Paige wasn't losing or backing down. She was following rules number one and two: keeping her head up and not giving up.

Knocking just as briefly as Doris had, Paige opened the other woman's door. Shane was on his back under her desk, and Doris was crouched in front of him. If he happened to look, he'd see everything under her short flared skirt.

Disgust rolled through Paige. Her fingers clamped on the door instead of slamming it as she wanted to. "Doris."

The woman jumped, then spun, pushing to her feet. She didn't even have the decency to flush or look guilty. She looked annoyed. *Tough.*

"Yes?"

"I need to look at the final tabulation of the luncheon."

Doris eyed her with suspicion. "You just checked it yesterday."

"I need to check it again," Paige said firmly. "Do you have a problem with that?"

"Got it." The monitor and tower's lights came on. Shane came from beneath the desk.

Doris swung back to him on her long legs. "Oh."

"A couple of connections came loose," Shane explained. "You shouldn't have any more problems. If you'll give Paige the report she needs, you can start on that report you need to do."

Lips tight, Doris dug through the files on her desk and shoved the file at Paige. "Here."

"Thank you." Taking the folder, Paige turned to leave, felt Shane's hand on her arm. Returning to her office with Shane beside her, she noticed the surprised but approving smile of the receptionist.

"We're even," Shane said, once inside her office.

She frowned. "Even?"

"You rescued me," he said with a grin. "I thought I'd be stuck under that desk."

Paige laughed, immensely pleased at the notion of rescuing a self-sufficient and resourceful man like Shane. "I did, didn't I?"

"You did." Lifting his hand, he took her other arm, staring down into her upturned face. "I like hearing you laugh."

"There hasn't been much to laugh about lately," she said, her voice and face serious.

"We'll have to change that." He gently pressed his lips to her temple. "See you this afternoon."

Shocked, she stood there as he left. Slowly her hand lifted to the spot his lips had touched. The kiss had been sweet, tender, comforting even. And somehow she knew that before long she'd know what it was like to kiss her Black Knight for real.

She couldn't wait.

Shane knew before he had taken two steps away from Paige that he had made a tactical error. The surprise on her face just before he'd gently kissed her, the look of wonder and pleasure when he'd raised his head, sealed both their fates. His heart had constricted painfully in his chest.

No woman had ever looked at him that way before,

as if he was all she desired, every fantasy and thought fulfilled.

And he was there under false pretenses.

He didn't curse or hit the steering wheel as he pulled out of the parking garage of her office building. Neither would help him feel any better about the situation. Paige deserved honesty. She'd see his help as thinking her incompetent to make her own decisions. He didn't think her mother would fare much better.

He stopped at a red light in the bustle of early-morning traffic. Shane hadn't thought of what would happen after Russell was exposed. No, that was a lie, his conscience prodded. Somewhere, in the most secret part of him, he had thought there might be a chance for him and Paige to get to know each other better.

With a lie between them, that wasn't likely. And he only had himself to blame.

He pulled through the traffic light, heading for the downtown office of Jericho's investigation firm. As of last night Shane had the dates and places of Russell and Alisha's last two meetings, but he wasn't ready to give the information to Paige. She'd see one liar exposing another.

And it would shatter her.

He wanted her to figure out by herself what a bastard Russell was, to realize that he was using her love for her father to further his cause for them to get married, and thus get his grimy hands on her money. Somehow Shane knew that was the only way for this to play out. Any other way would wound her deeply, and destroy any chance Shane had.

Shane walked a dangerous tightrope. He cared about her, worried about her. There was no sense saying he didn't. His returning early and, now, the kiss were proof.

He wasn't a philosophical man, but holding her was like holding a little bit of heaven. He wasn't going to let her go. He went after what he wanted. He didn't mind bending a few rules or laws to accomplish his goal. Turning on his signal, he turned into the underground parking lot of the building of Jericho's firm.

The only course Shane saw was an addendum to his plan. Save Paige, and then take her for himself.

The first part was easy. The second part was going to take work, but he had no intention of failing.

Chapter 11

Paige hummed softly as she pulled into the driveway of her mother's house. She couldn't wait to see Shane. She enjoyed just looking at his powerful build, his gorgeous face—both got her heart pounding. She glanced over at the package in the passenger seat and frowned. What had been a sure buy at the sports store now nagged her with apprehension.

Perhaps the black midriff-baring top and spandex shorts were a bit too revealing. She could have worn her sweats. She would have looked presentable, but not exciting or alluring. For the first time in her life, she wanted to look sexy for a man, for Shane. To somehow make his heart pound the way hers did for him.

Nearing the house, she saw the cars in the driveway and wanted to groan. Leave it to Russell's mother to ruin her day. Just then, Shane came out the front door and down the steps. He wore a long-sleeved white shirt and black slacks. He didn't look happy. While it was uncharitable of her to say, Russell's mother could try the nerve of a saint.

Stopping behind Tess's convertible Mercedes, Paige emerged from the car. "You seem upset."

"I see I'll have to work on my poker face." He smiled down at her, his hand gently sweeping over her unbound hair. "Not me, but your mother thought you might be. You have visitors."

"I recognized Tess's car, but not the other one," she told him.

"Let's walk." Curving his long arm around her shoulder, he didn't stop until they were on the other side of a seven-foot, cone-shaped boxwood by the corner of the house. He turned, placed his hands on her upper arms, and stared down into her face. "I'm not sure who drove, but both of the other women have beady eyes," he said.

As usual he didn't move back and she didn't ask him. Her excuse, and it was a good one, was that she was still trying to understand what was going on between them. "Beady eyes? Mother sent you out here?"

"In a matter of speaking. Russell's mother kept asking when you'd arrive. Your mother said she wasn't sure but, in any case, you and I had plans for the evening."

Paige barely kept her mouth from gaping at the implication. "Mother said that?"

He grinned. "She did. Caused quite a stir."

She just bet it did. "Why were you there?"

"Bad luck," he confided. "I happened to be going to the kitchen for a bottle of water and Mrs. Crenshaw saw me."

Paige remembered their meeting at the church. Without thinking she placed her hand on his chest in a gesture of comfort. "I'm sorry."

"I survived. Actually, the other women who left earlier were pretty nice," he told her, his hand resting on top of hers.

Paige felt his heart pound beneath her hand, knew her heart rate was just as erratic. Then it hit her. She shut her eyes. "Oh, no."

"What?" he asked, grasping her arms.

"The women are members of Mother's garden club." She shoved her hand over her head. "But they should have been gone hours ago."

"Mrs. Crenshaw said she couldn't leave until she saw you were all right. She said she'd promised Russell," Shane told her, not even trying to hide his disbelief.

Paige's mouth tightened. "The other two women are probably Gertrude Osgood and Emma Franklin, two of the worst gossips in the county. I'm sure they want all the juicy details, considering they're always talking about their supposedly perfect children."

"They give you a hard time?" he asked, his gaze sharp.

"Mother. I avoid them. Mrs. Osgood's daughter is married to a man who'd rather play golf than work at the executive position his father-in-law gave him, while she has one affair after the other. Mrs. Franklin's sons are in high political offices. Both have been investigated for kickbacks, for good cause from what I hear."

"Your mother is too much of a lady to point that out," Shane said.

"Exactly," Paige told him, not bothering to keep the anger at bay. "Russell's father is on the city code commission and, while not in their league financially, Mr. Crenshaw carries a lot of political weight. They wouldn't think of angering his wife."

"What they can't use, they abuse. You father carried a lot of weight and your mother comes from a wealthy family," Shane said. "He should have stopped it."

She glanced away. "Father wasn't always proud of us."

Cursing softly under his breath, Shane pulled her into his arms. "He should have been."

Eyes closed, Paige wrapped her arms around him, pressing closer, enjoying the comfort he offered just as she'd known she would. "He had his reasons with me, but Zach is brilliant."

Shane pushed her from him, his eyes hot. "Crap. There's nothing wrong with you, now or then, and I don't want to hear you say it again."

Startled by his fierce reaction, she stared up at him. He looked angrier than she'd ever seen him. And his anger was for—her. "Is . . ." She had to swallow before she continued. "Is that another rule?"

"Yes," he snapped.

"Well, I guess that settles it." She wanted his arms around her again, but hopefully that would come later. She stepped back. "I need to say hi to Mother, greet our guests. The clothes I plan to wear for our session are in the car. I'll get them and meet you where?"

The corners of his sexy mouth kicked up. "In the garden room by the Japanese garden, but can I tag along for now?"

"I wouldn't have it any other way."

"Hello, Mother," Paige greeted warmly as she entered the room.

"Hello, Paige," her mother replied, concern flickering in her eyes. "Didn't you have an appointment?"

"I wanted to say hello to our guests," she said, placing her hand on the back of her mother's wing chair and facing the other three women in the room. "Mrs. Crenshaw, Mrs. Osgood, Mrs. Franklin. The meeting is running a bit late, isn't it?"

Russell's mother set her teacup on the side table, pressed her hand to her enhanced breasts. "Hello, Paige. I couldn't bring myself to leave without seeing for myself that you were unharmed." Her accusing gaze flickered to Shane, arms folded, standing by the double doors leading into the solarium. "Russell was concerned, and I am inclined to agree."

Mrs. Osgood's and Mrs. Franklin's ears probably twitched, Paige thought. "I appreciate your concern. Please put your mind at ease. I was perfectly safe, but the incident showed me that I need to know more about self-defense. Shane is going to teach me some moves this afternoon."

Mrs. Osgood eyed Shane as if he were a bug that had wandered into her path. "Joann, Paige might be easily influenced, but you must know it would make more sense to have a qualified person instruct her."

Paige pressed her hand to her mother's shoulder to keep her quiet. She had defended Paige enough. "How would you know if Shane isn't qualified?"

"From what I hear, he's an unemployed computer person."

"You mean unemployed like your husband when he lost his job when the newspaper he worked for as a reporter folded? He didn't have any experience selling furniture, but your father loaned him the money to start his own business." Paige folded her arms.

"My husband's success has proven my father made the right decision. If you want a job done right, hire a professional," Mrs. Osgood continued.

"I guess your daughter took your advice. How is she coming with the lessons from the tennis pro at the country club?"

The other woman's eyes bugged. Her cup rattled on the saucer.

"I was at the club last week and they were looking for both of them because he was late for his next appointment, but no one could find either of them. Before that, she took lessons from the golf pro." Paige's eyebrow lifted. "I wonder which sport she'll take up next."

"They, at least, have credentials," Mrs. Osgood commented. "What does an out-of-work computer person know about self-defense?"

"You might have a point. Some people adapt. Others can't. Your son-in-law took a position with your husband's company as vice president when he left his previous job as an electronics salesman. I hear he's on the golf course almost daily instead of in his office. Since he enjoys golf so much, I wonder why he didn't teach your daughter when she took up golf last year?"

Paige didn't wait for an answer, but asked the other woman, "Mrs. Franklin, how are your sons?"

The matronly woman pressed against the back of her chair. "Fine, thank you. Paige, we don't want to keep you."

"Please tell Henry and Ralph that I'm sure things will work out for them this time, just like the other two times. Now, if you'll excuse me, I need to change. Good-bye." Paige walked from the room without looking back. Shane gave her a thumbs-up sign as she passed.

"Joann, just because Paige has few personal social contacts or social graces, or so it seems, there is no reason to insinuate those lies about my boys are true," Mrs. Franklin said. "I thought you had taught her better."

"I totally agree, Emma. I can't believe you let her talk to us that way," Mrs. Osgood said, her double chin quivering.

Joann stood. "I can't, either. I should have said it first." She ignored the other women's outraged gasps. "It occurs to me that I don't have to suffer one more moment of your snide comments about my children for business reasons."

"I'm president of the garden club," Mrs. Osgood said. "You *were* next in line as vice president to take over at the end of my term next month."

"One word from us, and you won't be accepted in our circle," Mrs. Franklin threatened. "There's a Women's League luncheon at the Zodiac Room tomorrow. The governor's wife will be there."

Joann calmly folded her arms. "You both always did have an inflated opinion of yourselves. Why don't we just test your theory? In the meantime, you've overstayed your welcome."

Noses in the air, the women rushed from the room. "Did you have something else to say, Tess?"

"I, er, I've never seen you or Paige this way."

"Long overdue." Joann took the other woman by the arm and led her to the door. "Drive safely."

Tess opened the door and stepped onto the porch. "I hope you know I had nothing to do with what just happened."

"Of course not. You wouldn't jeopardize Russell and Paige getting married," Joann said.

Tess brightened. "Then you do understand that they belong together."

"I understand nothing of the sort and will do everything in my power to see it never happens." Joann smiled. "But I don't think I have to worry about that *now*."

Russell's mother gasped. "You'd rather see her with *that* man than with my Russell?"

"Right the first time." Reaching out she closed the door, feeling better than she had in a long time.

Paige stared at her reflection in the mirror. The top cupped her small breasts, bared her thankfully flat stomach. The short pants, just above her knees, fit like a second skin, exactly as they were supposed to. She adjusted the straps to the top and, for a fleeting second, wished her breasts were a bit larger, then she chastised herself.

She wasn't bemoaning another thing about her body. She was the way she was. Grabbing the towel off the bed, she went down the stairs and met her mother on the way out the terrace door. For a long time, they stared at each other. Her mother spoke first. "I'm proud of you."

"I'm not," Paige said. "I left you to defend us, me, all these years."

"To anyone besides those two, you and Zachary don't need defending. You're both intelligent, wonderful, and successful individuals working in fields you love. I'm proud to be your mother," Joann said. "You made me realize I don't have to suffer them any longer."

A shadow crossed Paige's face. "Daddy?"

"He loved you and Zach, but he had high standards and business was important," Joann told her.

Paige realized for the first time how difficult it must have been for her mother not to defend her children because of her husband's business. "Mother." Paige went into mother's arms, hugging her. "I do love you."

"I know." Joann hugged Paige back. "But it's good to hear it. Now you better go. Shane is waiting."

Paige blushed. "I'm not sure how long we'll be."

"Take as long as you want, and don't worry about dinner," her mother assured her. "I've drunk enough tea and nibbled enough not to want anything else tonight. Macy left lasagna on the island and salad in the refrigerator."

"Thank you. Good night."

"Good night, Paige."

Paige watched her mother climb the stairs. She still

carried secrets, nothing was settled between them, but for tonight things were better than they had been in a long, long time. For now, that was enough.

His gaze trained on the terrace door, Shane sat cross-legged on the grass outside one of the dozen or so thematic garden rooms on the grounds of the estate. Paige and her mother were both coming into their own. About time.

He'd heard the threats of the two women and planned on making a phone call tonight to ensure that Mrs. Albright would be treated with the respect she deserved. Her husband might not have used his wealth to defend her and her children, but Blade and Daniel would have no such problem.

Powerful men made powerful enemies. Mrs. Osgood and Mrs. Franklin were about to learn that lesson, and so would any other woman who threatened the Albrights. Tread lightly or suffer the consequences.

Paige stepped through the terrace door and paused. She had a death grip on the white towel thrown over her right shoulder, her lips tucked between her teeth.

She was the most beautiful sight he had ever seen, so perfectly proportioned. The black top cupped her small breasts the way he yearned to do, bared the enticing indentation of her navel where he planned to dip his tongue. Her legs were slender, shapely. It didn't take much to imagine them wrapped around his waist as he surged into her moist heat.

Shane closed his eyes, drew in a breath, let it out slowly. He'd worn a long T-shirt and sweatpants to help hide his unruly body, but nothing would help if he didn't get his mind under control. When he opened them again, Paige hadn't moved.

She was nervous, but she had to get over that and

come to him. The workout outfit she wore probably wasn't helping. Paige dressed conservatively. Baring, revealing clothes weren't her thing. She was too conscious of trying to fit in, of failing, of wanting to be liked. He closed his eyes again, took a deep breath.

Come on, Paige, you can do this.

Opening them again, he saw her walking slowly toward him, no longer gripping the towel. He let his gaze hungrily sweep over her, leaving no doubt that he found her desirable. She moistened her lips, but she didn't tuck her head.

"Have a seat."

She dropped gracefully to the mat, then crossed her legs, their knees almost touching. "I thought you were going to teach me to be less of a cowar—" She stopped when his gaze narrowed. "Be more assertive."

"I am. It starts with the mind," he told her. "Unless you believe in yourself, believe you can defeat your opponent, you never will."

"We might be sitting here a long time," she quipped.

"If I believed that, I wouldn't waste my time," he said, staring straight at her. "You fight for others; you can fight for yourself."

She jerked the towel off her shoulder. "It's easier for me that way. Always has been."

"Because you care," he said. "You know how it feels not to belong, just as I do." He could see her retreating until the last four words.

She leaned toward him, bumping their knees. "You said you weren't in foster care."

"I wasn't," he said, trying not to let the bitterness heat his temper. If he had to bare his soul to help Paige, so be it. "My parents, and I use the term loosely, thought their job was done once I was old enough to walk. I raised myself. Worked from the time I was nine, selling cans to earn money for clothes and food. And they always wanted a share."

"Shane." Her voice quivered as much as her hand on his thigh.

"Once you've been down that low, the only way to go is up," he told her.

"Crap." She leaned over and took one of his balled fists in her hands. "We both know the way you chose was the hardest. If I have to stop being a wimp, you have to stop talking nonsense."

"My champion," he teased, a weight lifting off his chest. He should have known better. Paige cared about the person.

"You've been mine enough times," she said and then, as if realizing how close they were, she released his hand and leaned back.

Shane let her retreat. For now. "Every time you think of stepping back, don't. It'll take time but soon it will become second nature."

"The way it is for you," she said.

"Yes."

Her expression grew serious. "I want that, but I don't want to hurt people's feelings."

"They don't mind hurting yours or using you," he said tightly. "Let them, and they'll continue."

She slowly nodded. "All right. I'm ready."

"Close your eyes." He waited until she complied, then said, "Think of something or someone that will make you stop pulling back."

Her face curved into a beautiful smile. "Got it."

"Paige, the image is supposed to be one that will inspire you."

"I know." Her expression didn't change.

Suspicion entered his mind. "It wouldn't happen to be a person you're thinking about, would it?"

She blinked one eye open. "Might be."

He shook his head and stood to his feet. "Open your eyes and stand."

Paige unfolded her legs and pushed upward. "What's next?"

"If the occasion arises that you have to protect yourself, I want you to know how. A knee is good in close contact, but that might not always be the case." For this, he'd have to touch her, danger and pleasure all in one. "If someone reaches for you, use their momentum to push them away from you and, when they turn, hit the bridge of their nose with the heel of your palm as hard as you can. Reach for me, and I'll show you."

She hesitated, chewed on her lower lip.

"I won't hurt you," he assured her.

"It never crossed my mind that you would." She shifted from one foot to the other.

"Find the image, and come for me."

The words had no more left his mouth than she lunged. He gently tapped her shoulder instead of hitting her. She whirled. His hand came up, shooting over her head. She didn't stop as he expected. She barreled into him. His other arm came around her bare waist, dragging her to him, her breasts flattened against his chest, his mouth hovering seductively close to hers. "You were supposed to stop."

"Guess I forgot," she said, her voice breathless.

He wanted to forget, to kiss the moist, tempting lips so close to his. He didn't dare. One kiss would never be enough. Of that he was certain. He wanted too badly to drag sweet moans from her, to feel her tremble in his arms.

Slowly he released her, saw the disappointment in her face, which mirrored his own. This might be the toughest training session he had ever conducted.

* * *

Paige accepted that she was no Wonder Woman two minutes into the hand-to-hand combat session. Stepping out of the shower later that night, she dried and put on her pajamas. He had the most beautiful body. He was grace in motion, while she was clumsy, forgetful. His fault.

With his arms wrapped around her or his eyes staring into hers, her brain short-circuited. At least the other safety tips, like not leaving a building unless her car keys were in her hand in order to quickly get into the car or use on an assailant, or keeping a spare set of keys in the kitchen, she remembered.

Once finished with the session, they'd eaten the lasagna and salad in the kitchen. It had been relaxing instead of tension-filled as her time with Russell was becoming. Although her hormones went crazy around Shane, it was an exciting crazy. She was acutely alive around him, as if she had waited her entire life for him to find her and free her emotions, enthrall her body.

Grabbing her laptop from her desk, she climbed into bed and turned it on to check her e-mail. There would probably be several from Russell. He always expected her to answer immediately. Since she checked e-mail frequently, she usually did. Today she had other things, rather more specifically another man, on her mind.

Russell's mother's presence that afternoon, and her gossipy nature, might have unknowingly done Paige a favor. Mrs. Crenshaw probably couldn't wait to tell her only child and son how out of character and trashy Paige was acting. Paige grinned. This was just the beginning. She hadn't gotten the kiss she so desperately wanted from Shane, but she would.

Scrolling through her e-mails she saw at least five messages from Russell. All marked URGENT. She moved the cursor to delete, then decided to read the last one. By the end of the e-mail she was steaming. He'd crucified Shane and continued his tirade on how gullible and inept she was.

"Crap," she said aloud. Who did he think he was! She'd give him a piece of her mind that would make his hair curl. She was tired of being nice. Nice had gotten her squat!

The phone rang just as she moved the cursor to hit REPLY. She lifted her hand, hoping it was Russell or his nosy mother calling. Angrier than she ever remembered being, she rolled, reaching for the phone on the bedside. The laptop slid off her lap. Screaming, she frantically grabbed for it.

And missed.

She cringed on hearing the whack as it hit the hardwood floor. Scrambling out of bed, she picked up the computer just as the phone stopped ringing. Opening the top that had slammed shut, praying as she did.

The screen was black.

Chapter 12

Clutching the computer, Paige hung her head. All the data for the Masquerade Ball had been on this laptop. There was no way she could recall all the names or, more important, the amount of each contribution, the corporate donors.

She was screwed. She'd—*Shane*. His name and image popped into her head.

Surging to her feet, she clutched the computer to her chest, took two steps before she recalled that the connection line to the telephone jack was still plugged in. Placing the laptop on the bed, she took off running and didn't stop until she stood in front of Shane's door.

She rapped, called his name. "Shane!"

The door swung open. "Paige, what's the matter?"

Her hand froze in midair. Her breath snagged. Her brain fuzzed. She opened her mouth but nothing came out . . . and no wonder.

Shane wore only snug-fitting jeans. His magnificent chest was bare. Lord, he was built. Well-defined muscles delineated his wide chest, then flared to a flat stomach before disappearing into his jeans. Her fingers actually tingled with wanting to touch his, glide over his taut skin.

"Paige?" he questioned, reaching out to take her arm.

The contact jarred her senses. She swallowed, swallowed again. "I need you," she blurted, then rushed on as his eyes blazed. "I dropped my computer," she clarified.

"Let me get my shirt and shoes."

"Please come now." She grabbed his hand and raced back to her room. This was no time to let her hormones run wild. "You have to help me."

"What about your backup file? Zip drive?" he asked, following her into her room.

She wildly shook her head. "I don't have either of those."

"You don't have— Where is it?"

She went to the bed, picked it up, and gently handed it to him. "Please. All the data for the Masquerade Ball is on this computer."

He hit the power button. The screen remained blank. He looked back at her. "I need to get a tool kit and some other things out of my room. I'll be back."

"Do you . . . do you think you can fix it?" she asked.

He swept his hand up and down her trembling arm. "I'm going to do my best. I won't be but a minute."

True to his word, he was back shortly. Paige noted he'd pulled on a shirt, but hadn't taken time to button it, and he remained shoeless. The man even had sexy feet, long and narrow. Taking the computer from her, he crossed his long legs, sat down, turned it over, and began to take the back off, placing the screws and guts on a page of newspaper he'd brought back with him.

All Paige could do was watch and pray. She marveled that he appeared to have no difficulty handling the tiny screws with his large hands, and that he never paused. It was as if he had done this a thousand times, then she realized he probably had. Head bent in concentration, he had the determined look of her Black Knight. He was certainly built like one. Smooth golden skin rippled over corded muscles as he worked.

Paige licked her lips, then wickedly wondered what he'd do if she had the courage to lick *him*.

"How did this happen?" he asked without lifting his head.

With difficulty she pushed Shane's magnificent chest and her forbidden fantasies from her mind. "I reached for the phone. The laptop was in my lap," she said, angry at herself for forgetting.

"You aren't that careless or the clumsy type," he said, never pausing as he lifted something—she didn't know what—out of the laptop.

She couldn't stick to the lie she thought of telling. How could she when Shane made her feel as if she could do anything, be anything? "I'd just finished reading an e-mail from Russell when the phone rang on the night table. I thought it was him calling. I was so angry I reached for the phone without thinking."

His head came up. Dark eyes stared at her intently. "Must have been some e-mail."

She gritted her teeth. "It was."

Down went his head again as he laid more of the laptop parts on the newspaper. "What he thinks or says doesn't matter."

"He made me angry, and now I might have messed up the biggest fund-raiser of the year for the foundation."

"I see you forgot rule number three about finding your center."

"Then, but not later."

His head came up again.

"You're here," she said softly.

His eyes darkened. "You make me—"

"What?" she asked, leaning toward him in blatant invitation. She wanted his mouth on hers. She wanted his kiss.

Down went his head again. "Stop distracting me."

She grinned like a loon. Imagine her distracting a man like Shane. Then she saw her poor laptop and her smile died.

"Stop clenching your hands," he said, examining a specific part of the computer. "You're forgetting all the rules."

Paige uncurled her hands. She'd stopped being surprised that Shane was so aware of his surroundings, aware of her. "I might forget the rules, but not the man who taught them to me, the man who makes me believe."

His hand flexed on the tiny screwdriver. "Paige." There was a warning in his voice.

"Positive thoughts," she said, her smile returning.

Paige was a distraction and a delight. Shane was becoming too used to both. She'd moved from in front of him to beside him as he reassembled the computer, bringing with her the sweet fragrance that always lingered on her. She was a temptation that he was tired of fighting.

He might have bent a lot of rules in his day, but jumping the daughter of the woman you were asked to help, with her only a few doors down, was too far on the wrong side.

"I bet it's fixed this time."

Shane tightened the last screw before he lifted his head. This was the third try. She scooted closer each time, showing her distress, and also her confidence in him. If it took all night he was going to repair the computer. "One way to find out." He hit the on button.

Paige leaned closer, her hand clamped on his thigh,

leaning closer at the familiar flash of light, the sound of the system booting up. One by one her icons popped up.

He placed the laptop in her lap. "Check your files."

She hesitated for a moment, then moved her finger over the pad to open the file. MASQUERADE BALL came up. Silently she scrolled down to the end of the page, then she closed her eyes.

"Is it all there?"

Carefully, she placed the laptop on the floor and launched herself into his arms. He could have stopped the momentum of their bodies, but it was no more than a passing thought after her lips touched his. He landed with his back on the Oriental rug, Paige sprawled on top.

Desire exploded. His arms wrapped around her, dragging her closer, taking the kiss from sweet to hot and hungry in a heartbeat.

His tongue delved into her mouth, greedy and insistent, claiming her. Her tongue eagerly met his as she clung to him. His blood heated. The mating of their tongues was like nothing he had ever experienced before—fierce, passionate, intense. It was as if he had been waiting his entire life for this one kiss, this one very special woman.

He had to touch her. His hands roamed over the gentle slope of her slim back, her firm hips, and stayed there. She was as perfect in his arms as he'd imagined, dreamed. Before temptation caused him to press her against his thick arousal, his hands moved upward.

One temptation he couldn't resist. He slipped his hands under the soft white top and felt warm, bare skin from her shoulders to the soft swell of her hips. He'd never felt anything softer or been tempted more. He caught back a moan of pure pleasure. The softness of her yielding body and the intoxicating sweetness of her mouth were almost his undoing.

Need slammed into him. He ached for release. She tested his control as no woman ever had, teased his senses to the breaking point.

If he didn't stop now, he wouldn't until he'd made her his. Reaching for his own center, his own control, he set her away from him, watched her eyes slowly open, felt himself harden even more at the unquenched desire in their gray depths, to be replaced by uncertainty as she realized she was sprawled wantonly on top of him, his body hard and ready for hers.

"I guess this means it's fixed?" he said, using all of his control to make his voice and pose casual as he sat up, holding her loosely in his arms.

She flushed and smiled at him. "Thank you."

He'd walk through hell for her smile. "Thank me by keeping a backup file on your computer here and at the office."

"I'll take care of it tomorrow," she told him.

"Tonight." Setting her too-alluring body away, he pushed to his feet. "I have an extra flash drive in my room. I'll show you how to back up all your documents."

Crossing her legs, she stared up at him. "I bet your company hated to lose you. Nothing throws you."

His gaze went to her lips, the hard tips of her unbound breasts pushing against the soft cotton pajama top. "I wouldn't be so sure about that." He started from the room, but not before he saw Paige grin.

The next morning Paige practically floated into the kitchen. She'd felt energized, invincible, and it was all due to the man watching her with unblinking eyes. His sizzling gaze swept over her like silent caressing fingers, heating her body. One day, she promised, she'd return the favor, only her hands would actually be on that glorious body of his.

Last night he had taken her mouth with consummate skill and gentleness. She'd felt his hunger for her, but also his control. His kisses might pleasure her, his hands make her restless with desire, but he'd never take more than she was willing to give. He was chivalrous, tempting, confident, and he wanted her.

Her champion, her Black Knight.

She'd dressed for just this moment in a metallic tank over an open-weave linen double-layer skirt with a raw-edge handkerchief hemline. A brown three-inch leather belt with a gold buckle hung loosely over her waist. On her feet were her new chocolate wedge sandals with thin leather straps around her ankles.

Since she couldn't touch him, her gaze swept greedily over him. Her heart actually skipped a beat. In a black polo shirt and jeans, Shane looked dangerous and delicious. She shivered slightly, taking the chair he held for her, glad her mother had yet to turn. "Good morning, Shane, Mother."

"Morning," he said, taking the seat next to her as usual.

"Good morning, Paige," her mother said as she bent to take a dish out of the oven. "Shane said the practice went well."

"It did, but I'm no Wonder Woman," she confessed, making a face.

"Just as long as you can defend yourself . . . if necessary," Shane said. "If not, run."

She tilted her head to one side, knowing the move flirtatious, enjoying him watching her. "You wouldn't."

"I've had lots more practice and experience." His face hardened. "I mean it, Paige."

"I promise," she said, not wanting him to worry. "Mother, that smells good."

Joann set the egg-and-ham quiche on a metal trivet on the table. "I hope it tastes good." She took the seat that Shane rose and held for her. "I haven't cooked this dish in a long time." Bowing her head, she blessed the food.

"I can't imagine you making a bad meal." Shane accepted the quiche Joann passed to him.

Paige's mother smiled with pleasure. "Thank you. Paige is a good cook as well."

"Oh?" Shane said, his interest obvious.

Paige picked up her fork. "Mother taught me, although I haven't done any cooking in a while. It seemed easier to eat out or order in."

"And you don't have to clean up," he said, a teasing light dancing in his dark eyes.

"That's why the dishwasher in my condo had a pot scrubber," she said, smiling back at him. It took a moment for her to realize her mother was staring at them. Paige said the first thing that popped into her mind to get the conversation going again. "Shane fixed my computer last night."

"What happened?" her mother asked, concerned.

"I accidentally knocked it off the bed," she admitted. "I was frantic because it had all the information for the Masquerade Ball, but Shane saved the day, and then backed up all of my files."

"You're lucky he was here," her mother said casually.

"And today Paige is going to back up the files in her office so that if it happens again, she won't worry." Shane picked up his cranberry juice.

Paige drank her juice, watching him over the rim of her glass for the sheer pleasure it gave her. "I was kind of hoping that you'd come in and oversee me as I do it."

"Will around eleven be all right?" he asked, his gaze on her mouth, which was painted a soft berry color.

Remembering his insistent mouth on hers last night, her body went from simmer to aroused. She quickly finished the juice, hoping it would cool her down. No such luck. "Yes. Well, I have to go." Striving for normal, she rose. "Thanks for breakfast, Mother. See you later, Shane."

He stood. "I'll see you to the car."

"That would be nice." She had to get a grip.

"Excuse me, Mrs. Albright." Shane took Paige by the arm and walked her outside to the garage. He opened her car door for her. "Drive carefully."

"I will. See you at eleven." On tiptoe she kissed him on the cheek, then slipped into the car and pulled away with a smile on her face. Not too much of a grip, though.

Shane shook his head. A fearless Paige might be a handful. She'd looked so sexy in the sassy skirt that made him want to slip it and the tank top off to find the fragrant skin he knew waited beneath.

Returning to the kitchen, he speculated on how long it would take to make the thought a reality . . . until he saw Paige's mother watching him.

He was caught, lusting after her daughter. Heat climbed up his neck. He'd never experienced embarrassment before but, with Paige, he was experiencing a lot of firsts.

"Paige seemed happier than I've seen her in a long time," her mother said, watching him closely over the cup of coffee she raised to her lips.

Sharp woman. Shane took his seat and picked up his own coffee cup. "I think I should move out."

Unlike the first time he'd suggested moving, she simply continued to stare at him. "Oh."

Shane, who had never met the parent of a woman he took out, let alone wanted as desperately as he wanted Paige, barely kept from ducking his head. "Yes."

She set her cup exactly in the center of the saucer without looking. The simple act took practice. Her ancestors had been people who made their own way, helped others while doing it, unlike his, who took with both hands when no one was looking. "Do you mind telling me why?"

Now came the tricky part. "There's no reason for me to stay here. Russell is out of town, and when he returns, he'll find that the relationship between him and Paige has changed."

"Thanks to you."

Shane, who had dealt with the deadliest, most unscrupulous people on earth, fought to maintain eye contact with Paige's mother. He was quickly learning that mothers could be fierce opponents. He should have remembered that from Sierra's mother, Ruth.

"Have you told Paige yet?"

"No," he said.

"Why?" she asked, staring intently across the table at him.

She was like a pit bull. Once she got something in her mind, she didn't let go. No one had to tell him she'd take a chunk out of his backside if she thought he'd hurt Paige. She'd used him to get rid of Russell because she hadn't wanted to cause a deeper rift between herself and her daughter. With Shane, that wasn't a factor. "It seemed right to let you know first."

Joann snorted delicately and straightened. "What reason for moving are you going to give her?"

"You were gracious enough to allow me to stay, but

I don't want to wear out my welcome." He was ready for that one.

"And the real reason."

This time he wasn't as ready. Caring about a woman could cause a man a lot of trouble, but he wouldn't have it any other way. He met Paige's mother's stare head-on. "I care about her and feel it's best I move out."

"I see." She picked up her cup, then put it down. "If Trent and Daniel didn't trust you, you wouldn't be here. You've shown me you're a man of his word, a man to be reckoned with. No offense, but you're not an easy man. Paige has planned her wedding to her Black Knight since she was nine years old. Make-believe and fairy tales were how she coped in a world that was too often unforgiving and harsh. It was how she survived."

Shane didn't like the way the conversation was going. He wasn't talking marriage, and he realized that was exactly what she meant. Playing around with Paige was out. It had to be forever or nothing. "I understand."

"I'm grateful for what you've done. I even insinuated that you two might be interested in each other," she said.

"To make Russell and his mother angry," Shane said, feeling his gut tighten.

"Yes." Unflinching from the unflattering truth, she leaned across the table. "You're nothing like him. If I had to choose, you'd win hands-down. But I also know you have a life with Blade. Paige's life is here."

He stood, pushed his chair in, his temper simmering beneath the surface. "So I'm good enough to help, but not good enough to touch her?"

She came to her feet, her eyes angry. "That's a stupid, judgmental thing to say. I wouldn't care if you scrubbed floors for a living if you really loved her. I won't let her love you and then lose you. She'll love deeply. She doesn't know any other way." Tears sparkled in her eyes. "That won't happen to my baby. I won't let it."

His anger left as swiftly as it had come. He circled the table, taking her into his arms. Trent's father had been the love of Joann's life. They'd had one night and never seen each other again. The man was dead, and Joann had only a memory.

"I'm sorry."

"Neither of you can control how you feel about the other. I know that better than anyone." She lifted her face. "But there is a point of no return. If you don't plan to stick around, don't do that to Paige or yourself."

Awkwardly, he brushed the tears from her face. This was definitely not going the way he'd planned. "I don't know what to say."

"There's nothing to say." She moved out of his arms. "I know you won't hurt Paige intentionally."

"Maybe I should go," he said slowly, ignoring the churning of his gut at the thought. "I could send someone to monitor the situation."

"But it wouldn't be you." She smiled sadly. "You're the one who makes Paige's face light up. You're her Black Knight."

"Mrs. Albright—"

She held up her hand, stopping him. "Paige deserves happiness. I don't want my fears getting in the way. And there will be no moving out."

"Mrs. Albright—"

Again she stopped him. "If you moved out, do you really think that would help the situation or escalate it?"

He felt his face heat. Damn.

She picked up her coffee cup and his. "Shane, besides

white roses, Paige likes Swiss chocolates and lemon sugar cookies."

"Why are you telling me?" Shane asked.

She smiled patiently. "You're a smart man. I'm sure you'll figure it out."

He was afraid he had. Paige's mother had gone from warning him off to trying to help him court Paige. He didn't court women. "I—"

"I'm sure you have other things to do than watch me clean up the kitchen." Joann stacked the breakfast plates and took them to the sink.

Shane knew when he was outmaneuvered. Shaking his head, he departed for the garage. He cared about Paige, wanted her, but he wasn't this Black Knight her mother had talked about. His eyes shut. Now he understood those trusting, enamored looks of Paige's.

Damn. What a mess!

Worse, he didn't know how to fix things or who could help him figure out what to do. Emotions were involved. When that happened, there were too many variables to come to a logical conclusion.

Blade, in love with Sierra, would tell him to go for it. Rio would fix him with one of his enigmatic stares and say nothing. Shane didn't even want to think of asking Sierra, who wouldn't be shy about telling him exactly the same thing Blade had, only she'd try to stick her nose in things to make sure they happened.

Looked like he had to handle this on his own. And he hadn't the foggiest idea of how.

As he climbed inside the rental it occurred to Shane that, for the second time in his adult life, he didn't know what to do. Both times it was because of the same woman.

Chapter 13

"You look fabulous in that outfit," Jackie commented as Paige entered Jackie's office shortly after arriving at work that morning.

"Thanks." Paige took her usual seat in front of Jackie's desk. She'd been getting compliments all morning. Even Doris had looked at her with envy. Paige couldn't keep the grin off her face, then or now. It just showed what the right man could do for a woman's spirits.

"Not what you typically wear," Jackie commented, studying her closely. "I don't need to guess why."

"Probably not," Paige said with unabashed honesty. "I came in to thank you again for the carpet. It looked great in the apartment. I can pick up the tile this evening if it's convenient."

"It is." Jackie folded her hands on her desk. Her round diamond engagement ring flashed on her left hand. "I hope you don't mind my saying this, but I'm glad you and Russell are a thing of the past. I could never reconcile the two of you together."

Paige thought briefly of what her father wanted, then mentally pushed the thought away. "It's definitely over. I sent him an e-mail this morning. I had hoped we could remain friends, but I'm not so sure."

"Since I know you don't like confrontations, I can

imagine this isn't easy." Jackie leaned back in her chair. Sunlight glinted on her red hair and made her freckles more evident. "At least you didn't have to wait until you were my age to meet someone. Sometimes I was afraid it wouldn't happen."

"To tell you the truth, so was I," Paige confided.

"Looks like we both got lucky. Why don't you come around seven for dinner and bring Shane? You can see the new floors and what I've done to the house."

"I'd love to, but I'm not sure if Shane has any plans. He's coming to help me back up my computer file, and I'll ask him then."

Jackie lifted one eyebrow. "I've been trying to get you to do that for months."

"Last night made a believer out of me." Paige explained about dropping the computer, but kept the torrid kiss to herself. Some things were meant to be private.

"You certainly picked a winner this time." Jackie smiled across the desk at her.

Paige's brain latched on to *this time*. Now that Russell was out of her life, she was discovering what her friends thought of him. Shane was accepted. Russell had tried to rush her to the bedroom and then the altar. Shane wasn't rushing her anyplace. In fact, at times, she wished he'd speed things up a bit. "We've only been on one date."

And had one mind-altering kiss.

"If you didn't believe there was a possibility of others, you wouldn't have that twinkle in your eyes," Jackie told her with a brisk nod of her head. "I just hope he's not as slow as Aaron. He's still a little touchy about my executive position, the house, and my salary."

Paige slumped in her chair, her happy disposition wiped out in an instant.

"What?" Jackie asked, her voice raised in alarm.

"Shane is between jobs," Paige lamented. The agency had adopted the more positive term instead of *unemployed.*

"Surely he has prospects." Jackie folded her hands on her neat desk. "He's marvelous with computers and has the body of a Greek god. Even Veronica at the luncheon tried to latch on to him."

"She changed her mind when she learned Dr. Thompson had more money." Paige tucked her lower lip between her teeth. "He's just looking at the job market here. What if he decides to relocate someplace else?"

"Then, you, Paige, will just have to show him what he'll miss if he does," Jackie told her.

Paige said nothing. Her first test of overcoming her fear after Shane's instructions last evening, and she'd fallen flat on her face. The image she needed to create to help her was the very man who might break her heart.

Something had changed. Shane recognized it the moment he walked into Paige's office for their appointment. She smiled at him, but it was a far cry from the playful teasing of that morning. More telling perhaps was that, after he'd downloaded the first file, she had left him alone to back up the rest of the files, saying she had to run an errand. She was too well bred and polite to leave a person trying to help her. Yet that was exactly what she had done.

He was pretty good at figuring people and situations out . . . except when it came to Paige. Finished with the last file, he left her office to find her.

"Good morning, Shane," Jackie greeted, coming out of her office.

"Good morning, Jackie."

She stopped in front of the assistant's desk. "Paige said you were coming in to back up her files. Long overdue, I might add."

"I just finished her files and was going to look for her," he told her. "She's not with you, I see."

A frown flickered across the other woman's face. "She left?"

"She said she had an errand to run," Shane explained, but to him it was thin. Paige had agreed to the appointment time. She wouldn't run out on him . . . unless she had a very good reason.

"I'm sure she'll be back soon." Jackie's smile returned. "In the meantime I'll show you around."

"Thank you, but perhaps another time. I have to leave."

"A job interview?" Jackie asked, then rushed on when he didn't immediately respond. "I mean, you're so knowledgeable around computers. And like Aaron said, the city is booming. You'll have more offers than you know what to do with."

Shane could have smacked himself on the head. Rio certainly would have. Some cover. "I'm still weighing my options."

"Of course," she quickly said, obviously embarrassed.

"Please tell Paige I'll see her later. The zip disk is on the right-hand side of her computer. Good-bye." Trying to figure out where and why Paige had disappeared, Shane headed for the elevator. Passing an open door, he caught a flash of movement. Paige.

He stepped inside the room. She whirled abruptly, her gray eyes huge in her troubled face. "What happened between this morning and now?"

"I—"

He saw the lie forming. He closed the door and advanced on her. "Did Russell get to you?"

"Russell?" she cried incredulously. "He had nothing to do with this."

The pounding in his brain only lessened marginally. "Do you mind clarifying what *this* is?"

"I—"

His patience was nearing the breaking point. "Paige, don't think. Just spit it out."

"With your skills, you could relocate anyplace."

Me. Shane had never felt on shakier grounds or more at a crossroads. He had run out of time to decide if he planned to see where the attraction between them led—or take the corporate jet back to Santa Fe. He knew it wouldn't be the happily-ever-after Paige's mother said she wanted.

And then what? He'd still miss her, want to be with her. But she was the type of woman who wanted forever, and he was a man who wanted no strings.

"I need to get back to my office." She started past him, and he caught her arm.

"I didn't expect this to happen," he said quietly.

"You think I did?" she asked just as quietly, finally looking at him. Her soft mouth trembled.

His other hand lifted to cup her exquisite face. "No. I imagine not." His thumb stroked her smooth skin. "I have no intention of leaving for the time being, but I want you to know up front that I'm not much on long-term relationships."

Her gaze remained fixed on him. "That's a shame because that's the only kind I want." She walked out, leaving him staring after her.

Paige made it back to her office by sheer force of will. She might eventually see the humor that the man who had just hurt her so deeply was the man who taught her to keep her head up.

She should have known he wasn't for her. Shane was a fierce protector, intelligent, assertive. He'd want a woman his equal.

A knock sounded on her door. Hope surged through her. She quickly ran her hand over her hair. "Come in."

Jackie stuck her head in, the anxious frown on her face deepening on seeing Paige's miserable expression. "Can I come in?"

Her throat suddenly too tight to speak, Paige nodded. She would not cry.

Jackie rounded the desk to lean back against it and stared down at Paige. "I just saw Shane leave. He had the look of a man I wouldn't want to cross. When Doris saw him from behind, she called his name, but the dangerous expression on his face when he turned had her scurrying back to her office."

"His scary look."

"Since he's obviously p.o.'ed and you're not at your best, I take it things didn't go well in the break room," Jackie said softly.

Paige linked her fingers. "No. He's not into long-term relationships."

"Paige." Jackie drew out the name, then caught the back of Paige's high-back leather chair and spun her around to face her. "Weren't you listening to me earlier? Some men don't know what they want until a woman shows them."

"Women have tried changing men's minds before with disastrous consequences." She didn't know from personal experience, of course, but all the talk shows and numerous articles she'd read on relationships said as much. It was best to cut her losses now. Somehow she'd get over him.

Perhaps in fifty or sixty years.

Jackie tsked. "You can't change a lying, cheating, no-good man who'd rather spend your money than his, drive your car instead of getting one or getting his repaired, who wants to stay at your place rent-free and expects you to be ready to cook and have sex whenever he wants. You can't tell me Shane is like that."

"No, of course he isn't," Paige said, aghast. "What woman would want a man like that?"

"Plenty, including me. Until one morning I looked at the lazy bastard sleeping while I was getting ready to go to work." Jackie's mouth tightened. "I was so scared that I'd never find anyone that I settled for anything-in-pants."

"I'm sorry," Paige said, reaching out to touch Jackie's arm. "I didn't mean to make you think of unpleasant memories."

Jackie patted Paige's hand in reassurance. "You haven't. That was actually a proud day. I was late to work that day because I threw his lazy behind out. After that it was a long dry spell, but I wasn't accepting just anything-in-pants. If he couldn't step up to the plate and come correct, I kept walking."

Paige believed her. There was a fierceness about Jackie that she admired. "You're a strong woman."

Folding her arms, Jackie smiled. "I'd like to think so, but the right man can make the smartest woman act like a fool."

"That I believe." Shane had certainly tied her in knots and made her act out of character. All for nothing.

"But the right man can also make a woman float on air," Jackie mused, her face dreamy, she ran her thumb over the half-carat diamond center stone in her engagement ring.

"Been there, too," Paige confessed.

"And you're giving up?"

Paige squirmed in her chair. Jackie's words were almost a challenge. Part of Shane's rule number two popped in her head. *Never give up.* "I'm not sure what else to do."

"I'd say, continue what you're doing. You look sensational this morning and we both know why. I bet Shane noticed."

Paige brightened a bit at the thought. "He couldn't keep his eyes off me."

"You see. We already know other women are trying to get his attention, but he's interested in only one woman."

Paige sat up straighter in her chair. "Me."

"You."

"Is that how you changed Aaron's mind?" Paige asked.

"Just showing him that being with him was the most important thing to me went a long way, too." Jackie leaned over and whispered, "A little massage oil in the right places cinched the deal."

Both women burst out laughing. "Don't forget where you purchased it," Paige said, imagining her hands all over Shane's muscled, gorgeous body. She quivered and got a bit light-headed at the thought.

"No way. It's the first thing I plan to pack for our honeymoon." Jackie sighed. "Only six more weeks and I'm Mrs. Aaron Baskin."

In six weeks Shane could be gone. "Jackie, I'm going shopping for a few things at lunch. Care to come along?"

Jackie chuckled. "Shane won't know what hit him until it's too late."

Paige grinned. "That's the idea."

When the limousine carrying the governor's wife arrived at Neiman Marcus for the luncheon, Shane was stationed by the first-floor elevator. He'd already been cleared by her security and assured by a call from Daniel that morning that the "situation" would be handled. The governor's wife would support Mrs. Albright. Shane was there to remind her.

The governor's wife might go along with the plan, but she might also conveniently "forget." He'd learned she liked doing things her way. Women were unpredictable.

One woman in particular was Paige. He'd blown it at her office, but he planned to rectify things as soon as he saw her tonight. A babble of excited voices interrupted his thoughts and alerted him that the governor's wife was inside the store and heading for the elevator being held for her.

A throng of security guards and press followed the elegantly dressed woman every step. They entered the elevator. Shane followed. Two guards blocked the press and onlookers from entering after him.

"Might I say that your husband is doing a commendable job as governor, and has the support of many?" Shane said, staring straight ahead.

"So I've heard. What is your name?" she asked, removing her large-rimmed Chanel sunglasses.

"Shane Elliott," he answered, looking down at her. She stared back. This woman wouldn't back down from anyone. Things just got a bit dicey.

"Well, you're about to learn what my husband learned many years ago. I don't do lip service."

His gaze didn't waver. "A woman who loves her children more than anything in this world needs your help against those who'd rather tear someone to shreds than reach out a helping hand."

The elevator door slid open. Turning away, she stepped out of the elevator and met the welcoming committee. In front were Mrs. Osgood and Mrs. Franklin, who gushed and presented the governor's wife with a large bouquet of red roses.

Shane followed the security team off, but hung back as the women made their way to the podium. They were no more than twelve feet inside the Zodiac restaurant when the group stopped. He moved until he could see the reason.

The governor's wife stood in front of Mrs. Albright. The two were holding each other's hands and talking. The beady-eyed women's mouths were clamped tightly in anger. Shane wanted to roar with laughter.

The governor's wife said something to Mrs. Franklin, then continued to the head table, taking Joann with her. She was putting her stamp of approval on Mrs. Albright. He was about to leave when one of the security guards stopped him.

"Yes?"

The burly man leaned over and whispered, "She wanted you to know that if she hadn't agreed, you know what you could have done with the order to support Mrs. Albright."

"Please tell her thank you." Shaking his head, he proceeded to the elevator. Now if he could just solve the problems between himself and Paige.

Shane checked his watch a hundred times that day. The hours dragged by slowly as he waited for Paige to come home. They needed to talk. He shoved his hand over his head, paced in his room.

What would he say differently, do differently to make her understand? *I want your body, but I plan to leave when I get tired of it.*

Muttering a curse, he spun. He'd kick his own ass or any man's who ever even insinuated anything so heartless and cruel. He was caught between his desire for her and her desire for a lifetime.

One of them was going to lose, and it looked as if it was going to be him. He could probably seduce her. She was inexperienced, and he knew a thousand ways to pleasure a woman.

But even the idea left a foul taste in his mouth, a hard knot in his stomach. He'd cut off his arm rather than treat her so callously. There had to be a middle ground. Blade was the negotiator of their unit. This was all new to Shane. His expertise had been computers. Those he understood.

Computers were built by men to perform certain functions. They did no more or less than they were programmed to do. You didn't have to deal with emotions or logic, just hard facts and functions that never varied. You always knew what you'd get if you hit a certain key.

With Paige he was in the dark, making one mistake after another. He refused to believe there would be no common ground.

He checked his watch again. Five twenty. He whirled to the door. Paige should be coming home soon. He'd meet her outside and they'd drive someplace quiet where they could talk. He'd seen Macy earlier and told her they wouldn't be home for dinner—or supper, as they called it in the South.

He stepped out on the bricked porch and walked down to the flagstone driveway, not paying the least attention to the soothing waters of the large fountain directly in front of the front door. He'd make her listen. Paige was a reasonable woman, sweet and a bit malleable . . . or at least she had been.

Hearing the engine of a car, his head lifted. Even before the Lexus came into view, he knew it wasn't Page's Audi. Mrs. Albright waved as she continued around the side of the house edged with boxwoods toward the garage.

He checked his watch again, then he walked out a bit so the statue in the spewing fountain wouldn't impede his view.

Paige, where are you?

"Shane."

He spun around. Mrs. Albright stood in the arched doorway. She still wore the lavender Chanel suit she had on at the luncheon. "You aren't waiting for Paige by any chance, are you?"

"Yes," he answered, thinking the less said the better.

Frowning, she stepped onto the porch. "I thought she told you."

"Told me what?" He knew he wasn't going to like what she had to say by the uneasy expression on her face.

"She called me after I left the luncheon. She's gone out with a friend and doesn't expect to be home until late."

Stunned, he stared at her. Like mother, like daughter. Paige had outmaneuvered him. "How was the luncheon?"

Mrs. Albright smiled brightly. "Exactly as Bitsy and I planned."

"Excuse me?"

Mrs. Albright's smile turned into happy laughter. "The governor's wife's nickname. She and I have been friends since we were in grade school. I called her last night to tell her what was going on and asked for her help."

Shane shook his head. She hadn't needed him at all. What's more, the governor's wife had made sure he knew she followed her own conscience.

The night he and Paige had caught the thieves in her office, Shane had been bluffing when he'd thrown the Albrights' connections with the governor at the police officer to get the security guards to lower their weapons. "You mind if I ask why you hadn't sought her help before?"

Anger replaced the laughter. She rubbed her wrist. "There were repercussions for making waves. I had to protect Paige and Zachary."

Shane cursed silently. Marshall Albright had physically and mentally abused his wife, and used her love for her children to control her. "You're free now."

Sadly, she shook her head. "No. I have friends, good friends as Bitsy proved today, but Paige moves in the same circle. If word leaked out about Trent it would devastate her. Yet I want to shout to the world that he's mine." She swallowed. "He understands and has never looked at me with anything but love, although I gave him away a week after he was born."

"To protect him," Shane reminded her. "He realizes that."

Tears sparkled in her eyes. "Now I have to protect Paige. I think Zach would understand in time. He is worldlier than Paige. However, I can't risk telling either of them. I couldn't bear it if they turned their backs on me."

"But it's just as difficult not being able to acknowledge Trent," Shane said with certainty.

"Yes," she admitted. "But I won't lose hope. Somehow, some way, this will all work out. We'll all be happy."

Shane certainly hoped so. All of them were caught in an impossible situation. Time would tell if happiness or heartache waited for them.

Chapter 14

It was half past ten when Paige turned into her driveway. After their lunch and shopping spree, Jackie had suggested they change plans and stop after work to eat dinner and strategize. They'd decided to eat at the grill-and-tavern where Gayle served as the hostess, and Noah as waiter. It had been the right decision.

Gayle had seated them at a table near the window in Noah's section. Learning that Jackie had donated the carpet for their apartment, they insisted on taking care of her meal. As Paige expected, her friend and boss nixed the idea. It had been her pleasure, she told them. But she couldn't resist the chocolate dessert Noah served after they finished their meal, and neither could Paige.

It had been a fun, relaxing evening, leaving Paige feeling a bit more optimistic on the outcome between her and Shane. She might be inexperienced but, after sitting on the sidelines watching people for so long, she'd learned that what people did, didn't always match what they said. Russell popped into her mind as one of the talkers instead of the doers.

She'd tried to be non-judgmental because of her father's wishes. There was no comparison between the two men. Shane would always put her first, not himself. He cared, and she intended to do everything in her power to build on that.

Parking in the garage, she took the curved path to the back kitchen door. Her mother's bedroom lights were on and so were Shane's. According to Jackie, he wouldn't be pleased that they hadn't been able to talk or that she had blithely gone about her business while he was probably stewing in his own juices.

Paige wrinkled her nose and reached to unlock the back door. Shane wasn't the "stewing" type. The door jerked open.

Shane stood there and he had that hard, dangerous look that made men and women run. Paige smiled at him. "Thanks, but I had my key ready." Purposefully, she brushed against him and was rewarded by the sudden stiffening of his body. "Good night."

"Where have you been?" he growled, shutting the door with a sharp snap.

If there was one person who kept his cool, it was Shane. He was furious and not shy about showing it. Paige danced inside and lifted innocent eyes to his. "With friends. I had a wonderful time."

"You went shopping?" he asked, relief in his voice as he noted the clothes from a popular women's store in a plastic bag draped over her arm. "We need to talk."

She yawned, patted her mouth. "Maybe tomorrow. I'm tired. See you in the morning." She kept walking, feeling his eyes burning into her, fighting the instinct to run.

A little after eight fifteen the next morning, wondering if she had overplayed her hand, Paige continued downstairs to breakfast, her heeled sandals muted on the silk runner on the stairs. Last night she had half expected Shane to follow her up the stairs or at the very least be waiting for her when she came out of her room this morning. He'd done neither.

Her footsteps seemed unnaturally loud as she reached the Italian marble that covered the wide entryway. The sound probably coincided with her booming heart. She entered the kitchen and conversation stopped. Shane, who had been about to sip his coffee, jerked his head up. His eyes narrowed, then widened. Her heart boomed louder. Her mother lifted an inquiring brow.

Swallowing her uncertainty, Paige smiled and continued into the kitchen. "Good morning, Mother, Shane. I just came to say hello. I'm off to an early meeting."

"You're wearing that?" he asked, every word precise and as sharp as an ice pick.

Feigning innocence, she glanced down at the caramel off-the-shoulder top with banded-cuff voluminous sleeves. She could see her nipples outlined against the soft material. She fought to keep from blushing and let her gaze continue to the wide black leather belt and black tulip skirt that stopped four inches above her knees.

The saleslady said the draping of the blouse emphasized the breasts and made a man think of what was underneath. Shane was certainly watching. She just had to stay focused.

Looking back up, she shook her head in annoyance at him. "For a moment I thought I had the skirt on backward. Bye."

Paige hurried past Shane and out the back door. He looked ready to explode, and she didn't think her mother being there would help. Starting the car, she backed out of the garage and headed down the driveway. "If you think this is something, wait until you see me tonight."

Shane suspected what Paige was trying to do, and it angered the hell out of him, because it was working. Later that morning, he rode the crowded elevator, heading for her floor. He wanted to pace, but there was no room. He'd faced few problems in his lifetime that he hadn't overcome or solved.

Until Paige.

Running five miles and a rigorous weight routine that morning hadn't helped calm him down. He was afraid nothing would.

He'd never been jealous of a woman before, and now he was consumed by it. The supple material of her blouse left her breasts in-your-face tempting. The soft swell of flesh over the top of the fabric had made his pants tight and his mouth water.

And that skirt should be illegal in all fifty states and every country. It revealed too much of her sleek, softly muscled legs that he couldn't help thinking could hold him tight in her hot body.

This had to stop. IIe was all too human.

He stepped off the elevator of her floor and came face-to-face with his beautiful, seductive, driving-him-crazy problem. Paige and two men, both in their early forties and wearing dark tailored suits, were laughing and walking toward him.

Paige saw him, lifted an inquiring brow. "Shane, what a surprise. Did you come to see me?"

She was really pushing him. "Yes."

"Sorry, that's impossible. Please meet Mr. Jonathan Hayes and Mr. Hector Freeman, regional and district manager of the airline we're featuring at the Masquerade

Ball. Gentlemen, Mr. Shane Elliott, a friend of the family."

He made nice because they were. It helped that he'd seen a gold band on each man's hand, and she'd pulled the blouse up on her shoulders. "When will it be possible?"

"Perhaps tomorrow. Now if you'll excuse us, we have reservations for lunch." She stepped around him, the men moving with her, flanking her as they chatted for a few moments before the elevator door opened and they stepped on. Not once did she look back at him before the door closed.

Shane was left staring after them, and wondering again if he might have blown it. Perhaps Paige had moved on.

His mouth flattened into a thin line. He'd just see about that.

S hane wasn't home when Paige returned from work at half past six that evening. If she hadn't dropped off the tile for Noah and Gayle's kitchen floor at their apartment, she would have arrived forty minutes earlier. She missed Shane, and was already tired of the game she was playing. Tempting a man might work for some women, but not her. She wanted honesty in a relationship.

From her casual inquiry to her mother, she learned he hadn't been back since he'd left that morning. During supper, she couldn't concentrate on what her mother was saying and had to ask her to repeat herself several times.

Paige wasn't surprised when her mother asked, "Do you want to talk about it?"

Once, when Paige was a preteen, they'd talked about boys, dating, even her wish for a Black Knight, but that was long ago, before these "feelings" erupted that she didn't know how to handle.

She didn't have a chance to ask her mother's advice at the time, because she hadn't dated until she was a senior in high school—and then no more than a few times.

Now she was too embarrassed. "No."

"If you change your mind, I'll be in the garden or in my room," her mother answered.

Her mother didn't push, but, being a smart woman, she had to know that Shane had something to do with Paige's inability to concentrate. Paige wondered briefly if her mother would mind her dating a man who was between jobs.

Silently she helped clean up the kitchen, then went to her room to work on the ball. Two hours into it, Paige saved everything on the laptop and the disk drive. She was too restless to concentrate.

Sitting on the balcony off her bedroom, she thought of Shane waiting for her the night before, how she had blown him off then and this morning. Her actions now seemed inexcusably rude. Even cruel.

If you cared about a person you didn't want them upset or angry. She was getting a taste of her own medicine, and it wasn't very palatable.

Going inside, she went to her drawer and took out the tiny white bikini she'd purchased on her shopping spree with Jackie. Perhaps a swim would clear her mind. There was also the possibility that Shane would see her in the suit and put them both out of their misery.

Changing into her swimsuit, she called her mother to tell her she was going for a swim, grabbed a terry-cloth robe and large towel, and went to the pool. Dropping everything on the chaise lounge, she dove, cutting smoothly, cleanly into the Mediterranean-blue water of the rectangular pool.

She'd been swimming since she was five, but she hadn't made the cut for the swim team in junior high or high school. There weren't many things, besides her high school diploma, her college degree, and her job, that she had gone after and obtained.

Why did she think Shane would be any different?

"What are you doing swimming alone at night?"

She went under. Spluttering, regaining her balance and hopefully her poise, she glared at him standing majestically at the edge of the pool. With his beautiful chiseled face, wide shoulders, and muscled legs, she could look at him for hours and never get tired. She'd been so deep in thought that she hadn't heard his car engine.

"Not wanting to be scared to death and drown, that's for sure," she finally answered, wiping the water out of her face.

Kneeling, he stuck his callused hand out. "Come on out. You shouldn't be swimming alone."

"I'm not. You're here," she told him, treading water smoothly, enjoying just looking at his powerful build. Tonight he had on jeans and a white knit shirt, emphasizing his wide chest and biceps. Even in the dim lights surrounding the pool, he looked positively mouthwatering.

"Paige, my patience is not what it used to be where you're concerned, so I suggest you do as I asked." It was a command that brooked no argument.

She frowned at him as a memory surfaced. "You like giving orders."

"Only when necessary." He stood up. "If you don't come out, then I'm coming in."

"You're bluffing," she said, excitement rushing

through her. She'd dreamed of seeing Shane with his shirt off again so she could look to her heart's content, which would be a very long time.

His hands went to the polo shirt, pulling it over his head, tossing it carelessly on top of the things she'd left on the lounge. Hard golden-bronze muscles rippled. Her breath caught in her throat. He was absolutely the most beautiful thing she had ever seen.

His reached for the leather belt of his sinful jeans, unfastening, unbuckling, then never pausing or taking his eyes from her, he undid the first button of his jeans, reached for the second button.

Temptation and curiosity vied with decorum and modesty. She caught a glimpse of black silk briefs. Excitement pulsed through her. Unfortunately, sanity prevailed as he reached for the third button. "You made your point." Swimming to the edge of the pool, she reached out her hand to him. His callused one closed around her, solid and sure. She sighed with regret to see he'd redone the jeans. Darn it!

She could tell the exact moment he saw the top, then the high-cut bottoms of her bikini bottom. His hand flexed, his grip tightened. His gaze jerked up to hers, blazing with fire and desire, his breathing changed, grew faster, labored.

Paige gulped and remembered a fable from childhood about the peril of playing with a tiger. She gulped, opened her mouth, but nothing came out. Then she couldn't speak.

His hot, hungry mouth crashed down on hers, and everything else ceased to exist. He angled his head, deepening the kiss. He devoured her mouth. She relished every precious second, every thrust of his tongue, every gliding motion, every bite on her lips.

Finally, her hands were free to touch his bare chest,

feel the incredible heat and muscled strength. She found touching only made the wanting worse. Fire and need splintered through her, leaving her trembling in his arms.

Her breasts felt tight, her nipples hurt. Arching, pressing against him only increased the slow needy ache between her legs. She wanted him too badly to be embarrassed by her erotic response to him. He made her daring. A first.

His avid mouth blazed a fiery trail from her mouth, her throat, the slope of her shoulder. Her body trembled even more as his warm breath stroked her skin just above the swell of her breasts.

Touch me. Kiss me, her mind screamed.

His hand undid the tie to her top, his hand cupping her aching breast, making her legs quiver, wild desire curling through her. The slow hungry lick of his tongue on her distended nipple pulled a low moan of pleasure from deep in her throat. The needy ache intensified below her waist.

Wanting more, her hands clutched his head to her. He gave her what she wanted, pulling the rigid point into his mouth, suckling greedily. Her knees buckled.

Sensation ricocheted through her. She felt herself being lifted, carried. All she could do was hold on tightly. Then she felt the grass at her back and Shane's glorious weight on top of her.

She expected him to continue driving her insane with need, taking her on a sensual journey that not even in her wildest dreams had she imagined. But suddenly he sat up, bringing her with him. Placing her in his lap, he wrapped his arms around her and held her tightly.

She could smell the sweet fragrance of the roses, see their shifting outline in the night breeze from the tall lamps stationed throughout the garden rooms. Something was wrong. Shane's hold was almost desperate. His body trembled against hers. Somehow she knew he feared few things. Alarmed, she tried to push out of his arms. She couldn't budge him.

"Shane, what's the matter? Are you sick?"

A ragged chuckle was her answer.

"Shane, you're scaring me," she said, finally able to put enough distance between them to look into his taut face. "Are you ill? Did you go to the doctor?"

His forehead rested against hers. "I'm not sick."

"But you were trembl—"

"Because I'm fighting making love to you." Now she was the one trembling. His large hands cupped her face. "I care for and respect you and your mother too much for that."

Paige briefly closed her eyes. Her little teasing had almost resulted in disastrous consequences. But in her defense she hadn't realized a kiss could cause your body to burn out of control. She'd forgotten the few kisses she'd experienced in the past the second they were over. After last night, she should have known Shane would be different.

She enjoyed his kisses, enjoyed being in his arms, but she didn't want to cause him discomfort. Her unsteady fingers tied the strings of her top. "I'm sorry."

He lifted her chin. "I'm not. You didn't know how much I want you."

"But I knew how much I want you," she whispered, wanting him to know he wasn't in this alone.

"Paige." Her name was a guttural sound on his lips. He took her mouth again, kissing, nibbling. Then she was beneath him, reveling in the hard, muscled strength of his body pressed against her. He slid his leg between hers. She felt the unmistakable hard ridge of his desire, pressed wantonly against him. Need overshadowed reasoning when he held her.

Suddenly his head lifted. Muttering a curse, he groaned and rolled away from her to lie on his back. Blowing hard, he stared at the sky.

Beside him, but not touching, she glanced over at him, then up at the star-filled night. Shane touched her and she forgot reason. Her mind shut down and her body took command. "Is it always like this?"

"No." He groped for her hand.

If she had to wait for her body to awaken, she couldn't have wished for or dreamed of a better man. "I'm glad."

"I am, too. Now that we're talking." He tugged on her hand and she obediently turned her head toward his. "I missed you."

"I missed you, too." She rolled toward him and he did the same. "I was out here because you weren't here and I couldn't concentrate."

His hand smoothed a damp tendril of hair from her forehead. "I flew to Dallas this afternoon on business."

Alarmed, she came up on her elbow. "You aren't going to relocate there, are you?"

"I told you I'd be here for a while and I meant it," he said.

"For now . . ." She glanced away and sat up, wrapping her arms around her knees. "We're back to square one."

Shane came to his knees, tugging on her hands until she was on her knees facing him as well. "Not quite. We know we miss each other, that we're explosive together, that despite how we look at relationships, we aren't going to turn our backs on this."

"We aren't?"

"We aren't," he repeated firmly, his thumb grazing

the top of her hand. "Otherwise you wouldn't still be here with me, tempting me far more than I ever imagined possible."

She leaned over and brushed her lips softly against his. "How did you get so smart?"

"I wish. You had me not knowing up from down. A first." His arms went around her waist, and he brushed a kiss across her waiting lips.

"I wasn't so sure myself. Which isn't a first, but these feelings are." She leaned against him, felt his arms close securely around her. "Scary and exhilarating. I don't want to be hurt, Shane."

"Baby." He pulled her closer to him. "We'll take this as slow as I can stand it. All right? But it would help if you went back to dressing the way you used to."

She lifted her head and smiled as he had intended. "I'll think about it. It just might keep you on your toes."

"And in a perpetual state of arousal."

She giggled. His laughter joined hers.

Standing, he pulled her to her feet, then wrapped his arm around her waist. At the chaise he helped her slip on her robe and pulled on his shirt. Hand in hand they walked back inside and up the stairs.

"Tomorrow is Saturday. What do you say we take your mother to breakfast and give her a break from the kitchen? Afterward, I have a surprise for you," he suggested at her door.

"What kind of surprise?"

He tweaked her nose. "You'll just have to wait. Dress casual. No skirt. Call your mother and let her know about breakfast. We can leave around nine."

"I will," she said. "By the way, I did tell her I was going to the pool."

"But if you had gotten into trouble, she wouldn't have known," he said, his eyes serious.

He was right. As usual. "Next time I'll wait until you can swim with me."

"Be sure and wear this suit."

The lusty need that had yet to completely disappear fluttered low in her body. "I will. Good night."

"Good night." He pulled her into his arms again. His lips brushed against hers, then settled firmly to claim her mouth. She locked her hands behind his neck and gave in to the arching pleasure that only he could give her. And wonder of wonders, she gave him just as much. She felt powerful and lucky, two things she had never experienced before. But then, she'd never been kissed by a man like Shane before.

His hands swept possessively over her, branding her as his. She wouldn't have had it any other way. Both were breathing heavily when he lifted his head. If she didn't leave, he might not let her. Heck, she might not let him.

She opened her door. "I'm glad we had our talk."

"Me, too. Night, honey. Sleep well."

"I will now." Entering her room, she whirled around in a circle. Her Black Knight had come home.

Chapter 15

An amusement park. Paige couldn't believe it when he got in line with all of the other cars on the road leading to the popular Six Flags Over Georgia. "No wonder you told me to dress casual."

"I thought we both could use a little fun and laughter." He pulled into a parking space and opened her door.

Hand in hand they joined the people headed for the ticket booths. "I always lamented that I never had a date take me here." She smiled up at him. "I'm glad now. I'd rather share the first time with you."

His eyes darkened and she realized he was thinking of them making love for the first time. "My thoughts exactly."

Paige blushed, but she didn't lower her head. Smiling, she stepped aside and waited while Shane purchased their tickets. He wanted her, but he was willing to wait even though he had to know she was his for the taking. He was putting what she wanted ahead of his own needs.

How could she not love him? The certainty of that question scared her. She had no idea on how to get him to love her back. She only knew that she wasn't going to turn away from what they had.

He came back to her, taking her hand, an impish

grin on his gorgeous face. "Now let's go have some fun."

"Lead the way."

Paige continued to surprise and delight Shane. He'd been concerned about the more adventurous rides, like the Pirate's Ship that swung like a crazy pendulum hundreds of feet into the air. She'd screamed, clutched his neck, and hidden her face against his shoulder, but when they exited the ride she was smiling.

"What's next?" she asked.

Next had been the Cyclone, a double-loop roller coaster. He didn't remember ever having so much fun. He'd forgotten how. Blade worked hard. Subsequently, Shane and Rio did the same. Of the three of them, Shane was the most laid-back—until Blade had married Sierra. Until then none of them had a life outside business. Shane hadn't thought he wanted one.

Until now. Until Paige.

Together they were both experiencing the same wonderful feelings for the first time, which made the occasion unique and special. It was almost six when Paige and Shane decided to leave.

"Paige, we have one stop to make," Shane said as they strolled between hawkers trying to get him to stop and play a game of chance and win a prize. He was looking for one thing in particular.

"Are you going to win me a stuffed animal?" she asked, an impish smile on her beautiful face.

"Our day of firsts wouldn't be complete without it." He stopped in front of a stand filled with an assortment of stuffed animals. One of them was bigger than Paige. "A giraffe, panda bear, or teddy bear?"

"Panda," she said, grinning up at him. It was the largest of the three.

"Panda bear it is." Her hand still in his, he went to the counter. "What are the rules to win the panda?"

The crafty-eyed man grinned at them, revealing two gold front teeth. "Here's a man who knows how to please a lady." He stuck out his tattooed hand palm-up. "Five bucks for three darts. If you get them all, you get a pick of the bottom shelf. Five bucks more and all hits gets you the second shelf. Five more with all hits, and the panda on the top shelf is yours."

Shane reached for his wallet. "You must have had him a long time."

The man chuckled. "Almost like a family member."

"Let's cut to the chase." Shane placed a twenty on the scarred board. "Nine darts."

The twenty quickly disappeared into one of the pockets of the man's dingy apron. "You sure you don't want me to keep the five to get you started on the next round?"

Paige stuck out her hand for Shane's change. "Thank you, but he won't need it."

"You hear that, folks?" the man called loudly to people passing by. "This little lady thinks her man has what it takes to go the distance the first time." He placed the five in Paige's hand, then began motioning people over. "Step up, folks, and see him not disappoint his lady."

"He won't." On tiptoes, she kissed Shane on the cheek. "You just get my panda bear ready."

"Man, are you in trouble if you don't come through," a male bystander said.

"I wouldn't want to be in his shoes," another male called out.

"Well, I'd trade places with her," laughed a woman.

"Thank you, but I'm staying exactly where I am," Paige told the woman. She playfully winked at Shane, who grinned back. "Now please step back and give him room."

Shane shook his head. Paige smiled at him, confident that he'd win that panda. With a flick of his wrist, he sent the first dart flying into a balloon. The sound still lingered as he sent another, then another, each finding its target until all nine darts were on the board, the tattered remains of the nine balloons hanging from them.

The crowd erupted into applause. The hawker looked from the board to Shane as if still not believing what he'd just witnessed.

"My panda, please." Paige handed Shane the five and lifted her arms toward the man.

"How about double or nothing?" the man said, picking up nine darts.

Shane shoved the money into the front pocket of his jeans without taking his eyes from the man. "You wouldn't be trying to renege on the rules, would you?" Planting his hands firmly on the weathered boards, he leaned forward. "I'd hate to disappoint my lady."

The man almost fell over his feet scrambling for the stuffed animal. "No. No. Here it is."

Shane plucked the animal from the man and handed it to Paige. Her arms tried and failed to go around the bear's fat waist. He chuckled. "I better take him for now."

She seemed almost reluctant to turn the bear loose. "Thank you."

He leaned over and kissed her on the cheek, curving his free arm around her waist. He wasn't a demonstrative man, but he found he liked touching Paige, holding her. He wasn't going to deprive himself of the pleasure. "Thank you for the inspiration and the faith. There was no way I was going to leave without your prize."

She laughed up at him. "That man found out when you showed your scary face."

He glanced down at her, her head on his chest as they headed out the exit gate. "I see it doesn't scare you."

She looked up at him, her face suddenly solemn. "I think it might have, if I didn't know the other, gentler side of you."

Releasing her, he handed her the stuffed animal and deactivated the lock on the car door. "No one has ever called me gentle before."

"That's because they don't know you as well as I do." She handed him the stuffed animal to put in the backseat. "Which is all right, because no one knows me as well as you do."

"Paige." His arms went around her, pulling her to him, taking her lips in a kiss that was both passionate and tender.

"I'll always be thankful for Mother extending you an invitation to come to Atlanta."

His expression didn't waver as he opened the passenger door to seat her. He went around and got into the driver's seat. He'd almost forgotten that he was on borrowed time—and before the clock ticked down, he'd better find a way to tell Paige what had really brought him there.

Paige was definitely walking on air. She supposed being in love did that to you. She and Shane had a long way to go, but at least they were on the road. It was incredible being with a man who understood you so well.

She suggested they drop the panda off at her house before they went to supper. She couldn't help the childish delight she experienced on seeing her mother's face when she'd awkwardly carried the giant panda into the house. "Shane won this for me."

"I better take it upstairs." He laughed. "We're going back out to dinner where Noah and Gayle work. Do you want to join us, Mrs. Albright?"

"No, thank you." She smiled at Paige, brushed her hand over the head of the panda. "So you finally got one."

"I sure did." She handed the stuffed animal to Shane's waiting hands and explained. "When Mother took me to another amusement park, I used to envy the girls and women walking around with those stuffed animals."

"No wonder you didn't want to turn the thing loose." Shane followed her up the stairs.

"That's all right," she said, opening her door. "I found out what those girls and women probably already knew. It's much nicer holding on to the man who won it for you."

His eyes darkened. He put the animal in front of her desk, took her hand, and started back downstairs. "Let's get out of here before you get us into trouble."

Laughing, she followed him down the stairs and they were off again. Shane gave her confidence she'd never known.

"You think Gayle will be able to seat us in Noah's section?" Shane asked as he led her across the crowded parking lot of the grill-and-tavern. They had to park in the very back. The lot was full.

"I hope so." Paige stepped through the door he held open. People edged over to make room. Inside, it was even more crowded and noisy. From the bar area to the left, two wide-screen TVs blared sports programs. "It will be good to see them again."

"How many?" the hostess asked, smiling over the wooden podium.

"Two," Shane answered. "Is Gayle working tonight?"

"Yes," the friendly young woman answered. "Would you like to be seated in her section?"

"Section?" Paige repeated. "She's a hostess."

The young woman suddenly looked uncomfortable, pulled on her ponytail. "She was reassigned yesterday after closing."

"Is Noah here?" Paige asked, wondering what was going on.

"Yes." The hostess looked relieved. "He's training her, so I can seat you in their section."

"Thank you." Paige and Shane moved away to wait for their table. The small area was crammed with people waiting as well. "She was so happy to get the position. She had been afraid that she wouldn't because of her full figure. She confided in me that for one of the few times in her life, her weight didn't matter," Page said tightly.

A man in a long-sleeved white shirt passed in front of them, heading in the direction of the bar. Paige went after him, catching the man by the arm. "Ron, why was Gayle reassigned?"

He looked from her arm to her angry face to Shane standing behind her. "Come with me, please."

Silently they followed him to his office in the back. He didn't sit or ask them to. Introductions were brief. "To answer your question, Paige, it wasn't working," Ron told her.

"What happened?" Paige asked, trying not to let her temper get the best of her.

Ron folded his arms across his barrel chest and leaned back against the desk. "She's too shy. I need someone bright and bubbly out front. To tell the truth, I'm not sure how she'll make it as a waitress. My wait staff have fun, sit at the booth, remember the orders instead of writing them down. I put her with Noah, who's a natural at charming people." He shook his head. "Hard to believe they're twins."

"She needs this job. But more than that, she needs to build her confidence," Paige told him.

"Paige, everybody here carries their own weight. As the manager, it's the only way I keep down the BS. I'm sorry."

"How long does she have?" Shane asked, his hand on Paige's shoulder.

Ron hesitated. "She's with Noah tonight. She's off tomorrow. I'll know by the end of her shift Wednesday if she'll make it."

"That's not enough time," Paige protested, anger building within her. "Give her a fair shot."

"I am," Ron said, his own irritation building. He raked his hand through his hair. "If she wasn't one of your kids, and Zach wasn't a good buddy, I never would have hired her. Paige." His voice softened. "Some people are cut out for this. She's not one of them."

"Thank you. Come on, Paige," Shane said. "Our table is probably ready."

"If it isn't, it will be." The manager straightened. "I'm sorry, Paige. I know how much this means to you and to them, but I have to think of the other employees and the customers."

She stopped him with a hand on his arm. "I could pay you—"

"Paige, no," Shane cut in. "That's not the way. Gayle has to do this on her own."

Her hand slipped away. "I know . . . it's just . . ." So much like when she hadn't fit in. She knew too intimately what Gayle must be feeling. Paige didn't want that for a young woman who had already been through so much.

"I understand, Paige," Shane said. "Come on."

Silently they followed the manager back into the restaurant and waited while he checked the seating arrangement against the list of customers.

"This way, please." Ron grabbed two menus and walked to a bustling area of the restaurant, seating them in a section of raised booths. Paige and Shane were barely seated before Noah came back from the kitchen area. An unsmiling Gayle followed behind.

Gone were the white blouse and black skirt she'd worn the other night when Paige and Jackie visited the restaurant. Tonight she wore a tan-colored T-shirt with the restaurant's name embossed across the front. Paige ached for her. The clinging shirt emphasized her body's shape, the generous breasts she'd always tried to hide or downplay.

Noah saw them immediately. Instead of the usual smile, he stopped and gave an almost imperceptible shake of his head.

"Whatever you're feeling, don't let it show." Beneath the table, Shane squeezed her hand. "She has to know you have confidence in her, and that if this doesn't work, you'll still be there."

"Of course I will."

"For what it's worth, I'll be there, too."

She squeezed his hand back. "It means a lot."

Noah reached their table, propping his hand on the wooden back of the booth, and faced them. Gayle hung behind him. Paige unfortunately knew why. She thought she had failed.

"Hi, Gayle, Noah. I see I got lucky again to be in your section," Paige greeted.

"Welcome back, Paige. Shane, glad you came," Noah greeted.

"Hello, Paige. Shane." Gayle swallowed, bit her lower lip, then tucked her head.

"Hi, Gayle," Shane said, glancing briefly at the menu. "What's good on the menu? I'm in the mood for beef. How about you, Paige?"

"Fish is good," Paige answered.

Gayle looked at her brother, then edged a bit closer. "The grilled rib eye is a favorite. It's ten ounces and served with a loaded baked potato. Paige, I think you'd like the grilled seafood platter served on a bed of rice with a side of coleslaw and a creamy Cajun sauce."

Shane handed Gayle his menu. "Make my steak rare, please."

Paige folded her menu. "Perfect."

Gayle clutched the menus to her chest. "What would you like to drink and can I get you an appetizer to start?"

"Sweet iced tea for both of us. Since you're so good, why don't you surprise us with an appetizer?" Shane said. "We've been out all day, so make it a lot."

"You can mix or match up to three appetizers," she said. "You sure you don't want to look at the menu again?"

"Not me. You, Paige?"

"Nope. We trust you."

"I'll go turn this in." Still clutching the menu, she went to a computer near their table. She didn't hesitate as her hand moved over the screen.

"She's good on the computer," Shane noted.

"She's spent a lot of time by herself. It became her escape," Noah said, his voice worried. "I'm concerned about her. Maybe this will let her know she can do this. Thanks." He moved away to the table behind them.

"You know what I think?" Paige said.

Shane played with a lock of her hair. "Nope, but I can't wait to hear it."

Paige turned firmly toward him. "I think Gayle needs to find her center."

It was difficult for Shane to watch Gayle. He knew it had to be much more difficult for Paige and Noah. Perhaps if she had had the waitress job initially, she might have gotten through her shyness. But being demoted put a big dent in her pride, made her feel as if she'd let Paige and Noah down. Like Paige, Gayle had to learn that her first responsibility was to like herself, regardless of what people said or did.

"Can we have some water?" the man from the table next to them asked.

"Good luck," called a woman from the booth in front of Shane and Paige's. "We've been waiting for our checks for five minutes. I've never had service this bad."

"No." Shane didn't move when Paige pushed him to get out of the booth. "Both of them have to learn to take the good customers with the bad."

Gayle filled the water glass, set the pitcher on a ledge, then rushed up to the table with the woman complaining about her check. She handed a bill to each of the five women sitting there. "Sorry it took so long. I didn't know you wanted the meals rung up separately."

The woman who had spoken grunted and held up her receipt. "This is wrong."

Shane saw Gayle cringe and look around for Noah. He was taking an order for a large group. Gayle's helpless gaze went to Paige.

"Can't you hear?" the woman asked snidely. The other women at the table laughed.

Moistening her lips, swallowing, Gayle turned back to the woman. "How is the bill wrong?"

"My salmon was thirteen ninety-nine. You have another dollar ninety-nine on here and three six ninety-nine and I only had two drinks, not three," she said.

"Is there a problem?" Ron asked, stopping at the table.

Paige had a death grip on Shane's arm. Two tables over, Noah straightened from taking an order.

"Your waitress overcharged me," the woman snapped. "I guess she needs her hair done." More laughter sounded around the table.

Shane had to make himself stay seated and hold on to Paige. "She's the one who needs a hairstylist, with a weave from hell—not to mention the nerve to go braless in that ill-fitting halter top."

"Paige!" Shane shushed.

"Can I see the bill, please?" Ron asked.

"Sure." The woman flicked it to him. Crossing her legs in her short denim skirt, she explained again about the overcharges.

"Gayle, what are the charges for?" Ron asked.

Gayle swallowed. "She substituted a baked potato for the rice, added a dinner salad after the original order. I know she had three margaritas because Noah said sometimes people forget and to keep a cheat sheet in my pocket when I turn in the order to the bar." She pulled out the small spiral tablet and handed it to him. "It has the table number, the seat, the time."

Ron turned to the woman and handed her the bill. "It's correct. How would you like to pay?"

Paige applauded. The woman jerked her head around. Paige continued, would have stood if there had been room.

The woman slapped her credit card on the table. "I want the carbon copy."

"Of course." Ron picked up the credit card. "I'll personally take care of this for you. Gayle, you can get the other customers, please."

Gayle picked up the payments from the other women. Passing Paige, she smiled.

"She did it! She did it!"

"Yes, she did," Shane agreed, but he was unsure if that one episode would give Gayle the confidence she needed. It had been his experience that once wasn't always enough. It certainly hadn't been that way with Paige, but she was too happy for him to remind her of that.

"Paige, you're needed in the foyer," Mrs. Olson, the church usher, whispered as she leaned across Shane during Sunday-morning services while the announcements were presented on the three screens in the sanctuary.

Paige stiffened; her first thought that it was Russell. He'd sent her daily e-mails that she deleted without reading, until Friday—then nothing.

Her reluctance must have shown on her face because the usher continued, "He said his name was Noah, and that it was an emergency."

The moment Mrs. Olson mentioned Noah's name, Paige was rising. Shane, sitting next to her at the end of the pew, rose as well, taking her arm. So did her mother, sitting beside her. Clutching her purse, Paige quickly left the sanctuary.

"I think Gayle is in trouble," Noah said the instant he saw Paige, his face and voice frantic.

"Why? What happened?" Paige asked, trying to

remain calm. The obnoxious woman diner might have been proven wrong, but Gayle's night hadn't run smoothly after that incident. A couple of diners had complained about slow service or requested "the guy training you."

Seeing how worried Paige was and how badly things were going for Gayle, Shane had suggested they come back to take Noah and Gayle home. No matter what any of them said to Gayle in the car, her answers had been flat and one word. At their apartment, she had thanked them and gone directly to her room.

"After you guys left last night, I banged on her door until she let me in. She said she might not be the best waitress, but a man she'd met just before closing told her she'd be perfect for his modeling agency. He said he could practically guarantee her a six-figure salary in a year." Noah slid both hands into the pockets of his jeans. "She wanted to be a model when we were kids. I thought she had put it out of her mind. She was all excited. I made the mistake of saying the guy was conning her."

"Noah," Mrs. Albright admonished.

"I know. Seeing her crushed expression was worse than anything you can say to me." He shook his dark head. "She just turned away, saying she wasn't pretty like I was, but everyone didn't think that way."

"What happened then?" Paige asked.

"I let it drop because I didn't want to argue with her or hurt her feelings after all that had happened at the restaurant. Then this morning when I got up, she was gone."

"What time was that?" Shane asked.

"A little after ten," Noah said. "She usually wakes me up when breakfast is almost ready because she knows I like sleeping in the morning."

"Maybe she just went for a walk," Paige suggested, fighting her own growing concern. Gayle was too naive and trusting. She always believed the best of people, plus she wanted to be able to help Noah with expenses. She'd see the modeling job as an answer to her prayer, and not the possible danger.

Noah shook his head again. "Gayle is a homebody. If I didn't drag her out of the house, she'd never leave. I just know she's gone to meet this guy. Being reassigned as a waitress hurt her deeply. She saw it as being a failure. If the man had the right words, he could talk her into anything."

"Any idea who this man was or where his studio might be?" Shane had a bad feeling about this.

"No. All I know is that he was a customer last night. He wasn't in our section. Apparently he spoke to her when she went to the bar to get drinks while I was busy."

"Then possibly one of the other waiters will remember him." Shane pulled his cell phone from his jacket. "Let's go outside. Do you have any of the other employees' contact information?"

"I don't know how to contact anyone except the manager." Noah waited until Paige and her mother went through the door, then followed. "I should have kept my mouth shut and just gone with her."

Once they were out the front door, Shane activated his phone. "Her only form of transportation is the bus." He looked at his watch. "The same bus driver should still be on duty. Do you have a picture of her?"

"Yes. We took one together the day we signed the lease for our apartment." Noah blinked, swiping the back of his hand across his eyes. "There are all kinds of perverts running around. If anything happens to her . . ."

"Don't borrow trouble," Shane told him. "Let's go get that picture."

Noah nodded. "It's at the apartment."

"Let's go." They hurried down the steps of the church.

"When we left last night, Gayle didn't want to talk. You said she was excited when you went into her room after we left. What changed?"

"I don't know," Noah said slowly as they walked through the parking lot. "She was smiling when she finally answered the door."

"Gayle doesn't have mood swings," Paige said.

"Not that I've noticed," Shane said. "Someone caused it. Does Gayle have a landline in her room or a cell phone?"

"A cell, but she left it on her nightstand. We decided that was the best way to save mon—" Noah stopped abruptly. "You can find the number for the guy if she called him."

"Just as soon as you give me the number." Shane listened to the number, then hit SPEED DIAL for Rio.

"Urgent," Shane said as soon as Rio answered. "Cell phone number 555-976-9223 made a call between twelve thirty-five and one thirty this morning, probably to another cell phone. I need the name and address of that phone's owner."

"Working."

Rio didn't ask questions, just went after the information requested. He would also be faster than the police, who would have to ask for authorization first. "If he rents or owns any properties in Atlanta, I want to know about it."

"Got it."

Shane replaced his phone. "It will take time to get

the information. In the meantime we'll go to the police to get help finding the MARTA bus driver. And to ensure they prioritize this, we'll need help." He looked at Mrs. Albright. "I think it would be a good idea if you called Bitsy. They won't blow off the governor's wife."

Chapter 16

Just as Shane expected, the police were all too ready to help. Less than ten minutes after the call from the governor, a patrolman had spoken to the bus driver for the route by Gayle and Noah's apartment. The man had remembered speaking to Gayle because she was a regular. He'd dropped her off at the MARTA station downtown.

"She could be anywhere," the division captain told them after receiving the report. "I'm sorry. There's no way to track her now."

"You can't just turn your back on her," Noah yelled, advancing on the policeman.

Shane grabbed the young man by the arm. "That's not going to help Gayle. He's right, and you know it."

Noah's fists clenched. "He could be hurting her."

Shane heard Paige's gasp and put his hand on the young man's trembling shoulder. "We have to stay strong and keep our heads clear if we're going to help Gayle. If she is in trouble, she's counting on you to come get her."

He nodded. "I'd do anything for her."

"And she knows it, Noah." Paige touched his other arm. "We'll find her."

"Shane, isn't there something you can do this time?" Mrs. Albright asked.

He wasn't concerned about her letting *this time* slip. Gayle's safety was what mattered. They both knew she was recalling his help when Sierra was kidnapped. "Ron and his staff couldn't give us any information." His cell phone vibrated.

"Excuse me." Shane stepped outside the door and answered his cell phone. "Yes."

Rio gave him the man's name and address. "Good hunting."

"Thanks." Shane opened the door, giving the information to the surprised police captain. Shane knew the police were still probably trying to get a supervisor to okay the release of information. Rio had gone through the back door. "I'll meet you there. Send a patrol car."

Closing the door, he quickly left the police station. Running wasn't a good idea, and the only reason Noah and Paige caught up with him by the time he reached his rental was that he'd forced himself to walk.

"Mother is taking a taxi home," Paige said, opening the passenger door and getting inside. Noah dove into the back.

Arguing would only waste time and solve nothing. Neither was going to budge. "Fasten your seat belts."

Turning on the navigation system, he gunned the engine. Thankfully the Ford answered his need for speed. He hit the freeway going seventy miles an hour. They were twenty minutes away from the address Rio had given him, for one Lee Berger. A patrol car could be in the area and get there first, but Shane wasn't counting on it. The governor's involvement would speed things up, but there was no way to know if a police car was clear to respond.

"I don't know what the situation is. The man could be legit, but in any case I want both of you to stay in the car," he ordered.

"No way," Noah said from the backseat.

Shane flicked a glance in the rearview mirror at the worried young man. "If there is trouble, I need to focus on Gayle and nothing else. Her safety, if there is a problem, depends on it." He came off the freeway. Berger's address was five minutes away in a mixed commercial-residential area.

"Shane's right, Noah." Paige twisted toward the backseat. "I didn't listen once and might have been seriously injured if Shane hadn't acted quickly. Let him handle things. He's a former Army Ranger."

Shane braked hard in front of the two-story building. Time for talk was over. In the distance he heard a police siren. He didn't know if they were heading there or someplace else. He had no intention of waiting. On the glass front BERGER'S PHOTOGRAPHY was written in faded gold cursive writing.

"Stay here."

Not waiting to see if they followed his order, he quickly got out of the car. It took less than three seconds to get past the locked door. The dingy front room held cameras on tripods, lights, backgrounds.

Seeing the stairs off to the right, he started to climb them, careful to be quiet. He heard Gayle's voice five steps from the landing.

"This isn't what I expected. You said you owned a prosperous modeling agency."

"I do," a male voice said. "It's just not on the sign. No sense pouring all the profits back into a building. Once you sign the contract and I take the pictures, I'll be able to shop you around. Just sign. Here."

"I'm sorry. I'm not signing a contract turning over all rights to my photographs. I've seen beauty queens and actresses get into trouble for doing that."

Shane relaxed. Gayle was holding her own.

Reaching into his pocket, he switched his cell phone to vibrate and sent Rio a text message about Lee Berger. Risking going to the top of the stairs, he peeked around the corner and saw Gayle in a pretty white dress sitting across the table from a man in his early sixties. The man ran his hand over his balding pate.

The loft-style room was a living area with another camera and background set up to the far left. Through a partially opened door Shane could see a rumpled bed. Another door across the room was closed.

Easing back down the stairs, Shane sent a text message to Paige telling her Gayle was all right, trust him, alert the police, and stay in the car. A message came in from Rio on Berger. NO ARRESTS. NO COMPLAINTS.

The guy had a clean record, but that didn't mean he couldn't pose a threat to Gayle. Shane would let her handle things unless Berger pushed too hard. She needed to know she could take care of herself. Shane retraced his steps.

"I think I should go home," Gayle said.

"No. No. You said you wanted to be a model. Tell you what, why don't I take some pictures of you and you can see for yourself how good you look? You're a fresh face. A designer's dream. They'll be clamoring for you. We'll have our pick of assignments." He stood. "You can change in that room over there."

"W-what?" her voice wobbled.

"Standard procedure," he said easily, rounding the table. "I need head shots." He lightly touched the collar of her dress. "This would ruin the look."

"Mr. Berger, I-I don't know about that."

Tell him to go to hell, Gayle.

"There's a robe in there," he cajoled. "Full-figured models are coming into their own. You're an attractive young woman, proportioned just right to make companies from clothes designers to beauty products sit up and notice. The camera is going to love your face."

"I'm not sure about this anymore."

"You better," he said, his voice harsher. "It's a cinch you won't last long at that restaurant and then what? You said you needed that job. What will happen if you lose it?"

Shane heard a faint noise on the stairs behind him and guessed correctly that it was Noah and Paige. A hard look didn't stop either of them. He put his finger to his lips, then caught Noah's arm. When the young man looked Shane in the eyes he shook his head once. Releasing him, Shane stepped in front.

"I'll find another job," Gayle said, but her voice lacked confidence.

"Doing what?" the man asked. "I watched you. You're a shy one. Who is gonna hire you? The modeling world don't care if you're full-figured or that you're shy. I'm betting you will come alive in front of the camera. You just go and change clothes and I'll show you."

Gayle slowly stood. Paige's fingers dug into Shane's arm through his long-sleeved white shirt. With his other hand he kept a tight grip on Noah. Gayle had to do this on her own.

"I'll go check the camera." Smiling, Berger rushed across the room.

Gayle took another step toward the room, and then stopped. "I can't."

The man whirled around. "What do you mean, you can't?"

"I can't do this."

"Don't be a baby. Grow up. I'm giving you the chance of a lifetime," he riled. "Now go put that robe on."

She stepped back. Her chin lifted. "No. I'm going home."

"And how do you propose to do that?" he taunted. "There's no train near here, no bus. Be sensible. Let's do the photos and I'll take you back to the train station."

She took a wide berth around him. "I'll get home. Paige will come. I don't have to do anything I don't want to."

"That's telling the bastard," Noah said as he stepped forward. Since Shane agreed, he let the teenager go.

Seeing her brother, Gayle covered her face. Tears glittered in her eyes. "Noah."

Noah had been going for the man but changed directions; Paige didn't. Shane matched her steps in case she needed a little help.

"You're lower than slime. Intimidating a young woman. I don't believe this is the first time." Paige pulled out her cell phone. "I'm calling the police. It will be interesting to see what they find when they search this place."

"No!" The man grabbed for the cell phone. Paige completely skipped fainting and shot her hand out with the phone, hitting the man in the nose. He howled. "You broke my nose!"

"Be glad you didn't touch her, or that wouldn't be all you have broken." Shane picked up the moaning man and shoved him into the sofa chair. "Call the police, Paige."

Two patrol cars, including one with the police captain, arrived within minutes of Paige's call. He hastily explained that a five-car pile up on the freeway had prevented them from arriving earlier.

"She broke my nose," the man wailed. "I want to press charges."

"You lunged for me," Paige said. "I simply protected myself. You weigh twice as much as I do."

The man's eyes glittered with rage. "You bi—"

Shane struck without warning, grabbing the man by the collar of his shirt, lifting him off the sofa until his feet dangled. "Don't even think it."

The man's eyes bulged. His mouth worked like a fish out of water.

Shane dropped him. The man hit the chair and shrank back.

"Miss Mathis, would you like to take a seat and tell me what happened?" the police captain asked gently.

Gayle's trembling increased. She bit her lip, tucked her head.

"Nothing happened," the man said, keeping a wary eye on Shane.

"Miss Mathis, I need to hear it from you," the police captain said.

"Gayle, you can do this," Paige said, giving the young woman an encouraging hug.

"I met him last night at the restaurant. He was sitting at the bar. He said he owned a modeling agency. I called him after I got home and agreed to meet him at the train station." She looked at Noah, tears sparkling in her eyes. "I was so stupid to believe him." Her gaze fell to the floor in front of her feet. "When I refused to change into a robe to take head shots, he said he wouldn't take me home, that I had no choice."

"She misunderstood me." Berger motioned to stand, then sank back into his chair at a menacing glare from Shane.

"You're a liar!" Noah raged. "We all heard you."

"Noah is right, Captain Weller." Paige kept her arm around Gayle's waist. She hated to upset Gayle more, but it had to be said. "Sometimes photographers have a

Web camera in the dressing room to stream live video to the Internet. It happened to another young woman I helped. Please check."

Gayle whimpered. "Oh, no."

"You need a search warrant for that," Berger yelled.

"All I need is probable cause, and I'd say I have it," the police captain said, motioning one of the patrolmen with him to go into the dressing room.

"You got no right!" Berger yelled. "Just take her. I was just trying to help her. Just go."

"I want to go home," Gayle said, her voice cracking. "Please, Noah."

Her brother hugged her to him. "In a minute, sis."

Paige took Gayle's hands. "You've been very brave so far. Just a little while longer."

Gayle swallowed. "I guess."

The officer came back out. "I didn't see anything."

"Mind if I have a look?" Shane asked politely.

Paige had a feeling he'd asked out of courtesy, but one way or another, he was looking.

"Why don't we both look to make it official?" Captain Weller said.

Shane stepped over the threshold of the small room and stopped. The only furniture in the room was an overstuffed chair and a trifold mirror.

"Well?" Captain Weller stopped behind him.

"If there is a camera, it's fixed." Shane went to the chair, sat down, and looked at the cluster of flowers over the trifold mirror in the corner of the room. "Strange place for flowers, don't you think?"

"If there's a camera hiding in there, Patrolman Jenkins, his sergeant, and I will have a long talk before the day is over." Captain Weller went back outside and returned with a straight-back chair from the kitchen

232 *Francis Ray*

table. "You're probably itching to do this, but I need to be able to testify about my findings. If we're right, I want to nail him to the wall and make it stick."

Shane held the back of the chair. "I don't care how it's done, just so he pays."

Climbing on the chair, Captain Weller stared at the black center of a sunflower. On closer inspection he could see it wasn't wax, but glass. He cursed softly under his breath. "I hope I give the bastards watching a heart attack when they see my badge. Slimy perverts."

"The computer equipment has to be behind the mirror," Shane said. "There's no telling how many unsuspecting women he's filmed."

Captain Weller stepped off the chair. "Miss Mathis wasn't one of them. She stood up to him."

"Because she knew Paige would be there for her," Shane said proudly. Paige had made a difference in the young woman's life. She was Gayle's center. And his.

"She's a feisty one. I wouldn't want to make her angry."

"On that we agree," Shane said. Yet he had a feeling that he wasn't going to be able to prevent it when she learned he was hiding a secret as well.

Paige couldn't believe her mother was waiting for them outside Gayle and Noah's apartment. Paige had called her after Shane's initial phone call to tell her that Gayle was all right, and again when they were leaving Berger's studio.

"It's almost three, and I'm sure no one had thought about food," Joann said, holding up two large take-out bags from a popular Italian restaurant. "I know you like pasta, Gayle; and Noah, there's plenty of lasagna and salad."

"Thanks, but I'm not hungry," Gayle managed between sniffles.

"Of course you are." Joann gave Noah a meaningful look. "Noah, please open the door. Paige and I can set the table."

"Sure thing." His arm around his sister's trembling shoulders, he climbed the stairs and opened the front door, then led her to the kitchen. He pulled out a chair for her.

"Let me help you, Mother." Paige took one of the bags and began unloading the food.

"Oh, mercy," Joann said. "Shane, I forgot drinks. Would you and Noah mind going to the store and getting some soft drinks?"

"Not at all." Shane caught Noah's eye when he was about to protest leaving his sister. "Noah can direct me to the nearest store. Be back in a jiff."

"Gayle, why don't you get those bamboo place mats we found at the estate sale?" Joann removed a container of salad. "Your home is beautiful. You have such an eye for detail and color."

"It didn't keep me from being a fool." Gayle's eyes flooded with tears.

"There's probably very few women on this planet who haven't believed the wrong man at one time or another." Joann pressed her hand gently on Gayle's shoulder. "The thing is to learn. You learned."

Paige sent her mother a look of appreciation. Gayle had broken down when she learned there was a camera in the room where she was supposed to change. Shaken as well, Paige had let her cry, but now tough love was in order.

"Mother is right, Gayle. You made a mistake, but you also kept your wits about you and refused to be intimidated."

234 *Francis Ray*

"I was so scared." Gayle sniffed.

"Shane said there's nothing wrong with being scared," Paige knelt in front of the trembling woman. "You didn't let that fear keep you from standing up to that creep."

"That took courage," Joann agreed, coming to stand by Paige.

"I knew you'd come get me." Gayle looked at Paige, then her mother. "You always told us your mother said there was nothing so bad that you or your brother couldn't tell her. You wanted us to be the same way with you, to know you'd be there no matter what."

Paige glanced up at her mother. In the past two weeks she had remembered that more and more. "And she always was."

Joann placed her hand on Paige's shoulder. "You and Zachary made it easy, just as Gayle and Noah have done. Love is better when it's shared and returned."

Paige felt her throat tighten. "Yes, it is."

"I want to be loved." Gayle's hands tightened in her lap.

Paige covered Gayle's hands with hers. She was talking about a man. "We all do. Give it time." She wasn't sure how her mother would feel about what she was about to say, but Gayle needed to hear this. "I'm twenty-seven and for the first time in my life there's a man I like being around. Just talking to him is enjoyable."

"Shane," Gayle whispered.

Paige looked up at her mother. "Yes."

Her expression unreadable, Joann went back to preparing the table. "Your young man will come, Gayle. When he does, don't let anything or anyone stand in your way."

Paige stared at her mother. She had a longing, a regret in her eyes that Paige didn't recall seeing before. Despite the problems they might have had, her mother missed her father.

"Yes, ma'am." Gayle stood and opened a cabinet drawer to get the place mats. "I don't think I want to go back to the restaurant."

"Why?" Paige asked, placing the brass napkin holder on the table.

"I'm a disaster," Gayle admitted. "I'm not comfortable around a lot of people like you are."

Paige put one hand on her hip. "Neither was I at first, but I liked helping people. I'm still not the best in large crowds." She grinned and folded her arms. "I have a new strategy when I doubt myself. I think of something that empowers me. You could do the same thing at the restaurant. If you stood up to that creep, you can handle the customers there."

"If you decide to quit later, at least you would have tried," Joann said. "There's no worse feeling than knowing you failed without trying."

Again Paige caught the sadness in her mother's voice. Without thought, she rounded the table and placed a comforting arm around her shoulder. "Mother."

Joann's smile was strained. "Paige always tried. Nothing held her back."

"And you were always there to help me go on when I failed," Paige recalled fondly.

"I'm your mother and I love you. Where else would I have been?" Joann swept her hand over her daughter's hair.

"You two are lucky to have each other," Gayle said. "Just like I am to have Noah."

Each other, Paige mused. For so long, it had been just her and her mother. Zach was protective of her, but he was older and had his own friends and interests. It was only later that Paige's father had deemed her worthy of his love and time.

"Paige, are you all right?" her mother asked.

She shook the unfair thought away. Her father had been busy. Some fathers didn't know how to relate to their young daughters. "Fine. Let's get this table set before Shane and Noah return."

As if on cue, the front door opened. Noah came through first, heading straight for his sister. "I love you, you know."

His sister blinked back tears. "I know. I'm sor—"

"No." He placed the twelve-pack of Pepsi on the kitchen counter. "You trusted the wrong man one time. Too many times to count I knew I was wrong and did stupid things anyway. If ever you can top me, then we'll talk."

"Oh, no." Gayle closed her eyes. "The newspapers."

"Taken care of," Shane said. "Captain Weeler wasn't anxious for the press to find out one of his men had missed finding the camera. Plus he didn't want it getting out that the governor was involved."

"Governor," Gayle said in a strained whisper. "I don't understand."

"Why don't we sit down and eat, and Paige and Mrs. Albright can explain it?" Shane said, crossing his arms. "You don't mess with the Albright women."

Chapter 17

"Thank you again, Shane. If you hadn't been here, things might have turned out differently," Mrs. Albright said in the foyer of her home a little after eight that night.

"You helped." Shane looked at Paige. More and more she was coming into her own. "You both did. Noah and Gayle are lucky to have you two in their corner."

"We're lucky to have *you*." Paige looped her arm through his.

Her mother's gaze went to their linked arms. Paige's hold tightened. She stepped closer.

"I think I'll go up and call Bitsy to give her a report on how Gayle is doing. Good night, Paige. Shane," Mrs. Albright said.

"Good night, Mother." Crossing to Joann, Paige hugged her. "Thank you. Sleep well."

Her brow arched, Mrs. Albright glanced over her daughter's shoulder at Shane. "That might depend."

"Mrs. Albright," Shane called when she started to turn away. There was something he needed to say. "I won't abuse or take advantage of you or Paige." He'd rather face a crazed gunman than get on the bad side of the mother of the woman he cared about more with each passing second. She had to know that with one word she could send him to hell. Without Paige, that was exactly where he'd be.

"People often say what they think you want to hear," Mrs. Albright said, her gaze as direct as his.

"Mother, please," Paige said, obviously distressed. "I make my own decisions."

"She loves you, and that gives her the right to have her say and be concerned," Shane said. "I can be gone in ten minutes."

Paige cried out in alarm. "No!" She pulled him around to face her. "You're not going anywhere."

He looked back over his shoulder at her mother. Mrs. Albright had the last word in this. They both knew it.

As the silence lengthened, Paige faced her mother. "Trust me to know what I'm doing."

Shane felt his stomach knot. "Paige, you and your mother's relationship is too important for anything or any man to come between. Why don't you go to bed, and tomorrow we'll talk?"

"You'll be gone if I do."

He almost smiled. Paige learned fast and was nobody's fool.

"The only person who is going anyplace is me . . . to bed," Joann said. "Paige, of course I trust you. Shane, if I thought you weren't to be trusted, you wouldn't be in my house. Good night."

"Good night, Mrs. Albright," Shane called as she went up the stairs. "Thank you."

"We both know how you can thank me."

Ouch, Shane thought. She could have left that out. "Paige, I guess you better go to bed."

Paige walked her fingers up his chest. "It's not even nine."

His hands closed over hers, trapping her hand against his chest. "Paige. You heard your mother."

"I did." Freeing her hand she slid both arms around his neck, leaned against him. "Although it's kind of cute, I can't believe you're afraid of my mother when you can make men shake in their tracks."

His hand grasped her waist to keep her from sinking closer. "Paige, behave. You know where this is leading if you continue. We both have to face your mother in the morning."

Her lips brushed across his, bit. He groaned, felt his lower body stir. *Behave*. He was just a man and all too weak where Paige was concerned.

"We didn't have any problem this morning."

His face heated. He could not believe she was teasing him. He pulled her into the great room. "I've created a monster."

Her body sank against his, her breasts, her thighs flush against him. "Complaining?"

"I'm not that big a hypocrite or fool." His mouth took hers. He angled his head to deepen the kiss. She opened for him, arching against the hard line of his body, her tongue swirled against his, pleasuring him. He could gladly lose himself in her kisses, her arms. He had, and he would again and again.

Much later that night, Shane let himself into his room and called Rio. "Your quick work saved the day."

"Paige?"

It wasn't like Rio to ask questions, but then, Shane hadn't been acting his usual self in the past few months, either. "No. One of the teenagers she's helping transition from foster care. The phone number belonged to a creep photographer with a Web camera in the dressing room."

"If the person in jeopardy had been Paige, I'd be on my way there with a lawyer," Rio commented, his tone flat.

Shane rubbed the back of his neck. "So I'm protective of her."

"If only that was all."

"Rio, you don't understand."

"Since I'm reasonably intelligent, why don't you explain it to me?"

Shane paced. "It's not that simple."

"Sure it is. You're just making it complicated" came the laconic answer.

"It *is* complicated," Shane almost shouted, then he sat on the side of the bed.

"I'll say. Do you realize you've completed your initial assignment and you're still there?"

He did. "I told you, it's complicated. Paige is so giving and sweet. I don't want to hurt her."

"Damn. You, too."

The horror in his best friend's voice—the man whom *nothing* got to—somehow made Shane feel better. "You know they say things come in threes."

Rio grunted. "Funny."

"I mean, I'm not ready to marry or anything, but I enjoy being with her. I won her a panda bear at the amusement park yesterday," Shane said proudly. "She—" There was a click followed by a dial tone.

Grinning, Shane disconnected. "Rio, when your time comes, I'm going to remind you of this conversation."

Tuesday morning Paige woke up with a smile. A man in a woman's life certainly made it more interesting. While she bathed and dressed she couldn't help thinking how much fun it was to tease a man, especially a man like Shane. He was so incredibly complex. One moment tender, the next dangerous, the next kissing her until her body simply melted, then heated, tingled, wanted.

Yesterday he'd sent a five-pound box of Swiss chocolates to her office. She'd shared with the office staff and kept a grin on her face the rest of the day. Of course she'd save some to feed him. If she closed her eyes she could still taste the sweetness of the chocolate mixed with that of Shane. Incredibly delicious and addictive.

He'd helped her to be more self-assured. He was good for her and, she hoped, she was good for him.

"Paige?"

Whipping an egg into the batter mixture, Paige glanced around. She'd decided to show Shane her cooking skills. "Good morning, Mother. Please have a seat. We're having banana Foster crêpes this morning."

Joann sat at a breakfast table already set for three. "You got up early."

"Yes." Paige poured the thin, yellowish batter into the sprayed skillet. "I wanted to surprise Shane with breakfast."

"You really like him, don't you?"

Paige took her eyes off the sizzling batter to look at her mother. "Yes." She didn't think her mother was ready to hear that it went deeper than *like*. She loved Shane.

Joann picked up her cup and saucer and went to the coffeepot. "Have you considered that he might decide to relocate someplace else?"

"I have." Paige turned over the crêpe with a hand that had begun to tremble.

"And?" her mother pressed when Paige didn't say anything further.

"I refuse to think about it too much or I'll . . ." She couldn't prevent the quick rush of tears in her eyes, the stinging in her throat.

"Paige, honey. This isn't a fairy tale where wishes come true. It's not like you not to face reality." Joann set the cup aside.

"Mother, I believe in Shane. I can't explain it, but somehow I knew from the day he arrived that he would be important to me." She slid the crêpe onto a plate.

Joann studied her daughter for a long time, then briefly closed her eyes. "I don't want you hurt the way—" Biting her lip, she glanced away.

Paige frowned. "The way who was? Zachary and Carmen?" Her brother had had a fiery relationship with the tempestuous socialite before he moved to Los Angeles. Alone. Carmen had refused to leave Atlanta and go with him. "He's successful and loves what he does. He doesn't have to put up with a spoiled woman like Carmen. He's happy."

"What if Shane found a job someplace else?"

Paige sprayed the crêpe pan again. "It will work out somehow. I have to believe that."

"For both your sakes, I hope you're right," Mrs. Albright said, but her voice lacked conviction.

"Have you considered what will happen when you have to leave?" Mrs. Albright asked the moment Shane returned to the kitchen after walking Paige to the garage to see her off to work.

"I have, but I don't have an answer," he confessed.

Mrs. Albright shook her head. "You can hurt her worse than Russell ever could."

"I'd never hurt her," Shane said, angry that she thought he would.

"You think leaving won't hurt her?" Mrs. Albright challenged. "She has no defense against this. She thinks it will work out because of the way you both feel. Trent's father and I are proof that that doesn't always happen. I would have died for him, but I was doomed to live without him." She *had* almost died when she'd faked Trent's death to save his life.

"History is not going to repeat itself."

"I'll hold you to that. I'd hate to have summoned you here to save Paige, and see you end up destroying her."

Shane wouldn't allow that to happen. Somehow he'd find a way. He had to.

A little past eleven that morning Paige was trying to decide the best time to check on Gayle when she heard the knock on her office door. She'd spoken by phone with Gayle twice on Monday. She hadn't made a decision, but from what Paige had learned from Noah, the job wasn't becoming any easier for Gayle. Unlike Noah, Gayle was insecure, shy, and self-conscious about her weight. The incident with the photographer made her even more insecure.

Paige had been the same insecure way with an older brother who everyone adored and looked up to. People saw her and wondered where she'd come from. Zach helped by including her when possible. Noah did the same thing with Gayle. Yet Paige knew that eventually you had to face the harsh realities of life on your own.

Paige ignored the second knock and chewed her lower lip. Would it be better to go by the restaurant for lunch or wait until later that afternoon to go by her apartment?

Gayle planned on going in today, but it was any-one's guess how her shift would go. The manager said he'd give her until Wednesday, but if things went badly today, he might not wait.

The knock came again.

"Come in."

The door opened. Shane filled the doorway. Paige didn't even realize she had moved from behind her desk until his arms closed around her, his mouth found hers. Things blurred pleasantly. The man could certainly kiss.

"Hi," he said, staring down at her.

"Hi." How could just looking at a man make your heart beat faster, shut out the world, make you feel in-vincible?

"I think we need to talk."

Her warm mood evaporated. Her hands clenched on his arms. "About what?"

"Us."

Gazing up into his serious face, Paige couldn't tell if she was going to like what he said or not. "Go on."

Letting his arms fall, he caught her hand and went to sit on the love seat by a dark oak bookshelf filled with books, photos, awards, and crystal. "You've never asked me about my looking for a job or job prospects."

She tensed. "You found a job?"

"As I said, I'm keeping my options open. My check-ing account and savings are enough that I don't have to worry about it for quite a while." His hands flexed on hers. "You go to work and I stay at the house. It never seemed to bother you."

Some of the tension eased out of her. "I know after helping the foster kids and others find jobs that it can be difficult. Besides, you're not the freeloading type. You help without being asked. You've never hinted for a loan, always paid for us going out." Her hand ran over his callused palms.

"You're used to hard work. I don't figure an ex–Army Ranger would be lazy or shiftless. Mother said her former roommate spoke very highly of you. Macy marvels at how neat you keep your room and bathroom. You're the perfect houseguest."

"I don't know about perfect." His thumb grazed over the pulse in her wrist, causing it to beat even more wildly. "I've enjoyed being here. It's the first time since I was a kid that I didn't have a schedule to follow."

Her heart twisted. He hadn't had an easy life. "I'm glad you decided to spend it with us."

"Me, too. Do you have time for lunch or do you have another appointment?" he asked.

She glanced at her watch. "I have an appointment in an hour at the Carrington Estate where the ball is being held. Before you came in, I was trying to decide if I wanted to drop by the restaurant now or later to check on Gayle."

"Neither."

Her brow lifted. "You can't be serious?"

"I am," Shane said patiently. "She knows you're behind her. She doesn't need you checking up on her."

Her shoulders straightening, Paige pulled her hands back into her lap. "I'm not checking up on her. I'm supporting her."

Shane folded his arms. "A matter of semantics that amounts to the same thing. In any case, it would have the opposite effect. You can't hold her hand. She has to sink or swim on her own."

Paige's hands clenched. "Some lessons are painful."

Shane's hands closed over hers. "Life isn't pretty or easy at times. Hopefully one learns from those lessons."

"It would be so much easier if I could just tell her," she lamented.

"On whom?" Shane asked. "Don't you think your mother would have spared you any unhappiness if she could have?"

"She was in the front row at every tryout where parents were allowed. The moment my name was announced I could hear and see her yelling for me." Paige's mouth curved. "No matter where I finished, she'd still be just as vocal and proud."

"Exactly. And now you don't give up because you learned not to," he told her. "It might seem harsher to let a person learn on their own, but occasionally it's the only way."

Paige's head twisted to one side. "Are you talking from experience?"

"Yes."

"Any regrets?"

"Plenty, but it's the only way," he said, finality in his words.

Paige blew out a breath. "Since I can't go support Gayle, why don't you come with me and keep my mind off what might be happening at the restaurant?"

He grinned wolfishly. "How can I resist such an interesting proposition?"

Her heart rate kicked into overtime. It was going to be a fascinating afternoon.

Shane thought, and not for the first time, that he didn't think he'd ever tire of being with Paige. For almost an hour they'd toured the main rooms of the Carrington Estate, fifteen thousand square feet of luxury on three levels with beautifully landscaped grounds, a small lake, and a helipad. He hadn't gotten bored or restless, as occasionally happened when he'd been with Blade while he conducted business.

Paige and the executive manager of the property, Charles White, both had notebooks, and both were taking and comparing notes. For the first time Shane realized the massive undertaking she'd planned.

"Here in the main ballroom is where the French-themed dinner will be served, you'll note the beautiful gilt artwork on the domed ceiling, the five eight-foot crystal chandeliers," Charles said proudly. "Your guests will enter from the first floor, have their passports stamped by a host of attendants fluent in French, and come down either of the white spiral staircases." He spread his arms wide. "This area will be transformed into a Parisian street scene with charming sidewalk cafés, streetlights, couture stores, and a pastry shop. Mimes will stroll the perimeters. The replica of the Eiffel Tower will be at the farthest end."

"The photographer?" Paige questioned.

"Will be stationed there to take photographs," Charles confirmed. "The photographs will be available within an hour and given in a three-by-five Waterford crystal frame at no charge as another memento of the night."

Shane whistled. "That's going to be costly."

Paige smiled. "The tickets are three thousand dollars each. It's for charity, but I wanted the guests to feel they're getting their money's worth, so when I ask them next year they'll be eager to attend." She faced the executive manager. "We know they'll enjoy the French cuisine. The chef is sensational, the food fabulous."

Charles smiled. "You charmed the chef so much during your taste test that when he heard you were coming today he prepared a luncheon for you. If you'd like,

you and your guest can enjoy it on the terrace over-
looking the cascading pools and gardens."

"Won't you join us?" Paige asked.

"Thank you, but with the ball less than two weeks
away, I have a lot of work to do," he said.

"Everything is coming together just as I planned."
She looked up the graceful staircase. "I can't wait to
see the guests' expressions when they see what you've
created."

"Thank you, but this room is only the beginning, as
you know." He tucked his bound leather notebook to
his chest. "Your guests will also be transported to London, Rome, and Monte Carlo. At each stop they will
see a landmark synonymous with that great city."

"It will be a night to remember," Paige remarked. "A
night of romance."

"My staff and I at Carrington Estate will certainly do
our part." He turned to Shane and extended his hand.
"Now, if you'll excuse me. I have a few phone calls to
make. Lunch will be served outside."

"Thank you," Shane said.

"Good-bye, Charles." Paige turned to look back at
the sweeping staircase.

Shane curved his arm around her waist. She laid her
head on his shoulder. "How long have you been working on this?"

"A year," she answered without lifting her head. "My
debutante ball was held here my senior year in high
school. Luckily I had come into a bit of my own by then,
so I had fun. Mother and Father were so proud of me."

He kissed her on the forehead. "Of course they were."

"Mother planned to take me to Europe the summer I
graduated from high school, just as her mother had
taken her. Daddy thought I was too young," she said,
her voice full of regret.

"What happened?" His hand gently rubbed up and down her arm.

Paige burrowed closer to Shane. "Mother fell. She was so badly bruised it was an effort to walk. Father said she was clumsy. She kept apologizing to me. I told her it didn't matter, that I was just sorry she was in so much pain."

Shane had no doubt Mrs. Albright's husband caused the injuries. He hoped the sadistic bastard roasted in hell. "Did you ever go?"

"No," she said quietly. "So when I came up with the idea of the ball, I knew immediately the cities I wanted."

"So you'd finally take that trip together."

Turning in his arms, she smiled up at him. Her finger grazed his lower lip. "I think Mother will be pleased when she sees the destinations."

"Monte Carlo is a bit of an unusual place to take a seventeen-year-old."

She chuckled. "I added Monte Carlo because it always seemed so romantic in the movies. I imagine driving on the cliff in a red convertible, playing baccarat, midnight suppers."

One day he'd take her there. "You'd have beginner's luck and walk away with a bundle."

"Perhaps. The ball will be the culmination of so much. I dreamed of returning here one day and having my—" She straightened abruptly. "Why don't we go outside? I'm sure we'll be served shortly."

He caught her by the arms when she attempted to move away. "What were you about to say?"

She moistened her lips, started to tuck her head until his hands on her arms tightened with just enough pressure to let her know he wanted an honest answer, and to remind her to always keep her head up. "I planned to have my wedding here. Last year I finally realized that day might be a long way off and decided to hold the Masquerade Ball here instead."

His gaze, locked on her, didn't waver. "You've dated Russell since then."

"Russell is a friend. Make that *was*," she said. "He could never touch my heart the way I want the man I'll marry to."

"Paige." Shane pulled her roughly into his arms. "If another man touched you . . ."

"Why would I want another man when you're here?" she asked.

He lifted her head, stared down at her. "I wish I could promise you that I'll always be here. I can't."

For a brief moment, sadness flickered in her eyes. "You're here now. That's enough."

"And when it's not?" he questioned, not moving away.

"I'll let you know." She hooked her arm through his. "A certain man taught me to go after what I want."

Later that night Shane walked the grounds of Mrs. Albright's estate, seemingly impervious to the warm, gentle rain that soaked his shirt and pants. Deep in thought, he ignored the moisture. He'd been in worse. The situation he found himself in with Paige was a different matter entirely.

He only had himself to blame. At Riviera Maya, when Mrs. Albright came to ask for his help, he'd been so sure he could handle whatever threat Paige might present to his peace of mind. He'd been proven wrong in spades—and worse, the stakes had just gotten higher.

Paige wanted forever. He knew that, but seeing the wistful look on her face as she stared up at him at the Carrington Estate, then the flush of embarrassment when she talked of wanting her wedding there one day, he was hit squarely in the face with reality. He'd told Rio he wasn't thinking about marriage, and he wasn't.

Yet the thought of her coming down that staircase to another man made Shane's gut twist painfully, rage shimmer inside him. And even knowing he didn't feel the same way, she still looked at him as if he were the only man on the planet, the only man for her.

His mind didn't think of forever in terms of being with a woman. But he'd never felt for another woman what he felt for Paige. Protective, lustful, and, yes, hopeful. At any other time he would have been anxious to get back to work. Now he was content to get updates from Rio.

In the years he had worked for Blade, Shane had never been away from him this long, couldn't have imagined doing so until Paige entered his life. He took his job seriously, yet here he was, across the country with no great inclination to return to the life he once led.

No one asked when he might return, which in itself was telling. He was a stickler for details. He wanted to know who and what every moment. Now he was the one unable to comply with his own rules.

Rio reported that Blade and Sierra hadn't let the location change stop them from their honeymoon. Rio figured Blade would take another week before he emerged. When they did, Shane would have to return.

What Rio didn't say was that he didn't see how a man could spend so much time with a woman and not get bored. Obviously, Rio had a lot to learn about women. Paige was certainly teaching Shane a great deal.

The sound of Paige's bright laughter lifted Shane's downcast head. Dressed in a short-sleeved white blouse and black slacks, she ran lightly along the flagstone path heading straight for him.

His heart simply stopped.

She was so beautiful, and so loving and open. She deserved happiness. He realized at that moment he wanted that happiness with him. And his secret could rip them apart.

She didn't stop until she'd thrown her arms around his neck. She laughed up at him, rivulets of water running down her face. "I saw you from my bedroom window."

Pain sliced through him at the thought of losing her. Just short of desperation, his arm dragged her to him. "It's raining."

"I wanted to be with you," she said simply. "Why should I let a little rain stop me?"

His hands framed her face. "You're so beautiful."

The laughter ebbed. He felt her tremble. "I'm not, but thank you."

He frowned down at her. "Why would you say that?"

The smile came again. "Most beautiful women have more men coming on to them than they can count. I am pitiful in the date department."

"Because you've probably turned them down," he told her. "All except 'he who shall remain nameless.' "

She giggled as he intended, then sobered. "I'm busy with work and the foster program. I don't have time to date."

"Then I'm a double lucky man that you accepted my date and found the time to go out with me." He kissed her gently on the mouth, then curved his arm around her waist and started back toward the house. "Let's get you inside. I don't want you sick for your big night."

"I'm never sick."

Shane kept walking. "You have an escort for the ball?"

She stopped. "Not anymore."

"Any tickets left?" he asked. She was adorable with raindrops sparkling on her thick lashes. No one was escorting her down that staircase again but him. At least he could fulfill part of her dream. And just maybe, a part of his own unrealized dream as well.

"We sold out, but since 'he who shall remain nameless' never paid for or picked up his ticket, there is one left."

He grinned. "*Was*. I'll give you a traveler's check as soon as we get back."

She swept the rain out of her face. "That's not necessary. It's already paid for. It can be my gift—"

"No," he said, harsher than he intended. He cursed under his breath as she went still. "I pay my own way. I can afford the ticket." She simply stared up at him with enormous eyes. "Paige, honey, I'm sorry I yelled at you."

"I can see why men quake."

"I'd never harm you," Shane promised, hurt that she thought he might. "You believe me, don't you?"

"Of course." She leaned against him, her arms circling his waist. "For a moment I was back at a time I don't want to think about."

He barely kept from stiffening. "What happened? Were you hurt?"

"No," she said. "The incident just made me feel helpless and inept. I didn't like the feeling."

His thumb and finger lifted her chin. "You're neither of those two things. I'll have to put on my scary face if I hear you say that again."

"Can't have that. Besides, with you I don't feel that way." Her fingertips brushed across his damp lips. "With you, I think I can do the impossible."

"Exactly how I feel with you." His lips covered hers,

feeling them warm, soften. He gathered her to him, kissing her with leashed need and power. Desire rushed through him, shaking him to the very core. Each kiss took him closer to the edge, but he had no intention of depriving either of them.

He fed on her sweet mouth. Their tongues mated, dipped, and swirled, kiss after drugging kiss. It was just the two of them caught up in a maelstrom of need and passion. Insinuating his leg between hers, he let her feel his hard arousal. Trembling, she pressed closer, her arms tightening around his neck, her mouth as feverish as his.

His need strained to be free. He longed to feel her clench hotly around him, for him to drive into her satin heat. If he didn't stop, he'd take her here and now.

With supreme effort, he lifted his mouth and held her securely against his chest. His breathing as ragged as hers, his hand swept up and down her back, soothing her the only way he could. It was several minutes before their breathing returned to normal, her hands on him stopped being desperate.

He rubbed his chin against the top of her head. Even with the rain falling on them, their clothes wet, he enjoyed just holding her. "We better go back to the house while we can."

"I suppose," she said, regret in her voice.

Shane knew exactly how she felt, but he also knew she wasn't ready to take the irrevocable step. Once done, it couldn't be undone. For Paige, it had to be right. Too many times, things in her life had gone wrong. If he had to take a thousand cold showers, he wouldn't ruin her first time for her.

Silently they started back.

Chapter 18

"Are you going to be able to sleep if you don't hear from Gayle?" Shane asked as they climbed the stairs together.

"No." Paige stopped in front of her bedroom door. "Although I am trying to think positive."

"But you're worried." He dropped a kiss on her forehead. "Friends worry about friends."

"If it doesn't work out, she'll see it as a failure." Having stood where Gayle stood, Paige knew exactly how that felt. "Noah said things didn't go well last night. I don't think it had anything to do with memories of the photographer trying to use her."

"You and Noah will always be there to help her see differently."

But Shane might not be there. Panic clutched at Paige's heart. She didn't want to think of a time he wouldn't be with her. As her mother said, it wasn't like Paige not to face reality. But she'd never been faced with the possibility of losing the man she loved.

"Go inside and change into some dry clothes." Shane opened her door. "I'll meet you back downstairs. We can neck and find a bad movie on TV."

"You don't have to babysit me."

"I'd like to know how she did as well." He gently pushed her into the room. "Ten minutes."

"Ten minutes." Inside her room, Paige grabbed fresh undergarments, reached for a sundress, then chose a pair of slacks and a blouse instead. There was no sense in tempting fate.

Setting the clothes aside, she undressed and stepped into the shower. Shane had only to touch her and her body took over. He brought to life all the pent-up needs she had repressed for so long. She'd thought there was an abnormality in her, but it wasn't her, it was the men.

Shane was the *one*. He was the only man who filled her with desire, made her heartbeat quicken. For her, there wouldn't be another. If she had to risk it all for his love, so be it. She didn't want to look back on this one day with regrets, should-haves, if-onlys. She would know that she had held nothing back and take satisfaction from that.

For as long as she could remember, she had planned her wedding. She'd wear a beautiful white French reembroidered lace gown with pearls and Swarovski crystals, and come to her husband chaste. That was before Shane kissed her, before he made her body crave his touch. He could just look at her and she trembled with desire.

And never once had he taken advantage of her weakness. She wasn't sure if she agreed with his restraint. This achy need left her restless. With a trembling hand, she shut off the water, dried, and dressed.

The way things were going, she might never know the intimacy of his body, the heated touch of his bare skin against hers. Her hand curled around the handle of the hairbrush she'd picked up. She wanted that intimacy more and more. Shane wanted it, too, but he was holding back because he respected her and her mother. While she appreciated his restraints, she just wasn't sure she agreed with him any longer.

Perhaps she should have let him move out when he first suggested it, she mused as she brushed her hair. But making love wouldn't solve the real problem. Shane wasn't committed to her or to staying in Atlanta. Until he was, she was on borrowed time.

So make the most of it. Finished with her hair, she picked up her cell phone and went downstairs. Another thing about Shane she loved, she didn't have to dress up or wear makeup for his eyes to narrow and burn with desire. He made her feel seductive and desirable.

"I was about to come get you."

Just as he did now. His gaze, bold and hungry, swept over her. "Women have more to put on."

He slowly walked to her, like a knight coming to claim his lady. "You didn't have to bother on my account."

Her body tingled. "Shane."

His finger traced her lower lip. His warm breath flowed over her heated skin. "You make it hard for me to resist you."

Her forehead dropped on his muscular chest. She couldn't say it while she looked at him. "If you got a place . . ."

"We both know what would happen, and so does your mother." His arms closed around her, anchoring her to his taut body. "She trusts both of us."

Paige blew out a frustrated breath and accepted the inevitable . . . at least for tonight. "I can see why none of my friends live at home."

"There is that." Taking her hand, he pulled her toward the curved teal leather sofa and turned on the television. "There's not much on tonight. Joan Crawford in *Mildred Pierce*. Heather Locklear in *The Return of Swamp Thing*."

She sat, slipping off her sandals and drawing her feet

under her. The only light in the room was a lamp on dim
at the other end of the sofa and the TV. Necking seemed
a definite possibility. The news was just coming on.

"*The Return of Swamp Thing*. At least it led you to
believe there would be a happy ending for the Swamp
Thing and the woman he'd saved and loved. Mildred
loved her daughter too much, and they both paid for it."

Shane turned to her with the remote in his hand.
"Sometimes love hurts."

Paige knew that all too well. "I—" She gasped as
two women's faces filled the television's wide screen.
She grabbed the remote from Shane.

"What—"

"Shhh." Holding up her hand, she came to her feet
and increased the volume of the TV. Her hand clenched
as she stared at a picture of Dominique Falcon-Masters,
Trent's wife, and that of another woman. The resem-
blance between the two striking women was so strong
they had to be related.

"Today it was confirmed that a European fashion
magazine was the high bidder to publish the wedding
photos and story of billionaire real estate mogul Blade
Navarone's marriage to Sierra Grayson."

"We're missing the movie," Shane said.

Paige evaded Shane's hand reaching for the control.
Her gaze remained locked on the TV. She'd heard
about the secret marriage, but hadn't connected it to
Dominique.

"Dominique Falcon-Masters, cousin to the bride,
with a growing reputation as a photographer, and her
mother, Boston socialite and art patron Felicia Falcon,
will author the piece. The money will go to a Darfur
charity."

Cousins. Why hadn't she had his wife, Dominique,
investigated instead of concentrating on Trent?

A picture flashed on the screen of an incredibly handsome man staring down into the face of a beautiful woman. The love, the sizzle between them, leaped from the photograph. Grudgingly, Paige acknowledged that Dominique was indeed good. The picture was sensuously beautiful.

"The newlyweds, married July twentieth at the Navarone Riviera Maya resort in Playa del Carmen, remain secluded on the estate of Mrs. Navarone in Santa Fe, New Mexico."

"So that's where she was?" Paige whispered, her gaze glued to the TV screen.

"Paige, talk to me."

She swung around to Shane. So many conflicting emotions were running through her, but anger was at the forefront.

Shane wanted to curse on seeing the shattered look on Paige's face. Why hadn't Rio warned him? "Honey, are you all right?"

"I—excuse me." Tossing the control toward the sofa, she tried to run from the room. She'd gone no more than a few steps when Shane captured her arm.

It was risky, but he had no intention of letting her go. "We talk and you keep your head up. Remember?"

She looked away. She didn't want to talk. She was too afraid of what might come out.

"You wouldn't be this upset unless it was close and personal," he suggested carefully. "I want to help."

"Help?" The single word trembled over her lips. "Only Mother can do that."

His eyes narrowed on her face. There was one certainty that would help her cope with this. "Your mother loves you."

"Not enough." There, she'd said the painful words,

but then she couldn't meet the censure in Shane's eyes. "There's never any excuse for lies."

He was walking a dangerous tightrope. "You can't say that until you have all the facts."

"And she won't give them to me, and I'm tired of asking." Anger and tears sparkled in her eyes. "You didn't lie to me about how you feel about relationships."

His hands flexed on her arms. He'd lied about so much more. He didn't want to add more lies. Yet somehow he had to help her to understand. "Paige, you're obviously upset because of what you just saw on TV. Doesn't your mother's love and devotion for twenty-seven years weigh heavier?"

"Not anymore." Her voice shook, then firmed. "No matter what, I could always count on my mother to put me first, to be there."

His dark brow lifted. "You sound jealous."

"What if I am?" Trent didn't have any right to her mother. His absurd question was so far-fetched, it was ridiculous. But she knew there was something going on between them. "She's my mother, and I need her here."

"And that's where she is," Shane said.

Now. What about the times since her father's death? What about next week or the next? What drew her to Trent? She'd lost her father. She couldn't lose her mother. She wanted to explain to Shane, but didn't know how. "I don't feel like watching a movie. Good night."

"Running isn't going to solve anything," he said, disappointment in his face.

"I'm tired. Good night." She twisted out of his arms, and he let her go.

"You should know your mother will always be in your corner. She'd fight anyone who tried to harm you. She certainly warned me off. Twice."

That got her attention. Slowly, she turned to face him.

"I don't mind telling you I would have rather faced a barrage of gunfire." He shook his dark head. "Anyone who messed with you would have your mother to deal with. Mrs. Osgood and Mrs. Hamilton found that out at the luncheon. No more free rides at your expense."

"They had to give up their seats for Mother and a security guard who, of course, never sat. They were both embarrassed and livid." Paige had heard from a couple of friends who were there. Her mother had only said the luncheon had gone well. She wasn't the gloating type.

"Their own fault." Shane didn't have any pity for the two gossipers. "You can't tell me those two didn't spread what had happened here to anyone who would listen," Shane told her. "I bet they wished they'd kept their mouths shut when the governor's wife showed her support of your mother. And don't forget her help with Gayle. Your mother is firmly in your corner. No one can change that." He walked to her, taking her forearms in his hands. "Not even you."

Her head rested against his chest. "No matter how much I push her away, she keeps coming back."

His hand cupped her cheek. "Love will do that."

Her cell phone rang. If she hadn't been waiting for Gayle's call she wouldn't have answered, not with Shane staring at her like he wanted to eat her alive. "Gayle."

"I quit tonight," the young woman said.

Paige glanced at Shane. Love meant acceptance. "It was your decision to make."

"That's all you have to say? You aren't disappointed?"

"I believe in you, Gayle. You'll find another job."

"Thank you," Gayle said, clearly relieved. "I'm seriously going to look into decorating for people. I helped the man put the tile down in the kitchen. He said I did a good job. The home improvement store has classes, and it's on the bus line."

Paige glanced at Shane again. "That's a wonderful idea. You'd be great at it."

"I think so," Gayle said. "Good night, Paige, and thanks for giving me room to make my own decision."

Paige looked at Shane as he curved his arm around her waist. "You're welcome. Good night."

She disconnected the call and shoved the cell phone back into her front pocket. "She thanked me for giving her room. If you hadn't come by the office today, I might not have."

"You wanted her to know you were there for her."

"But it was the wrong approach."

"Don't beat yourself up over it," he told her. "I've lived longer."

"I can tell by the stoop of your shoulders and the gray hair," she quipped, hoping to get back to their earlier playful mood before she'd seen Dominique's picture.

"Old?" He tugged her closer. "Why don't we just see about that?"

His mouth melded with hers, soft, gently, then heated, his tongue delving into her mouth, sucking and tasting. With a low moan, Paige sank into him for a heart-pounding, body-altering moment, then she pushed away, rapidly blinking.

"I'm sorry. Good night." Biting her lower lip, she turned and ran from the room.

Feeling helpless, Shane let her go. By the time he reached the bottom of the stairs, she had disappeared.

He wanted to help her, but Paige didn't want to talk and there was nothing he could do. She was upset enough that she hadn't become suspicious about his lack of pointed questions.

Shane stopped at her door, knowing she was inside and upset. Paige needed to let it out, not keep it in, if she was hurt. For too long she'd been the little girl trying to fit in, to please everyone, and it had continued in the woman. Although she was getting better, she wasn't over her insecurities yet.

Blowing out a breath, Shane went to his room. There was time enough to warn Mrs. Albright in the morning. She'd spent enough restless nights worrying about Paige.

Unhooking his cell, he stared at a blank screen and cursed softly. He might have prevented this.

The cell phone linked him to Blade and his security team. He checked it frequently to ensure it was operating properly. Anything man-made could malfunction. No wonder he hadn't received a call from Rio.

He retrieved a second phone from his bag and activated it. Four messages. All from Rio. All urgent. The first one had come two hours ago.

Walking onto the balcony, he punched in Rio's number. He answered on the second ring.

"You all right?"

"Yeah. Dead phone."

Total silence stretch between them. Communication was paramount. They'd learned that as Army Rangers, and had incorporated it as the key directive of security. He had to be able to communicate with all of his men, and them with him. No matter what the circumstances. No exceptions. Forgetting was grounds for reprimand, and possible termination.

"Was the urgent message about the news broadcast about Blade and Sierra?" Shane asked in the silence. Rio had read the report of the night Shane tackled Paige, and knew Paige was searching for answers.

"Yes. You just checked in under the wire," Rio said.

"Glad you didn't call the firm I hired to check on me," Shane said. As second in command, it was Rio's responsibility to ensure that everyone, including Shane, was all right.

"Jefferson is on standby" came Rio's answer.

Blade's pilot. Shane blew out a breath. There was no way to tell *why* a phone wasn't being answered. Shane could take care of himself, but accidents happened. "It won't happen again."

"Paige."

There went that uncanny perception of Rio's again. A helpless feeling came over Shane. He didn't like it. Nor was he used to not being able to fix things. That was what he did, what he prided himself on. "We were watching the TV and she saw the news piece. She's hurting, and it's not going to get better until Mrs. Albright comes clean."

"Have you thought of what will happen when she does?"

"Yes." Shane's gut clenched. He'd be exposed. "It's for the best. Neither of them can go on like this."

"And if she turns against you?"

Rio didn't shy away from the tough questions. Shane wouldn't shy away from the equally tough answers. "Her happiness comes first."

"I thought you'd say that. Keeping both their secrets puts you in the middle."

"There's no other way."

"So you say. Night."

"Night." It was going to be a long one.

"Paige has connected you with Trent Masters."

Mrs. Albright gasped and swung around from the kitchen counter, the package of coffee falling from her hand. Shane caught the bag before it hit the tiled floor.

"How?" Shock radiated across her unlined face. Her hands covered her trembling mouth.

"We were watching television last night. There was a news story that a European magazine won the bid for Blade and Sierra's wedding story and photos. The wedding date was mentioned. Paige's happy mood changed immediately on seeing a picture of Dominique. She wouldn't explain, but she said enough for me to know you were involved," he explained. "My phone was down and Rio couldn't warn me. I'm sorry."

Her hands lowered. "I didn't want this to happen."

"It was a secret that, unfortunately, wouldn't be kept forever." He placed the coffee on the counter. "I don't know if she's figured it all out, but I do know that she's hurting. It's time for you to tell her everything."

"No." Frantically, Joann shook her head. "She doesn't understand. I'll lose her."

You're losing her anyway, Shane thought. "You've always been the one person she could count on. She doesn't like sharing you," he said cautiously.

Mrs. Albright gripped the smooth edge of the counter. "She was there the day Trent came to the house with Dominique, Luke Grayson, and his soon-to-be wife, Catherine Stewart. Marshall recognized Trent immediately because he looked so much like his father. Paige came home to all the shouting and heard Trent ask me if I was his mother," she confessed, barely above a whisper. "Marshall went into a rage. They left and Marshall called them con artists, and forbid us to mention the incident ever again."

"Please sit down." Shane helped the older woman to

a chair and got her a glass of water, tilting it to her lips when she made no move to drink.

"She and Zach were told their brother died in an automobile accident when the car I was driving ran into a lake, so she believed her father and didn't give any credence to what Trent asked. At least, I prayed she didn't." Tears sparkled in Mrs. Albright's eyes. "As you know, Stephen—Trent's birth name—wasn't in the car. I'd left him where I knew he'd be safe. I-I developed pneumonia from being in the water and was hospitalized afterward for a long time. My parents were devastated at the loss of their first grandchild. Do you know how guilty I always felt for that lie? It's a guilt I'll never get over."

Shane took her cold hands in his. "You had no choice. You saved Trent's life."

"I know. Marshall knew Trent wasn't his. The day I caught Marshall standing over Trent's crib with a pillow in his hands is one I'll never forget. And yet . . ." She swallowed. "I don't want to gain Trent and lose Paige and Zach. Then, too, Paige adored her father. I don't want her or Zachary to know what a cruel, heartless man he was."

Hearing the soft footsteps of the maid, Shane whispered, "Macy's coming," and moved away.

Mrs. Albright swatted at the moisture on her face, then stood and moved to the kitchen counter. Trembling hands pushed the bag of coffee aside.

"Good morning, Mrs. Albright, Mr. Elliott," Macy greeted. "How long will Paige be gone?"

"What?" Mrs. Albright swung around, gripping the handle of the carafe.

Macy frowned, took a step closer. "Are you all right?"

"Why would you think Paige is gone?" Mrs. Albright asked instead of answering the maid's question.

"I saw her leaving with her laptop and a suitcase when I came in this morning," Macy told her. "I was going to do the weekly grocery shopping later this morning and I wanted to know about meals for the rest of the week."

Mrs. Albright turned back to the counter. "I-I'm not sure."

The maid frowned. "Is everything all right?"

"Yes." Mrs. Albright stuck the carafe under the faucet and turned on the water.

With one last puzzled look at Shane, the maid left.

Shane saw Mrs. Albright's shoulders shaking. He walked over and shut off the water, took the carafe from her trembling hands. Tears rolled down her cheeks. "My baby's gone, and she might never forgive me."

It twisted his insides to see her crying because he knew somewhere Paige was probably in just as bad a shape.

The day had been long; the night would be even longer. Deep in thought, Shane walked the grounds of the Albright estate. Sleep was impossible. He hadn't even tried. It wouldn't be the first time Paige had kept him awake. He wasn't taking any bets that it would be the last.

Stopping near the Japanese garden room, he gazed up at Mrs. Albright's window. The lights were on and it was past one in the morning. She'd had a rough day. He could well imagine what she was going through. He had tried to help her get through the day by keeping her busy.

They'd gone to a garden center, had lunch at Noah's

restaurant, visited Gayle. Mrs. Albright had tried, but the sadness had never left her eyes. She hadn't been able to shake the possibility that Paige would never forgive her.

It had been the same for him when he and Paige were on the outs. He'd gone to Dallas to check on the security of Navarone Place to keep his mind occupied. It hadn't helped. He still thought of her, missed her. It wasn't lost on him that the job he'd once loved was no longer paramount to him.

When Paige had become the most important thing in his life, he didn't know. It didn't matter. She was the one—and he hadn't even known he was searching, hadn't even considered the possibility.

Perhaps it was because she needed him. There wasn't anything he wouldn't do for her. He didn't mind that she came to him with her problems. He needed her just as much. They were better together than they were apart. She needed to know and accept that as well. He hoped their time apart would teach her the same thing it had taught him.

They were meant to be together. He just had to figure out how.

He wouldn't even entertain the thought that once she knew why he'd come, learned that he was the man who'd taken her down on Trent's estate, she'd despise him. He wouldn't be able to function if he thought about it.

At least she hadn't gone far. He hadn't expected her to. Paige took her responsibilities seriously. Not only was the ball coming up, but there were Noah and Gayle to consider as well.

He'd known how to find Paige. She'd used her credit card to check into a suite at the Ritz-Carlton downtown. For Mrs. Albright's peace of mind, he'd told her and asked her not to call Paige. She needed time to work through her anger and her fear of being pushed aside.

Unless she overcame her lifelong fear and learned to trust unfailingly no matter how things might appear, she wouldn't forgive her mother or him, for that matter.

He'd give her tonight, but if she didn't call by tomorrow afternoon, he was going for her.

Paige Albright, what are you doing? Paige had asked herself that same question several times since she'd checked into the hotel suite yesterday morning. Thankfully, they'd had a vacancy. She had yet come up with an answer she was comfortable with.

Was she here because she was angry with her mother and tired of the lies, or because she was testing her mother's love?

Sighing, she looked out the wide expanse of glass. The Atlanta skyline stretched before her. She hadn't missed a day from work since she'd lost her father, and only twice before then.

She was definitely hiding. She didn't want to see the disappointment in Shane's face, or deal with the growing possibility that she had to share her mother with a stranger.

She'd briefly gone by the office to tell Jackie she would be working off site for the rest of the week so she wouldn't be distracted. She could be reached by her cell phone. Jackie wasn't fooled. There was no way Paige could disguise that she had been crying. Jackie had hugged Paige and said to call if she wanted to talk.

Talk wouldn't help.

Paige's gaze dropped to her computer screen, which listed all the things she had to do before the ball. The wondrous event had lost its magic. She felt . . . adrift. As if she were alone with nothing and no one. The other night, before the news program, she'd had such hope that her life would be the way she had always dreamed.

Until a photograph had snapped her back to reality.

Paige was never the one who walked away with the grand prize. She always lost. For a while she had let herself believe. She'd stuck out her neck and with it her emotions, and the results were what she'd eventually always gotten:

It had been chopped off.

Shane would leave her eventually. He was everything she wasn't. He'd want a woman who was as confident and self-assured as he was. She'd been naive to think he'd stay.

As for her mother, even if she didn't see Trent, Paige had no doubt he would remain a wedge between them. Love meant risks she wasn't sure she wanted to take. It hurt too badly when you were let down . . . and she always was.

A knock sounded on the door. She expected two deliveries, both from printing companies. Paige had hired Aaron to do the programs for the Masquerade Ball. Like the bank president, she saw no reason to penalize Aaron because of his association with Jackie. He did excellent work, but he didn't have the capability of printing on the gift bags, so she had hired a graphic design firm she'd used before. Her life might be in a mess, but she had no intention of letting it ruin the ball. Saving the file, she went to the door.

As she had thought, it was the messenger from the graphic design company. Signing, she accepted the package and tipped the smiling young woman one of the two ten-dollar bills she had shoved into the pocket of her slacks for that purpose.

At least somebody was happy, she thought, wincing.

She would not become cynical. Life was meant to be enjoyed. Ripping the envelope's tab, she pulled out the white, medium-sized shopping bag just as another knock came at the door. Sticking the bag and package under her arm, she pulled the other bill out of her pocket and opened the door. And froze.

"Hello, Paige."

Surprise turned to need. Shane looked incredibly handsome in a beige-colored sports jacket and white shirt. She gripped the doorknob. She was not throwing herself into his arms no matter how much she wanted to. She was facing reality. Sooner or later he'd move on.

"How did you find me?"

He shrugged the broad shoulders that she so desperately wanted to lay her head on. "Doesn't matter. Someone was worried about you."

She almost asked who when she caught a movement. Her mother stepped up beside him. Her eyes were red, her lids puffy. Paige forgot her anger and rushed to her. "Are you all right? What happened?"

Her mother trembled. Tears pooled in her eyes. "I— you . . ." Her voice trailed off.

"Mother, what's wrong?" Paige's heart lurched. She looked to Shane and forced herself to ask, "Is Zach all right?"

"Your brother is fine. She was worried about you," Shane explained.

Paige jerked her gaze back to the tear-ravaged face of her mother. Guilt stabbed her. She'd done that to a woman who loved her despite her inadequacies. Shame quickly followed. "Mother, I'm sorry." Paige hugged her, felt her tremble, the tears moistening the shoulder of Paige's blouse.

In that moment she realized Trent wasn't driving her and her mother apart; Paige was doing that herself.

Shane was right. She was afraid of losing her mother. She was an adult, but she still needed her mother's love and support. She'd been frightened of losing both and tried to distance herself.

"It's all right," her mother said, clutching her tightly.

"No." Paige lifted her head, swallowed the lump in her throat. Her mother didn't deserve this. "It's not all right, but it will be."

"Why don't we go inside?" Shane picked up the ten-dollar bill, the gift bag, and the envelope she'd dropped on the floor.

"Of course." Her arm around her mother, Paige stepped back into the suite. She felt awkward.

"Looks like you're working." Shane handed her the things he'd picked up.

Paige threw Shane a grateful look. "Yes, I'm finalizing plans for the ball." *And running away.* "This is the gift bag I had designed."

"You must be anxious to look at it," her mother said. "Please go ahead."

Paige smiled at her mother, the one person who always understood her so well. At least until Shane came into her life. Both waited patiently for her to examine the bag. Neither condemned her for disappearing without even a note. She had a lot to make up for. Trust worked both ways.

"I am. Thanks." Paige unfolded the bag and really looked at it for the first time. The four destinations of the event were there on each side, but missing were the dotted lines and image of an airplane with the premier sponsor's logo connecting the cities. "Oh, no!"

"What is it?" Shane asked, stepping to her side.

"The printer left off the major sponsor, the airline." Paige kept turning the bag in her hands in disbelief.

"Can they be done over?" Shane asked.

Paige shook her head. "I was able to purchase the bags at a deep discount because the company was going out of business. This order was shipped months ago." She shoved her hand through her unbound hair. "I've got to call the graphic company." She quickly crossed the room and picked up her cell.

The knock sounded on the door. "Shane, please get that. That should be the program. Hopefully, Aaron's company did a better job."

"Got it." Shane opened the door and signed for the package, tipping the messenger. Closing the door, he opened the package and crossed the room to Paige.

"Mr. Lott, please. Thank you," Paige said into the phone. As she waited on hold, she pulled out an eight-by-eight glossy black booklet featuring the Eiffel Tower and a Paris streetlight centered against a red background. On the front, bold letters spelled out BI-ENVENUE.

"Is it all right?" Her mother asked from her side.

"I know the word *welcome* is correct on the front, but my French is a little rusty for the other English translations inside the program," Paige said. "The correct spelling is at my office."

"I'll check." Shane held out his hand.

"Why am I not surprised?" Paige said, and gave him the program. Then, "Mr. Lott, this is Paige Albright. I've just received the bags and they're not printed properly." She described the situation.

In two minutes she knew what had happened, but not how to fix it. Although she wouldn't have to pay for the printing, that didn't solve the problem. She disconnected her cell.

"The printer used the wrong proof, the one before the airline decided to come aboard." She rubbed her forehead. "I courted them for six months before they decided to come on as the premier sponsor. The CEO and several major stockholders will be there, and their airline is only listed on the inside page of the program. This is a disaster."

"No, it isn't," her mother said, the last of her tears gone. "You'll just have to figure out how to showcase the airline in another way."

"Your mother is right," Shane said. "If the bag is out, what can you do with just as much impact?"

Paige stared at both of them. They were staring back at her with complete confidence when she didn't have a clue. She started to say she didn't know, but one look at Shane and she swallowed the words.

"I planned for the attendees to receive the bags at the beginning of the event so they could put their goodies inside from each city they visited. Seeing the airline images on the bag would emphasize that the airline served all the destinations," she said slowly.

"When the guests arrive, their first impression is of course the beauty of the magnificent estate where dreams are made. The second should be that this is happening in large part because of the contribution of this airline, which gives them wonderful service, but also gives back to the community. Then the next time they travel, they'll think of and want to support the company."

"So you want to give the guests an impression of the generosity of the airline as soon as they get out of the car at valet parking," her mother said. "Would a banner do the trick?"

Paige liked the idea immediately. "A welcoming banner could be placed at the arched entryway being erected for the guests to enter from valet parking to the double-door entrance. We could put one on the other side, too, so that when they leave, we can thank them for coming and hope they enjoyed their evening just as passengers are told at the end of every flight."

"Can you get a banner?" Shane asked.

"After the fiasco with the graphic design company that I've thrown a lot of business to over the years, you betcha," Paige said. "In case some people miss the banner, how about if we hire flight attendants to welcome them, handing them a boarding pass with a perforated section to register to win a trip anyplace the airline flies."

"The rich love free stuff just as much as anyone." Shane crossed his arms.

"Exactly." Paige smiled. "That should further solidify to the airline that the Carl Rowe Foundation appreciates their contribution, but also let the guests know it is the airline carrier of choice, not chance."

"I'll donate the ticket," her mother and Shane said at the same time.

"Thank you both, but I'll take care of it." How could she have forgotten that her mother, and now Shane, were always there for her? "However, I need you and Shane's help on another project."

"I hope this never gets out," Shane teased as they left the Carrington Estate. They had been busy since they'd left Paige's hotel that afternoon. Their initial stop had been to the graphic design firm.

Paige had been right when she'd said the graphic design company would do the banners; the owner had even agreed to design and print the boarding pass with the contest entries. Paige had been as gracious as Shane expected, reminding the man to be sure to put the name of his company on the back, and add that it was donating the boarding passes.

The next stop was to pick up the daisy-shaped boxes

and doilies from the container store and deliver them
to the gourmet cookie shop. Afterward they'd swung
by a retailer for several cases of chocolate candy bars.

"I think it would be a nice touch to put little gold or
red elastic bows on them," Paige had commented.

Of course her mother had agreed. Of course he had
agreed as well. Since the bows were already made, putting them around the candy bars had been a cinch. It
was another detail that would make the night stand out.
What was even better was listening to Paige and her
mother talk and laugh. He noted that Paige hadn't let
her mother fully see the gift bag. He reasoned she
wanted to keep the other destinations a secret.

Both knew nothing was settled, but neither was willing to disrupt the harmony between them. Neither was
Shane. It was almost ten when they pulled out of the
black iron gates of the Carrington Estate and headed
home.

"Thank you. More help is coming to finish up tomorrow, but I wanted to get a head start," Paige said,
sitting beside him in the front seat of his rental.

"In case another problem came up," Shane said.

She smiled at him. "Exactly."

"The Carrington Estate is beautiful and perfect,
Paige." Mrs. Albright's eyes remained red, but the
hopelessness in them had been replaced with happiness. "I don't think I've been back for an event since
your debut."

"Then it will be a night to remember for both of
you," Shane commented, enjoying their happiness.

"Shane, you can drop me off at the house," Mrs. Albright told him. "If you need any more help, Paige,
call me."

"I'm going to take you up on it." Paige turned
around in the seat to look at her mother. "In the mean-

time, I think I'll give up the hotel room and come home."

Her mother's smile wobbled. "I'd like that."

"It occurred to me too late that I should have kept this place," Paige said, moments after they entered her hotel suite. The curtains remained open, giving a beautiful view of Atlanta by night. The maid had turned down the king-sized bed. Swiss chocolates were on the pillow.

Shane's arms curved around her, kissed her upturned chin, her waiting lips. "I won't lie and say it didn't cross my mind, but your mother needs to know that you and she are all right."

Sighing, she placed her head on his chest. How she'd missed this, missed him. "We might not have been if not for you. You have a way of making complicated things seem simple."

"Old age," he bantered.

Chuckling, Paige lifted her head. "I think we had this discussion before. It went like this." Pulling his head down, she kissed him deeply, holding nothing back. As she watched him slip on those tiny bows with his long-fingered hands, she'd decided he was worth the risk. No matter what, he was there for her, and he did it willingly. She wasn't going to be a coward ever again.

He held her just right, kissed her as if she were his salvation. She knew he was hers.

Her hands tugged out his shirt. She wanted to feel his warm, supple skin beneath her fingertips, excite him as he excited her.

"Paige," he moaned, his hands cupping her hips against his hard masculinity. "Maybe you shouldn't do that."

She laughed, a sexy, throaty sound. In Shane's arms, his mouth and hands on her, she felt powerful and all woman. "I disagree. I missed you. Missed this." She nipped his earlobe, felt his shudder, his hands clench.

Helpless, she arched against him, powerless to do anything else. His desire didn't frighten her, it pleased her. She tucked her head.

"What?" He lifted her head. His dark eyes stared down into hers.

"I—"

"Say it."

There was a command in his voice, made deeper by his passion, but the underlying gentleness and patience was also there. "I'm shameless with you."

His eyes, dark with desire, narrowed. "Do you regret it?"

"No."

"I'm the same with you. I hear the water running in the bathroom and I imagine you stepping naked into the shower, the water flowing over your skin. I imagine I'm there with you, my mouth and hands caressing, pleasing you." His forehead rested against hers. "You enter a room and I can't get enough of just looking at you. Your laughter makes me wonder if you will be playful in bed or wild and untamed."

Her heart thudded, her breathing grew ragged, her hands fisted. "I want you and yet—"

He kissed her on the mouth, the barest touch of his lips on hers. "When it's time, you'll know." He stepped back. "I'll grab the laptop and you can pack."

She picked up her suitcase from the closet. Instead of packing, she crossed the room to where he was unplugging her computer. "Why do you put up with me? Another wo—"

He put his finger over her mouth, moving with that

fluid quickness of his that stunned her into silence. "For me, there is no other woman."

The suitcase dropped from her hand. Her entire body trembled. "I—" She had to swallow and try again. "I'm going to hold you to that."

His thumb replaced his finger. He grazed her lower lip. "I figured you would."

"Well, I guess I better go pack." Picking up the suitcase, she went to pack. Hot damn. She was Shane's woman.

Chapter 19

Paige knew she should be working, but she just couldn't concentrate. She'd turned on her computer when she arrived at work that morning, but little else.

It was Shane's fault, of course.

Shane's woman. She hadn't been able to get his startling admission out of her mind. From the torrid kiss he'd given her last night before she'd gone into her room, and the one this morning after he walked her to her car in the garage, he had no plans to let her. Good, because, as she'd said, she planned to hold him to it.

He grounded her, made her feel invincible. He might not be thinking of forever, but somehow she'd get him around to that. She refused to think otherwise.

A brisk knock sounded on her door. "Come in."

The door opened and the last person on earth she'd have expected came in. "Hello, darling Paige," Russell greeted.

Her good mood evaporated. She straightened in her chair. "Russell, what are you doing here?"

He quickly crossed the room and rounded her desk. She studied him with mild annoyance. "I had to see you," he finally answered, grasping her hands before she could evade him.

"But you're supposed to be in Beijing until next week."

"I couldn't stay." His hands tightened in despair around hers. "I was no good during the negotiations so I came home. I had to be with you."

Paige could only stare. Russell, like her father, always believed in business first and always. "But the e-mail I sent—"

"It doesn't matter," he told her, cutting her off. "You were reacting to my shameful e-mails. You'll never know how much reading them the next day made me want to slit my own throat, knowing that they cost me the only woman I'll ever love."

This time she pulled free. She wanted nothing from Russell, least of all his love. Even polite friendship was iffy. He'd crossed the line when he'd attacked Shane. "Russell, I've explained that I don't feel the same way."

"Your father wanted us together," he reminded her. "Doesn't his last wish mean anything to you anymore?"

Hurt and anger splintered through her. She shot to her feet. "How dare you say anything like that! I loved Father and you know it."

"Please forgive me, Paige." Standing, looking distressed, he shook his head, paced away, then back. "This entire situation hasn't been easy. I've loved you for so long. I thought if I was patient with you, you'd see we were right for each other and we'd unite our families as one."

"I'm sorry, Russell, but it can't be the way you want," she said.

"Because of Elliott," Russell retorted. "He's turned your head, made you forget who you are and what plans we had. What plans your father had for us. Marshall would have been so proud of our getting married."

An ache started in her head. "Please, Russell."

He grasped her hands again, his face frantic. "I looked up to your father. Admired him. I was honored that he thought I was worthy to marry his daughter. We can't let his last wishes go unheeded. It would be as if he hadn't mattered. As if you'd forgotten him."

The office door opened and closed. "Get away from her," Shane said tightly, crossing the room in ground-eating strides.

Wide-eyed with fear, Russell released her hands, and quickly stepped away. "What would your father say if he knew you were dating a man who is taking advantage of your mother and making a laughingstock of you? He doesn't even have a job."

Shane grabbed Russell's silk tie, ignoring his frantic attempts to free himself. "Say another word and you'll be spitting out teeth. Be thankful you're in Paige's office so you get a pass." His grip unrelenting, he pulled Russell to the door. "Come back here or to her house at your own risk." Opening the door, he released Russell, then closed the door and returned to Paige.

His heart lurched on seeing her pale face, her hands clenched tightly together. He'd seen Jackie when he'd arrived, and she'd told him Russell was in Paige's office. "Don't let his lies upset you."

"I loved my father," she said softly, her voice filled with anguish.

He was a cheating bastard, Shane thought, but he bit back the words. "But you can't let that love decide how you're going to live."

"But I can't ignore it, either."

"The hell you can't." He took her arms, pulling her to him. "You pushed your way into my life. You're not going to walk out of it again."

"Shane—"

"No. If you want to honor your father's memory, we'll find another way, but you're not going to sacrifice your life on a bastard like Russell." His voice was sharper than she had ever heard.

"Shane—"

His mouth on hers stopped what she had been about to say. There was anger, a hint of desolation in the kiss that she would not have equated with a strong man like Shane. Deeply concerned, she sought to soothe him. She opened for him, kissing him as greedily as he kissed her. Her arms went around his neck to hold him, to freely give him whatever he needed from her. In doing so, she received as well—passion for a lifetime, pleasure only he could give her.

His dark head lifted. She whimpered at the loss.

Her eyes opened to find him staring down at her. She saw the worry in his face before he veiled his emotions. Her fingers traced the lines in his forehead. A smile trembled on her lips. "One day I'm going to win an argument."

He crushed her to him. "Where do you want to go for lunch?" He lifted her away, a wicked grin on his face. "Or we could order in. I give a mean foot massage."

"And I'd take you up on the last offer if it wouldn't get us both in trouble." She kissed him on the chin, then grabbed her purse.

"How about tonight?"

She thought of the oil Jackie had mentioned and grinned. "Only if I can return the favor one day, only a little higher up."

His dark eyes glinted. "I can't wait."

Her office phone rang late Wednesday afternoon just as Paige opened her door to leave work. She groaned, debated whether or not to answer, then went to pick up the receiver. She hadn't been able to get her massage that night or the following night because several of the volunteers hadn't shown up to stuff the gift bags.

She and Shane had spent the last few nights working at the estate instead of driving each other crazy with desire. With Gayle and her mother helping, they couldn't even sneak a kiss or two. She'd promised herself that wouldn't happen tonight, but with the ball three days away she couldn't take a chance.

Retracing her steps, she picked up the phone. "Hello, Paige Albright."

"Paige, I'm so glad I caught you."

Russell's mother. Why hadn't she looked at the caller ID? She didn't want to speak to Tess any more than she wanted to speak to her son.

"Paige?"

"Tess, I was about to leave," Paige finally said. "If this is about Russ—"

"Of course it is!" she cried, her voice breaking. "He's miserable without you. He loves you."

"Tess, I don't mean to be rude, but this is none of your concern."

"I'm his mother. Of course it concerns me," she said. "He's lost. I've never seen him so despondent. You were his life."

Paige did not want to hear that. "Tess—"

"How can you just abandon him?" she interrupted. "Russell has always been there for you, even more so after your father's death. He helped you get through a difficult time."

Guilt that she had been trying not to feel nudged her. "I'm thankful, but it doesn't change how I feel."

"It should," she snapped. "Russell, not your mother's

houseguest, was there when you needed someone the most. Russell is the one your father wanted you to marry. You can't have forgotten that."

As if you or Russell would let me, she thought. "I haven't forgotten."

"You were always so sensible, Paige," she went on to say. "Some women like that type of shiftless man, but your father wouldn't have approved, and you know it."

The muscles of Paige's stomach clenched. She didn't want to think about what her father would have thought of Shane. "Tess, I don't love Russell."

"Great marriages aren't always built on love, but on other, more important considerations like being of the same social class, mutual respect, compatibility. You and Russell make the perfect couple."

"No, we don't, and I refuse to marry a man I don't love. I'm sorry, I have to go."

"Paige, please, just see him." Her voice broke. "He's miserable. You can't do less to help him now that he needs you. He helped you."

"I'll try to drop by," Paige said, feeling trapped.

"Oh, Paige. He'll be so happy," Tess told her. "Russell loves you so much."

Tired of saying she didn't love him, Paige just said "Good-bye" and hung up. If Shane found out, he'd be livid. Pushing away from her desk, she retraced her steps, digging for her car keys. She saw the bottle of massage oil Jackie had given her. Was she woman enough to use it?

She was happy now, but she knew how it felt to be lonely. Opening the door, she headed for the elevator. Everyone had gone home. She'd stayed to double-check with Charles, the valet service, and all the myriad other services hired to make the ball a success.

Once she arrived home, she wanted her entire attention
to be on Shane as his would be on her, not on the ball.

In a matter of minutes she was in her car and exiting
the garage. Her cell phone rang just as she pulled onto
the street. She looked at the screen and smiled. "I'm on
my way home."

"It's almost dark," Shane said. "Drive carefully."

"I will." It was nice having a man worry about you.

"Your mother went to dinner with friends."

Her body actually tingled. "I wish I could hurry, but
traffic is almost at a standstill."

"You just drive carefully. Bye."

She inched up and stopped. "You think I'll be distracted talking to you?"

"I'm not taking a chance. Bye."

She chuckled. "Bye." Disconnecting the call, she
drummed her fingers on the steering wheel, wishing
the traffic would speed up. She didn't want to waste a
moment.

She glanced out the window and froze. Russell and a
woman who looked oddly familiar were getting out of
a cab in front of the Marriott Hotel. After paying the
fare, he curved his hand around her waist and they entered. He was smiling. He certainly wasn't the grieving
man his mother had described.

Traffic began to move. Instead of continuing, Paige
put on her turn signal and pulled in behind the cab.
Grabbing her purse, she didn't wait for the valet but
went to him, pulling a ten from her wallet. "I'm in a
hurry."

"Sure." Pocketing the money, he gave her a ticket.

"Thanks." Paige rushed into the hotel, careful to remain out of sight. Russell was at the registration desk.
The woman sat in a chair near the elevator. Paige's

The Way You Love Me 287

heart pounded as Russell left the desk and headed for the bank of elevators. The woman rose. When the doors opened, they got on together.

Paige's hands clenched. The desk clerk wouldn't give her the room number, but she was friends with the head of the wait staff. Shane could get the information as well. She'd figured out that he'd traced her from the credit card she'd used to book her room. If she called him, he'd want to come. She wanted to do this on her own.

"Room service." Paige lowered her voice and knocked on the suite's door.

"That was fast," Russell said, opening the door wearing a white hotel bathrobe, his bare legs sticking out from the terry-cloth bottom. His eyes rounded in shock, his mouth gaping.

"Hello, Russell." Paige stepped past him. The woman she'd seen with him had on a white bathrobe as well. "I don't think we've met."

The woman gasped, scrambled up and ran to the adjoining bedroom, slamming the door behind her. "I guess she's shy."

"Paige, this, I—"

She turned to him. "Your mother called and said you were brokenhearted over me. I'll be sure to call her back and let her know you're recovered. Good-bye."

"Paige, I . . . She's just for—"

"Don't say it, Russell," Paige snapped.

"Men have needs," he said, his voice pleading.

"Real men like Shane control themselves," she said.

Russell's eyes chilled. "He's just playing you along. He's a nothing. A nobody."

Paige got in his face. "He's more man than you'll ever

be. He doesn't take, he gives. Every time I've needed him, he's been there. No excuses. I'd trust him with my life."

He sneered. "That's a bit melodramatic."

"And beyond what a selfish liar like you can understand," she said. "Everyone saw through you, but I trusted you, made excuses for you. No more. Now get out of my way before I do something we'll both regret."

He moved aside. "He's no better than I am."

"A snake is better than you are." Head high, she walked out of the room.

Shane was waiting for Paige when she pulled into the garage. She'd called him after leaving the hotel. Before the motor died, Shane opened the door. "You're all right?"

After unfastening her seat belt, Paige stood. "Why am I so angry? I didn't love him."

Shane's hands swept up and down her arms. Paige fumed. "But you trusted him."

"It wasn't the first time," she told him. "I remembered seeing her the day you arrived. She came off the elevator with Russell when I saw him earlier that day." Paige frowned up at him. "I'd seen her before. I think it was in Father's office building."

Shane didn't want her going there. "It's over."

Slowly she shook her head. "He made a fool out of me."

"No. He was the fool," Shane said hotly. "Forget him and move on."

She blew out a breath and leaned into him. "Mother never liked him, neither did Jackie or Noah, for that matter. What's wrong with me that I couldn't see through him?"

"You think the best of everyone. Remember, he

fooled your father as well," Shane said, not batting an eye at the lie. He'd bet anything her father had planned on getting something out of the marriage. Perhaps even a huge chunk of Paige's inheritance. Russell's parents probably knew about the inheritance as well.

"You're right. I'm putting Russell out of my mind." She curved her arms around his neck, fitting her body to his. "You'd never deceive me."

It took all of Shane's control not to flinch. "I'll always have your best interests at heart."

"Good. After dinner, why don't we take a swim and you can show me?" Her mouth pressed against his, sweet and tempting.

What she was doing was filled with danger, but so exciting and sensual that she had no intention of not continuing. Just looking at Shane wearing only brief black swim trunks, stretched out before her like a pagan offering, made her a bit light-headed.

Her jaw had become unhinged earlier when he'd first slipped out of his pants and shirt. If his face was gorgeous, his body was magnificent. His chest was scored, his stomach flat, his thighs strong.

She'd stared and concentrated on breathing. When she'd looked her fill and lifted her head, she found him looking at her the same reverent, greedy way. Her heart thundered in her chest.

"If I touch you now I'm not sure I can stop this time," he'd told her, his voice thick and strained with desire.

This startling confession from a man who had no obvious weaknesses awed her. She felt powerful and so blessed to have found the one man who moved her, touched her heart and soul.

Turning away from him, she'd dived into the pool.

He'd come in after her. All the time they were swimming, she'd been thinking about this moment when she'd get to freely run her hands over his magnificent body.

With an unsteady hand she picked up the small bottle of massage oil. "Ready?"

He twisted his head to stare up at her as she knelt beside him. His eyes were dark with desire on her. "I'm not sure this is a good idea."

Neither was she, but there was no way she wasn't going through with the massage. She wanted her hands on him. "You promised and you'd never break a promise."

His hands fisted, he looked away.

Opening the bottle, she poured a generous portion of the exotic-smelling oil onto the palms of her hands, rubbed them together. Taking a deep breath she placed her hands on Shane's bare back. Muscles and skin rippled.

His reaction radiated up her arm and settled low in her belly, leaving her restless, achy. She embraced the sensations. For so long she had thought she'd never feel desire that almost consumed her. But what made it heaven was knowing the man she desired felt the same way about her.

Without hesitation, she straddled him, her knees on either side of his hips, her body poised over his. Only her hands touched him. Immediately he tensed beneath her.

"Paige." He growled her name in warning. "Don't."

Despite need gnawing at her, she smiled. Yes, she affected him as much as he affected her. Her warrior. Her Black Knight. "I can't do it properly otherwise. Just relax." Leaning forward, she kissed his shoulder, felt him shudder. Her hands trembled as much as her body. "I like touching you."

"And I like it too much," he rumbled.

Her hand stilled, then began a smooth glide up his back, her thumbs almost meeting at his spine. "You're beautiful."

He snorted.

She laughed, accidentally settling against him, cradling him between her thighs. Heat and hardness radiated from him to the very core of her. "I—" was all she got out before she found herself on her back, Shane staring down at her, his face and breathing harsh in the night.

For a split second, she experienced a forgotten fear, then just as swiftly it was gone. This was Shane; she was his woman. He'd never hurt her.

She placed her hands on his broad chest, felt a shiver race through him. Her gaze on him, her fingertips stroked the warm, supple skin. "I guess I did it wrong. I'll get better."

When he didn't say anything, just continued staring down at her, she knew he was fighting making her his. With her mother in the house, that wasn't going to happen. "You're the first man I've ever wanted to touch, to give a massage to. Before you came into my life I used to think there was something wrong with me because I didn't feel attracted to men. I thought there was a malfunction in me. Another thing wrong in the long list."

"There is nothing wrong with you."

Despite the tense situation, her smile returned. He would defend her even against herself. "I know that now. So forgive me if I enjoy having my hands on you a bit too much."

"Paige." Her name trembled over his lips, then they

were on hers, hot and greedy. He devoured her mouth, his tongue retreating, then returning to ravish and excite her. With a groan of pure pleasure, her arms went around his neck, drawing him to her, enjoying the feel of his hard body on hers.

His thick arousal pushed against her stomach, causing it to knot, her nipples to harden, the place between her legs to throb. Restlessly, she moved against him, trying to appease the ache.

Shane sucked in his breath. His hand cupped her woman's softness. "Paige." His voice was sharp with unfulfilled desire.

She whimpered, lifted her hips to increase the pressure. Her fingernails bit into his naked shoulder. "More."

Abruptly he lifted to his head. In one smooth motion he stood, pulling her with him to her feet. Their harsh breathing was loud in the night. Several seconds passed before Shane spoke. "You better go inside."

Reaching for her own control, Paige tried to remember that her mother was in the house, and not how badly she wanted Shane's hands and mouth on her again. "What about you?"

"I think I'll swim for a while."

She shook her head. "You wouldn't let me swim alone. I'm not going to let you, either."

"Pai—"

"No. Since this is not one of those times that kissing will make it better, how about a walk? The trails around the garden rooms are a mile and a half. We could jog, but you'd leave me in the dust. Or we—"

A small smile curved his lips, then ragged laughter rippled from his throat. He hugged her. "My Paige. Always thinking of the other person." He brushed his lips across the top of her head. "What did I ever do to deserve you?"

My Paige. Her heart was so full she could hardly get the words out. "We're both lucky and blessed."

"That we are." Hugging her tightly to him, he stepped back, curving his arm around her waist. Together they went to where they'd left their clothes. Picking up her robe, he slipped the pink terry robe on her, tied the sash, then picked up his shirt and jeans.

She sighed loudly. He glanced up, his gaze questioning, his hands pausing on the snap of his jeans. "It seems such a shame to cover up such an incredible body."

His intense gaze held hers. "Same thing I thought when I tied your robe."

She started to reach out to him, then changed her mind. It was a good chance they'd end up back on the mat, and this time they might not stop. Instead she picked up the massage oil and slipped it into her pocket. "I don't want to forget this. We'll need it next time."

Shane grinned. "I am indeed a blessed and lucky man."

With the Masquerade Ball less than thirty hours away, Paige sat behind her office desk Friday morning checking and double-checking everything in her notebook against the computer printout. Every day a new problem came up, but thank goodness she'd been able to solve them all.

Today the last delivery for the gift bags—lemon sugar cookies in a box shaped like the petals of a daisy—was to arrive by noon from the gourmet bakery. She'd already hired Gayle to be at the Carrington Estate to receive the delivery, and supervise the cookies being placed in the gift bags. When Shane drove Gayle to the estate he was going to put the banners up.

Paige shook her head. She hadn't even thought of securing the banners until he'd mentioned it last night when she was going over her list with him. It was certainly nice having a man who seemed to think of everything.

Her door opened after the briefest knock and Doris strode in, an empty coffee can in her hand. "We're out of coffee."

The smile on Paige's face evaporated. She and Doris had never been friends, but the other woman had become cooler toward Paige since the first day Shane came to the office.

"We're also low on snacks," Doris added.

In the past Paige might have overlooked the other woman's curtness because she wasn't the only one benefiting from the goodies Paige purchased. No more. She wasn't being a doormat for anyone else. "I've been busy as you can see. Perhaps you or someone else would like to restock the break room."

Doris blinked. "What?"

"Perhaps you or someone else would like to restock the break room this time," Paige repeated slowly.

"If I had your money I wouldn't quibble over a few bucks," Doris snapped. "It's not as if you can't afford it."

Paige stared at Doris and realized that she was jealous of her. "Doris, I suggest if you want coffee or snacks, you buy them. Now, if you'll excuse me, I'm busy."

"That's selfish," she huffed, and turned, almost bumping into Jackie. "I-I . . ."

"Paige is the most giving person I know." Jackie bit off each word. "You talk about being selfish when you've never spent one penny to buy one item for the break room or bring a dish when we have potluck. But you always eat."

Doris flushed, bit her lips. "I-I always wake up too late to cook."

"So you claim." Jackie folded her arms. "Before you start pointing fingers or slinging accusations, I'd say you better look in the mirror."

Doris tucked her head and started from the room.

"One more thing," Jackie said. "I suggest, as Paige said, if you want coffee, you purchase it. Now, I'm sure you have work to do." Doris quickly left.

"Jackie—"

Jackie held up her hand, cutting Paige off. "I hate to admit it, but Doris made me realize how we've all taken advantage of you. I'm sending out a memo that we can either start a goody fund or everyone will have to bring their own."

Paige started to argue, then realized that people often better appreciated those things they had to make an effort to obtain. "All right."

Jackie nodded at the papers on Paige's desk. "Everything going all right?"

"Yes. I'm just checking everything now," she told her boss.

A knock sounded on the door. She glanced up and smiled at Shane, then she noticed the white bakery box in his hands. Frowning, she shot to her feet. "The bakery didn't get the size of the cookies mixed up, did they?"

"Nope. Hello, Jackie." Shane placed the twelve-by-twelve box in the center of her desk. "This is for you."

"Hello and good-bye, Shane," Jackie said, slipping from the office and closing the door after her.

Paige looked from Shane's smiling face to the cookie box. He said, "It won't untie itself."

Nodding, she undid the ornate silk organza bow, then lifted the lid. Her hand trembled. Inside was a large, heart-shaped lemon sugar cookie.

"Aren't you going to taste it?" He rounded the desk to stand beside her.

"Yes." She took his mouth, dipping her tongue, swirling, tasting him. "Delicious."

"Delicious." He kissed her again, then gently touched her cheek. "I'd stay and continue this, but I have to pick up Gayle and put up a couple of banners."

"Then we'll have to continue once I'm home."

His eyes darkened. "Don't be late." Kissing her swiftly, he strode from the room, closing the door behind him.

Paige sighed, then quickly went back to work. She planned on going home tonight on time.

Saturday morning, waving good-bye to Paige as she left to do a final walk-through at the Carrington Estate, Shane accepted that his life had taken a turn he hadn't foreseen. He knew his responsibilities better than anyone. He had worked all his life to achieve respectability and a certain amount of financial success, but that was no longer enough. He didn't want to think of a day he couldn't see her, be with her.

He'd worked with two men he had been honored to call his friends, but he needed something more. He needed Paige. She was so pleased with little things he gave her—the white roses, the chocolates, and the cookie she refused to eat.

She filled his life, made the days brighter, his life better. His purpose had shifted. Looking back, he knew it had happened the second his body had covered hers. His heart had known it. It had just taken his brain longer to accept it and stop fighting.

Now the problem became: How did he make Paige his? Nothing could be built on lies and deceit. He abhorred both, had worked to leave them behind with his shiftless family. One thing he understood and accepted, there could never be anything between him and Paige until she knew the truth.

The call wasn't his. And that presented a problem.

Taking the path from the garage he opened the back door to find Mrs. Albright still at the kitchen table drinking her coffee as he'd known she would be. "After the ball, I want to tell Paige the real reason I'm here."

Joann's head lifted abruptly. Her slim fingers flexed on the handle of the delicate cup in her hand. "Russell is out of the picture. Why can't we just leave things alone?"

"Because lies have a way of coming out," he told her. "Paige has a right to know the truth."

"Is that the only reason?" she asked, staring at him.

He didn't hesitate. "I care about her, and every time she says how much she trusts me, I feel like the underbelly of a snake."

"So you plan to return to Santa Fe?" she questioned, watching him closely.

"I'm moving out in the morning and getting a place. I plan on sticking around for a few days," he said slowly. Or longer. Blade would understand the new direction Shane's life had taken. Rio was another matter. "I want to make sure Paige understands."

Mrs. Albright rose and took her coffee cup to the sink. "Have you considered that she'll know that you knew about Trent?"

He'd thought of little else. "Yes."

She turned, her face and voice determined. "I don't want you to tell her."

"You can't keep running from the truth," he told her. "It will destroy you."

"Perhaps, but it won't destroy my relationship with Paige," she reasoned.

"What about my relationship with her?" he asked, keeping his gaze level. "If we don't tell her and she finds out later, she might see this as another occasion of people making a fool out of her."

"That's a chance I have to take."

"You're condemning me to take it right along with you."

"I'm sorry, but that is the way it has to be. There are too many variables." Turning back to the sink, she began rinsing the breakfast dishes.

Shane quietly left the room. He didn't agree with her, but it was her call . . . at least for tonight.

Chapter 20

The taupe-and-beige evening gown was designed to draw a man's attention and keep it. Swirls of silk were bordered by flesh-toned organza that, at first glance, appeared to be naked flesh. The material skimmed over the body before flaring at the knees in flirtatious ruffles with a foot-long train. One shoulder was bare, the other had a bouffant sleeve. The back was bare to the waist. With every movement, the gown shifted, beckoned. It was daring, a bit wicked—and nothing like the old Paige would have worn.

Underneath she wore only bikini panties and thigh-high stockings. On her feet were four-inch matching evening sandals. After she and Shane had visited the Carrington Estate the first time, she had changed her mind about wearing the dark pink taffeta gown with the flowing skirt. She wanted a complete departure from the reserved Paige. Tonight she wanted to be a little wicked. If the night worked out as she'd planned, she'd be a lot wicked when morning came.

Taking a deep breath, she picked up her jeweled evening bag and left the room. Her steps were slow on the stairs. She paused when she saw Shane waiting for her at the bottom.

Her heart stopped, then raced. He was incredibly gorgeous. The black tux fit his broad shoulders perfectly, emphasizing his muscular build. Any woman would take a second look at the body, but the gorgeous face would stop her in her tracks, just as it had Paige.

"You take my breath away."

"Good, because you do the same to me," she said, feeling bold and daring. She had a feeling that this night would change everything between them. She continued down the stairs, feeling his hunger, the desire he barely kept in check, with each stop.

"I don't plan on letting you out of my sight tonight," he said, drawing her closer, his mouth hovering near hers.

"I'll be busy."

"No matter." His thumb graced across her chin. "I want to kiss you so badly, but one taste wouldn't be enough and I'd undoubtedly mess up your hair and wrinkle the gown."

She moistened her lips. "You tempt me to let you do just that."

"I know." He blew out a breath and grabbed her hand. "Let's get you to the ball before your guests arrive." He opened the front door. "Your mother is coming later. Your carriage awaits."

She laughed, a warm melodious sound that went straight to his heart. "Carriage?"

"The word seemed to fit. You're awakening like Sleeping Beauty or Cinderella. Only at midnight, we'll still be dancing."

Paige looked at the black limousine, the uniformed driver waiting by the open door. How many times had she dreamed of her modern-day knight taking her to the ball? It was impossible to resist a man who fulfilled her fantasies. "Thank you."

"Thank you," Shane said, helping her inside. As soon as the driver pulled off, he opened a waiting bottle and poured two glasses, handing her one. "Sparkling cider for now, champagne for later. To a memorable evening and night."

Paige clicked her flute to his, her hand slightly trembling. "It has certainly started out that way."

"And it is only going to get better."

The Carrington Estate was ablaze with lights in the windows and thousands of twinkles in the trees surrounding the home. Paige was pleased to see the long line of red-coated valets waiting for the guests. Their limousine pulled up in front of the awning, and a waiting hand opened the door.

Shane emerged first, then helped her out. The strong callused hand curved around her waist the moment she straightened, sending goose bumps skipping up her spine.

"The banner looks good."

It took a moment for Paige's mind to grasp what he was talking about. Then she saw the sixteen-by-three-foot blue-and-white banner stretched beneath the arched entryway. On either side was an airplane with the sponsor's logo. The middle said WELCOME AND HAVE A GOOD TIME in English and French.

They had barely taken a step before one of the off-duty flight attendants Paige had hired approached. "Welcome to A Night to Remember Masquerade Ball. Enjoy the evening and please enter to win a trip to any of our destinations around the world. There will be someone in every city to take your entry. Good luck."

"Thank you." Paige accepted the white card and checked out the printing. Perfect. She handed it to Shane. "I can't enter, but you can."

Shane slipped the card into his pocket. He didn't say anything until they stood in front of the heavy double doors at the entrance. "If I win, what are the chances that you'll go with me?"

She turned, brushed her lips across his. "I'd say your chances are excellent."

His eyes darkened with desire. "I'll hold you to that."

"I'm counting on you to."

Shane kissed her on the cheek, then escorted her inside. They walked from London, to Paris, to Rome, and finally to Monte Carlo. Each destination was lavish and had its own unique charm and appeal. Although she'd never gambled in her life, the roulette table appealed to her. "I'm trying that before the night is over."

"Why wait?" Shane asked.

"I couldn't."

His eyebrow lifted over deep black eyes she could gladly drown in. "Why?"

She laughed. "Because I'm the chairman."

"All the more reason for you to check it out first to make sure everything works. Don't you think?" he asked the croupier.

The young man grinned. "Sounds reasonable to me."

"We don't have any chips."

"I'm sure the establishment will stake us," Shane said. The dealer obligingly pushed four fifty-dollar chips across the green felt.

"Place your bet."

She looked at Shane. He smiled and nodded. She took a deep breath, then placed all the chips on black 27, the date they'd met.

The dealer set the wheel in motion, sending the steel ball spinning. Then, as it slowed, it bounced, finally landing on black 27.

"I won!" Paige screamed, then launched herself into Shane's arms, laughing up into his smiling face.

"I'd say we both did." He stared down at her, his mouth inches from hers.

Her head rested briefly on his chest. "You make me weak."

His arms tightened around her. "I can't say that I'm much steadier."

"Your winnings, ma'am?" the croupier said. "Place your next bet."

Paige looked from the stack of chips in the man's hands and back to Shane. "I think I'll hold what I have. You can keep the chips, and thanks again."

Shane chuckled. "Where to next?"

She didn't even think of telling him he didn't have to go with her. She enjoyed being with him. "To thank Charles for his impeccable taste and attention to details, then outside. I don't want the cars getting clogged up. Thanks to you, we can scan the invitation into the computer or check by name. Charles and I thought it a good idea to have waiters at the entrance with a choice of chilled wines."

"You certainly know how to plan an event."

"Thank you. I guess it's from sitting home reading about them. And I like to see people have a good time."

"I certainly plan to." He nodded toward the entrance to the room. "Looks like your mother decided to arrive early."

They quickly crossed to her. Mrs. Albright looked lovely in a long mint-green sequined lace gown. Shane kept his arm around Paige's waist. She was delighted her mother had accepted that they were attracted to each other.

"Hello, Shane. Paige, you look beautiful," her mother said, looking happier than she had in a long time. Part of it, Paige knew, was because Russell was out of her life. She just wished his own mother would stop calling and making excuses for him.

"Thank you," Paige said. "I thought you were coming later with Bitsy."

"I decided to come early in case you needed me." Mrs. Albright looked around the beautifully decorated room and smiled. "I can see I was worried for nothing."

"Ms. Albright, is everything to your satisfaction?" asked Charles, dressed in a black tux. He joined the group, his notebook clutched to his chest.

"It's fabulous, Charles. Just as I envisioned." Paige turned to her mother. "My mother, Mrs. Albright. Charles White, the executive manager of the Carrington Estate."

"Good evening, I can certainly see you take great pride in what you do," her mother greeted.

"Thank you. It's a pleasure to work with someone like your daughter, who knows what she wants," he said.

Paige cut a glance at Shane, shivered when their eyes met. She had what she wanted, and tonight she was going to show him.

"Paige had her debutante ball here," Mrs. Albright told him. A brief frown touched her brow, then was gone.

Paige saw it and thought she knew why. "Mother, why don't I show you around before the place gets crowded? We can finally visit London, Paris, and Rome together."

Sheer delight crossed her mother's face. "I wondered if the cities were just a coincidence when I saw the bags. Thank you."

"I'll go check on the parking situation, if you'd like," Shane offered. "Charles can go with me."

"Thank you both. I'll meet you out front shortly." She glanced at the thin diamond watch on her wrist. "I want to be there to greet the first guests."

"You're certainly going to be running around a lot," Shane said.

"I'm used to it. See you in ten." Taking her mother's arm, Paige started toward another room. She felt Shane's searing gaze on her all the way.

The ballroom sparkled with lavish crystal chandeliers, the shimmering gowns, the jewels the women wore, the crystal and china on the table. Again and again people stopped Paige to tell her what a wonderful time they were having. As she'd guessed, Monte Carlo was popular, but the couture stores in Paris, with actual gowns for purchase, ranked a close second.

"Paige, you've outdone yourself," Jackie said, looking pretty in a long silver gown. Aaron, in a tux, had his arm around her waist. "Everyone is having a good time. I've even been asked if this could be a yearly event."

"I've already booked the estate," Paige confessed. "Aaron, you're down for the programs. I wish I could give it all to you, but I want to spread the business around."

Before she'd finished, he was already shaking his head. "I'm just thankful you included me at all. I've already gotten several inquiries for other jobs."

"That's wonderful," Paige said.

"It sure is," Shane agreed.

"If you'll excuse us, we're going to see if the line for pictures in the Eiffel Tower is shorter," Jackie said.

"Catch you later," Shane said. "We're headed back to the roulette table."

Aaron shook his sandy-blond head. "I wish you better luck than we had. Wiped us out in ten minutes."

"I have a secret weapon." Shane, his arm around Paige's waist, stared fondly down at her.

She was definitely walking on a cloud. She'd won

almost a thousand dollars at the roulette table before switching to baccarat and then craps. She was on a winning streak and feeling invincible, and it was all because of the man who hadn't left her side all evening. Things couldn't get much better, she thought . . . until she looked up and saw Russell's mother's furious gaze directed toward her. Again.

"Ignore her." Shane stepped in front of Paige to block out the other woman. He'd been guarding her from Tess all night.

"Trying to." Paige shook her head. "I just can't get over her trying to get me to forgive Russell after what he did or being so mean-spirited as to attack your character. Her behavior is inexcusable."

Shane's forefinger gently swiped at her jutted chin. "I have a thick skin."

She leaned closer and whispered, "Not on the places I've felt."

Shane sucked in his breath. His eyes heated, darkened.

"Excuse me, sir. Don't I know you?"

Shane and Paige turned around to see a tall, rawboned man with a shock of white hair. Shane wanted to curse, but his expression didn't change. He should have thought of the possibility of someone recognizing him. Things were too dicey with Paige for mistakes, especially with Russell's mother watching their every move.

"Hello, Mr. Gaines," Paige greeted warmly. "This is Shane Elliott, a house guest of mother's, and a close friend. Mr. Gaines is an investment banker."

"Hello, Mr. Gaines." Shane extended his hand. "I've only been in the city a short while."

"Perhaps you saw him at church or with me around town," Paige offered.

The older man frowned, his blue eyes studying Shane. "I'm usually good with faces." He chuckled. "I have to be in my line of work."

"I'm sure you'll remember," Shane said, hoping the man didn't remember that he'd flown out to Blade's headquarters in Tucson to try and interest him in a business venture last year. Blade hadn't been interested, but Shane had been in the office at the time. "In the meantime, if you'll excuse us, we were headed to the casino in Monte Carlo."

"That reminds me. I better find my wife before she buys something else." He lifted his flute. "Great party as always, Paige."

"Thank you, Mr. Gaines."

Shane glanced over his shoulder and saw Russell's mother making her way toward Gaines. Time might have run out for him and Mrs. Albright. "I thought this was over at one. It's half past."

"It was supposed to be, but people are still here," Paige said, staring at the throng of people who showed no signs of going home. The live band kept people on the dance floor or milling in groups. Luckily, the estate had a private wine cellar so there was no chance of running out of wine.

"I suppose you have to stay until the last straggler goes home," he said, only slightly relieved to see Mr. Gaines disappear into the crowd without Tess speaking to him.

"Yes." She faced him. "I'm sorry."

He smiled. "I'm not. I get to hold you in my arms that much longer."

When 2:00 AM rolled around and half the guests were still there, Paige and Jackie decided to shut down the band and stop serving alcohol, leaving the partygoers little choice but to finally leave. Among the last group was the CEO of the airline, Frank Tate, and his wife, Lisa.

"We had a fabulous time," Lisa said. "We've decided to go to Europe next month for our thirtieth wedding anniversary."

"I'm delighted you enjoyed yourself, but the generosity of Mr. Tate made this night possible," Paige said, meaning every word.

"Thank you, Paige, but you went beyond our contributions." He smiled fondly down at her. "The ticket to anywhere we fly wasn't part of our donation. It shows you trust our airline."

Pleased, Paige smiled. "I do. You're the airline of choice, not chance."

"Hmmm," he said, his thin face thoughtful. "I like that. Mind if I toss it out to our marketing team?"

Paige laughed. "Of course not. The foundation owes you so much."

"I'm always glad to help." The executive nodded to Paige and Shane. "Good night."

"Good night," Paige said, then turned to Shane. "I know it's late, but everyone should be out of here in half an hour."

"Then I'll have you all to myself."

A hot shiver ran through Paige. "I can't wait," she admitted. She had a surprise for him. The night would be all that she had ever wanted. She just had to be brave enough to reach out and take it.

Thirty-three minutes later Paige watched the last car head down the mile-long drive. A bus followed with the valets. In less than a minute Paige and Shane were alone. Her heart beat fiercely in her chest.

"You ready to go?" Shane asked.

She moistened her lips. "I want to show you something first." She glanced nervously toward the chauffeur, who stood by the limousine. There were several other cars there as well because the estate had guest suites available.

"Are you all right?"

"Wonderful." Taking his hand she started back through the entrance, but instead of going down the stairs, she went out a side door, then up an outdoor white stone staircase. Her body trembled, her heart thumped.

"Paige?"

"I want to show you something," she said, glad she didn't have to go much farther. His hand tightened on hers as she opened the French doors and stepped into the luxurious bedroom. A king-sized bed dominated the room done in pale shades of creamy beige and blue. A bottle of champagne peeked from a silver ice bucket.

"Pai—"

She pressed her finger to his lips, silencing him. then replaced it with her lips. He tasted of the after-dinner wine, rich and sweet and delicious. She concentrated on that, and not the wobbling of her knees.

Lifting her head, she reached for his black bow tie. His hands stopped her. "You wanted to wait."

"I want to be with you," she told him, meaning it. If they only had one night, she was taking it.

His large hand cupped her cheek. His thumb brushed across her lip. "What if I want to wait?"

For a second, she couldn't speak, couldn't breathe. "What—what do you mean?"

Pulling her hands from around his neck, he held them tightly in his as he stared at her. "Paige, I want to ask you something, but I have to settle something first."

Her thudding heart refused to steady. "Why—why can't you ask me now?"

His large hands tenderly palmed her face. "You don't know how badly I wish I could. You're courageous, beautiful, unselfish. You're so incredible. I never lived until I met you."

"Shane." She trembled as his hands lowered to circle her waist. "I was the one only half alive until you touched me, until I felt the connection with you, felt the sensual awareness that I had waited so very long to feel, and was so afraid I wouldn't."

"I'd fight the world for you."

Tears of joy sparkled in her eyes. "I know." Her lips touched his. She felt the warmth, the fire, and always the passion. "I'm your woman."

His nostrils flared, his hands flexed. "Never forget it. We better get out of here while I can."

"I won't forget," Paige said, allowing Shane to lead her back out the way they had come. She had been right—it was a night to remember.

Shane didn't sleep all night, but he had put the time to good use, he thought as he packed the next morning. Phase one of his plan was complete. Phase two was going to be a little dicey.

He didn't have to be a genius to know Paige expected him to ask her to marry him. That she would give up her dream of marrying with her virginity intact humbled him and convinced him all the more he had made the right decision when he'd spoken with Blade and Rio last night, and again this morning.

He wanted to marry Paige. It surprised him how much. He didn't want to think of her not being an integral part of his life. But it wasn't fair to ask her until everything was out in the open. Convincing Mrs. Albright was going to take some doing.

He knew it would be tricky for her to explain without divulging Marshall's abusive and adulterous behavior, but it was a chance she had to take. He just hoped letting her know he wanted forever with Paige would sway her.

Placing the last pair of pants in his bag, he zipped up the suitcase, then started from the room. He was leaving today and, tomorrow, regardless of how things went, he'd put the third phase of his plan into action.

In the hallway he heard voices. They weren't clear, but he could tell one was Paige, while the other belonged to a man. Earlier, Shane had heard Paige and Mrs. Albright going downstairs. He had hoped to meet with Mrs. Albright, but hadn't had the opportunity because of another conference call he'd had that morning.

A few steps farther on, Shane recognized the male voice as Russell's, then heard Gaines's name mentioned. Shane took off running. He thundered down the stairs three at a time to see Paige with Russell.

"You're so into trust, I thought you might like to know that Elliott has been lying to you," Russell said snidely. "Last night Mother found out from Mr. Gaines—"

"Russell, I don't want to hear anything your mother or you have to say," Paige said, trying to close the front door.

"But he's an imposter." The flat of Russell's hand kept the door from closing.

"I warned you, Crenshaw," Shane growled, coming off the bottom step.

Paige glanced over her shoulder. "Yes you did. Do you want Shane to help you to your car?"

"I'd be happy to." Shane started around Paige.

Russell yelped in fear and scrambled back. "Ask him about Blade Navarone."

Paige stiffened, then slowly turned to Shane. Her face was pale. "W-what is he talking about?"

Shane wanted to smash Russell's gloating face, but the coward jumped into his car and sped away. Vowing they'd cross paths again, Shane closed the front door and reached for Paige.

Her body trembling, she stepped back. "What did Russell mean?"

His heart clenched. "It's complicated."

"The truth is only complicated when people want to twist it for their own benefit." She wrapped her arms protectively around her midriff. "What is your connection to Blade Navarone?"

Shane hesitated. To admit he worked for Blade would lead to questions he couldn't answer. "You have to trust me."

"Why do people always ask you to trust them when they're hiding something?" She shook her head. "If you know Blade, then the chances are good you know Trent Masters."

Shane watched helplessly as his silence condemned him. "You'll know everything in time."

Her arms dropped to her sides. Her fists clenched. Her laughter was strained. "I must be the biggest fool in the world and the worst judge of character. First Mother, then Russell, and now you."

His gut twisted. "Don't compare us to him."

"Why?" She swatted at the tears forming on her lashes. "All of you obviously deceived me. What's the difference?"

He gave her the only truth he could. "The difference is that we love you."

She gasped. Tears flowed down her cheeks. "Don't you dare tell me that now! Don't you dare!"

"Paige." He crossed to her in two long strides, taking her into his arms, ignoring her feeble attempts to be free. His mouth covered hers. She resisted for a brief moment, then she opened for him, allowing him entrance, and kissing him back with all the passion he knew she was capable of.

Reluctantly he lifted his head and stared down into her tear-drenched eyes. The sight tore at his heart. "I love you, Paige. Trust me. Trust what you feel."

Her lips trembled. "More than anything, I want to, but why can't you tell me what I want to know?"

"Because I won't let him."

With Paige still in his arms, Shane turned to see Mrs. Albright a short distance away. His arms tightened around Paige's waist. He wondered if she realized she had stepped closer to him.

"Perhaps it's time," Mrs. Albright said softly.

"Why don't we go into the living room and sit down?" Shane suggested, crossing to Mrs. Albright and leading both women to the sofa. He moved a short distance away to give them more privacy, but he had no intention of leaving unless one of them asked him to.

Mrs. Albright's hands clenched and unclenched in her lap. She bit her lower lip.

"I'll get you some water." Paige made a motion to stand, but her mother grabbed her hands.

"No. This is just difficult," Mrs. Albright said, still clutching her daughter's hands. "I'm just not sure where to start."

"Why do you disappear at times?" Paige asked and felt her mother's hands tremble. A thread of fear swept through her. "Just tell me."

"I never meant to hurt you or Zach. Please try to

remember that." Mrs. Albright swallowed. Swallowed again. Her gaze locked on Paige. "There are no excuses for what I'm about to tell you, but it wasn't done lightly or selfishly."

Paige trembled as much as her mother. "This is about Trent Masters, isn't it?"

Her mother's hand jerked, but she kept eye contact. "Yes. A month before I was to marry your father I fell in love for the first time. I—I gave in to those feelings, and as a result, Trent was conceived."

Paige stiffened in shock, then jerked to her feet. "How could you betray Father in such a way?"

"Paige—"

"No!" Paige cried, cutting her mother off, her own tears falling. "I thought I knew you. I was wrong." Stepping around her mother, Paige headed for the kitchen and the spare set of keys Shane insisted they keep there in case they needed to leave the house in a hurry.

Shane. She swiped the tears from her cheeks. He'd lied to her as well.

Opening the drawer, she snatched the keys up and turned to find Shane, grim-faced, arms folded, standing in front of the kitchen door. She didn't care that he looked ready to break someone into little pieces. "Get out of my way."

"Your mother doesn't deserve this."

"Neither did my father," she retorted, brushing her hand ineffectively at the tears she couldn't seem to control.

"And what is it that she did to your father besides be the best wife possible, deferring to him even when it meant letting people take a swipe at the children she loved?" he asked her. "If you'd just stop and think, you'd realize that she was in an impossible situation.

Do you think for one second her parents would have called off the wedding? Would your father have let her?"

Paige knew the answer instantly. Her grandparents loved her mother, but they were also very old-fashioned and abhorred any hint of a scandal or gossip attached to the Wilder family name. Her father had been driven to succeed and had been unbendingly proud. He wouldn't have liked being jilted. The wedding would have gone on regardless of what her mother wanted. "No," she finally answered.

"Right the first time." Shane closed the distance between them. "Trent's father was an honorable man. If I thought I couldn't have the woman I loved, I would have used every dirty trick to have her. I wouldn't have left town and let another man marry her, knowing he could never love her as much as I did, knowing she'd be in his bed instead of mine."

Inexplicably her body stirred at the intensity in his voice, his eyes. "It shouldn't have happened."

He stepped closer, bringing with him the heat and temptation of his body. "Do you think for one second that, if I thought you were lost to me, I wouldn't have made love to you, binding you to me any way possible?" his voice low and husky.

She shivered. "You always stopped."

"Because we weren't racing against a clock," he told her. "I'd never let the woman I love, the woman who loved me, marry another man." His gaze sharpened. "But I guess that's the difference. I can be a selfish bastard. Neither your mother nor Trent's father was. They loved with everything. He died without ever marrying, but there are plenty of stories about how he helped any woman who needed it, no questions asked. He celebrated his love for your mother every day of his life.

How much do you think it hurt her to give their child away? She lost the man and the child."

Tears streamed down Paige's cheeks. This time for her mother and what she had gone through. She couldn't begin to imagine what that must have felt like. "I can't think of anything more painful."

"And the pain hasn't stopped. She can never openly claim Trent because of what people might say, not about her, but about you and Zachary. She wants to be able to enjoy and love all of her children. I say it's about time."

Shame and misery swept through Paige. Closing her eyes, she bowed her head. "I hurt her."

"Yes, you did." His fingers beneath her chin lifted her head. "But you can fix things. Loving someone isn't always easy, as I'm finding out. But without love, you're only half living."

"You're just like Mother," she said softly. "You always try to find the best in me."

"We both love you." His arms circled her waist. "And no matter how long you live or where you go, you'll never find anyone who loves you as much."

"Shane." Pleasure spiraled through her. Flinging her arms around his neck, she pressed her mouth to his, clung. The kiss was as sweet as it was gentle, then it changed. Crushing her to him, his mouth became hungry and demanding. She answered, savoring the taste of him, rejoicing that they still had a future. Slowly she lifted her head. "I love you."

His arms tightened. "I know, but it's good hearing you finally say the words."

She smiled, then sobered and grabbed his hand. "Let's go see Mother. I have to apologize." They quickly went to the living room to find Mrs. Albright unmoved from the sofa, her head bowed, her hands in her lap. The sight tore at Paige's heart. "Mother, I'm sorry."

Mrs. Albright's head abruptly lifted. She came to her feet. Her face was tear-stained. Joy replaced the desolation in her eyes. The women met in the middle of the room. "Paige, I'm sor—"

"No." Paige shook her head and stepped back. "I understand. You don't owe me any explanation."

"I don't want to find one child and lose another." Mrs. Albright's voice trembled.

"You won't," Paige promised. "I admit it was a shock, but I understand now."

"Come on and let's sit down. I want to tell you everything." Mrs. Albright retraced her steps.

"I guess the brother we thought died is actually Trent," Paige said when they were seated.

"Yes. I didn't know until Trent was born that he wasn't your father's. His complexion and eyes were dark, unlike anyone in our families. Your father knew he wasn't his. Shortly after I brought Trent home from the hospital, I made the decision to give him up for adoption and faked his death so no one would know. He was raised in foster care."

Stunned, Paige stared at her mother. She might have wrestled with her own insecurities at times, but she couldn't have asked for a better mother growing up—or now. Giving up her child must have almost killed her. "I'm not sure I could have been as strong as you were."

"At the time I saw it as the only way, but not a day has gone by that I don't regret the decision." Joann swiped at the lingering tears in her eyes. "I hoped, prayed he'd be adopted, for someone to love him as I couldn't."

Paige ached for her mother. She loved fiercely. Unfortunately, she couldn't say that about her father.

Paige had to admit what she often forgot—that her father could be hard and unforgiving. No power on earth would have made him accept a child who wasn't his. Even with his own children, he had issues. Paige couldn't please him when she was young; Zachary couldn't please him as an adult. "Working with the foster program must have been a constant reminder."

"Not always," Mrs. Albright said. "I wanted to believe someone was helping him just as I helped others. I can't believe he has accepted me and doesn't hate me. I couldn't bear it if I lost you."

Once Paige might not have understood the kind of passion that consumed you until nothing else mattered, but loving Shane had made her a believer. "You're stuck with me. I'm sorry for what I said earlier."

"It's all right. I just ask one thing, that you let me tell Zach when it's time," Mrs. Albright said. "I want my children to be close, but I know it will take time to accept Trent."

Paige had another brother. She'd refused to believe that Trent asking her mother had any validity because his age hadn't added up, and because her father had said it was a hoax and to forget it. Desperate for her father's love and approval, even as an adult, she had done just that . . . until her mother started disappearing. "What about his father?"

"We never saw each other again," her mother said, regret and pain in her voice. "He died before Trent found me with the help of his wife's family."

"The Falcons."

"And Dominique's in-laws, the Taggarts. They're a close-knit family." Some of the strain left her mother's mouth. "He now has a family that loves and cares about him."

"I don't know how I feel about this," Paige said honestly.

"I understand, but please don't take it out on Shane. I hired him to find out all he could on Russell," her mother said. "I didn't fight for what I wanted when I was young, and, although I regret it, if I hadn't married your father, I wouldn't have had you and Zach." Her mother squeezed Paige's hands. "You two made life worth living."

Paige couldn't condemn her mother. In a way she admired her more than ever. She'd walked away from the man she loved and honored her marriage vows. As Shane had pointed out, she'd sacrificed so much. Paige knew she wasn't that strong. "Thank you for telling me. You did love Father, didn't you?"

"Just as much as he loved me," her mother answered, then looked at Shane, who was standing by the doorway to give them privacy. "Shane wanted to tell you long ago. He cares about you."

Paige glanced across the room to Shane, who gazed at her with love and approval. "I know. I'm a very lucky woman."

"If you love him, don't let pride or anything stand in your way."

"I won't." Paige kissed her mother on the cheek, then went to Shane. "Last night you said you had something to ask me today."

He took her hand. "Let's go outside." He didn't speak until they were sitting on a stone bench in front of the rose garden room. "You need to know something first."

"I have a feeling I'm not going to like this," she told him.

His thumb swept across the top of her hand in a

soothing motion. "Months back you went to Trent Masters's house to find the connection between him and your mother."

A frown darted across her brow. "How did—" Her eyes widened. She surged to her feet. "You!"

Shane came to his feet as well. "I was chief of security and communications for Blade, both private and for his resorts," Shane explained. "He and Sierra were visiting Trent and Dominique that night."

Paige's eyes narrowed. "I hated that man for humiliating me, for making me feel foolish and helpless."

He never broke eye contact. "Not any more than I've hated myself."

She stared at him for a long moment. "I wanted to sock you."

"You paid me back in other ways," he said. "My memory of you that night haunted me. I couldn't get the softness of your body, the smell of your perfume, your eyes wide with fear, out of my mind. Not many days went by that I didn't think about you."

"Is that why you came here?"

He took a chance and settled his hands on her waist. "Yes. I told myself it was to repay you for frightening you so badly, to help your mother once I found out Russell wasn't what he seemed."

Her eyes widened, she pushed against his chest. "You knew about that woman and you didn't tell me."

"You needed to learn on your own what a sleaze he was," he told her. "You needed to know you can take care of yourself."

"What if I hadn't found out? What if, when he came back, I forgave him?" she asked, watching him closely.

His eyes darkened, fury swirling in the black depths. "You belong to me. There is no way in hell I would allow another man to touch you."

Her brow arched. "Don't I have any say in the matter?"

"Since you love me, and you're my woman, no."

"It's a good thing or I'd show you the door." Her arms wrapped around him. "I guess I forgive you. I *was* trespassing."

Relief rushed through him. He pulled her flush against his body. "Why didn't you hire someone to get the information for you?"

"I felt bad enough that I had hired a private investigator to follow Mother. I didn't want to risk him finding out anything that could get her into trouble or embarrass her."

He kissed her on the forehead. "Even conflicted, you loved your mother and were smart enough to want to find out on your own."

"And I completely bungled it," she admitted with a wry twist of her mouth.

"But because you decided to investigate, I found a woman I couldn't forget."

"I'm glad I haunted you." Her smile turned into a frown. She glanced away. When her eyes met his again they were filled with sadness. "I guess you're flying back to wherever Blade is?"

"That depends on you." Taking her hand, he kissed her fingertips. "I'm not sure how a Black Knight would do this, but I can only say what is in my heart."

Her heart beat so fiercely she felt light-headed.

"Paige Albright, I'll love you with everything that is within me. Will you marry me?"

Tears streamed down her cheek.

His hand clenched on hers. "I hope those are happy tears."

She nodded. "Yes."

He pulled her into his arms, kissing her until both of

them were breathless. "I want to be there for you in good and bad times. To see you wake up in the morning. Hold you as you fall asleep."

"I love you so much, Shane."

His hands palmed her face. "I love you, too. It just took a while for my brain to catch up with my heart. I realize there are still things for us to work out, that you probably have a lot of questions to ask, but there's one more I have to ask first."

"What?"

"What date would you like to become Mrs. Shane Elliott?"

Epilogue

It took six seamstresses three months to create the exquisite one-of-a-kind stark white French reembroidered lace ball gown hand-sewn with pearls and Swarovski crystals. The gown weighed twenty-eight pounds. The seamstresses finished the dress and the matching twelve-foot train the day before the wedding and earned a sizable bonus.

Trumpets sounded as Paige appeared at the top of the double staircase at the Carrington Estate on the arm of her brother, Zachary. She was breathtaking. A hush fell over the three-hundred-plus assembled guests.

Paige and Shane's gazes touched, held, promised to love forever. Shane felt his chest swell with pride and thankfulness that above all men, she loved him. His life might have started with nothing, but today and all the tomorrows to come he was the richest and luckiest man alive. He had Paige and her love.

The moment her white satin shoe—embroidered with Swarovski crystals and pearls to match the dress— touched the stairs, the bridal march began. Her head high, her bearing regal, Paige came down the flower-entwined staircase to him. Emotions clogged his throat. He hadn't known he could love so completely.

His heart couldn't have picked better.

When Paige and Zachary were even with her

mother, they stopped. Paige bent to kiss her mother's cheek. Lifting her head, Paige's gaze flickered to her half brother, Trent, sitting with Dominique and Sierra with her mother, Ruth. Mrs. Albright had mentioned in passing that she owed Ruth for her help.

Paige's and Trent's first meeting a week ago had been brief and a bit awkward, but it was a start. Her inviting him went a long way toward Mrs. Albright's dream that one day all of her children would be together.

Straightening, Paige allowed Zachary to lead her to the bottom of the raised, curved platform. The minister stepped forward and said, "If there is anyone here who has reason that this man and this woman should not marry, let him speak now or forever hold his peace."

Rio, one of Shane's two best men, cleared his throat. Shane cut him a look, saw Blade, his other best man, elbow Rio. Paige glared at Rio. So did her matron and maid of honor, Jackie and Gayle. Shane almost laughed. During the rehearsal, Paige had overheard Rio ask Shane if he was sure he wanted to get married. She'd marched up to a man who made grown men run and told him to mind his own business. The two had stared at each other until Rio had dipped his head slightly.

"Who gives this woman?"

"I do," Zachary answered. Kissing Paige on the cheek, he took his seat with his mother.

Shane descended the steps to Paige. "I love you," he whispered softly, then took her arm to face the minister. He couldn't wait to marry the woman he loved more than life.

The double-ring ceremony was beautiful and everything Paige dreamed. Her hand trembled slightly as

Shane slid on the platinum wedding band next to the flawless pearl-and-diamond engagement ring he had given her the day after he asked her to marry him. His wedding band was platinum as well. Both bands had their initials and wedding date engraved.

The elegant reception was absolutely perfect, with cobalt-and-white flower arrangements on each table, tulle-covered chairs, Waterford crystal and flatware, and hand-engraved table assignments. The wedding invitations had been hand-engraved as well.

For the reception she'd changed into a cobalt-sequined tulle knee-length dress with ivory grosgrain trim so she could move more freely. The tears didn't start to fall until she and Shane danced for the first time as man and wife.

Occasionally it remained difficult to believe that she had somehow captured the heart of her very own Black Knight. He was everything she had dreamed of—intelligent, loyal, courageous. He made her feel safe and cherished. He always thought of her needs first. Aware of her pending inheritance, he'd insisted on a prenup for her benefit. She'd refused and kissed him into a good mood.

Knowing that she didn't want to move and leave her mother, Shane resigned as head of security and communications for Blade and opened his own computer security firm near her office building downtown. His business was thriving, but they'd promised each other that, no matter what, they would be home by nine and never sleep apart.

They'd purchased a house—French in style with lots of rustic beams and weathered stucco on a wooded hill not far from her mother. Her life was absolutely perfect.

Shane kissed the tears away. "Have I told you how beautiful you are?"

She smiled up at him. "Every time you look at me."

His eyes darkened. "How much longer?"

Paige didn't flush or look away. She wanted to be alone with him just as much. "Probably an hour or two at the least."

"I thought so." He kissed her on the lips. "You're worth waiting for."

Paige laid her head on his chest. What if she wasn't? What if she was a dud in the lovemaking department?

"Paige?"

She forced a smile and lifted her head. "Yes?"

"What's the matter?" he asked.

He was too perceptive, but they were surrounded by over three hundred people. She bit her lip.

His head dipped, he whispered in her ear. "You belong to me. Trust me on this. It's going to be a night to remember."

She shivered, not from fear, but from anticipation. She kissed his chin. "I'm going to hold you to that."

"Why do you think we're staying at the Carrington Estate for two days before we take off to Monte Carlo?"

Paige's body heated. "Maybe we can leave in an hour."

Shane laughed and swung her around in a circle. She laughed back. With Shane, she never had to be afraid of anything. She wouldn't forget again.

Shane carried Paige into the elaborate wedding suite, kicking the door shut with his foot. Before the sound died, his hungry mouth was on hers. When he lifted his head, they were both breathing hard.

"I guess I should go change," Paige said.

"I guess." He set her to her feet.

Smiling up at him, she turned her back. "Could you unzip me please?"

Shane caught the tab and slowly inched it down to reveal fragrant, flawless skin. His breath hitched. He pressed a kiss against the elegant curve of her back, felt her shiver. "You're so perfect."

"I won't be but a minute," she said, slipping through the connecting door to the bedroom.

Shane removed his tie, shrugged off his coat, and saw the serving cart. On it was a note from Rio in what amounted to a monumental event. "Just in case."

Shane lifted the three domes to find an assortment of fruits, meats, and cheeses. A bottle of champagne was nearby. Rio was putting his stamp of approval on Paige. Just before the wedding he'd whispered to Shane that Alisha had decided she no longer liked living in Atlanta.

Russell no longer lived in Atlanta, either. He had been demoted and reassigned to his company's St. Louis office. The Beijing delegation hadn't liked his high-handed, pompous attitude. He'd cost his firm millions of dollars and was paying the price.

The bedroom door opened and Shane's breath caught again. Paige stood framed in a white gossamer negligee. His body stirred, hardened. He hoped he could take it as slow as he needed to for her first time.

"You ordered food?"

"Rio," he answered, going to her.

She smiled up at him as he pulled her into his arms. "That was nice of him. I think we're going to be fine. We have something in common. We both love you."

"Rio is a good man, but he's not into love," Shane said. "At least not yet."

Her head tilted to one side. "No offense, but it will take a very special and fearless woman to get him."

Shane smiled at her. "Blade and I were lucky. Rio will be as well. You didn't eat much at the reception. You hungry?"

"As a matter of fact, I am." Her hands began unbuttoning his pleated white shirt.

"You're sure you don't want to eat or have a glass of champagne first?" Shane asked, although food was the farthest thing from his mind.

She jerked his shirt out of his pants, ran her hands lightly over his chest, then pressed a kiss to his bare skin, swept her tongue over his nipple.

He sucked in his breath so hard he felt dizzy. "Guess not."

She looked at him with love and trust shining in her gray eyes. "You said I'd know when it was time. I don't want to wait another moment, another second to truly be yours."

"Good, because I'm holding on by a thread here." His mouth captured hers. His tongue probed and searched the sweet interior of her mouth, then moved to the tempting curve of her cheek, her shoulder, finding the lace of her robe.

Slowly, he slid the material off one shoulder, dropping kisses on her smooth bare skin, then repeated the process on the other shoulder. Her skin was like silk velvet, soft and beckoning.

He stared down at her looking so trustingly up at him, her breathing growing more labored, and hoped he could hold it together long enough to make this special for her. But she tempted him as no woman ever had. The long lace gown cupped her high rounded breasts. He almost groaned on seeing the outline of her nipple, the dark shadow between her legs.

His breathing unsteady, he picked her up and headed for the bedroom. He didn't stop until he was by the bed. The need to touch her, to taste, to be inside her body was overwhelming. He took one, then another slow breath until he was sure he had his emotions under control. He placed her gently on the wide bed.

For a long moment, he just stared at the woman he would love for a lifetime. Tossing his shirt aside, he toed off his shoes, unfastened and unzipped his pants.

All the time she watched him with unblinking eyes. "You're so beautiful." Leaning up, she ran her hand lightly over his chest. Air hissed out of his lungs. "I'm glad your head finally listened to your heart."

"No more than I am." He went down on the bed, drawing her under him. "Thank you for loving me, for trusting me." The words were barely out of his mouth before one hand palmed her breast, molding it, and his mouth took hers again. Then he moved purposefully downward. He wanted to touch and taste every inch of her.

He pulled the gown over her full, firm breasts. His eyes narrowed at the tempting sight. Dipping his head, his teeth and tongue stroked the nipple to hardness.

Paige twisted restlessly under him, feeling the sucking sensation in the core of her body. She burned. Caught between passion and need, she ached helplessly against him. His hand palmed the other breast, rubbing the sensitive peak between his fingers, then moved to the junction of her thighs to cup her woman's softness.

It wasn't enough. She whimpered, twisted, trying to increase the contact.

"Lift your hips."

She quickly complied. He pulled the gown off with one smooth motion. With her body clamoring for release, she never thought to be embarrassed. She stared up at Shane to gauge his reaction to seeing her naked for the first time. His eyes were dark, intense with passion. And she was the reason.

His breathing quickened. She was as perfect as he had imagined. He couldn't wait to taste all of her. Quickly he finished undressing and came back to her. He kissed his way down her elegant torso, the smooth dip of her navel, the inside of her taut thigh, the dimple behind her knee, the arch of her foot.

"Sh-Shane." Paige whimpered his name, wanting more, but not knowing how to ask for it.

He came back up, taking her hips in his hands, positioning her. He kissed the most intimate part of her. Her hands shoved at his head, then she clutched him, opening for him.

Her cries of pleasure urged him on. He felt her stiffen, her hands clasping his head. Coming to his knees, his hands cupping her hips, he thrust into her wet, waiting heat. The fit was tight and perfect. She clenched around him.

"Shane!" She cried out his name as her body spasmed in an orgasm that went on and on.

He thrust again and again until she was with him once more, her body hungry and needy again. Her legs wrapped around his waist; her head thrashed on the pillow. His mouth found hers, his tongue imitating the motion of his hips. Clinging to him, she matched him thrust for thrust.

She moaned with mindless pleasure. Each time he moved, he rubbed against her sensitive breasts, arousing her even more. Feeling him inside her, filling her, loving her was almost too much, too good.

He loved her. It was deep and hot and immensely pleasurable. Soon she felt the tightening of her body. She grasped him to her, felt him surge into her, the tempo increasing until she was spinning, reaching for completion again. She cried out his name. They went over together.

His breathing labored, his body spent and immensely satisfied, Shane rolled to one side, pulled Paige against him, then he tilted her chin up. Her eyes were closed but the blissful expression on her face made him want her all over again. "Are you all right?"

Her eyes opened. Love and happiness and a little devilment stared back at him. "The way you love me, I'm more than all right. You said this would be a night to remember and I'd say we're off to a good start."

Shane laughed and hugged her. He was the luckiest man alive. "And I'd never break my word to my woman, my wife."

"Good." Paige climbed on top of him. "I'll hold you to that."

William H. Ray

FRANCIS RAY (1944–2013) is the *New York Times* bestselling author of the Grayson novels, the Falcon books, the Taggart Brothers, and *Twice the Temptation,* among many other books. Her novel *Incognito* was made into a movie that aired on BET. A native Texan, she was a graduate of Texas Woman's University and had a degree in nursing. Besides being a writer, she was a school nurse practitioner with the Dallas Independent School District. She lived in Dallas.

"Francis Ray is, without a doubt, one of the Queens of Romance."

—*A Romance Review*